Jo & Rus ™

Published by

kaboom! ™

Designer
Chelsea Roberts

Assistant Editor
Michael Moccio

Associate Editor
Jonathan Manning

Editor
Bryce Carlson

Special Thanks
Whitney Leopard

Ross Richie CEO & Founder
Joy Huffman CFO
Matt Gagnon Editor-in-Chief
Filip Sablik President, Publishing & Marketing
Stephen Christy President, Development
Lance Kreiter Vice President, Licensing & Merchandising
Arune Singh Vice President, Marketing
Bryce Carlson Vice President, Editorial & Creative Strategy
Kate Henning Director, Operations
Spencer Simpson Director, Sales
Scott Newman Manager, Production Design
Elyse Strandberg Manager, Finance
Sierra Hahn Executive Editor
Jeanine Schaefer Executive Editor
Dafna Pleban Senior Editor
Shannon Watters Senior Editor
Eric Harburn Senior Editor
Sophie Philips-Roberts Associate Editor
Amanda LaFranco Associate Editor
Jonathan Manning Associate Editor
Gavin Gronenthal Assistant Editor
Gwen Waller Assistant Editor
Allyson Gronowitz Assistant Editor
Ramiro Portnoy Assistant Editor
Kenzie Rzonca Assistant Editor
Shelby Netschke Editorial Assistant
Michelle Ankley Design Coordinator
Marie Krupina Production Designer
Grace Park Production Designer
Chelsea Roberts Production Designer
Samantha Knapp Production Design Assistant
José Meza Live Events Lead
Stephanie Hocutt Digital Marketing Lead
Esther Kim Marketing Coordinator
Breanna Sarpy Live Events Coordinator
Amanda Lawson Marketing Assistant
Holly Aitchison Digital Sales Coordinator
Morgan Perry Retail Sales Coordinator
Megan Christopher Operations Coordinator
Rodrigo Hernandez Operations Coordinator
Zipporah Smith Operations Assistant
Jason Lee Senior Accountant
Sabrina Lesin Accounting Assistant

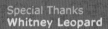

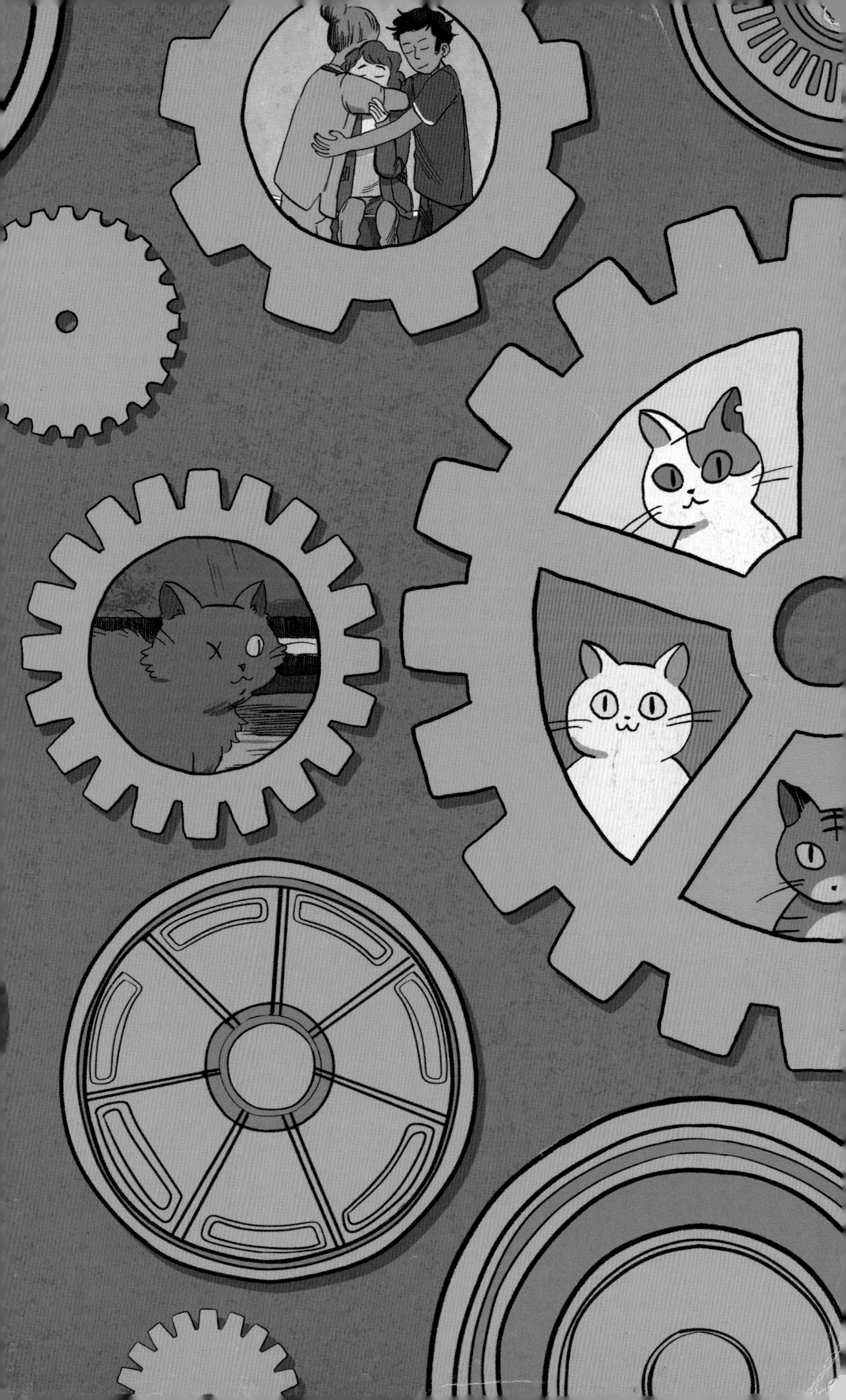

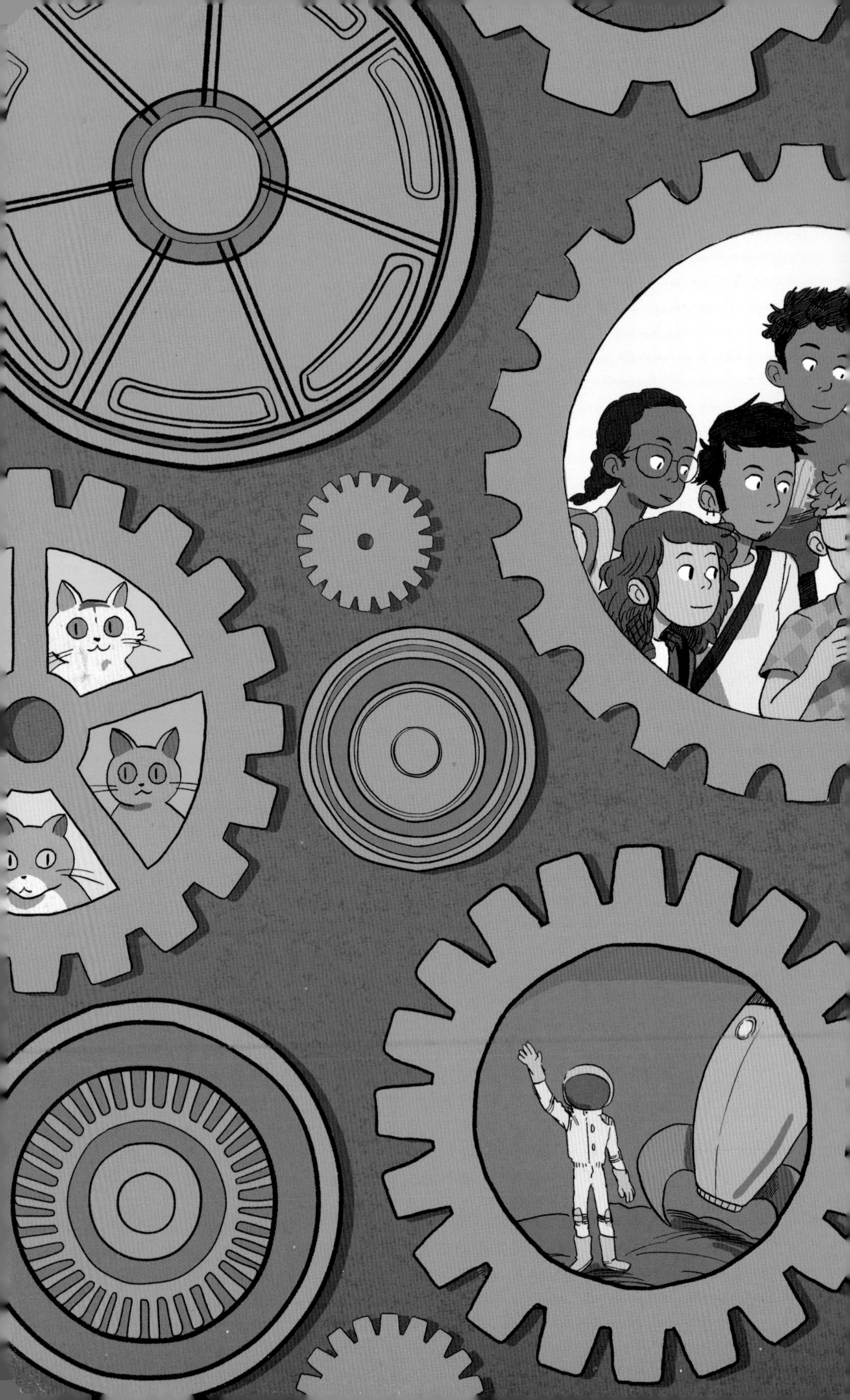

Jo & Rus ™

created by Audra Winslow

Written & Illustrated by
Audra Winslow

Letters by
Mike Fiorentino

Cover by
Audra Winslow

To Colin, the Rus to my Jo.

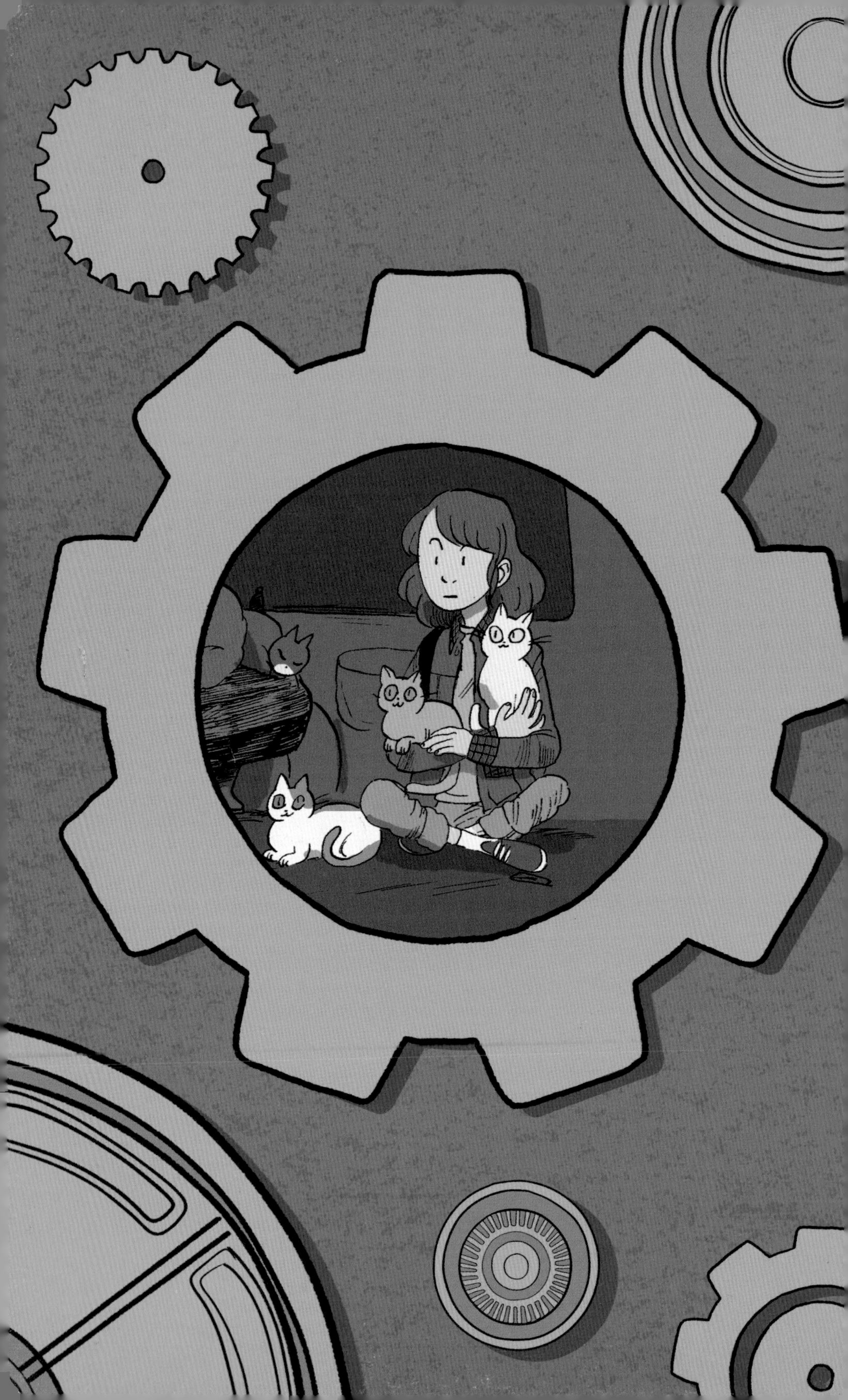

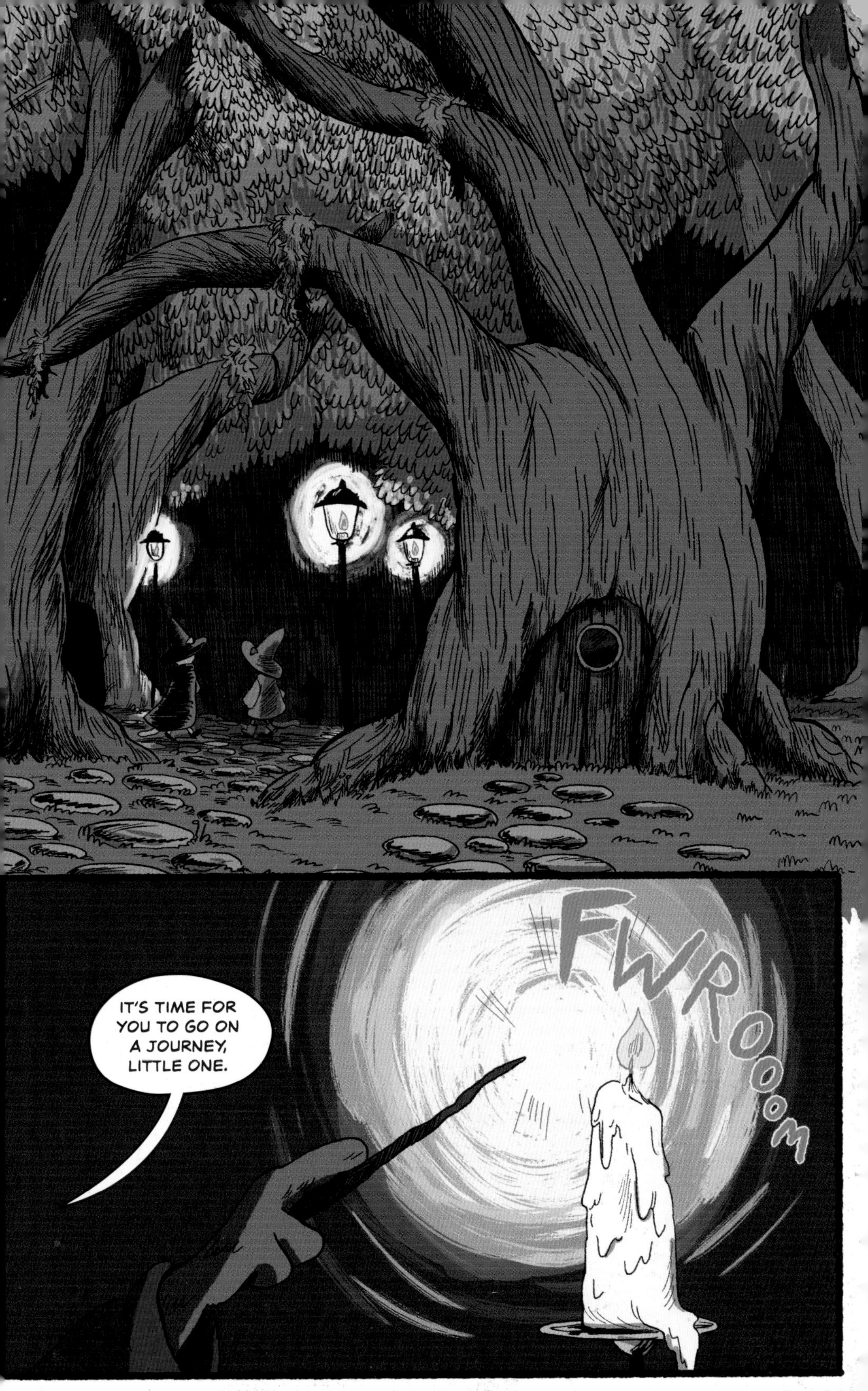
IT'S TIME FOR YOU TO GO ON A JOURNEY, LITTLE ONE.
FWROOoom

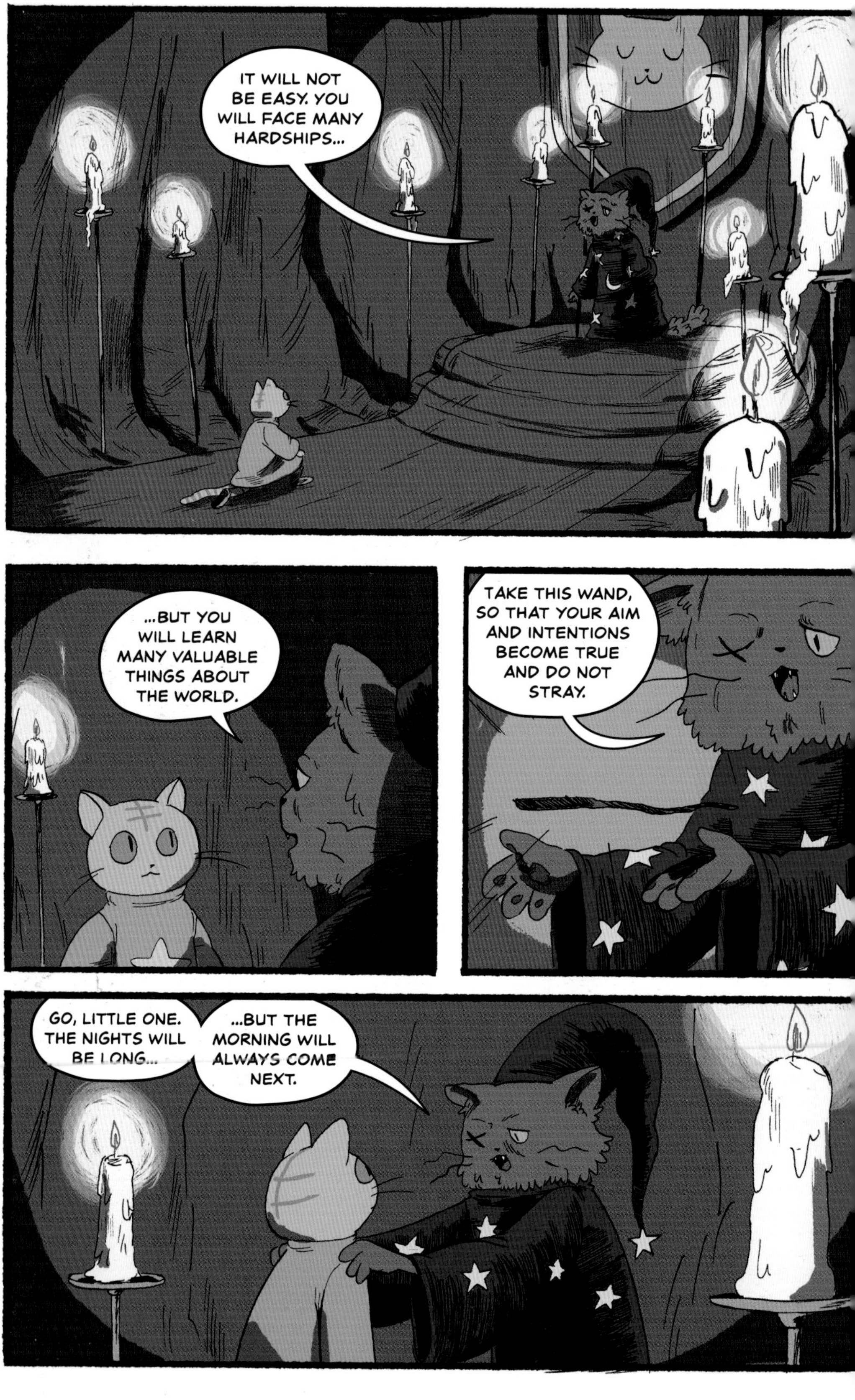
IT WILL NOT BE EASY. YOU WILL FACE MANY HARDSHIPS...
...BUT YOU WILL LEARN MANY VALUABLE THINGS ABOUT THE WORLD.
TAKE THIS WAND, SO THAT YOUR AIM AND INTENTIONS BECOME TRUE AND DO NOT STRAY.
GO, LITTLE ONE. THE NIGHTS WILL BE LONG...
...BUT THE MORNING WILL ALWAYS COME NEXT.

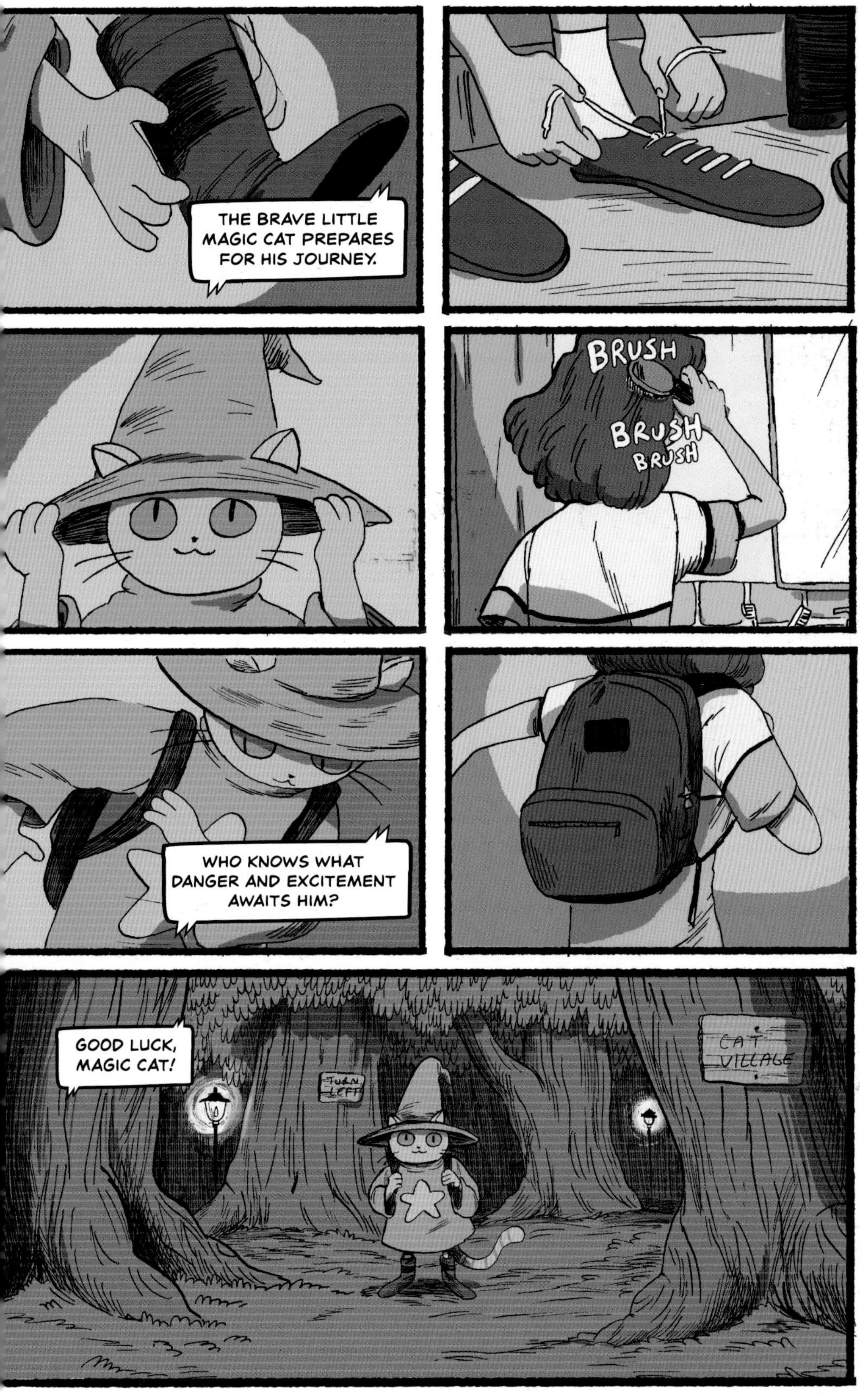
THE BRAVE LITTLE MAGIC CAT PREPARES FOR HIS JOURNEY.
BRUSH
BRUSH
BRUSH
WHO KNOWS WHAT DANGER AND EXCITEMENT AWAITS HIM?
GOOD LUCK, MAGIC CAT!
TURN LEFT
CAT VILLAGE

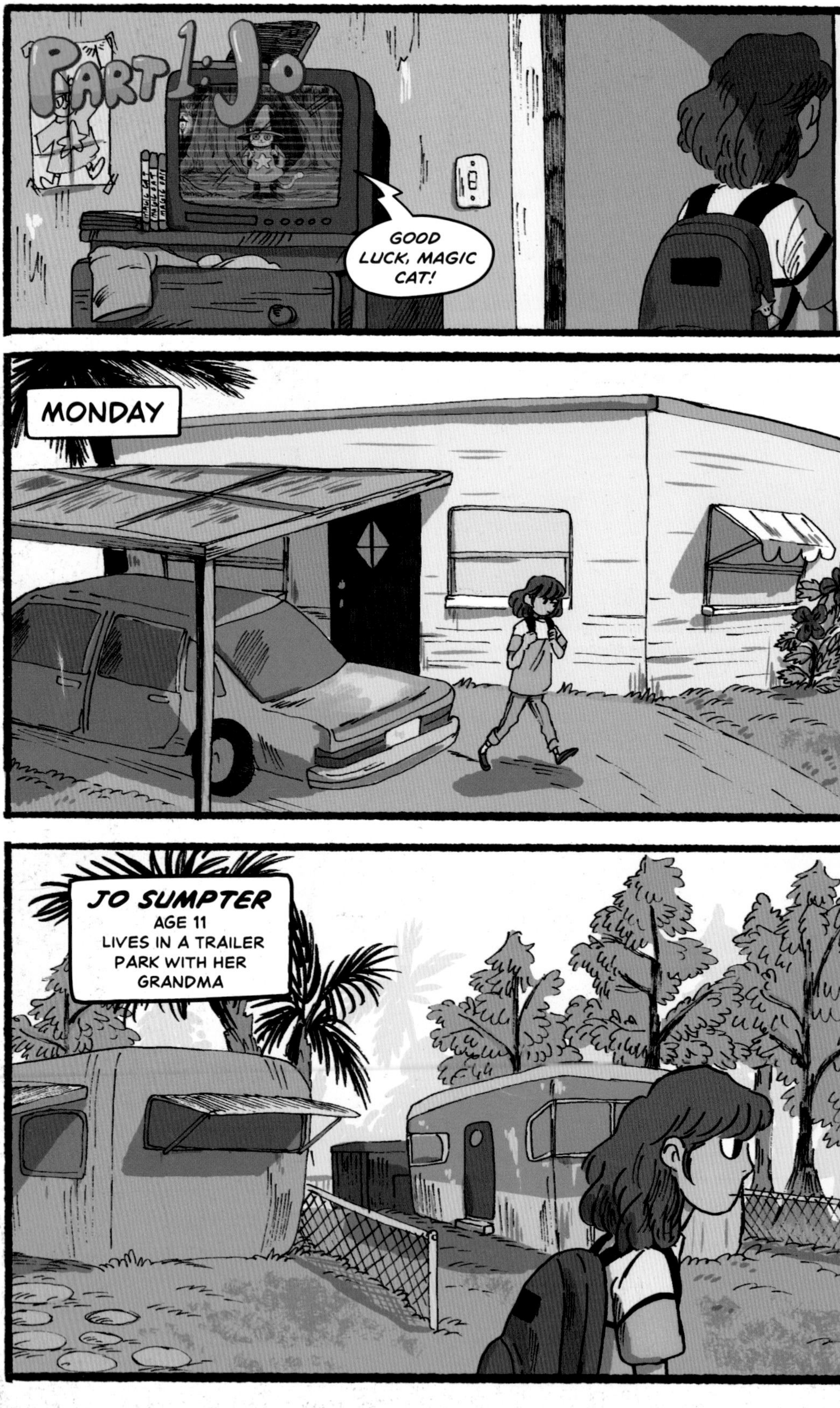
PART 1: JO
GOOD LUCK, MAGIC CAT!
MONDAY
JO SUMPTER
AGE 11
LIVES IN A TRAILER PARK WITH HER GRANDMA

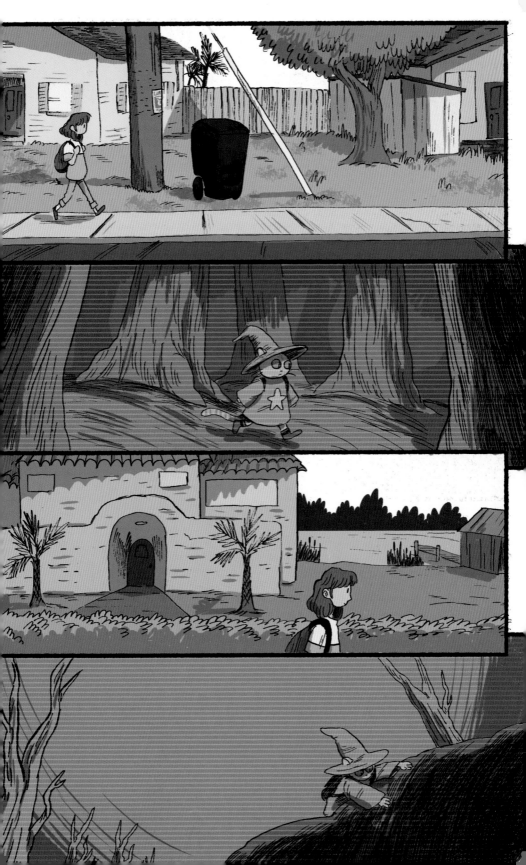

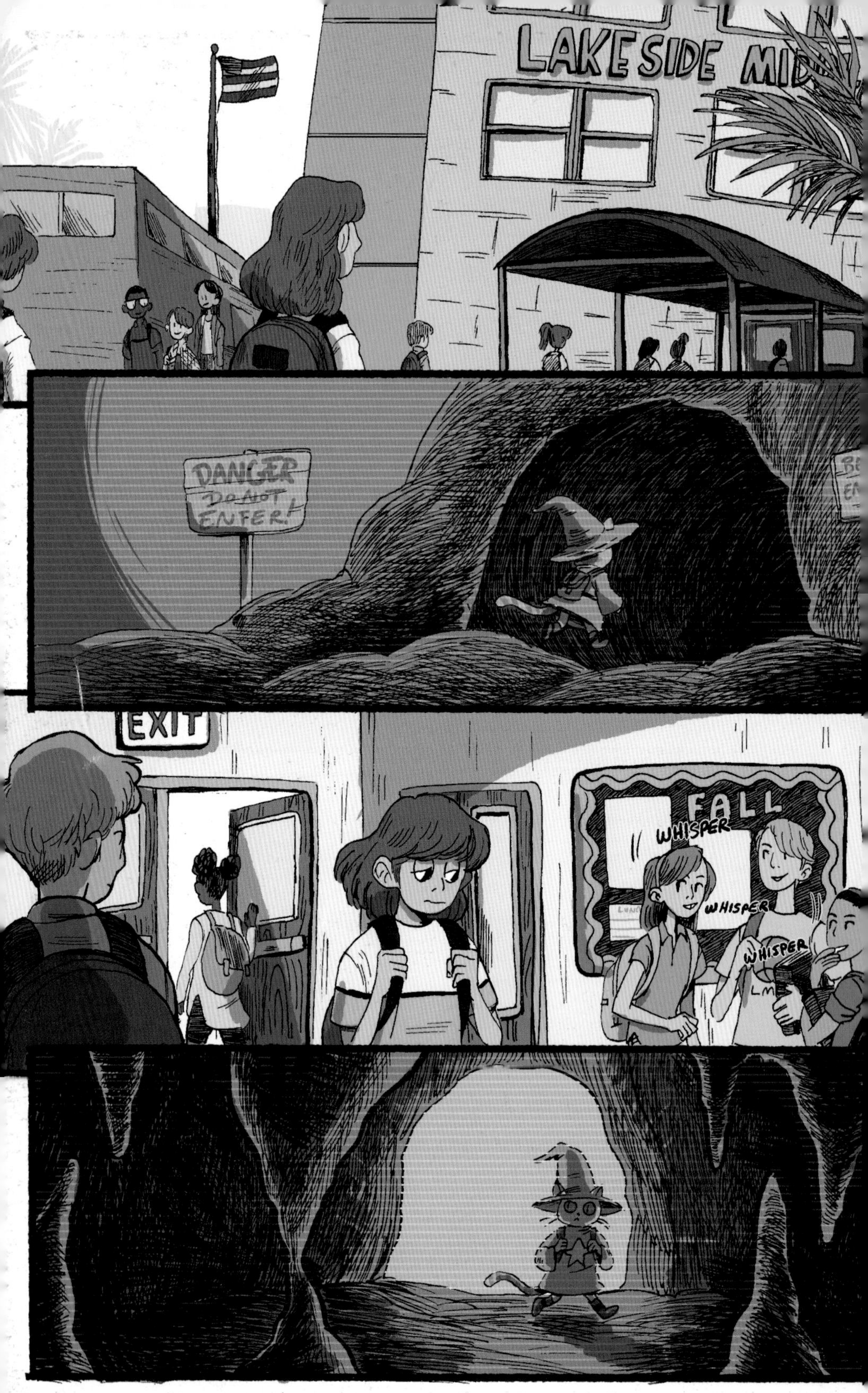
LAKESIDE MID
DANGER
Do NOT
ENTER!
EXIT
FALL
WHISPER
WHISPER
WHISPER

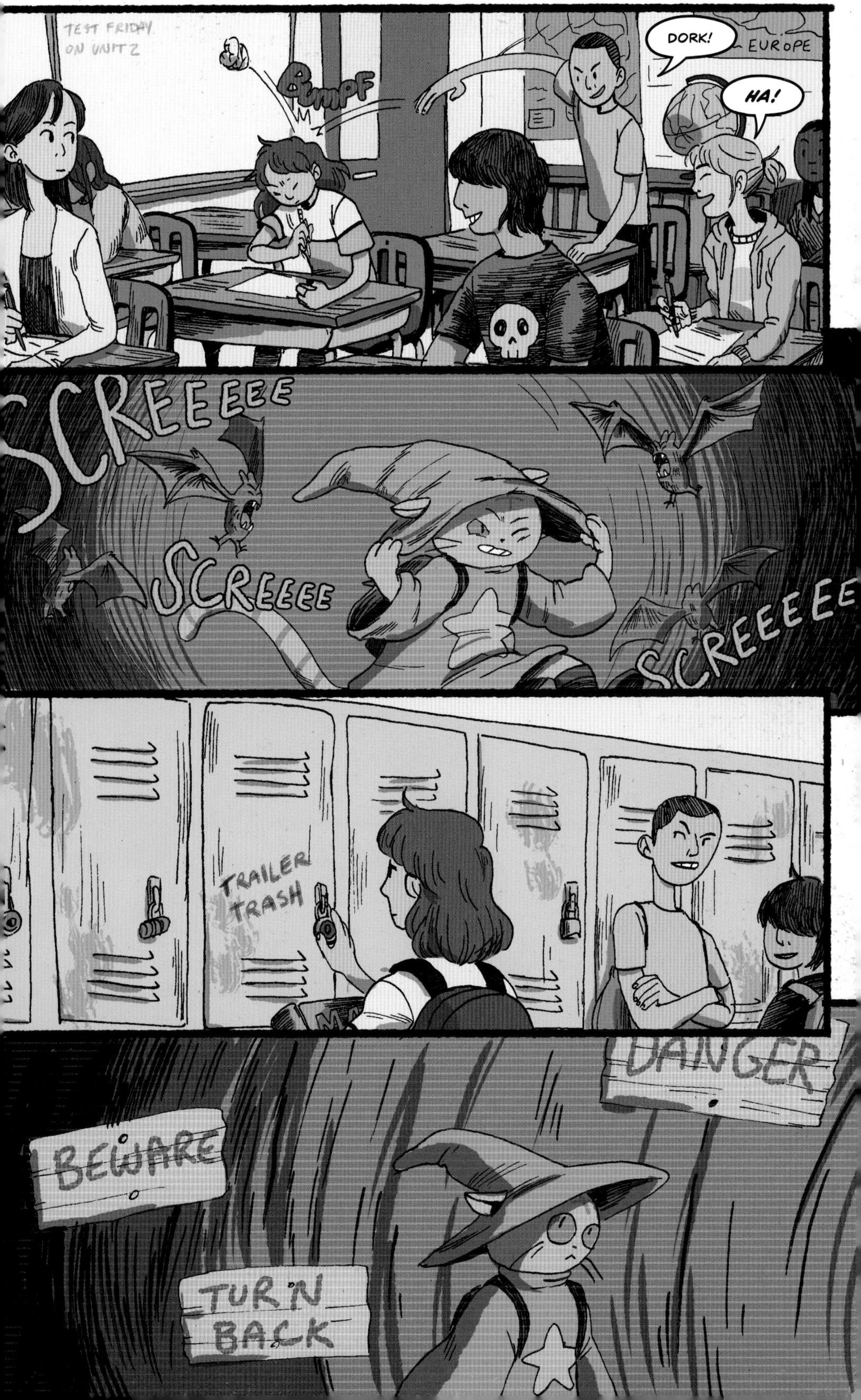
TEST FRIDAY
ON UNIT 2
BUMPF
DORK!
EUROPE
HA!
SCREEEEE
SCREEEE
SCREEEEEE
TRAILER
TRASH
DANGER
BEWARE
TUR'N
BACK

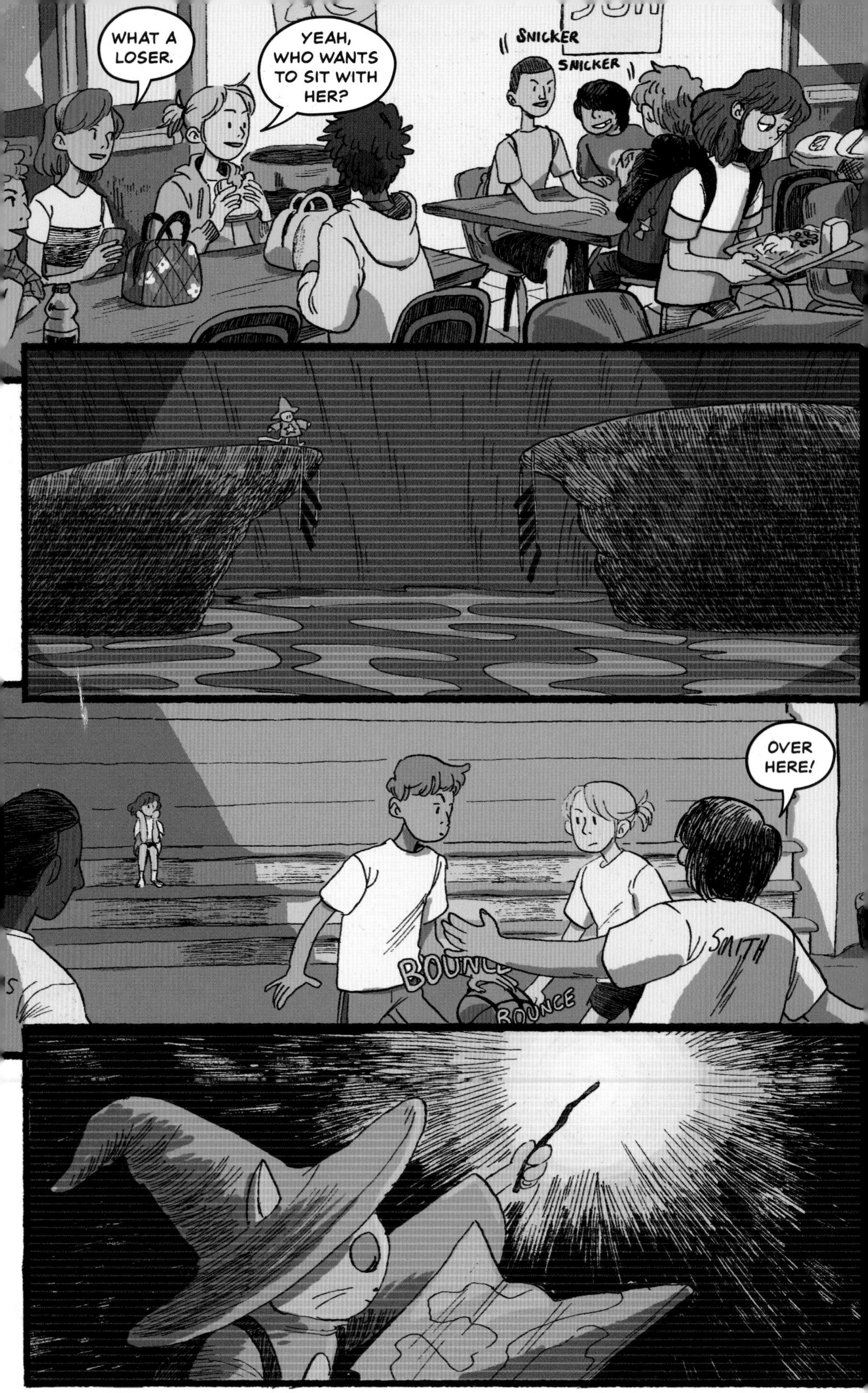
WHAT A LOSER.
YEAH, WHO WANTS TO SIT WITH HER?
SNICKER
SNICKER
OVER HERE!
SMITH
BOUNCE
BOUNCE

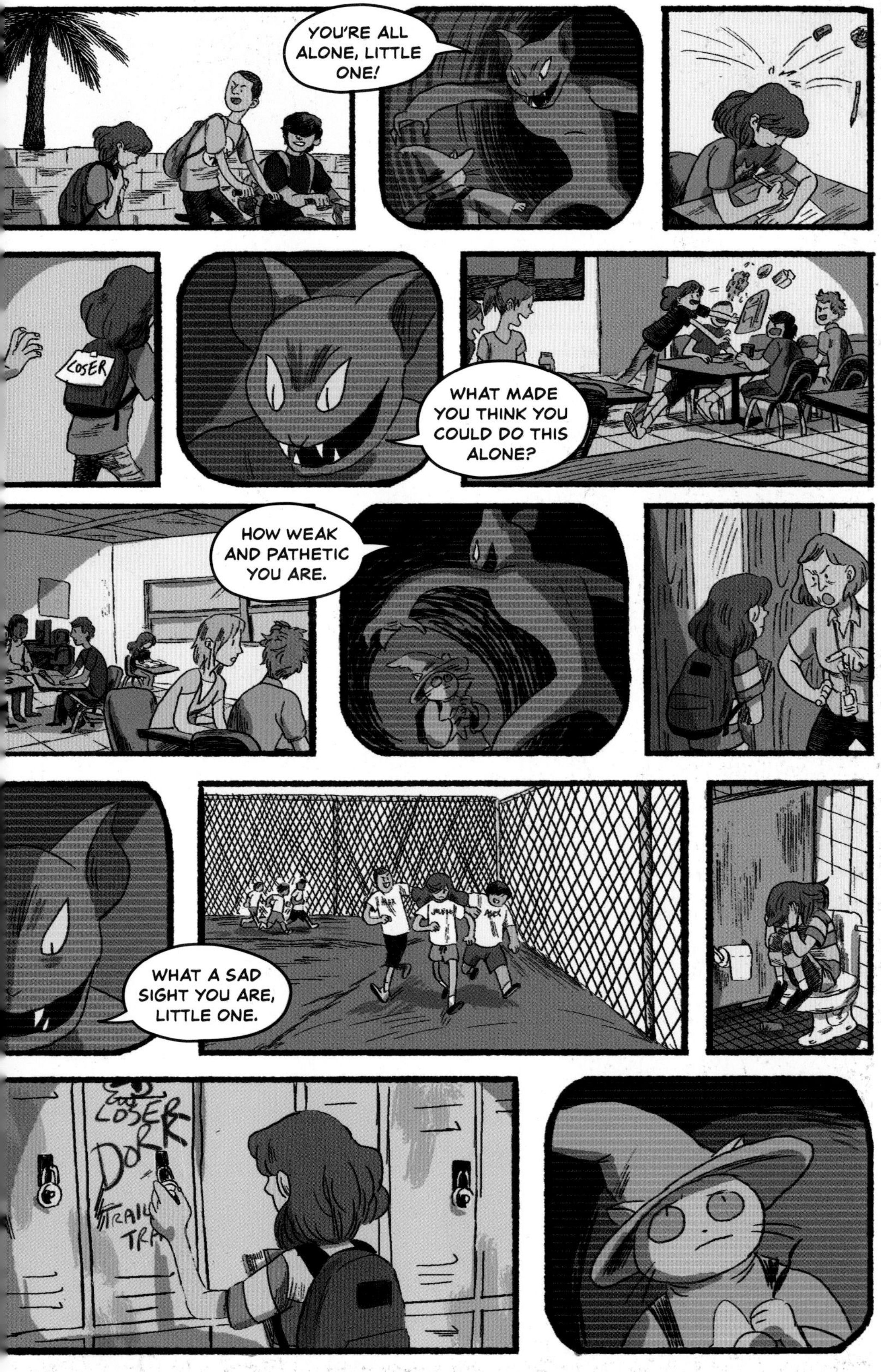
YOU'RE ALL ALONE, LITTLE ONE!
LOSER
WHAT MADE YOU THINK YOU COULD DO THIS ALONE?
HOW WEAK AND PATHETIC YOU ARE.
WHAT A SAD SIGHT YOU ARE, LITTLE ONE.
LOSER
DORK

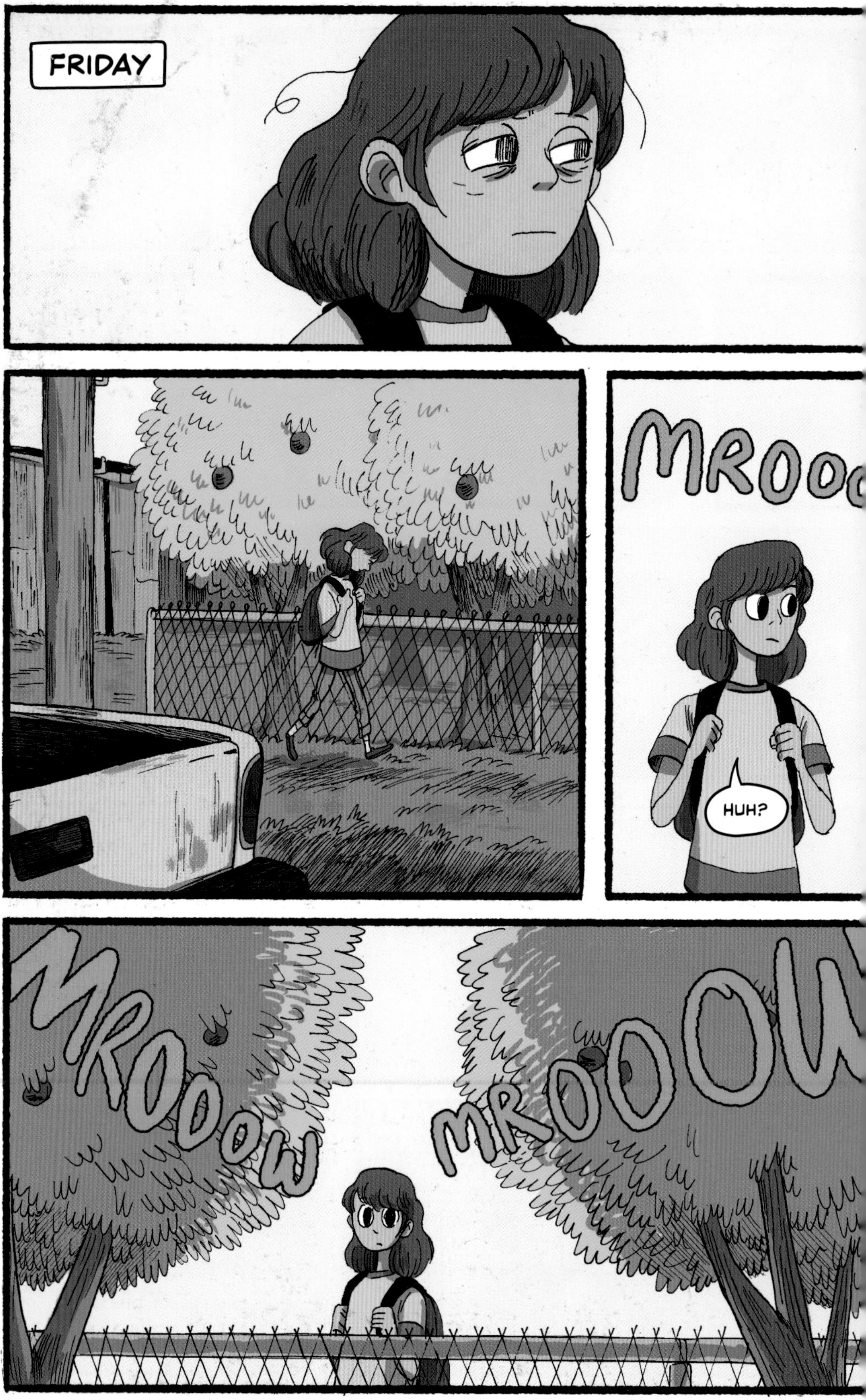

FRIDAY
MROOO
HUH?
MROOOW
MROOOOW

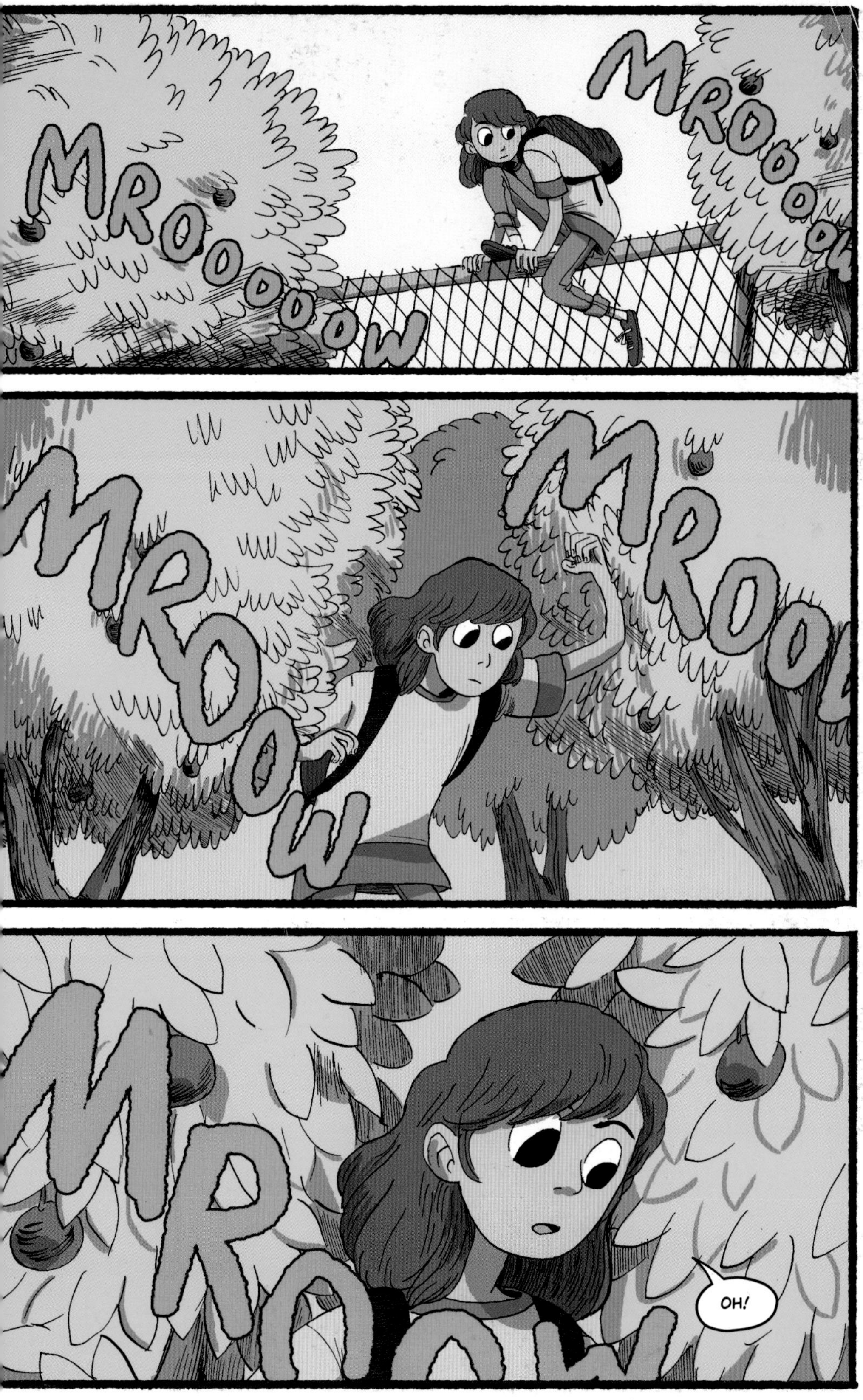
MROOOOOOW
MROOOOOW
MROOOW
MROOO
MROOOW
OH!

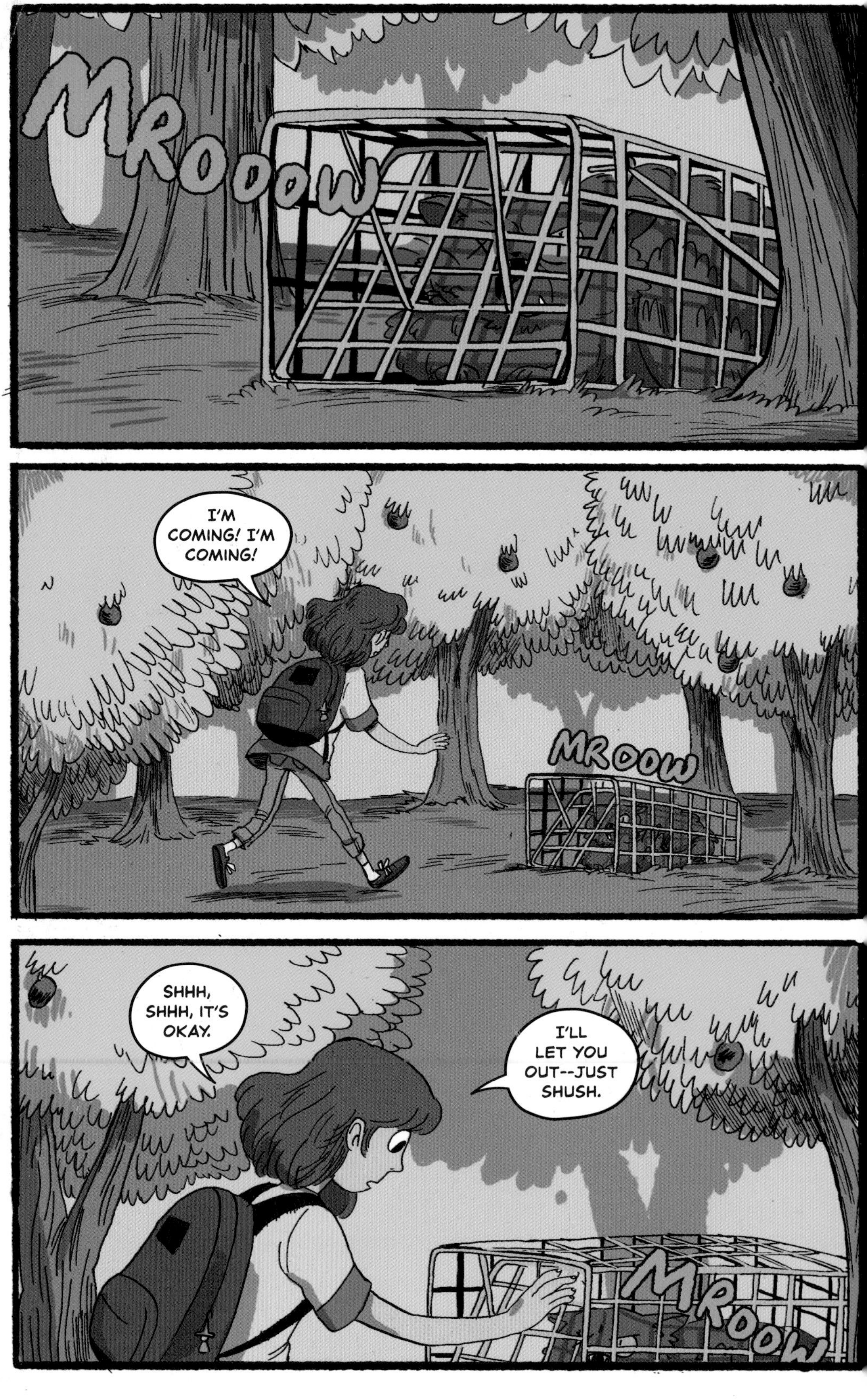
MROOOW
I'M COMING! I'M COMING!
MROOW
SHHH, SHHH, IT'S OKAY.
I'LL LET YOU OUT--JUST SHUSH.
MROOW

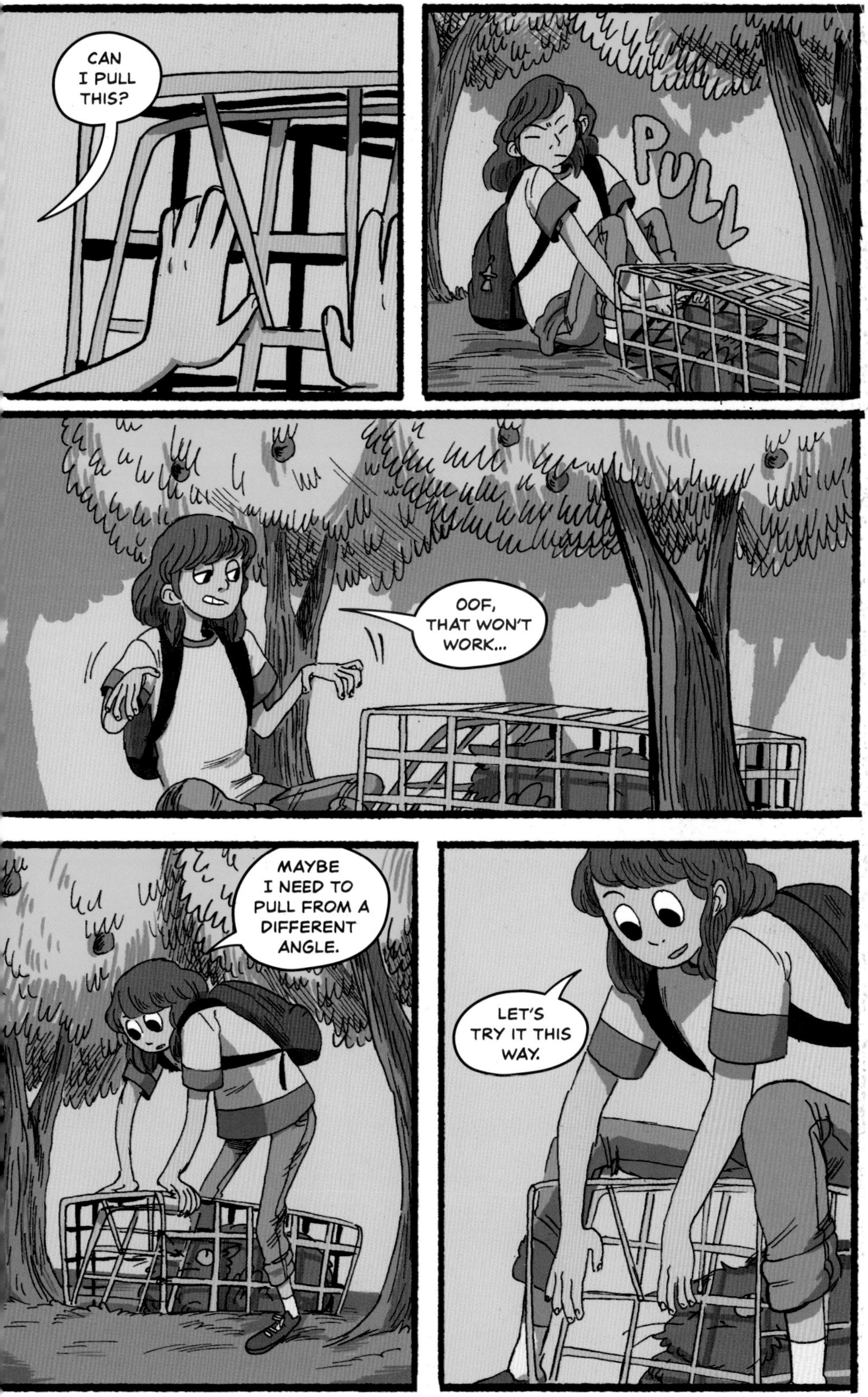
CAN I PULL THIS?
PULL
OOF, THAT WON'T WORK...
MAYBE I NEED TO PULL FROM A DIFFERENT ANGLE.
LET'S TRY IT THIS WAY.

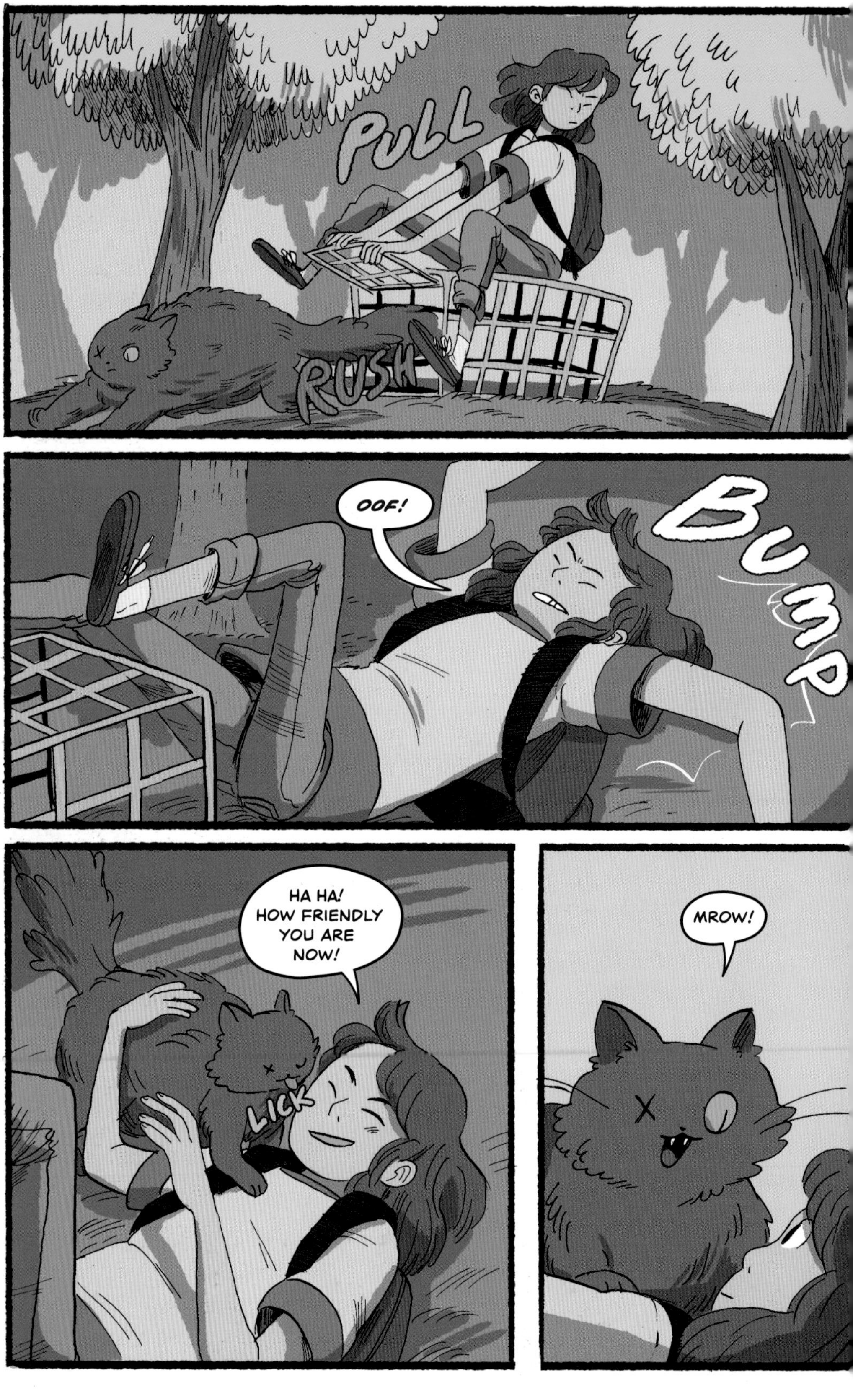
PULL
RUSH
OOF!
BUMP
HA HA! HOW FRIENDLY YOU ARE NOW!
LICK
MROW!

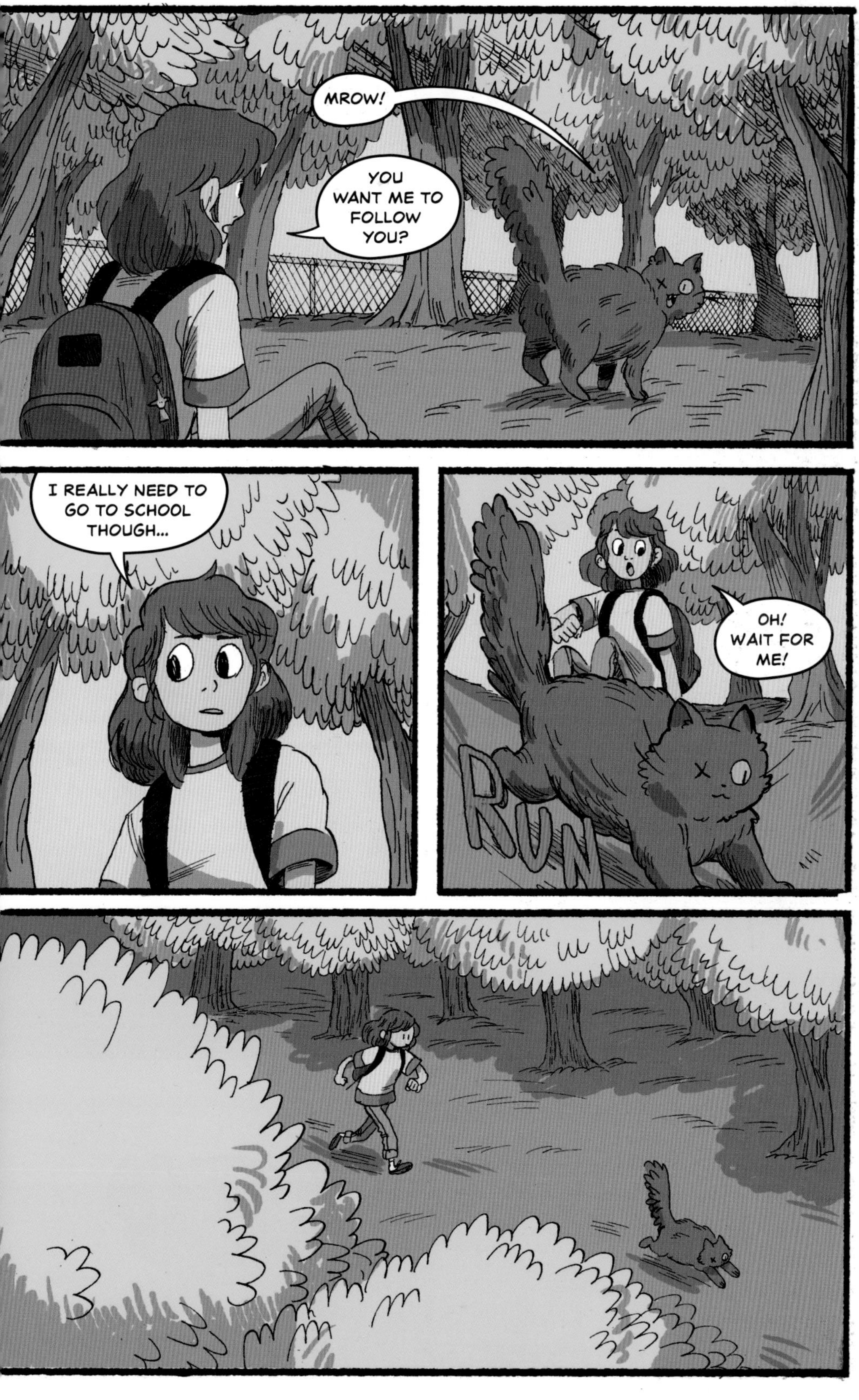
MROW!
YOU WANT ME TO FOLLOW YOU?
I REALLY NEED TO GO TO SCHOOL THOUGH...
RUN
OH! WAIT FOR ME!

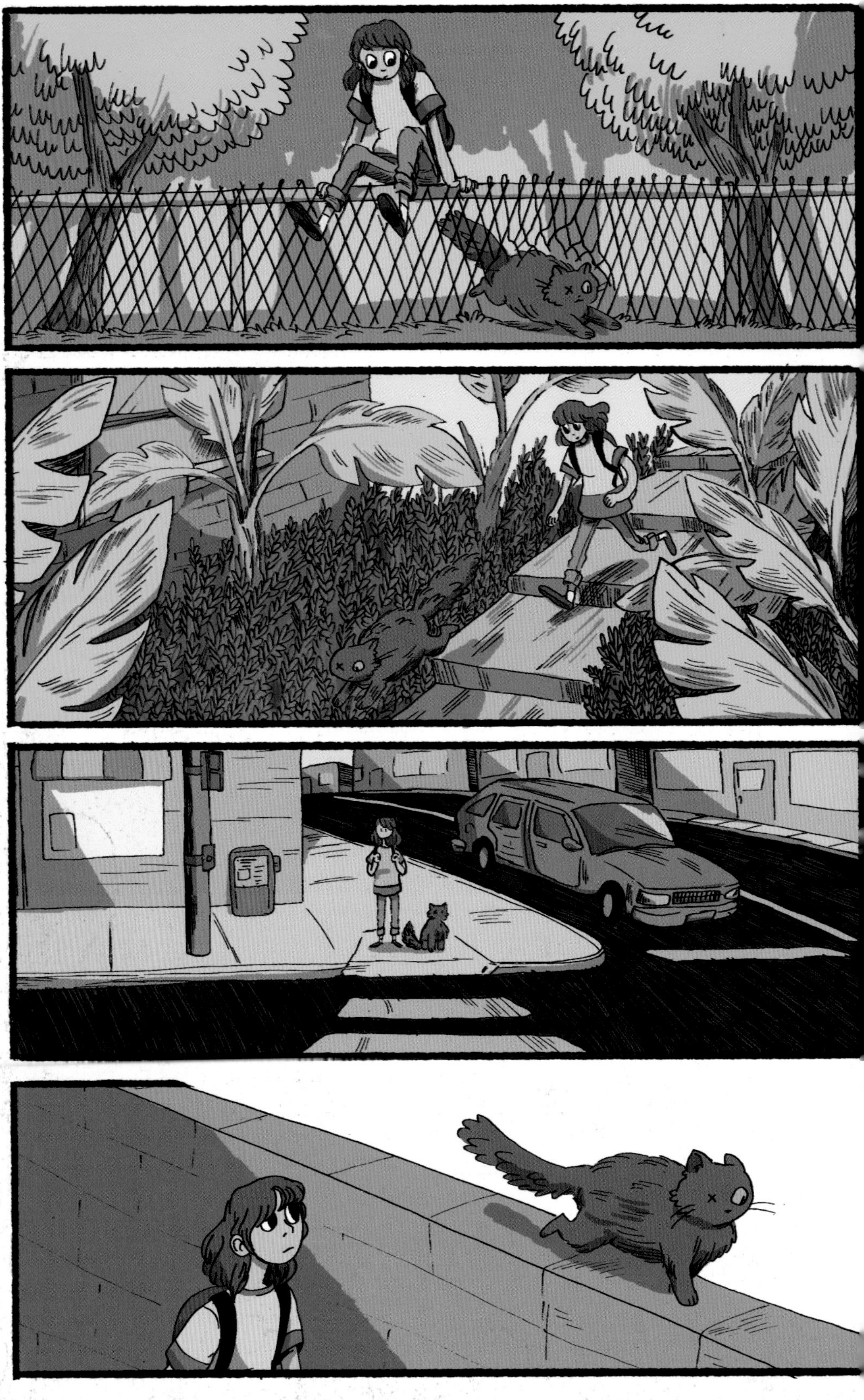

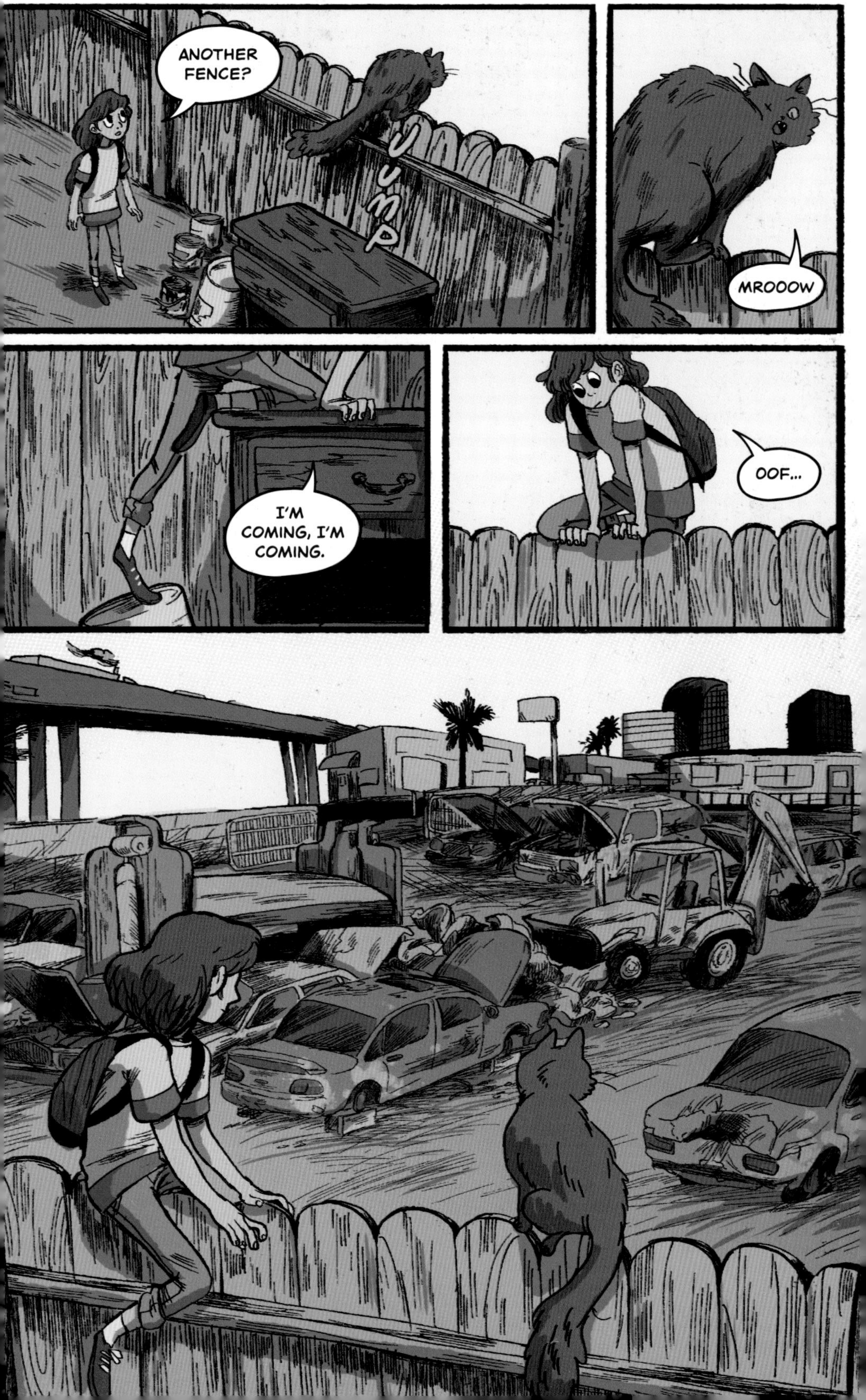
ANOTHER FENCE?
JUMP
MROOOW
I'M COMING, I'M COMING.
OOF...

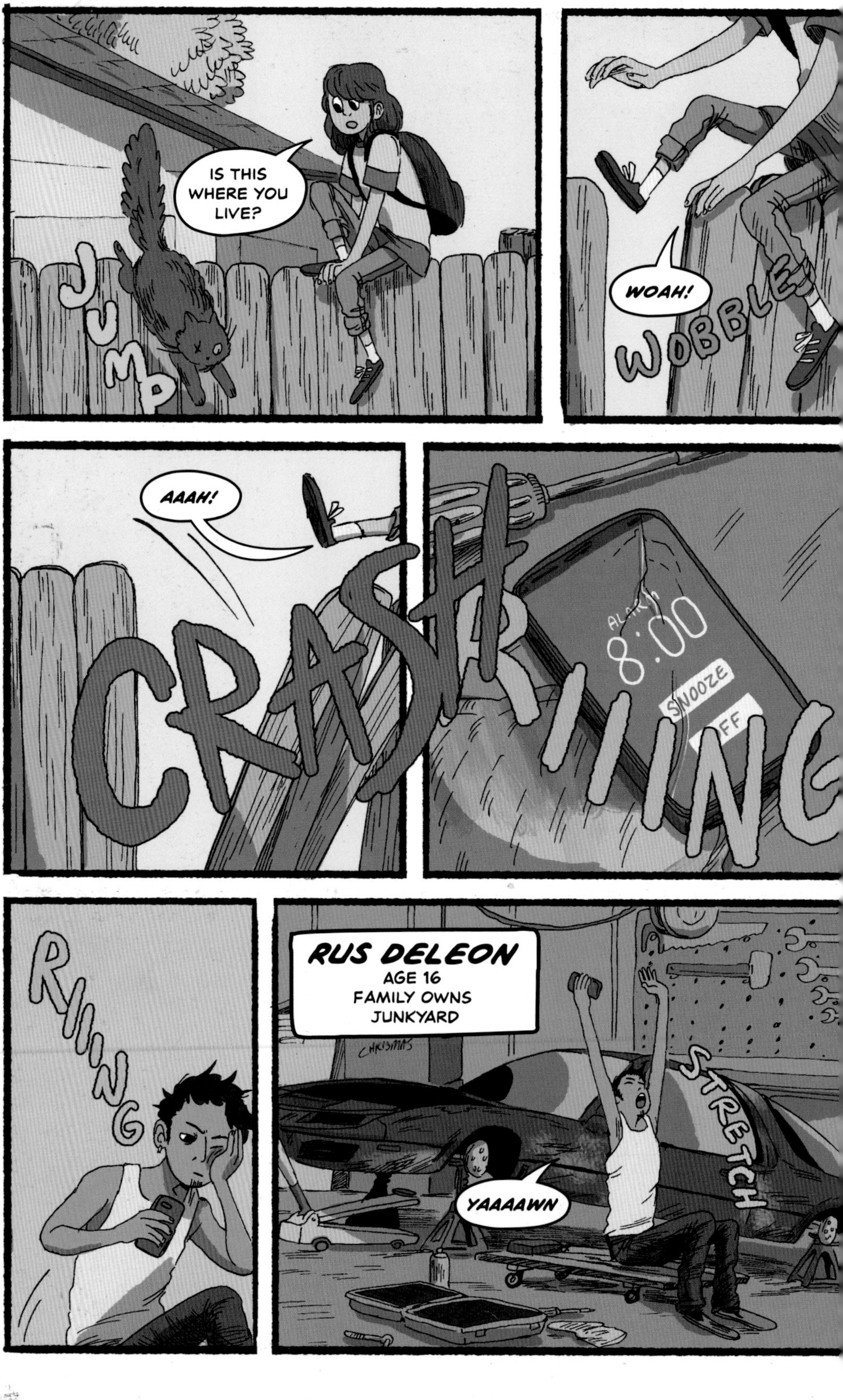

IS THIS WHERE YOU LIVE?
JUMP
WOAH!
WOBBLE
AAAH!
CRASH
ALARM
8:00
SNOOZE
RIIING
RIIING
RUS DELEON
AGE 16
FAMILY OWNS JUNKYARD
CHRISTMAS
STRETCH
YAAAAWN

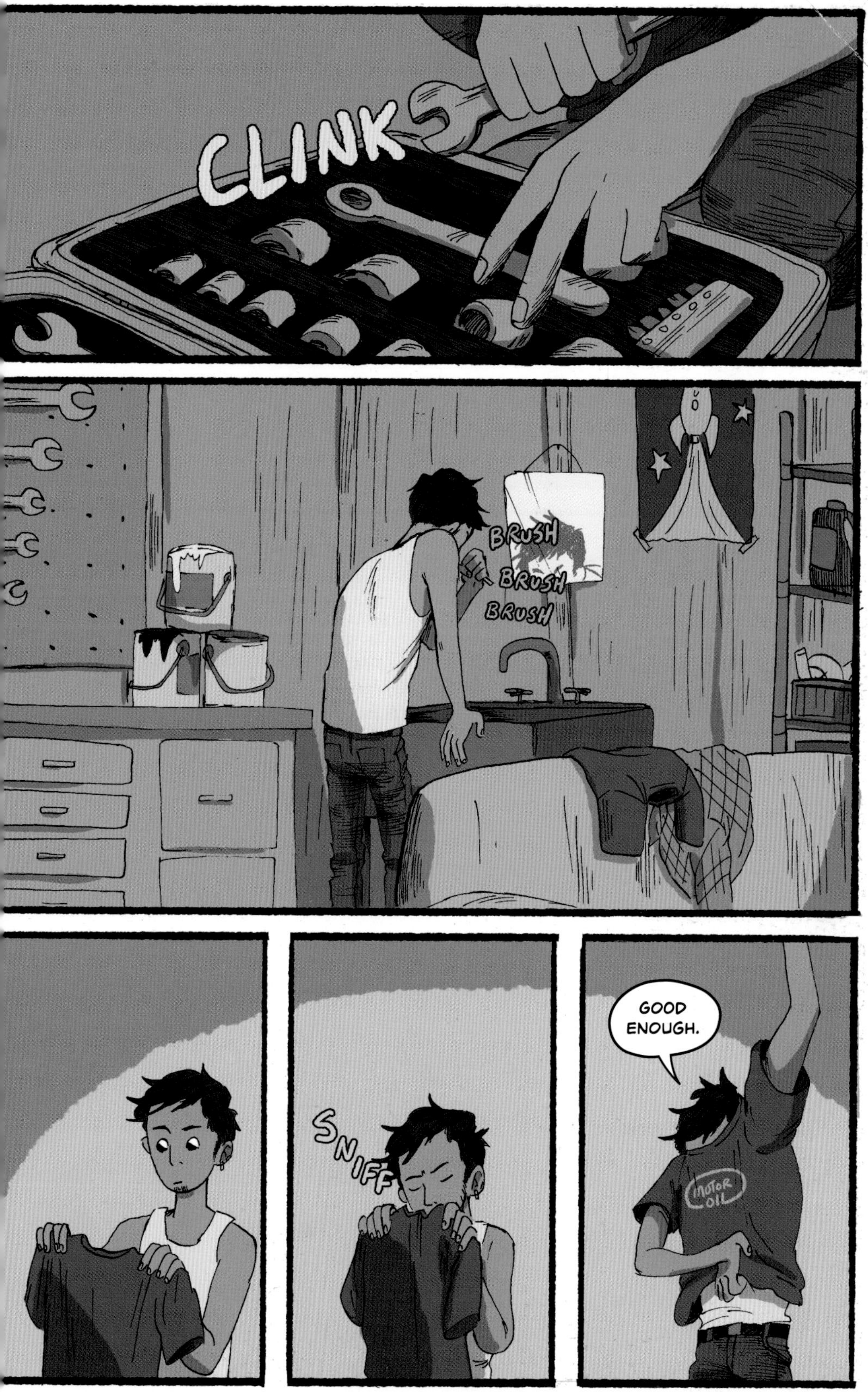
CLINK
BRUSH
BRUSH
BRUSH
SNIFF
GOOD ENOUGH.
MOTOR OIL

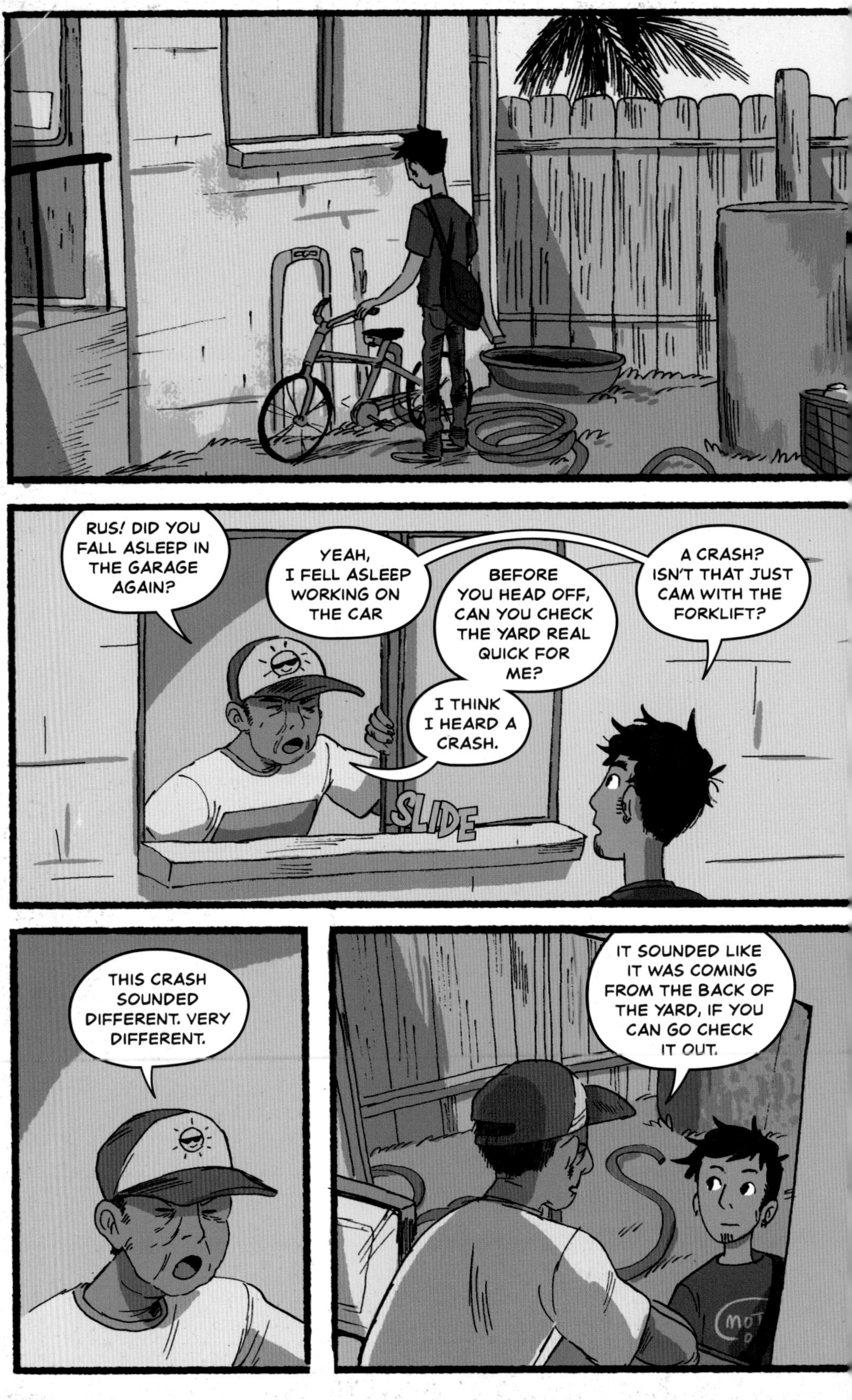
RUS! DID YOU FALL ASLEEP IN THE GARAGE AGAIN?
YEAH, I FELL ASLEEP WORKING ON THE CAR
A CRASH? ISN'T THAT JUST CAM WITH THE FORKLIFT?
BEFORE YOU HEAD OFF, CAN YOU CHECK THE YARD REAL QUICK FOR ME?
I THINK I HEARD A CRASH.
SLIDE
THIS CRASH SOUNDED DIFFERENT. VERY DIFFERENT.
IT SOUNDED LIKE IT WAS COMING FROM THE BACK OF THE YARD, IF YOU CAN GO CHECK IT OUT.

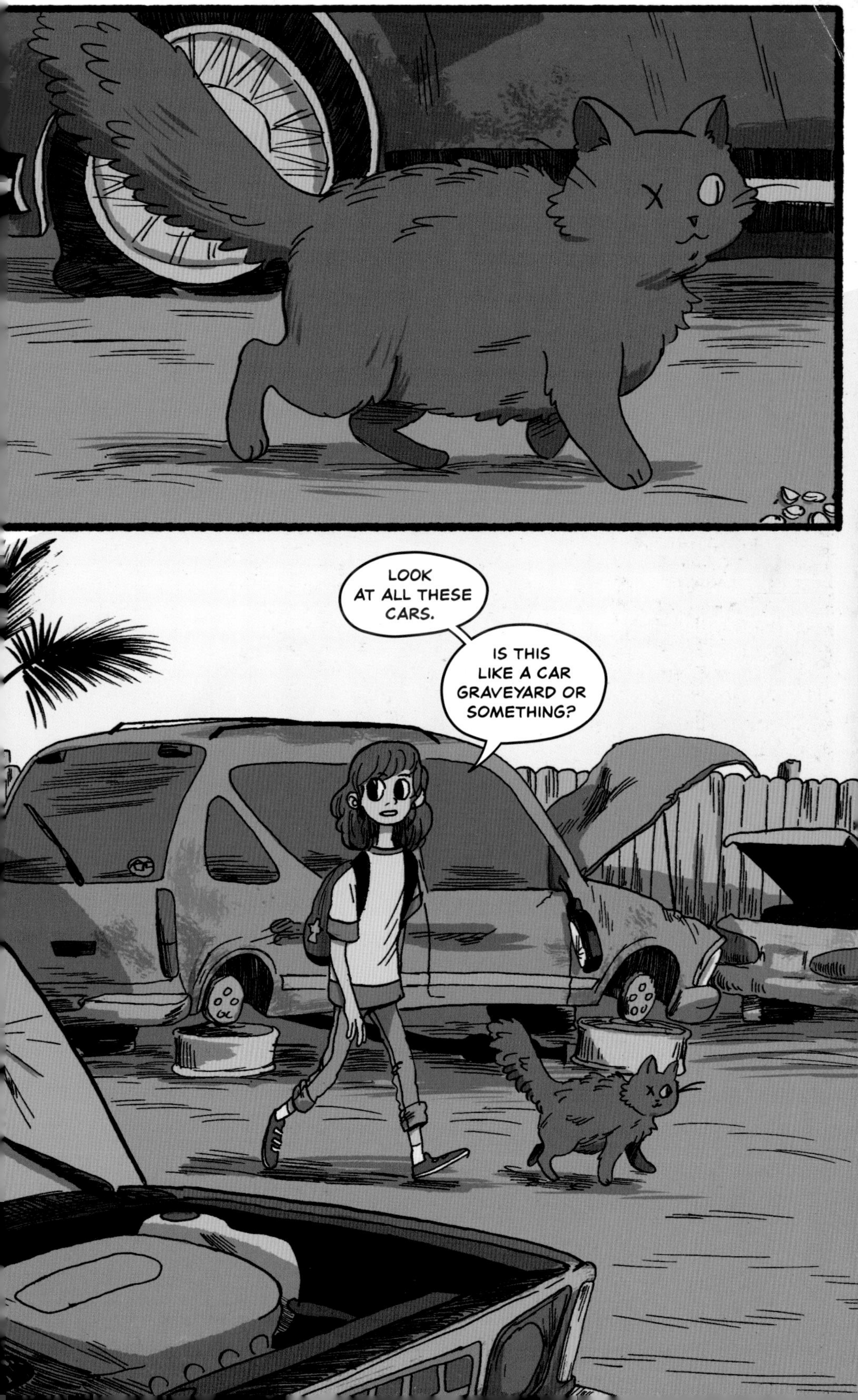
LOOK AT ALL THESE CARS.
IS THIS LIKE A CAR GRAVEYARD OR SOMETHING?

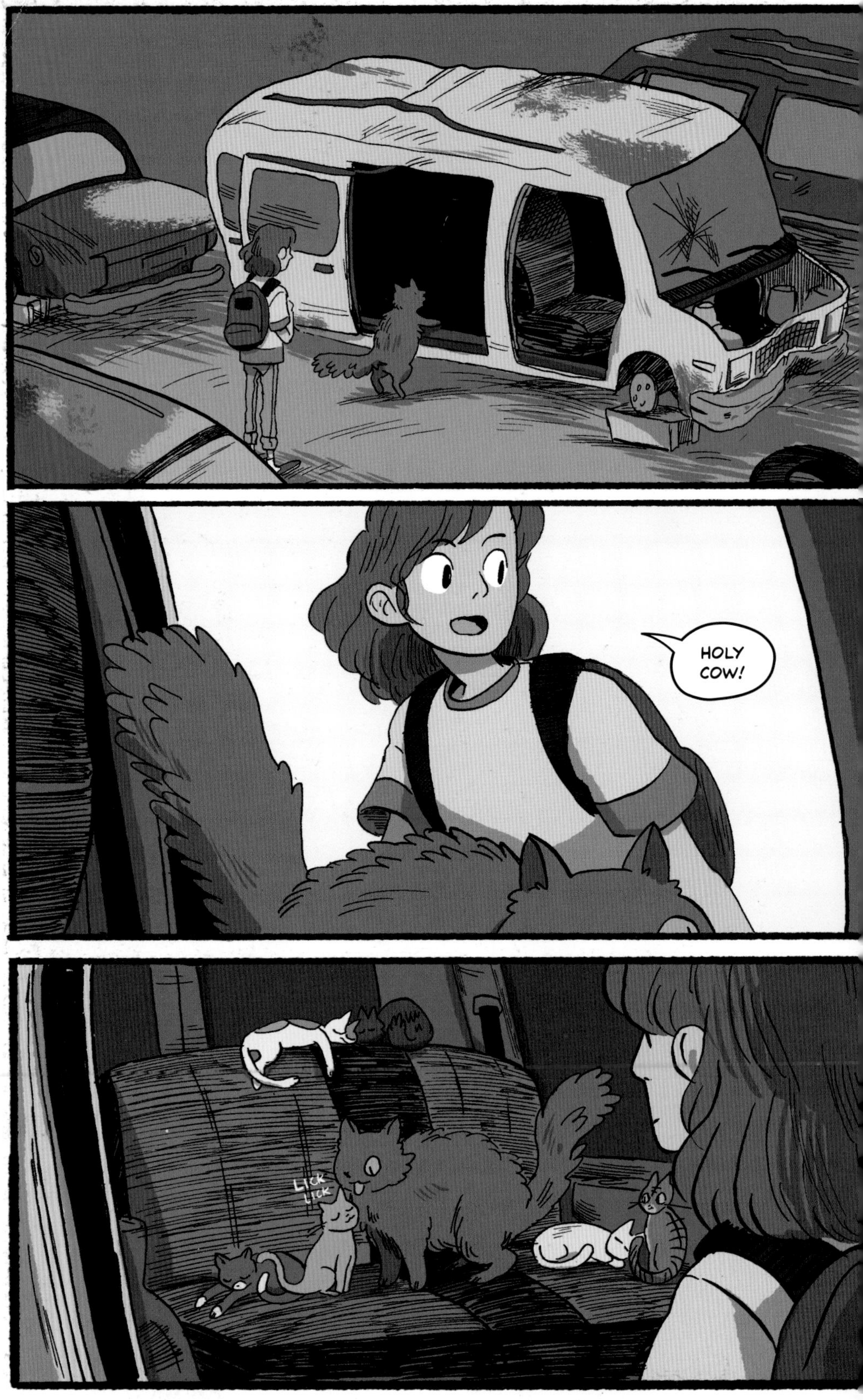
HOLY COW!
LICK LICK

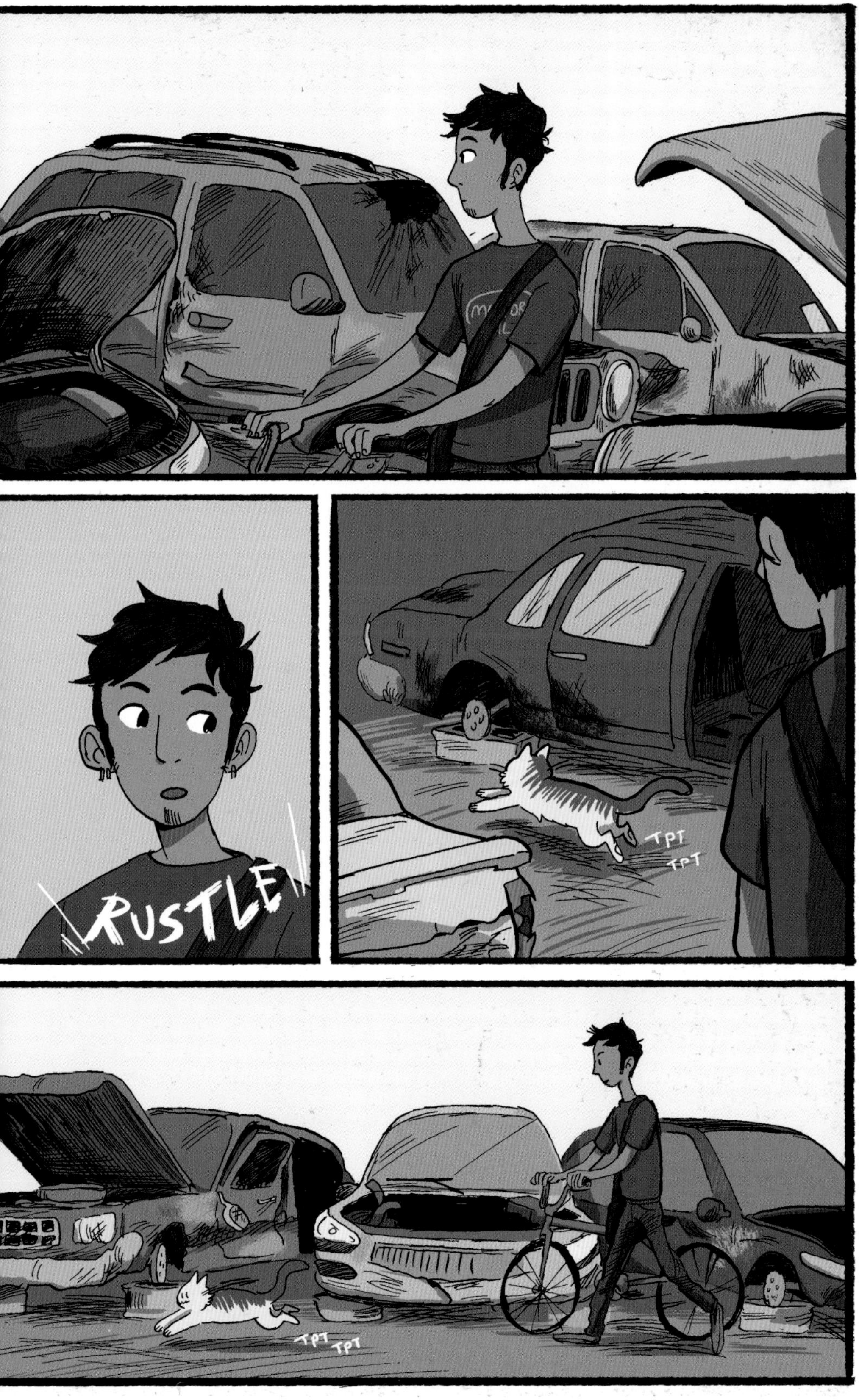
RUSTLE
TPT
TPT
TPT
TPT

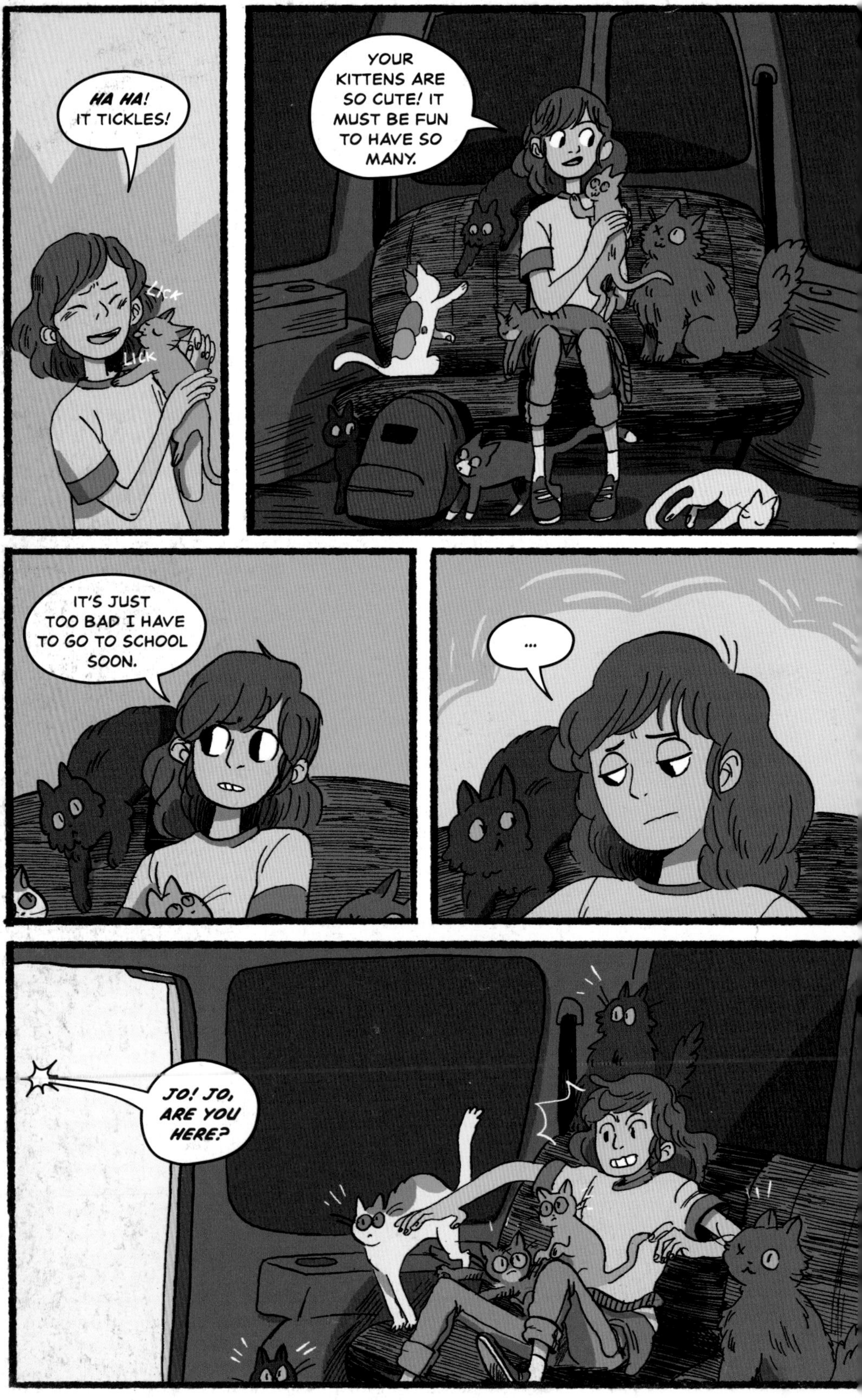
HA HA! IT TICKLES!
LICK
LICK
YOUR KITTENS ARE SO CUTE! IT MUST BE FUN TO HAVE SO MANY.
IT'S JUST TOO BAD I HAVE TO GO TO SCHOOL SOON.
...
JO! JO, ARE YOU HERE?

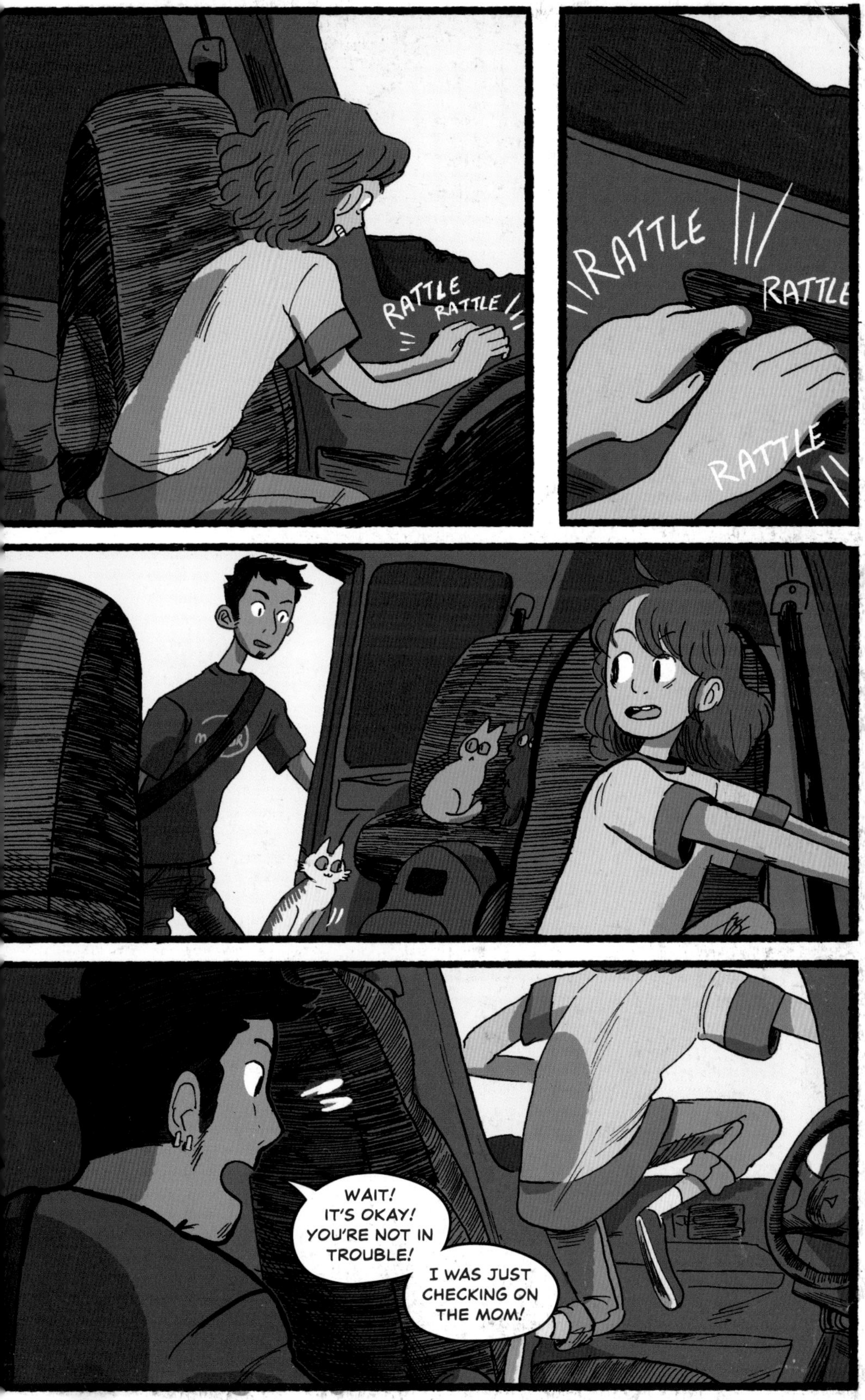
RATTLE
RATTLE
RATTLE
RATTLE
RATTLE
WAIT! IT'S OKAY! YOU'RE NOT IN TROUBLE!
I WAS JUST CHECKING ON THE MOM!

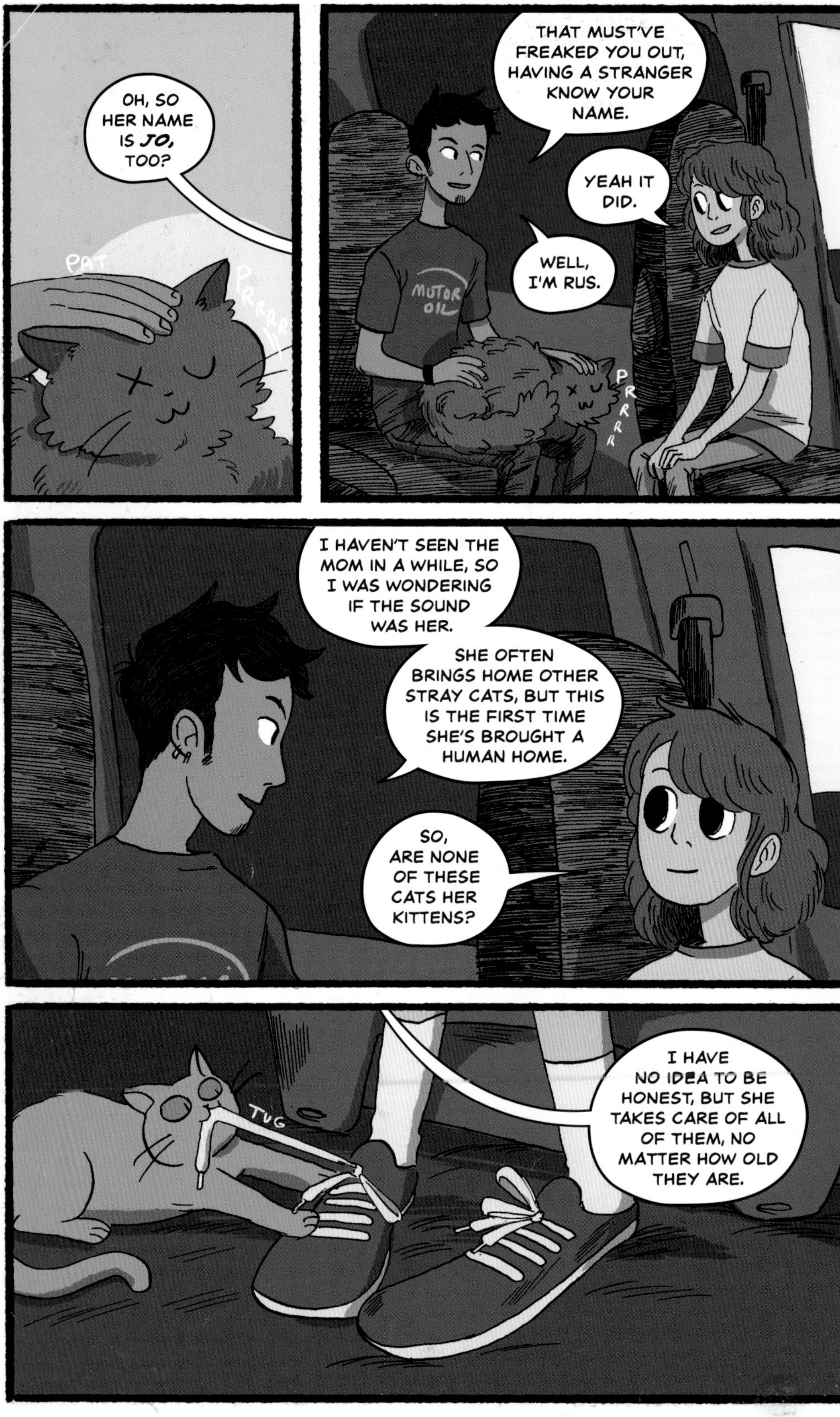
OH, SO HER NAME IS *JO,* TOO?
PAT
PRRRR
THAT MUST'VE FREAKED YOU OUT, HAVING A STRANGER KNOW YOUR NAME.
YEAH IT DID.
WELL, I'M RUS.
MUTOR OIL
PRRRR
I HAVEN'T SEEN THE MOM IN A WHILE, SO I WAS WONDERING IF THE SOUND WAS HER.
SHE OFTEN BRINGS HOME OTHER STRAY CATS, BUT THIS IS THE FIRST TIME SHE'S BROUGHT A HUMAN HOME.
SO, ARE NONE OF THESE CATS HER KITTENS?
TUG
I HAVE NO IDEA TO BE HONEST, BUT SHE TAKES CARE OF ALL OF THEM, NO MATTER HOW OLD THEY ARE.

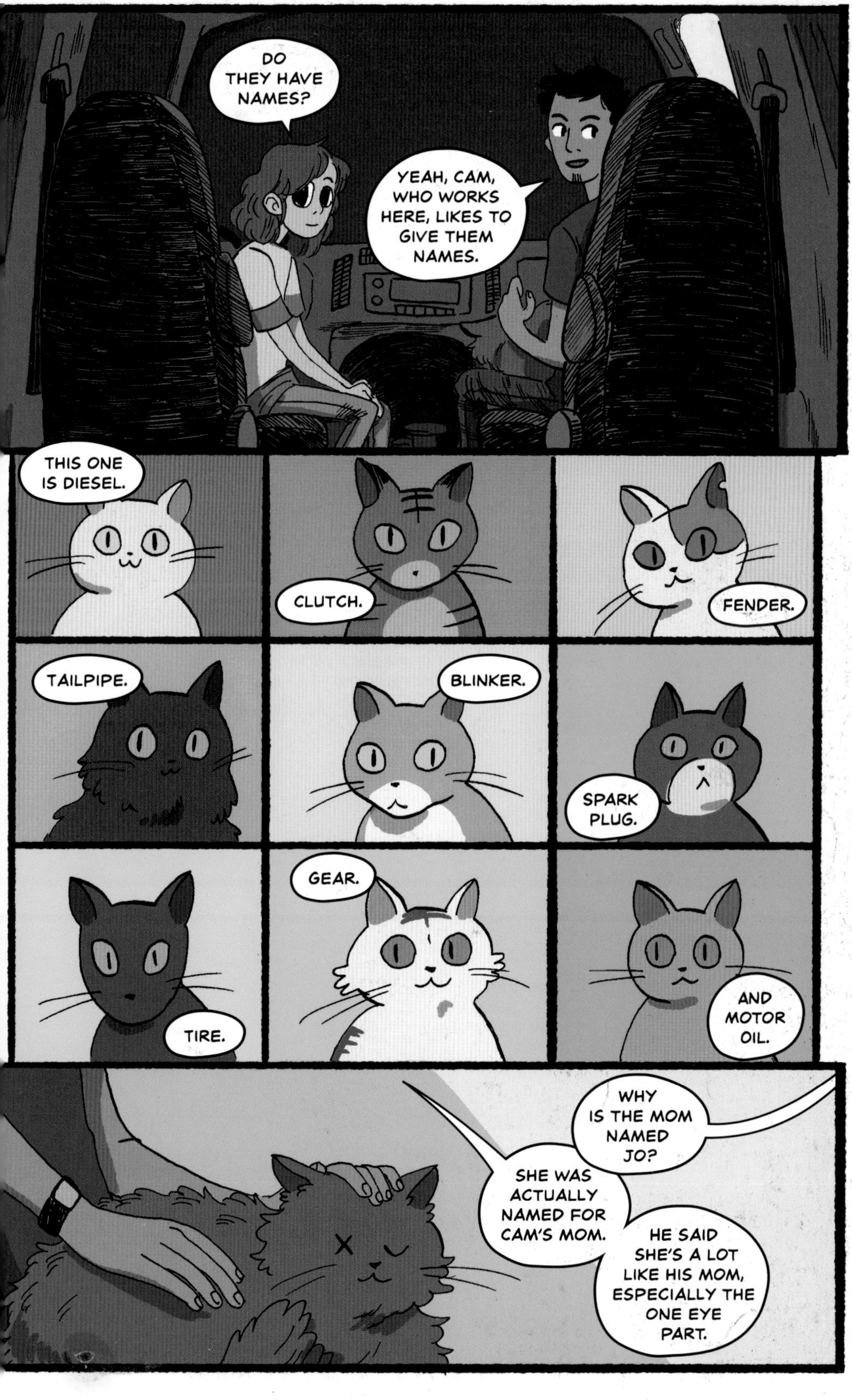
DO THEY HAVE NAMES?
YEAH, CAM, WHO WORKS HERE, LIKES TO GIVE THEM NAMES.
THIS ONE IS DIESEL.
CLUTCH.
FENDER.
TAILPIPE.
BLINKER.
SPARK PLUG.
TIRE.
GEAR.
AND MOTOR OIL.
WHY IS THE MOM NAMED JO?
SHE WAS ACTUALLY NAMED FOR CAM'S MOM.
HE SAID SHE'S A LOT LIKE HIS MOM, ESPECIALLY THE ONE EYE PART.

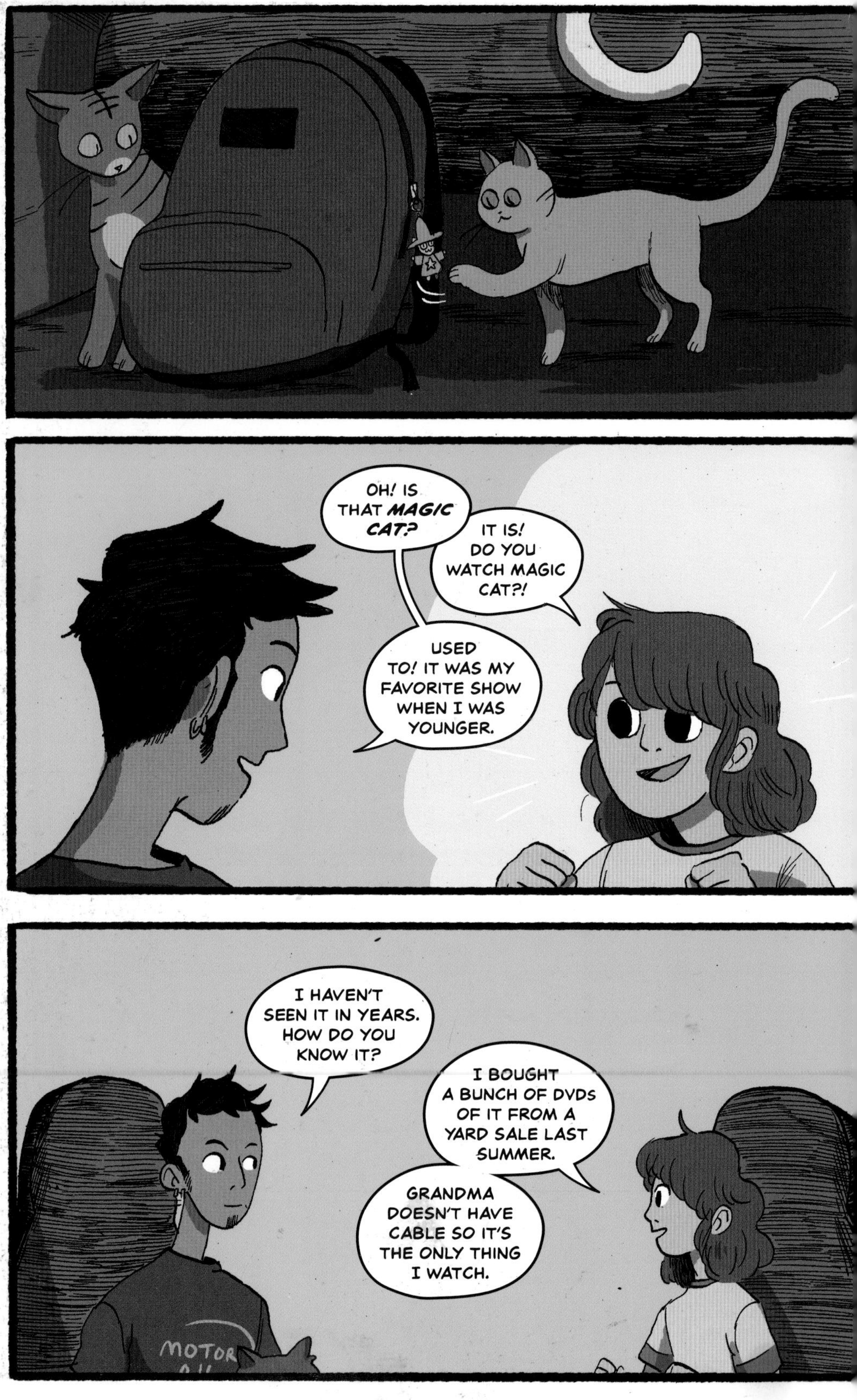
OH! IS THAT *MAGIC CAT?*
IT IS! DO YOU WATCH MAGIC CAT?!
USED TO! IT WAS MY FAVORITE SHOW WHEN I WAS YOUNGER.
I HAVEN'T SEEN IT IN YEARS. HOW DO YOU KNOW IT?
I BOUGHT A BUNCH OF DVDS OF IT FROM A YARD SALE LAST SUMMER.
GRANDMA DOESN'T HAVE CABLE SO IT'S THE ONLY THING I WATCH.
MOTOR

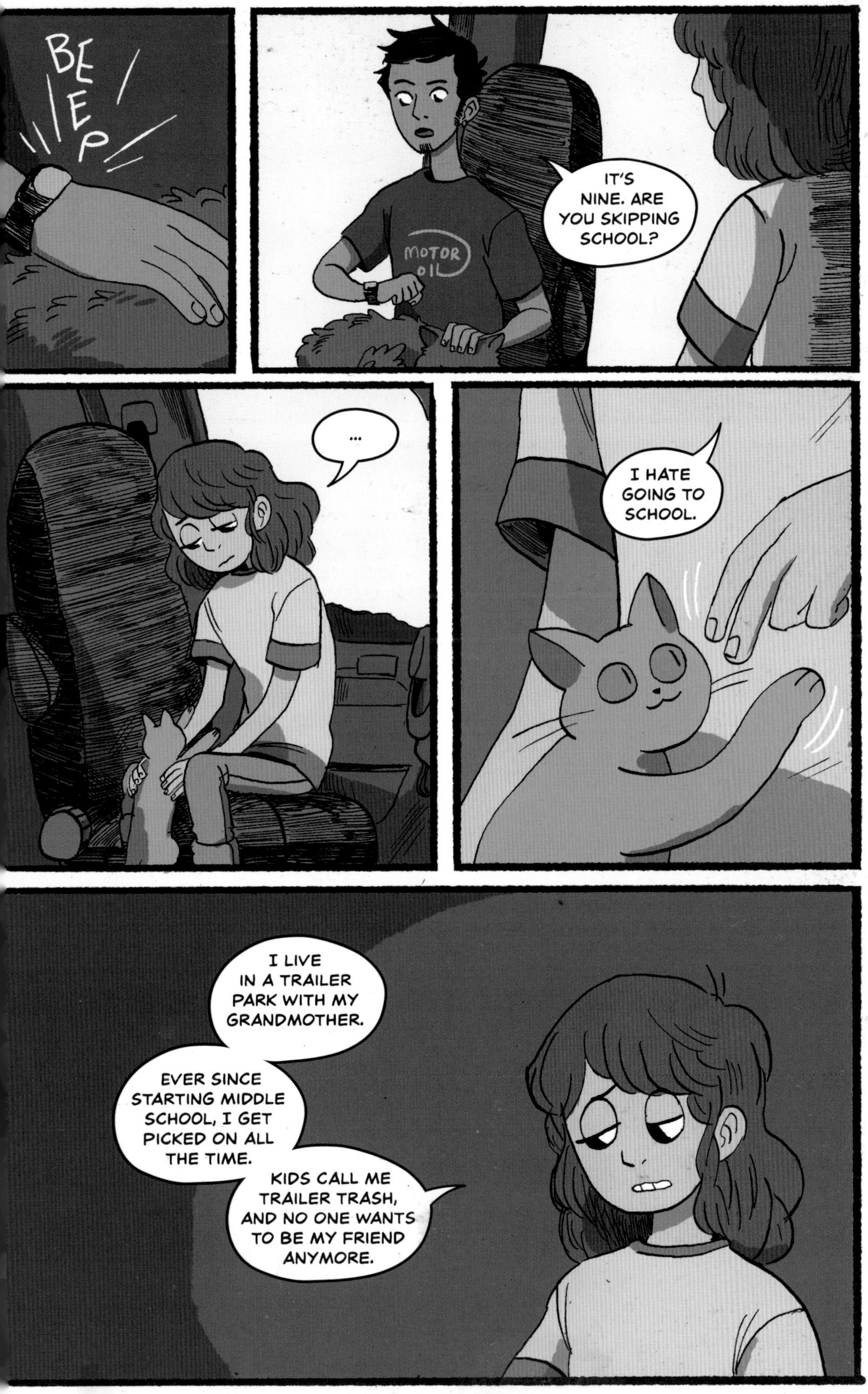
BEEP
IT'S NINE. ARE YOU SKIPPING SCHOOL?
MOTOR OIL
...
I HATE GOING TO SCHOOL.
I LIVE IN A TRAILER PARK WITH MY GRANDMOTHER.
EVER SINCE STARTING MIDDLE SCHOOL, I GET PICKED ON ALL THE TIME.
KIDS CALL ME TRAILER TRASH, AND NO ONE WANTS TO BE MY FRIEND ANYMORE.

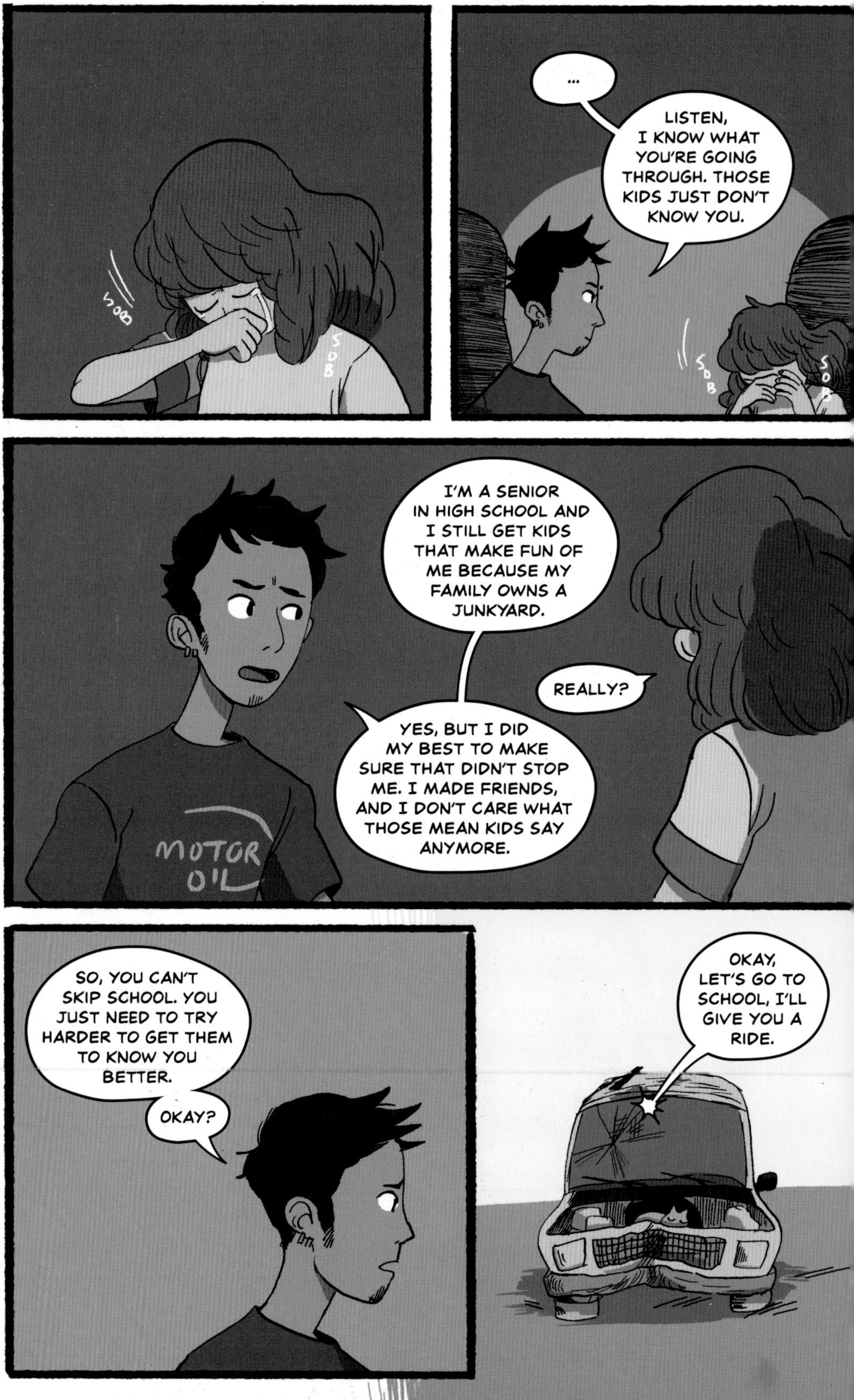
SOB
SOB
...
LISTEN, I KNOW WHAT YOU'RE GOING THROUGH. THOSE KIDS JUST DON'T KNOW YOU.
SOB
SOB
I'M A SENIOR IN HIGH SCHOOL AND I STILL GET KIDS THAT MAKE FUN OF ME BECAUSE MY FAMILY OWNS A JUNKYARD.
REALLY?
YES, BUT I DID MY BEST TO MAKE SURE THAT DIDN'T STOP ME. I MADE FRIENDS, AND I DON'T CARE WHAT THOSE MEAN KIDS SAY ANYMORE.
MOTOR OIL
SO, YOU CAN'T SKIP SCHOOL. YOU JUST NEED TO TRY HARDER TO GET THEM TO KNOW YOU BETTER.
OKAY?
OKAY, LET'S GO TO SCHOOL, I'LL GIVE YOU A RIDE.

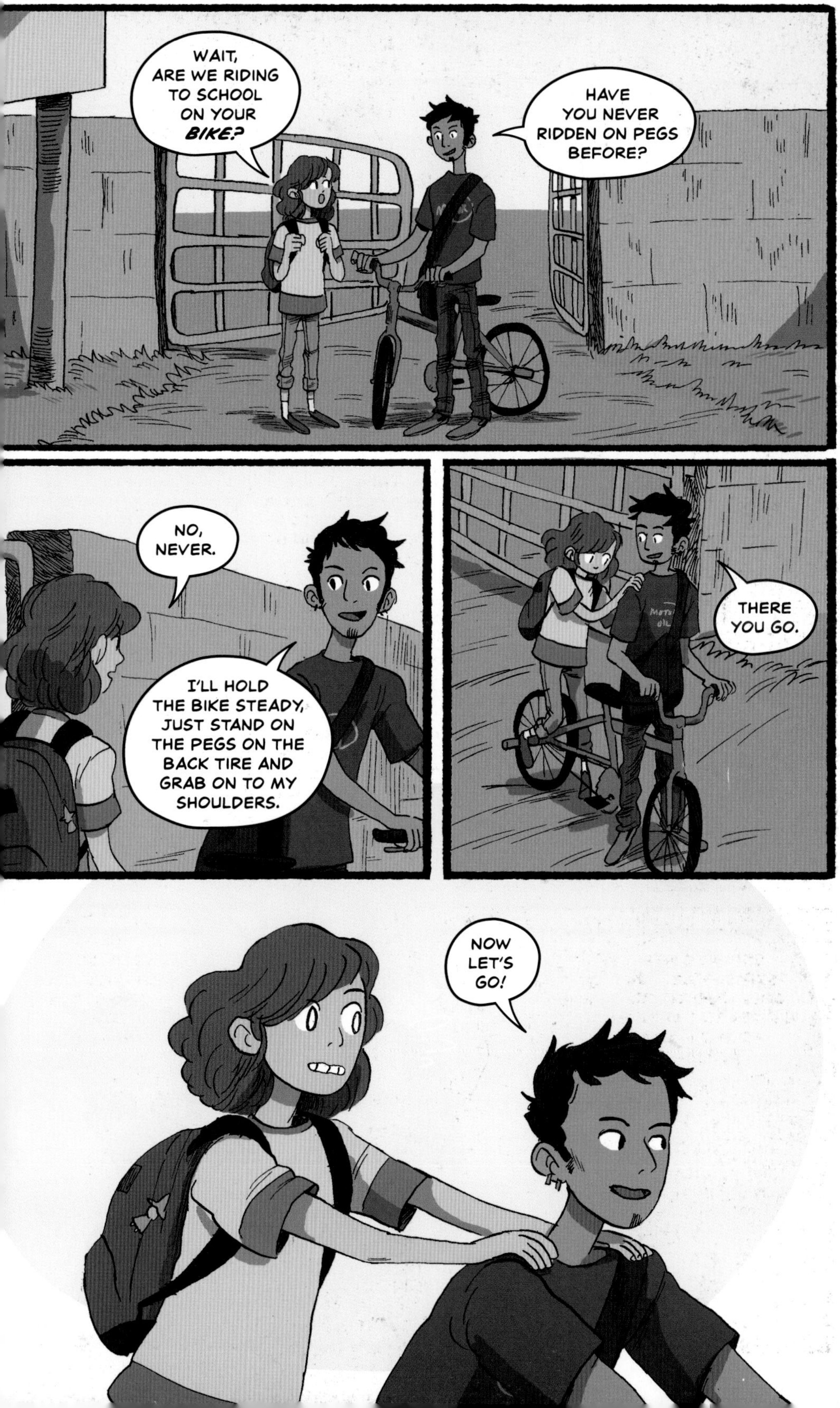
WAIT, ARE WE RIDING TO SCHOOL ON YOUR *BIKE?*
HAVE YOU NEVER RIDDEN ON PEGS BEFORE?
NO, NEVER.
I'LL HOLD THE BIKE STEADY, JUST STAND ON THE PEGS ON THE BACK TIRE AND GRAB ON TO MY SHOULDERS.
THERE YOU GO.
NOW LET'S GO!

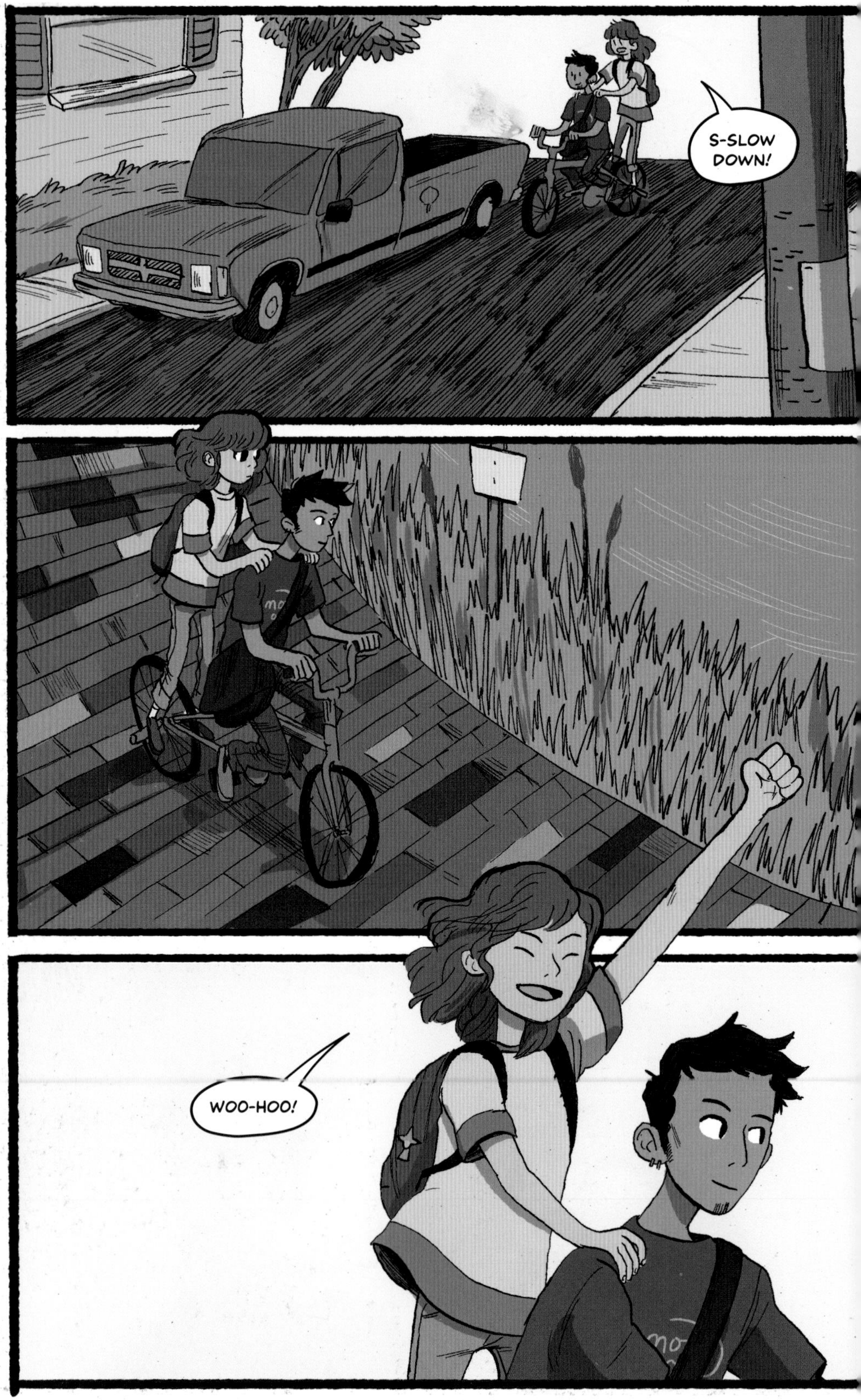
S-SLOW DOWN!
WOO-HOO!

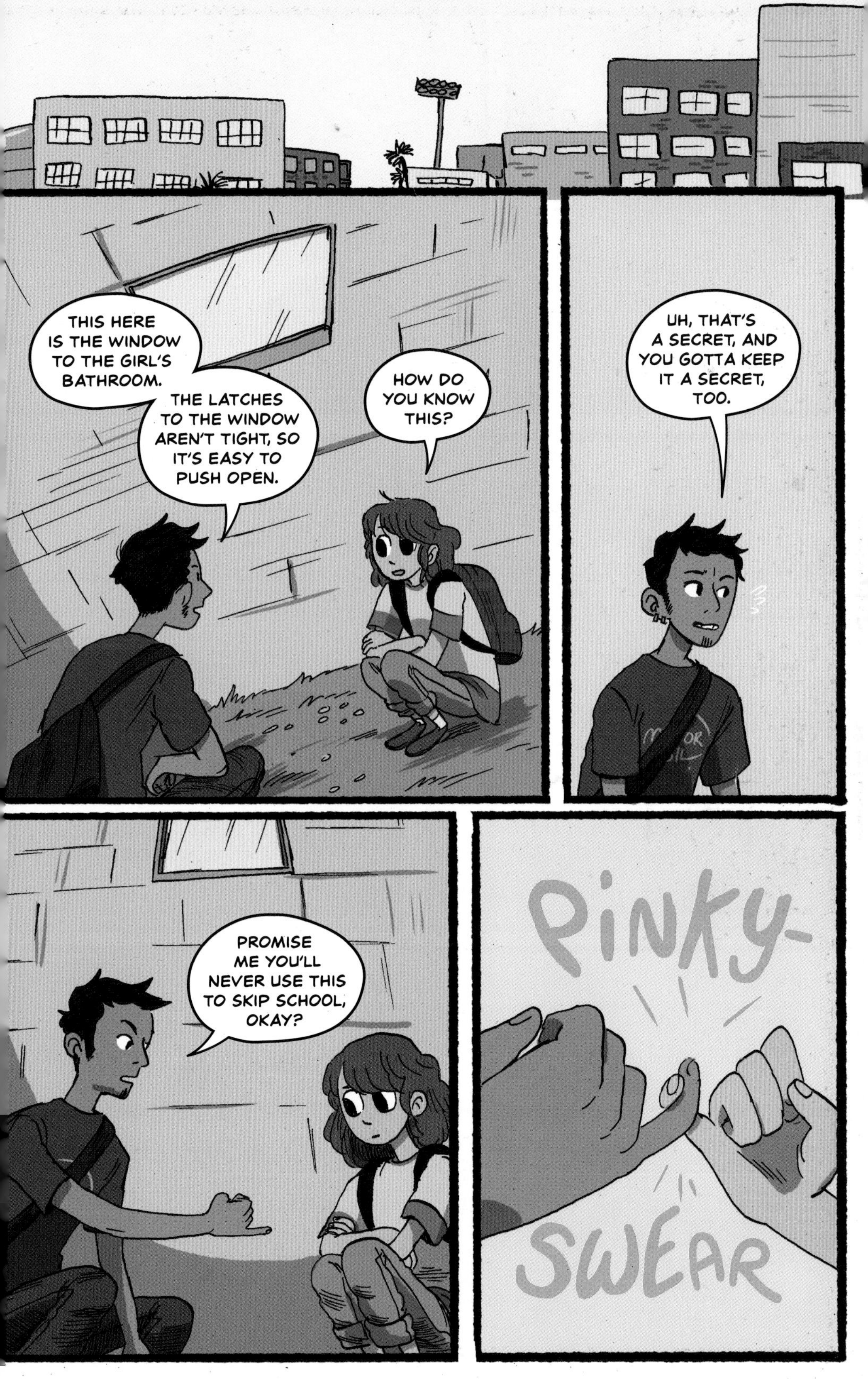
THIS HERE IS THE WINDOW TO THE GIRL'S BATHROOM.
THE LATCHES TO THE WINDOW AREN'T TIGHT, SO IT'S EASY TO PUSH OPEN.
HOW DO YOU KNOW THIS?
UH, THAT'S A SECRET, AND YOU GOTTA KEEP IT A SECRET, TOO.
PROMISE ME YOU'LL NEVER USE THIS TO SKIP SCHOOL, OKAY?
PINKY-
SWEAR

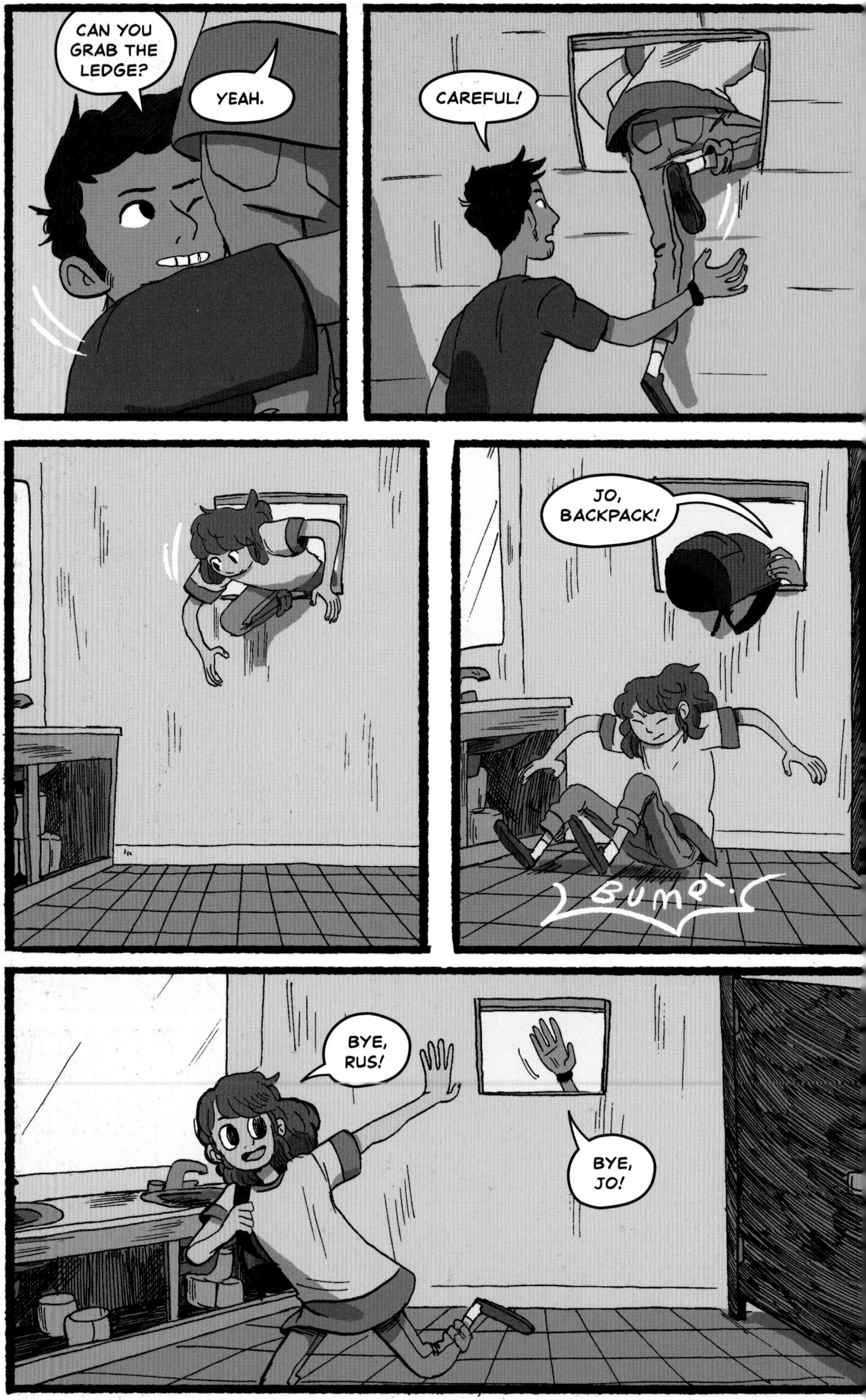
CAN YOU GRAB THE LEDGE?
YEAH.
CAREFUL!
JO, BACKPACK!
BUMP
BYE, RUS!
BYE, JO!

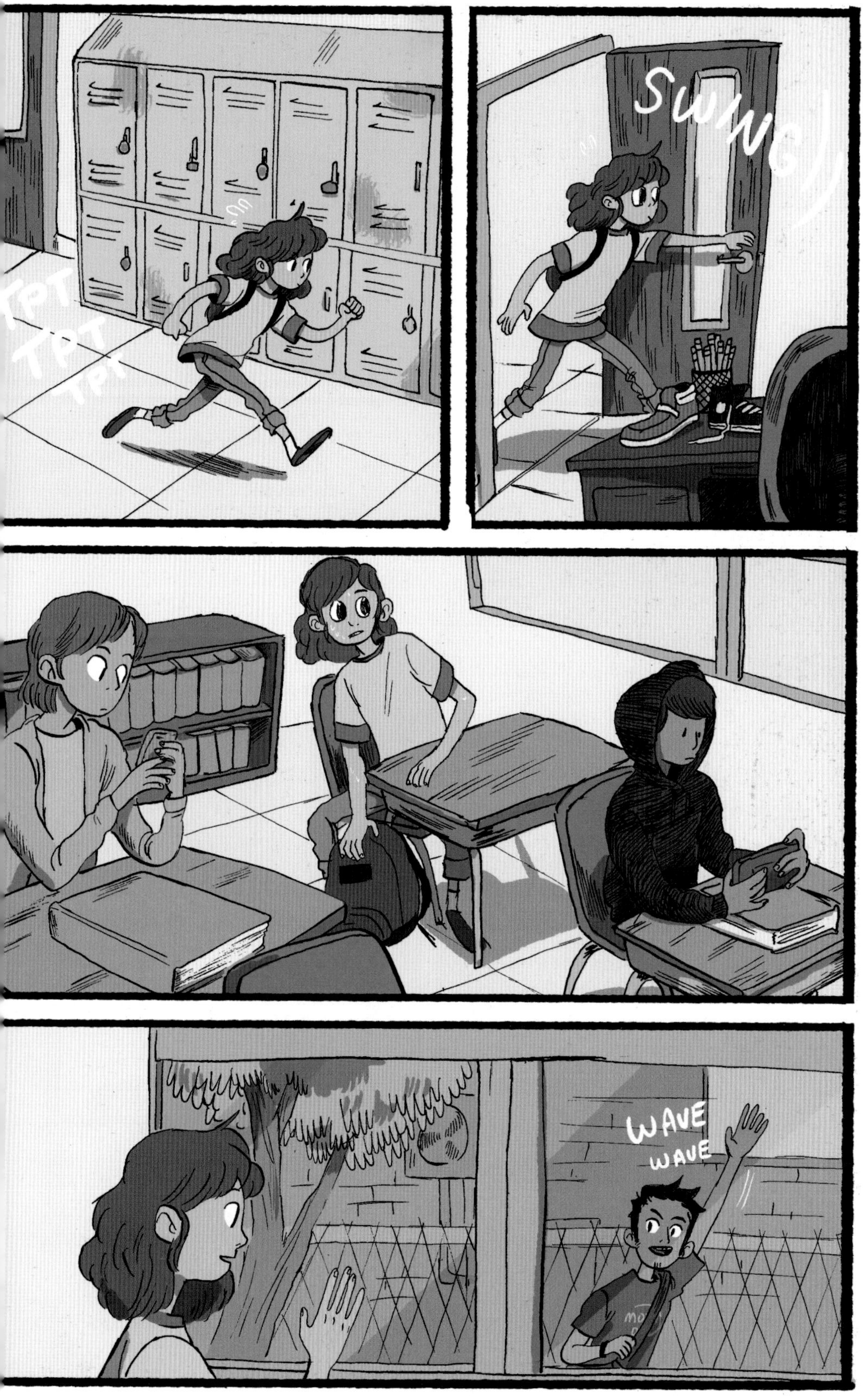
TPT
TPT
TPT
SWING
WAVE
WAVE

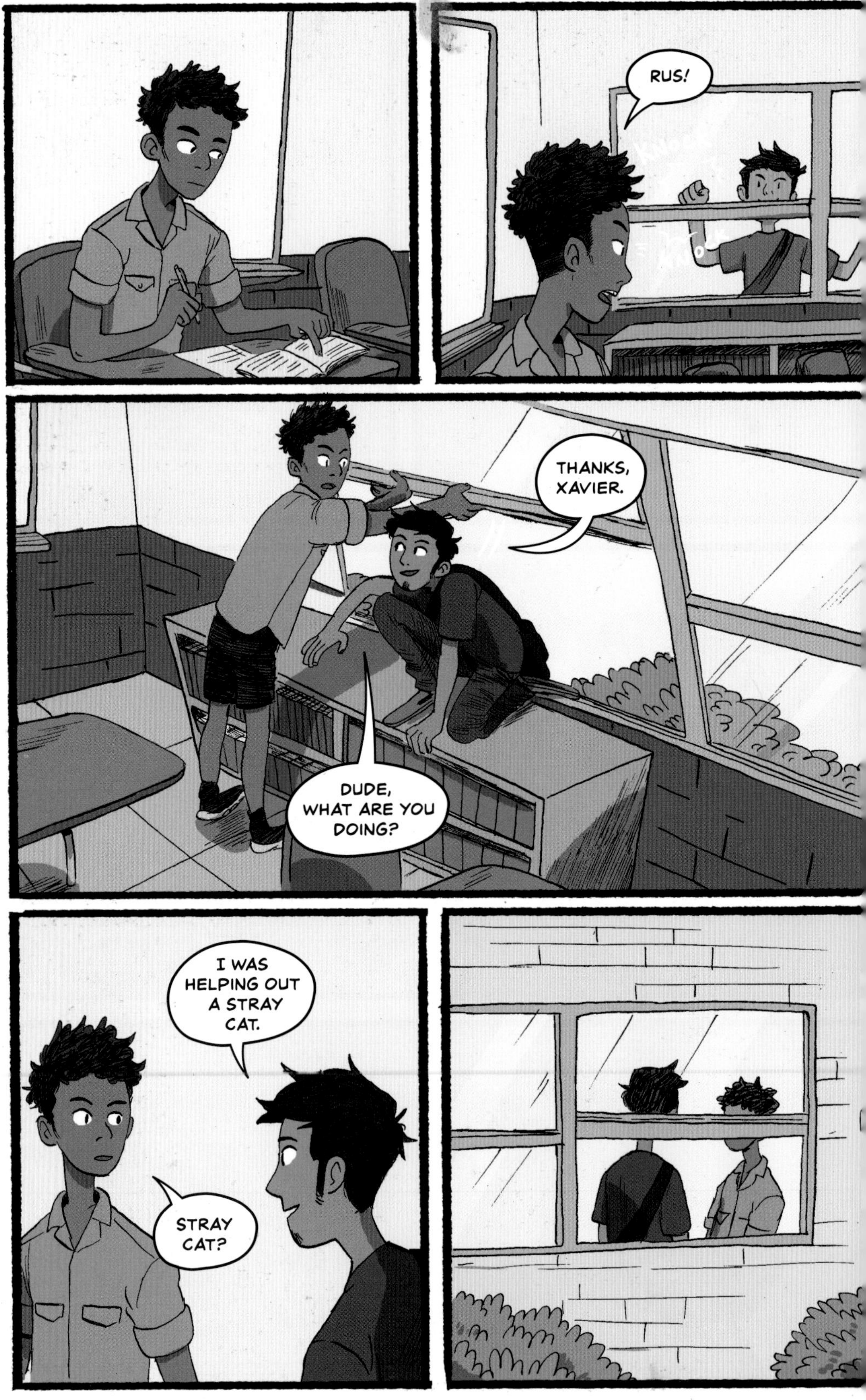
RUS!
THANKS, XAVIER.
DUDE, WHAT ARE YOU DOING?
I WAS HELPING OUT A STRAY CAT.
STRAY CAT?

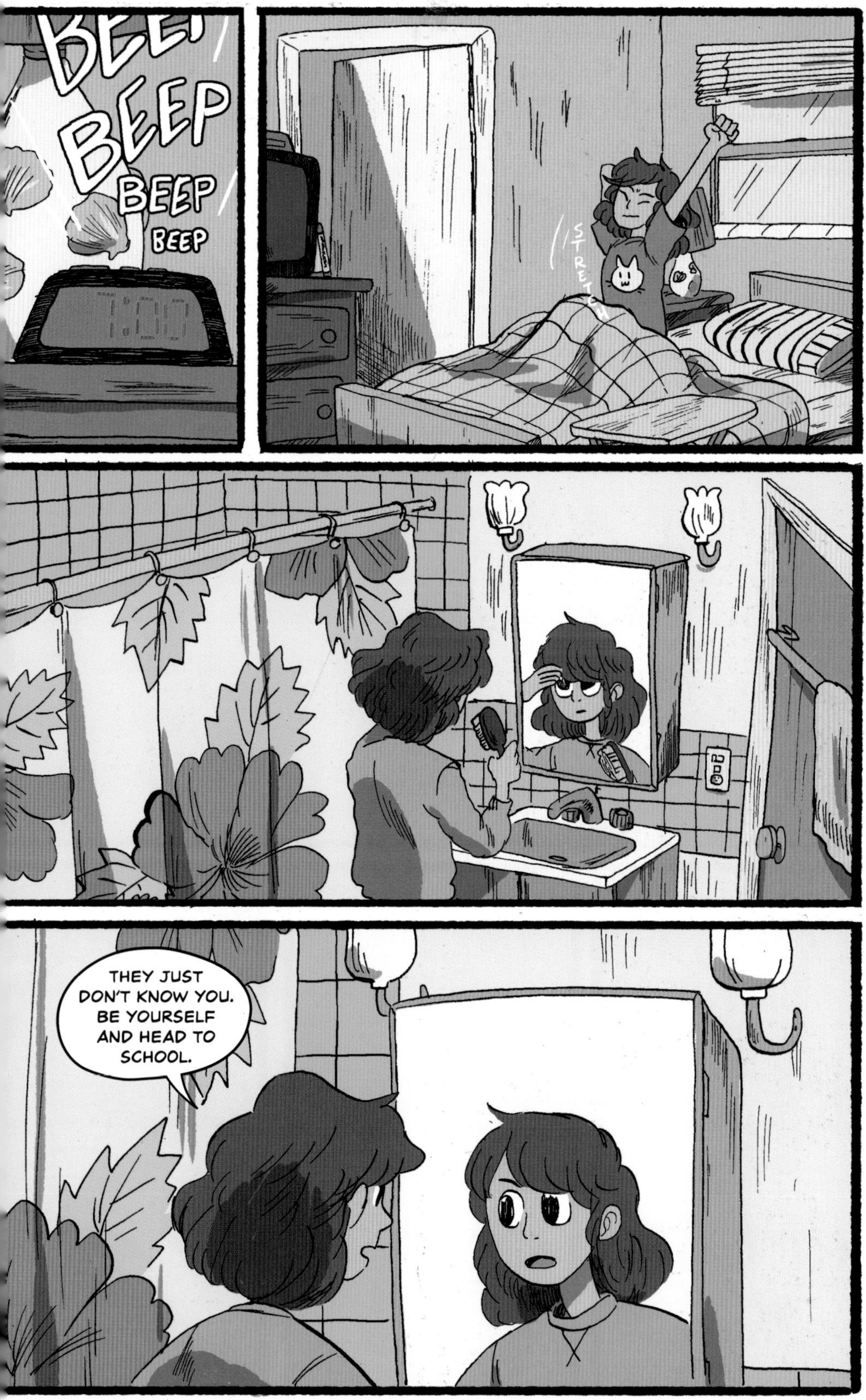
BEEP
BEEP
BEEP
BEEP
STRETCH
THEY JUST DON'T KNOW YOU. BE YOURSELF AND HEAD TO SCHOOL.

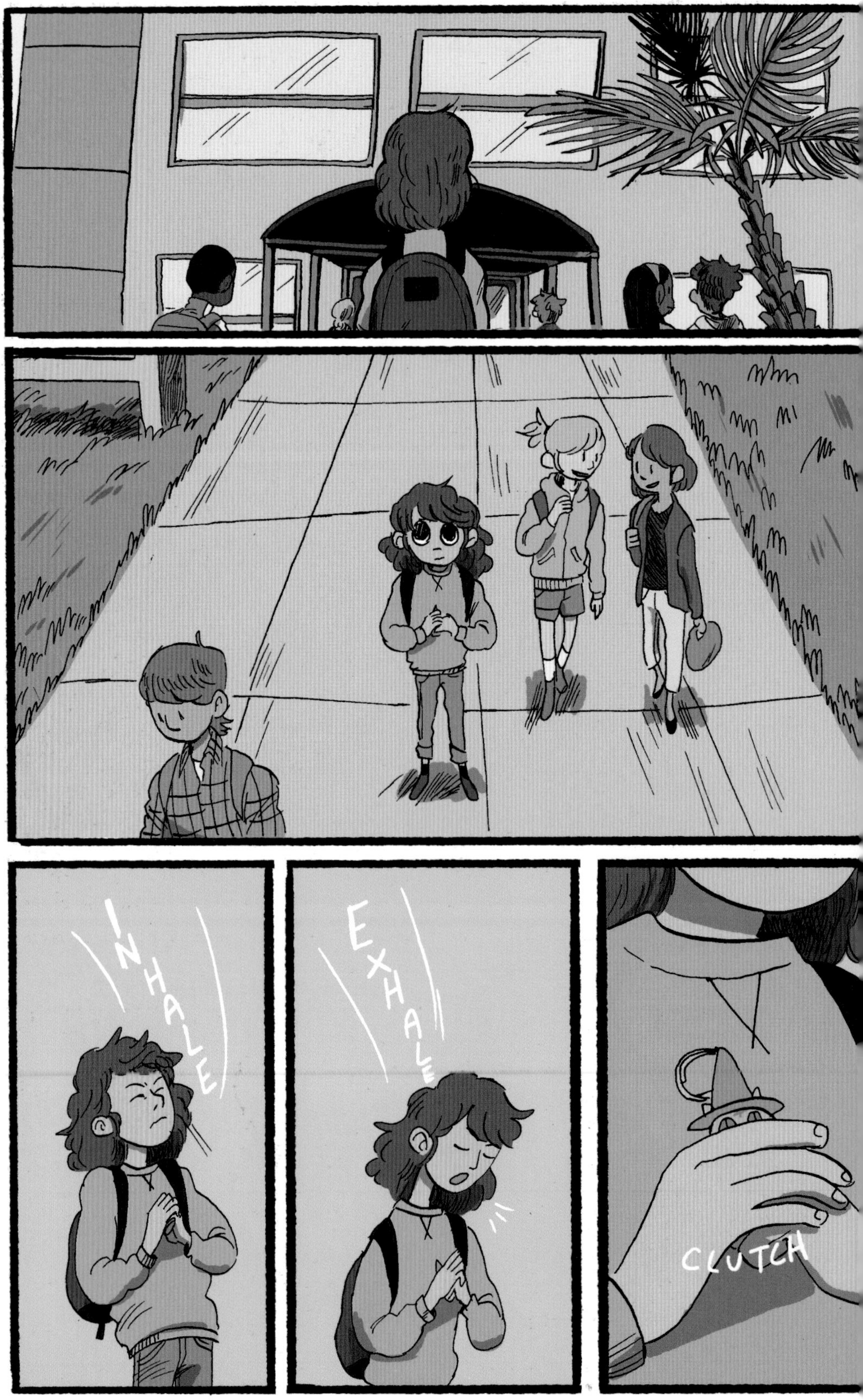
INHALE
EXHALE
CLUTCH

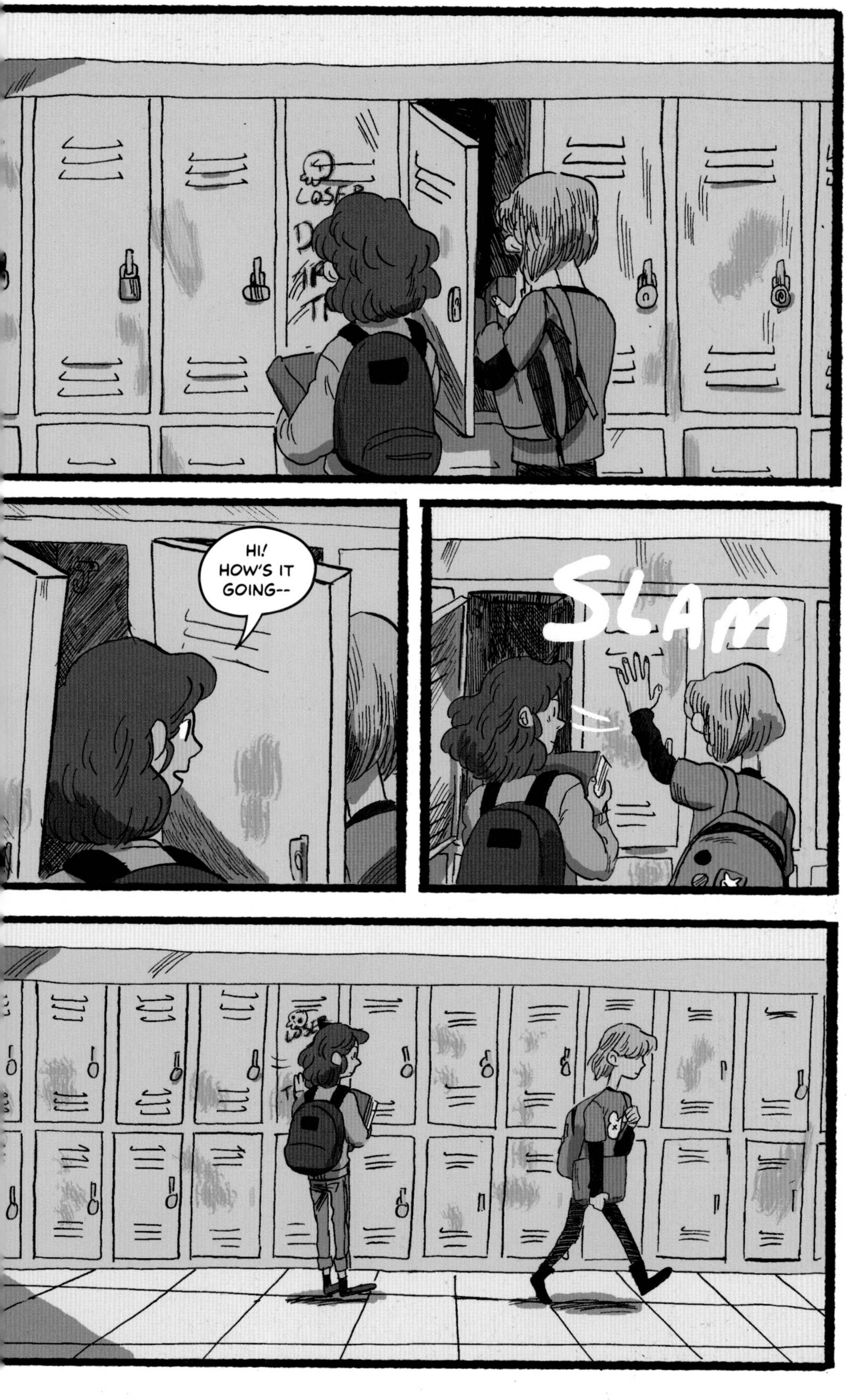
HI! HOW'S IT GOING--
SLAM

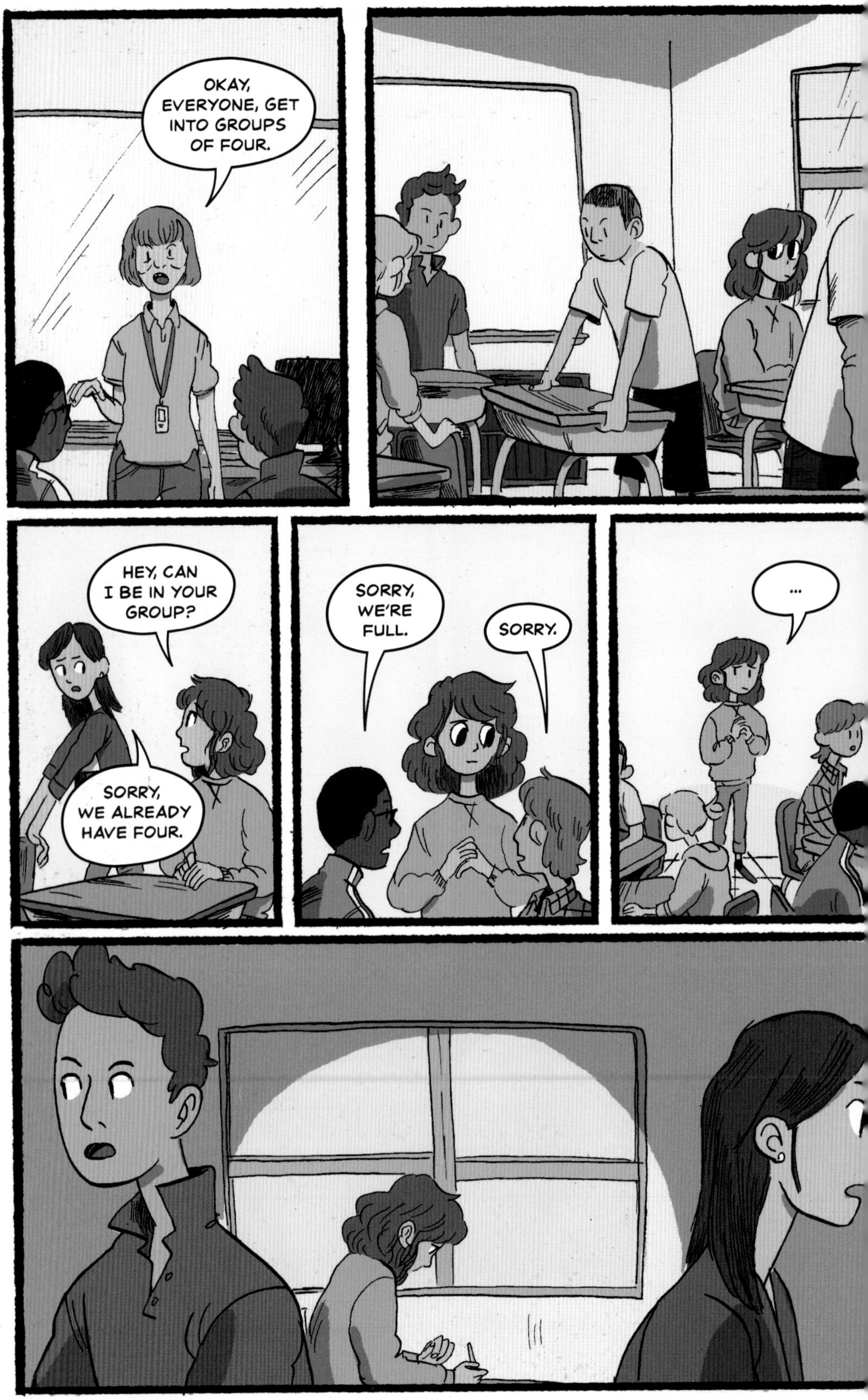

OKAY, EVERYONE, GET INTO GROUPS OF FOUR.
HEY, CAN I BE IN YOUR GROUP?
SORRY, WE ALREADY HAVE FOUR.
SORRY, WE'RE FULL.
SORRY.
...

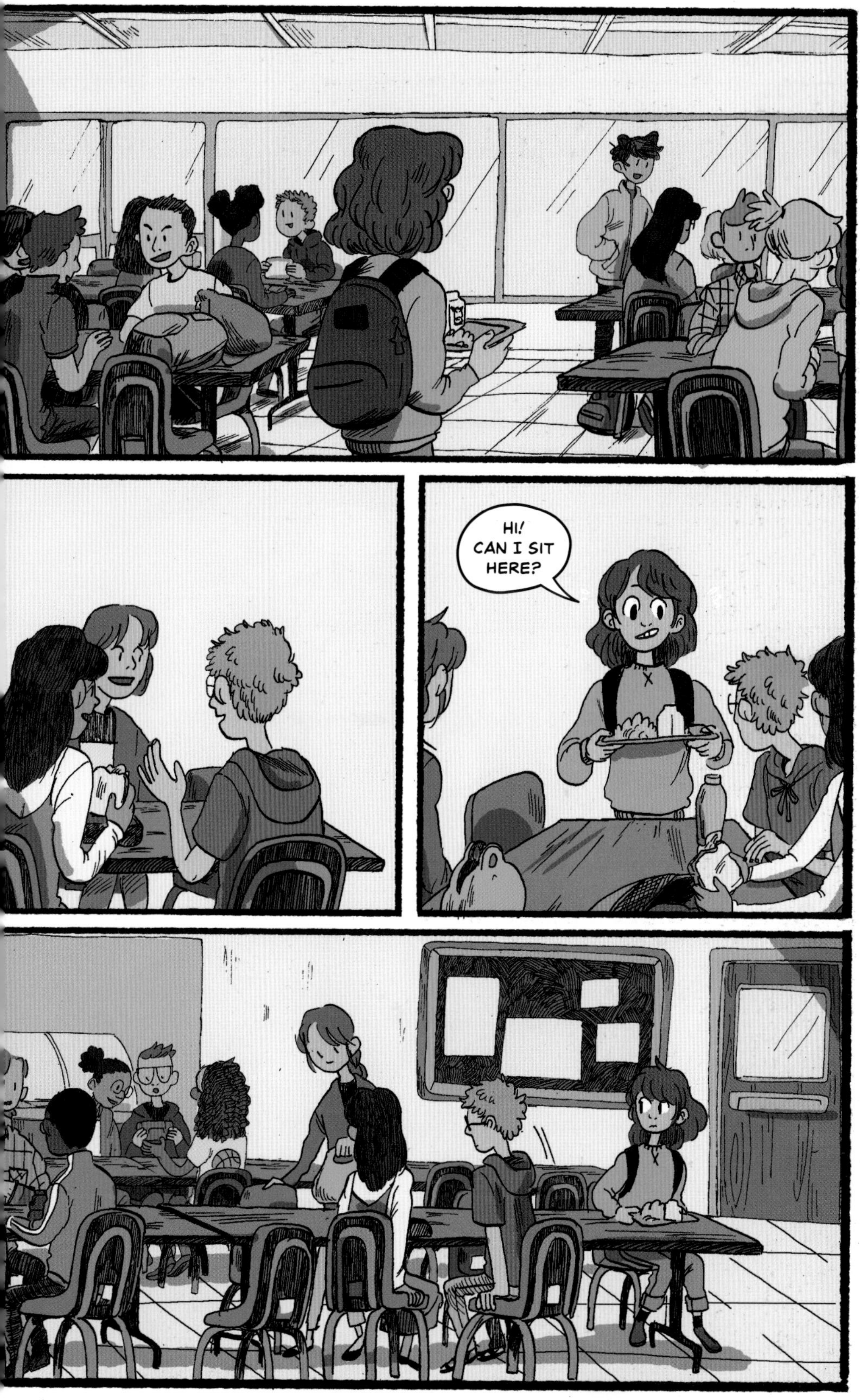
HI!
CAN I SIT
HERE?

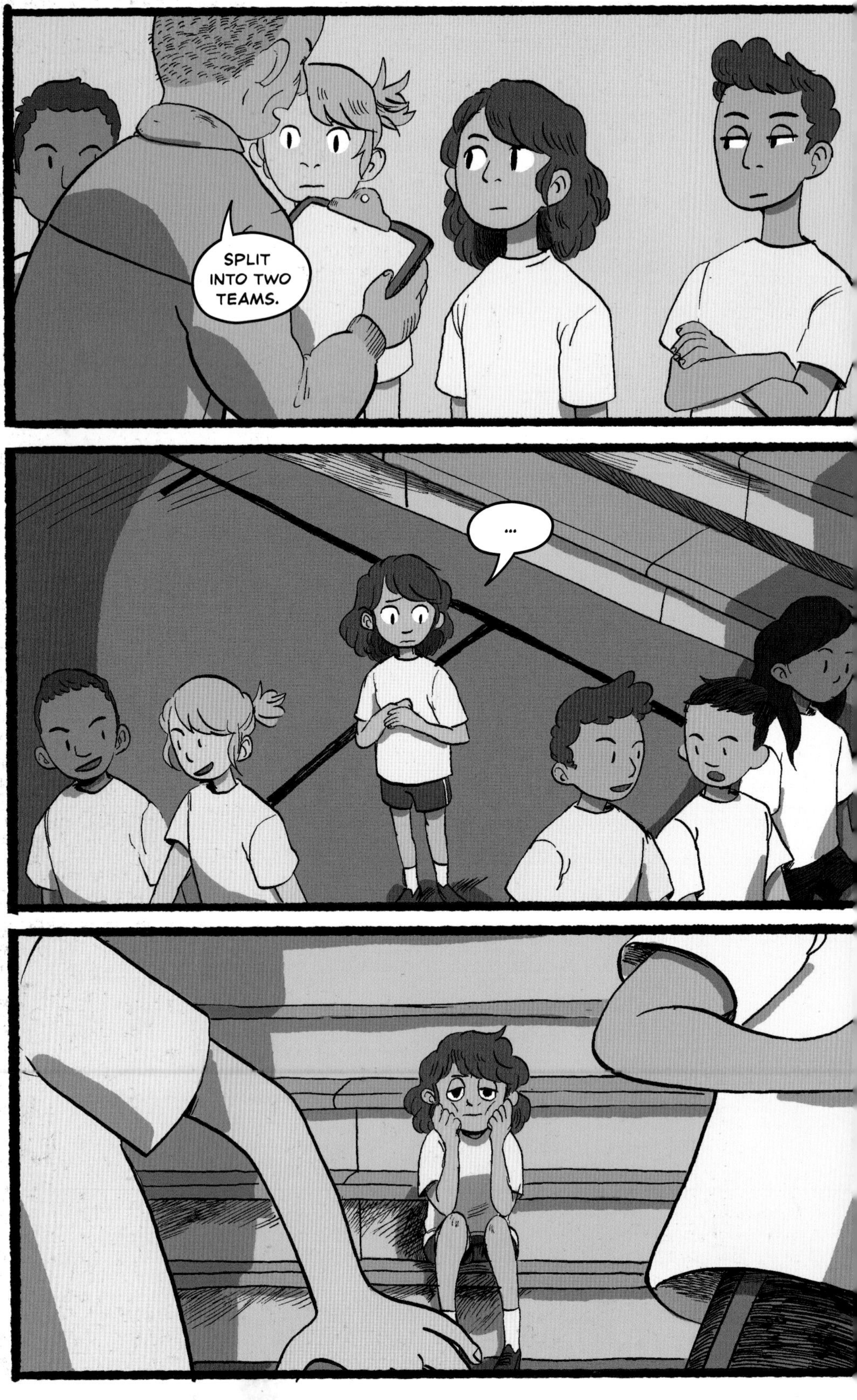
SPLIT INTO TWO TEAMS.
...

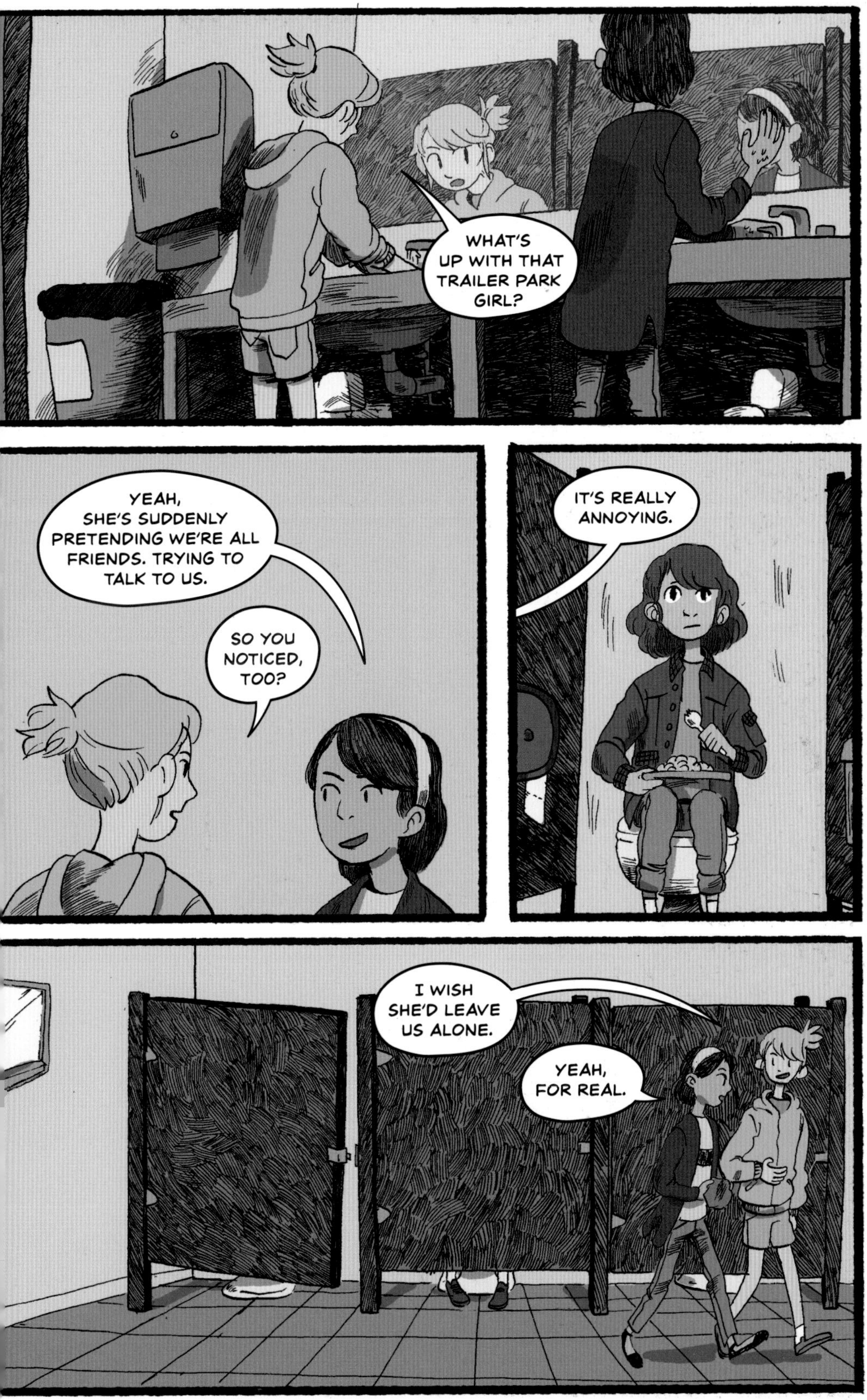
WHAT'S UP WITH THAT TRAILER PARK GIRL?
YEAH, SHE'S SUDDENLY PRETENDING WE'RE ALL FRIENDS. TRYING TO TALK TO US.
SO YOU NOTICED, TOO?
IT'S REALLY ANNOYING.
I WISH SHE'D LEAVE US ALONE.
YEAH, FOR REAL.

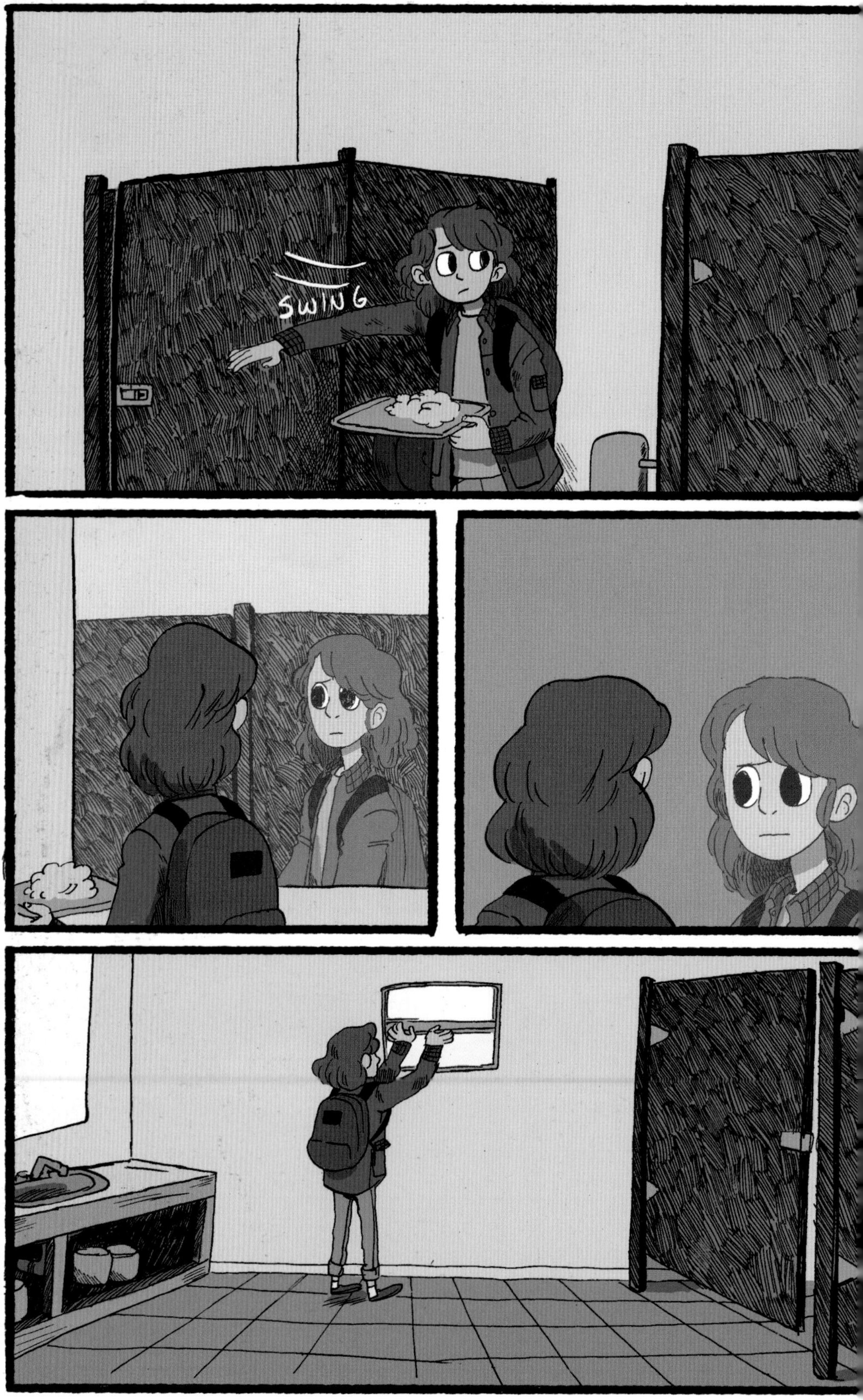
SWING

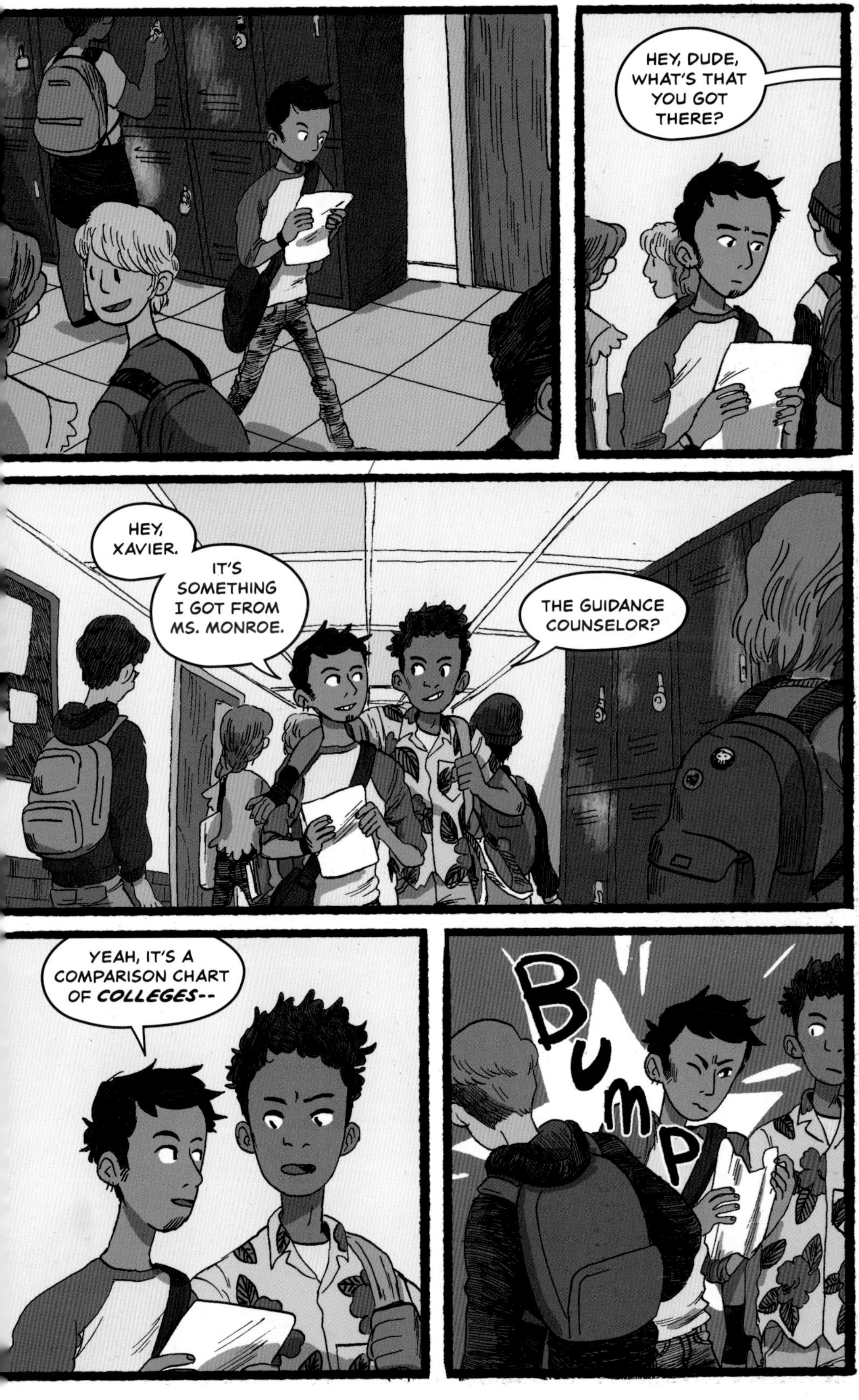
HEY, DUDE, WHAT'S THAT YOU GOT THERE?
HEY, XAVIER.
IT'S SOMETHING I GOT FROM MS. MONROE.
THE GUIDANCE COUNSELOR?
YEAH, IT'S A COMPARISON CHART OF COLLEGES--
BUMP

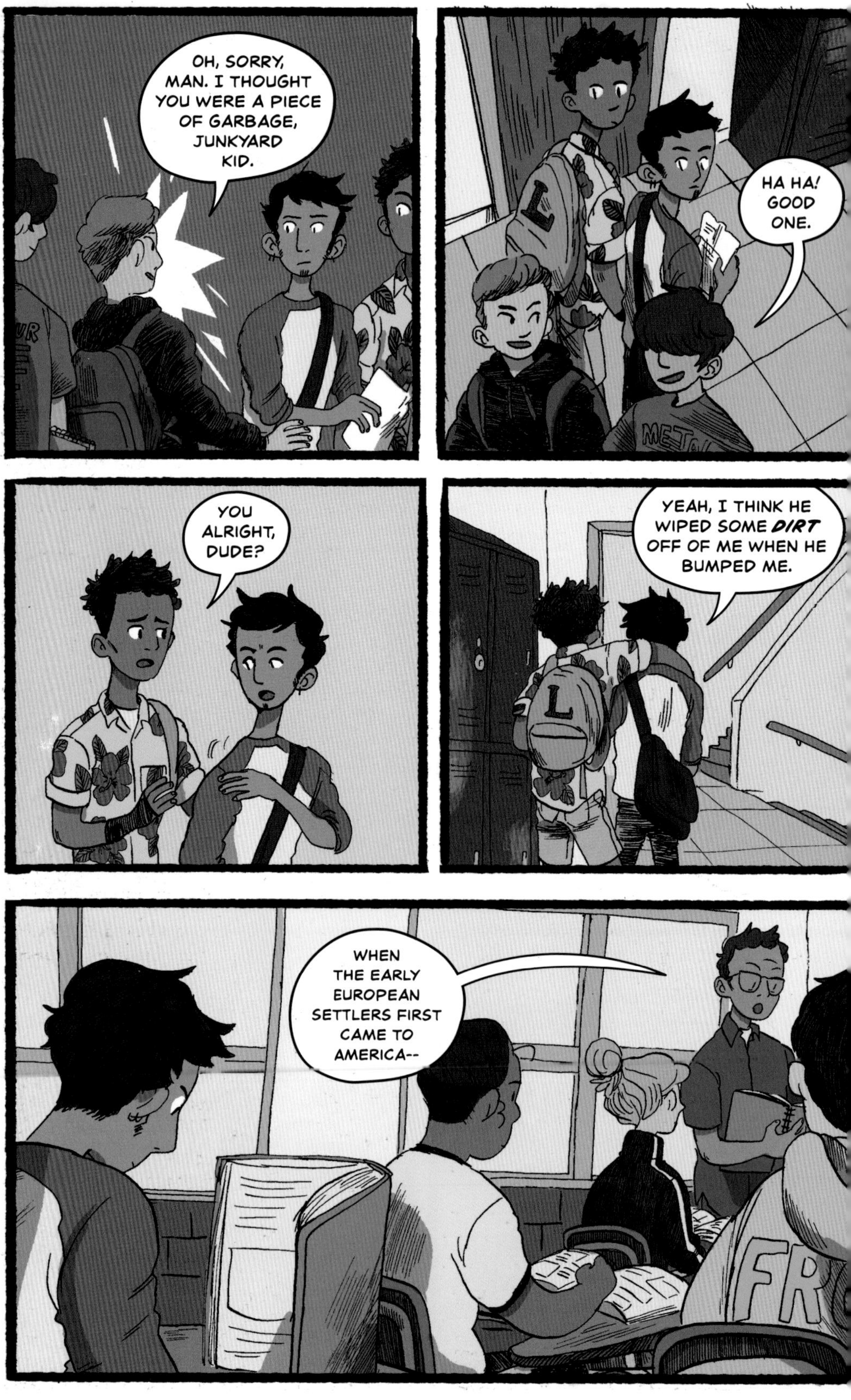
OH, SORRY, MAN. I THOUGHT YOU WERE A PIECE OF GARBAGE, JUNKYARD KID.
UR
HA HA! GOOD ONE.
METAL
YOU ALRIGHT, DUDE?
YEAH, I THINK HE WIPED SOME DIRT OFF OF ME WHEN HE BUMPED ME.
WHEN THE EARLY EUROPEAN SETTLERS FIRST CAME TO AMERICA--
FR

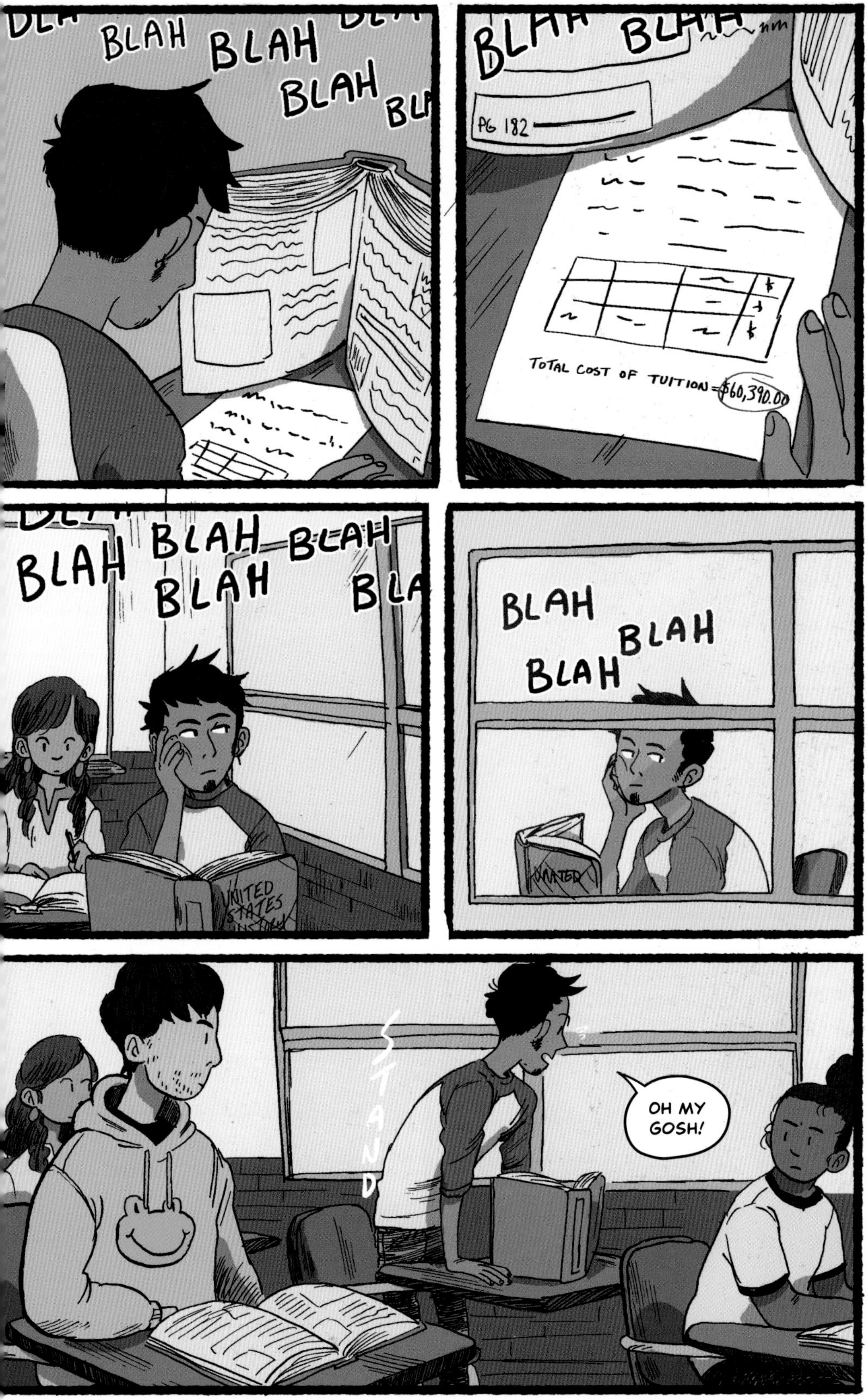
BLAH
BLAH
BLAH
BLAH
PG 182
TOTAL COST OF TUITION = $60,390.00
BLAH
BLAH
BLAH
BLAH
UNITED STATES
BLAH
BLAH
BLAH
STAND
OH MY GOSH!

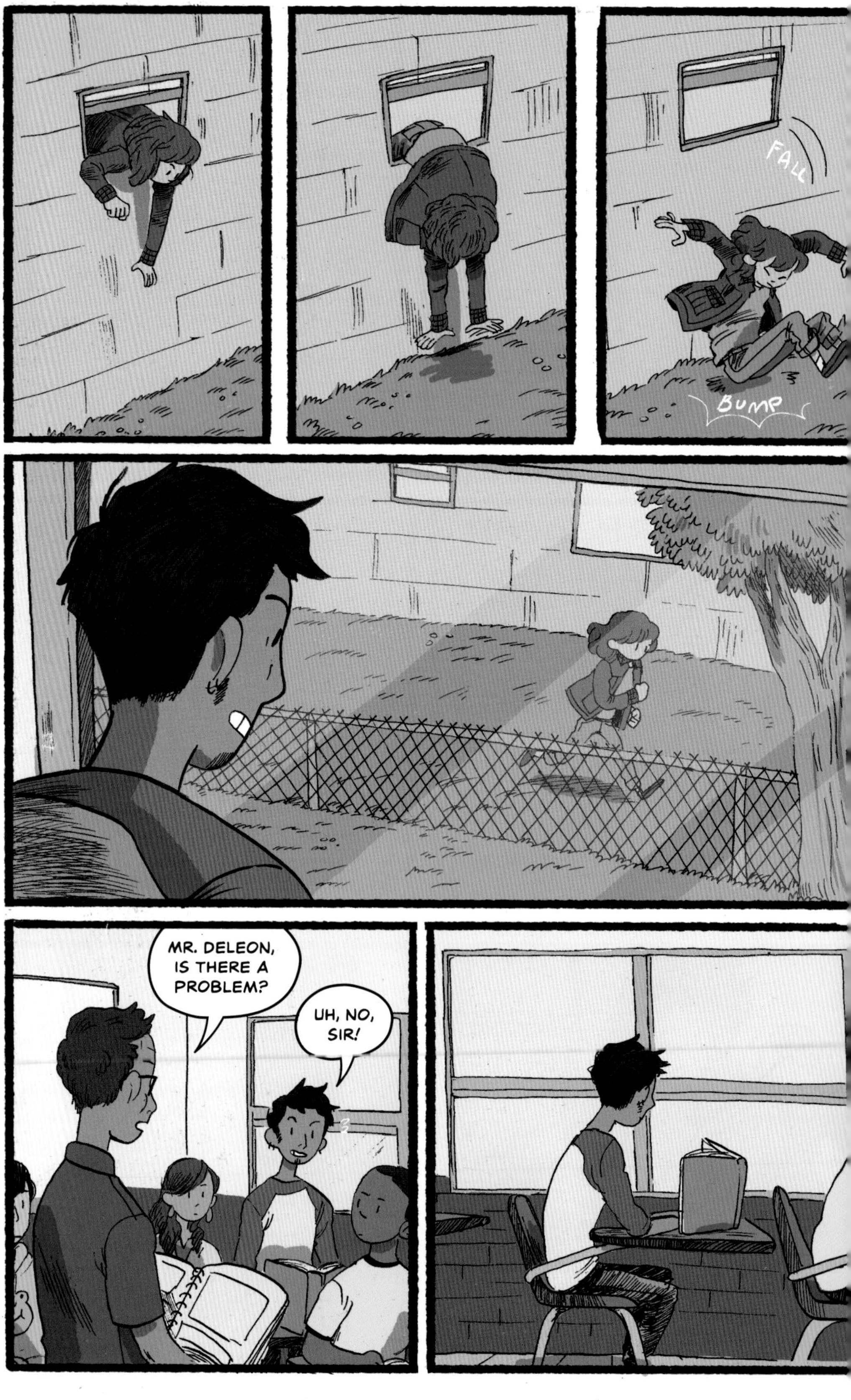
FALL
BUMP
MR. DELEON, IS THERE A PROBLEM?
UH, NO, SIR!

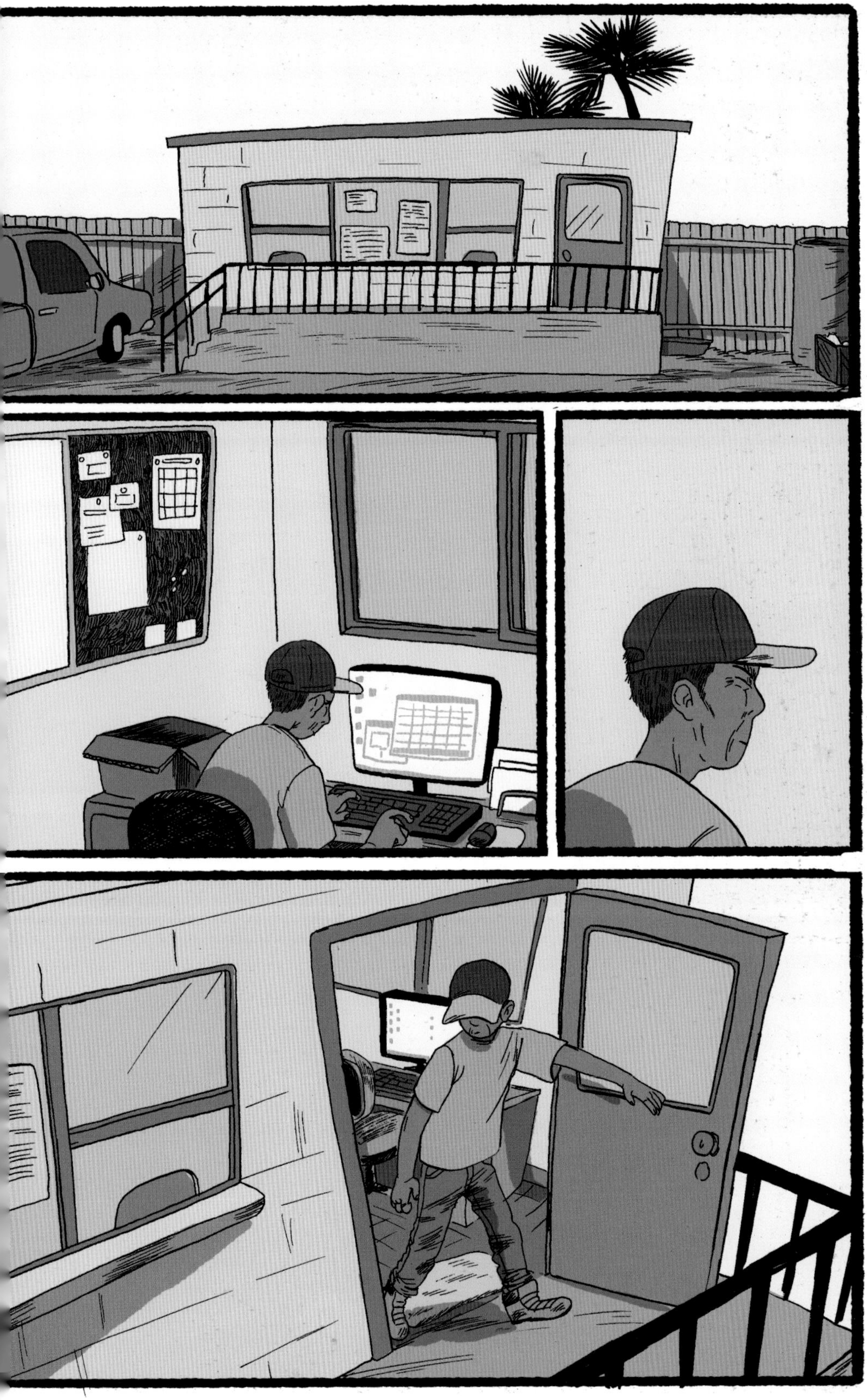

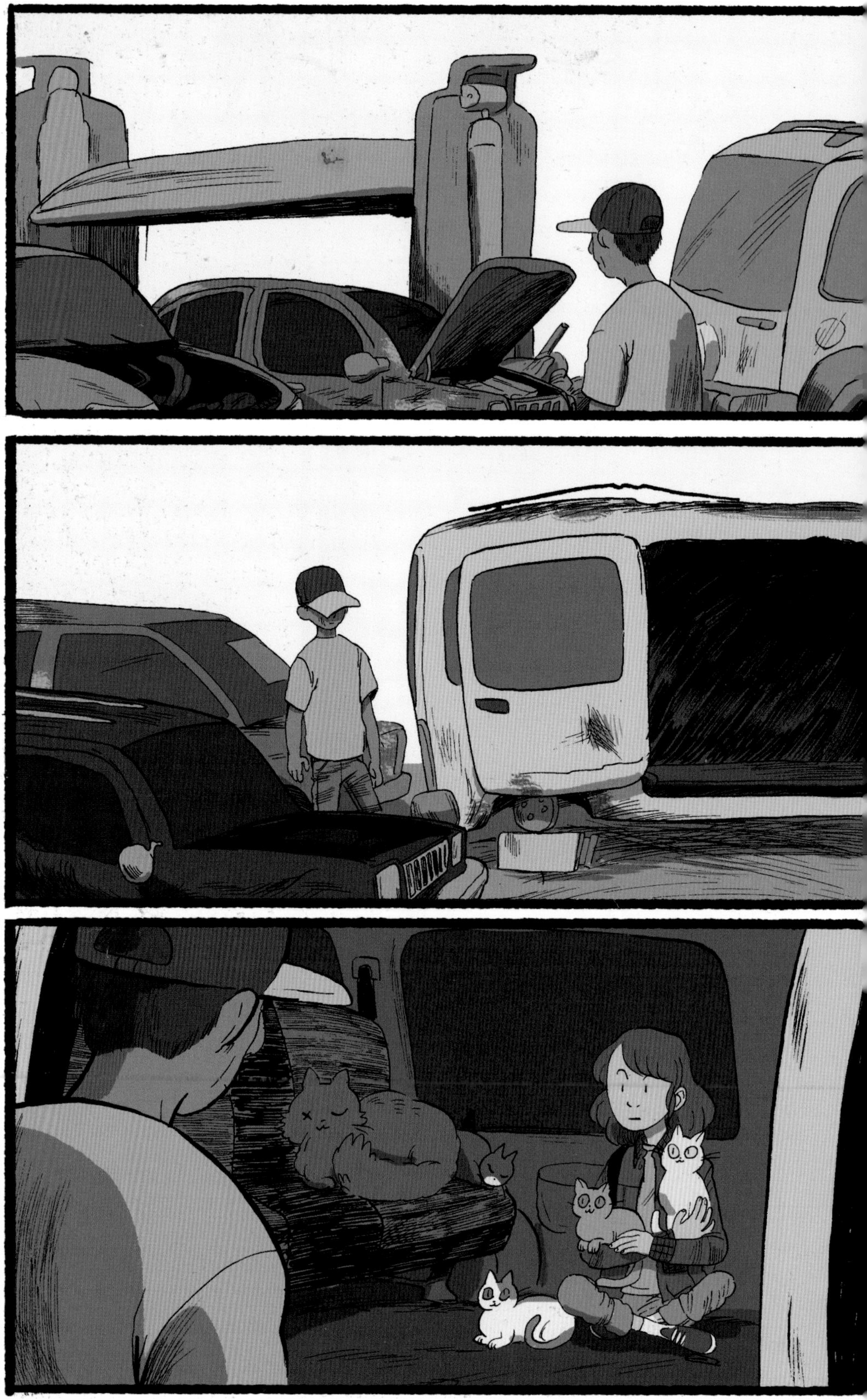

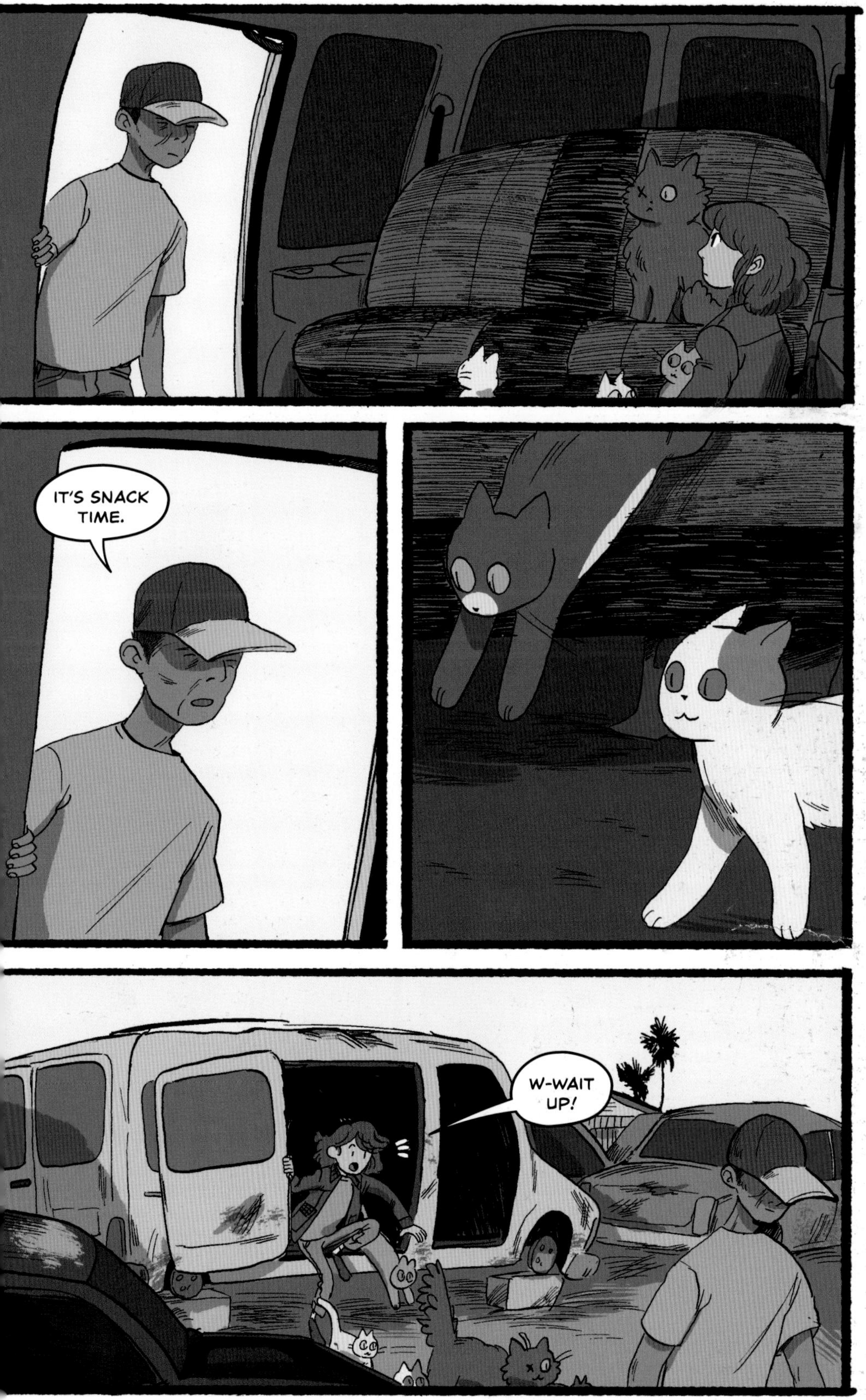
IT'S SNACK TIME.
W-WAIT UP!

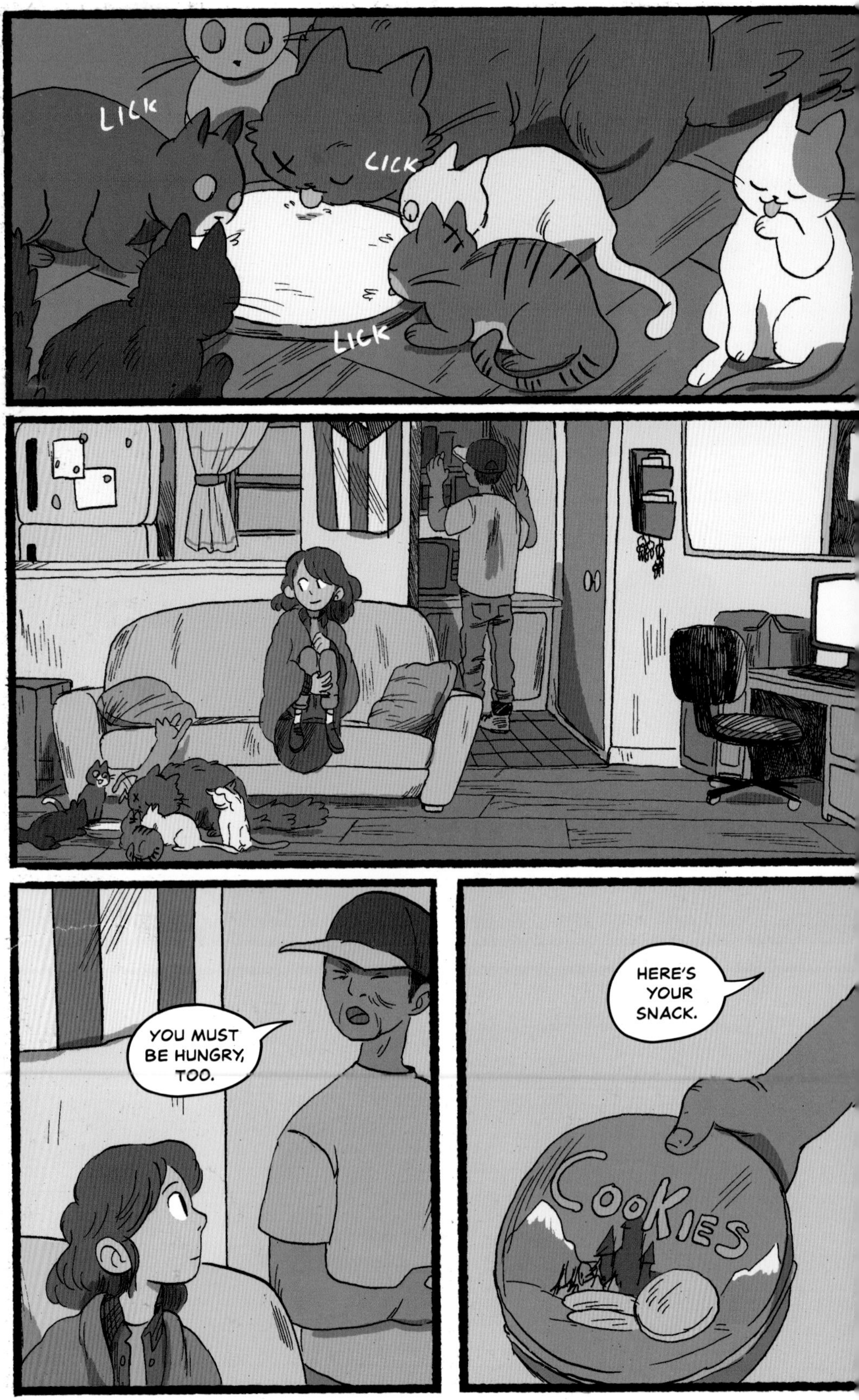
LICK
LICK
LICK
YOU MUST BE HUNGRY, TOO.
HERE'S YOUR SNACK.
COOKIES

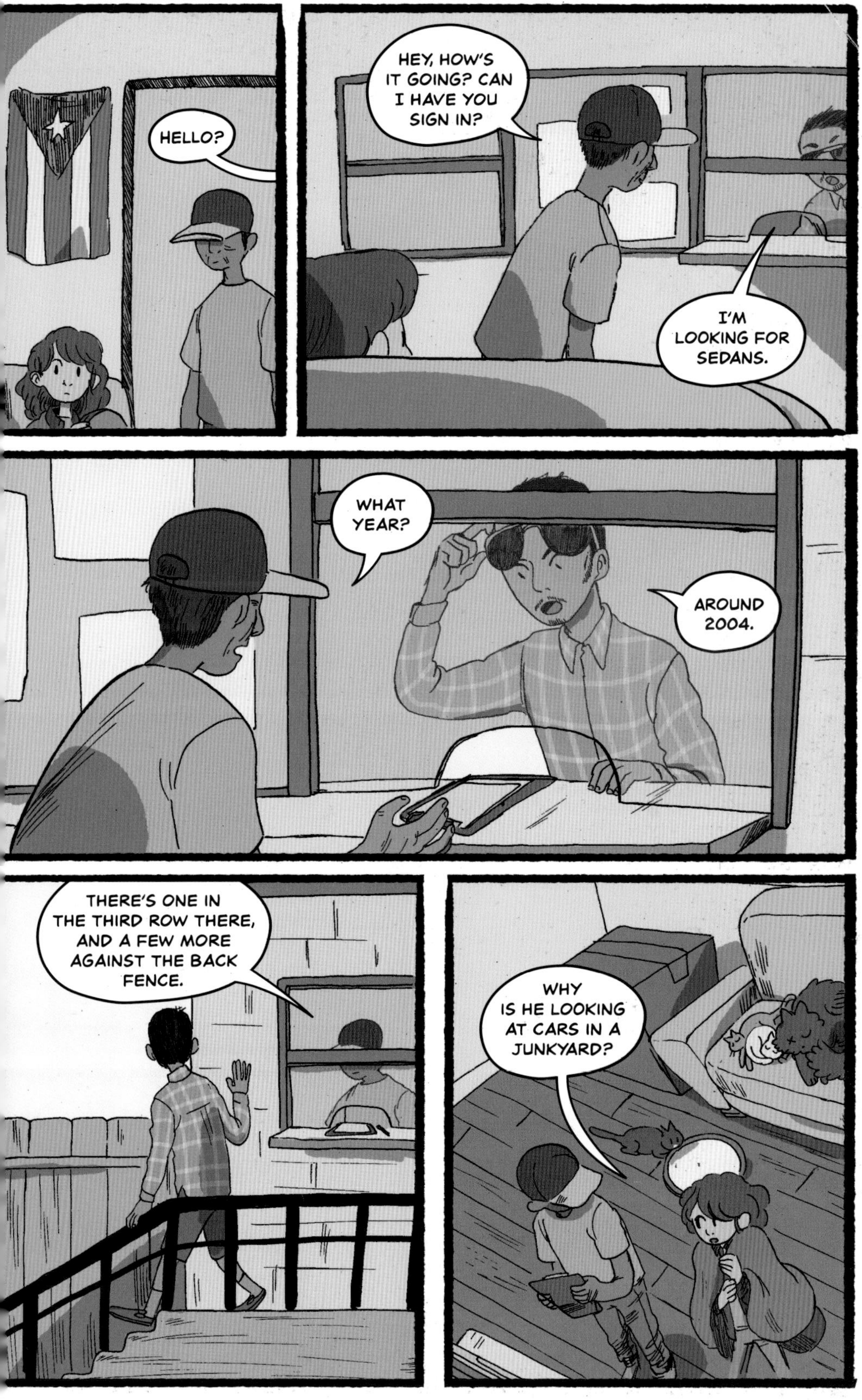
HELLO?
HEY, HOW'S IT GOING? CAN I HAVE YOU SIGN IN?
I'M LOOKING FOR SEDANS.
WHAT YEAR?
AROUND 2004.
THERE'S ONE IN THE THIRD ROW THERE, AND A FEW MORE AGAINST THE BACK FENCE.
WHY IS HE LOOKING AT CARS IN A JUNKYARD?

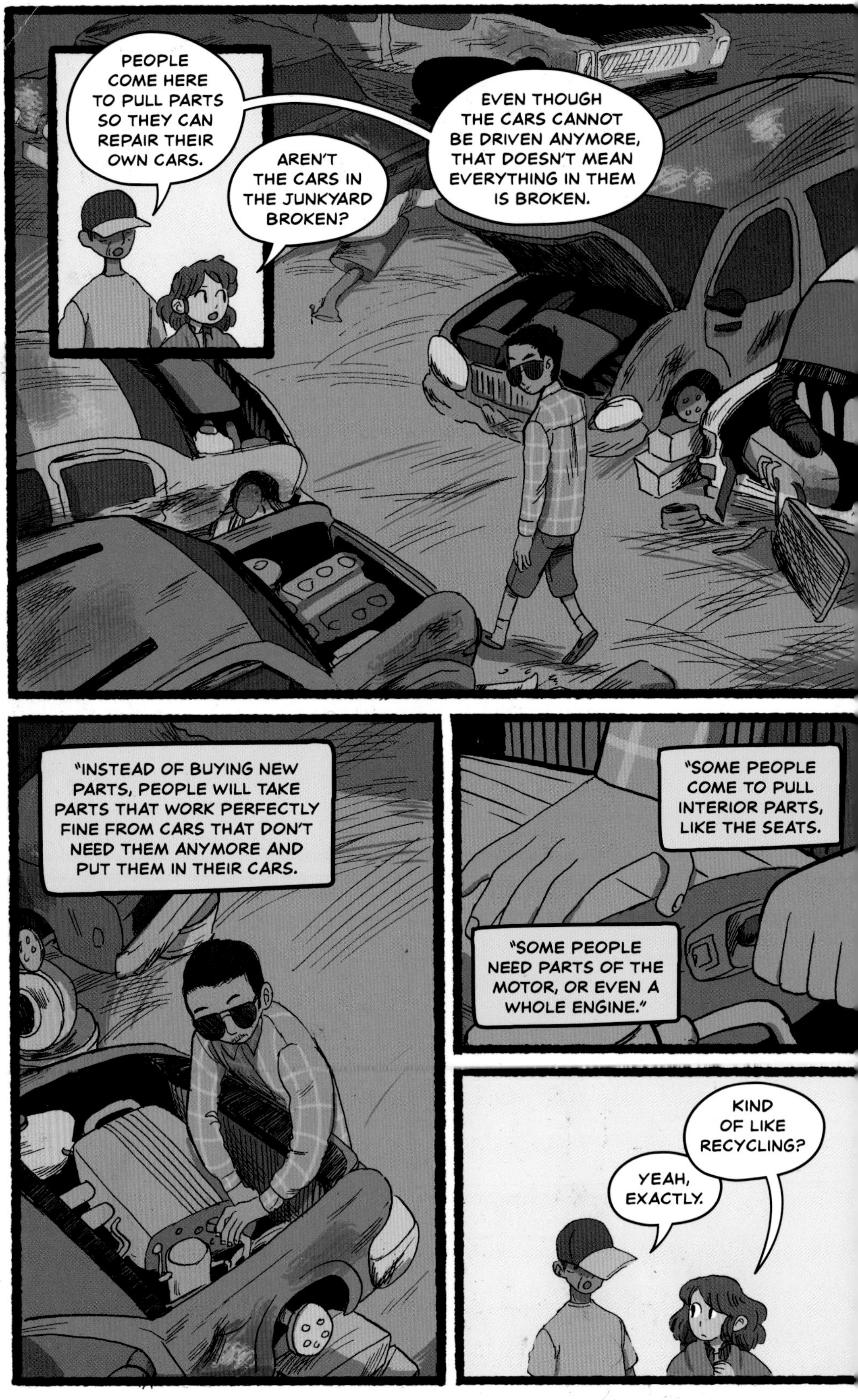
PEOPLE COME HERE TO PULL PARTS SO THEY CAN REPAIR THEIR OWN CARS.
AREN'T THE CARS IN THE JUNKYARD BROKEN?
EVEN THOUGH THE CARS CANNOT BE DRIVEN ANYMORE, THAT DOESN'T MEAN EVERYTHING IN THEM IS BROKEN.
"INSTEAD OF BUYING NEW PARTS, PEOPLE WILL TAKE PARTS THAT WORK PERFECTLY FINE FROM CARS THAT DON'T NEED THEM ANYMORE AND PUT THEM IN THEIR CARS.
"SOME PEOPLE COME TO PULL INTERIOR PARTS, LIKE THE SEATS.
"SOME PEOPLE NEED PARTS OF THE MOTOR, OR EVEN A WHOLE ENGINE."
KIND OF LIKE RECYCLING?
YEAH, EXACTLY.

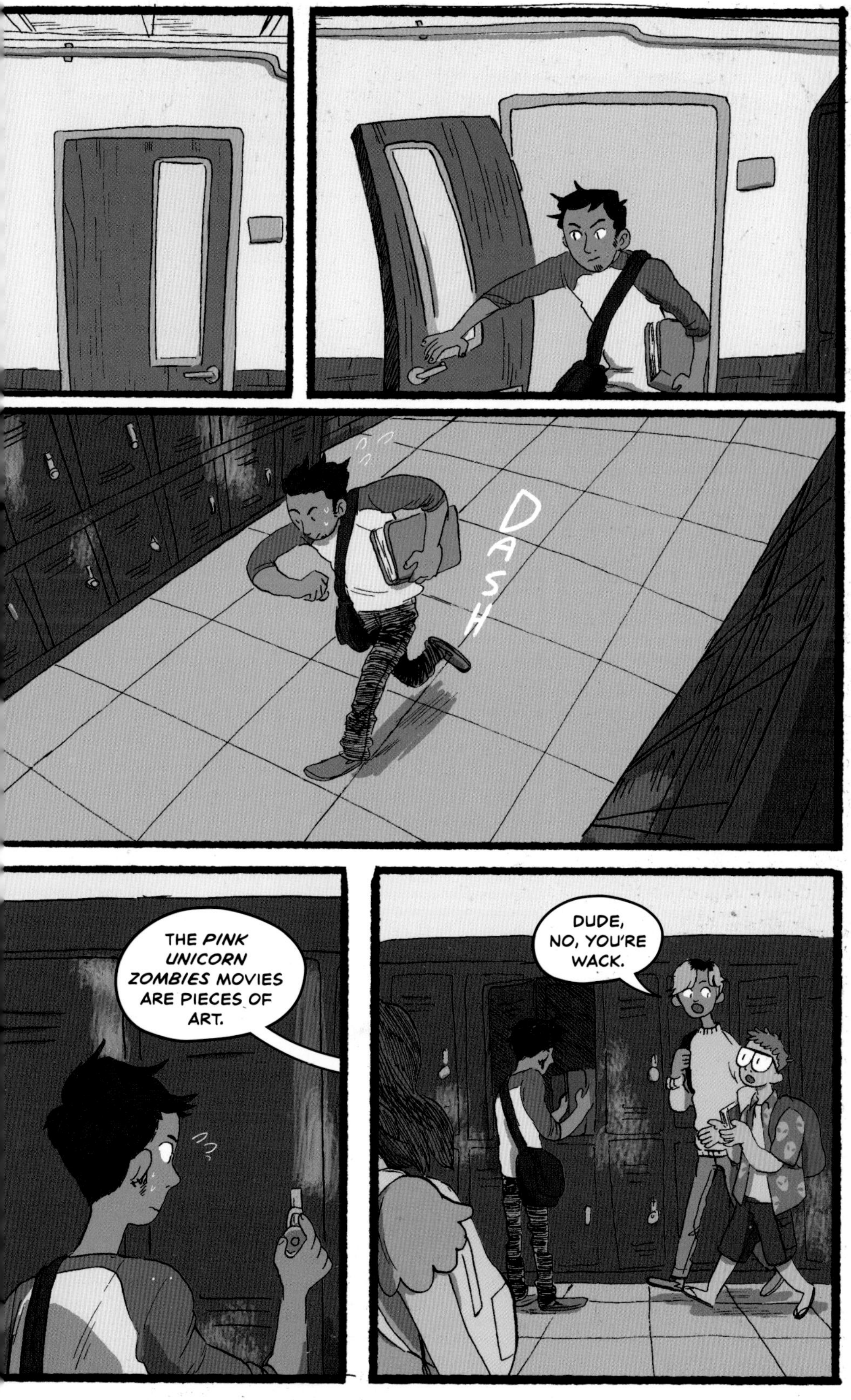
DASH
THE *PINK UNICORN ZOMBIES* MOVIES ARE PIECES OF ART.
DUDE, NO, YOU'RE WACK.

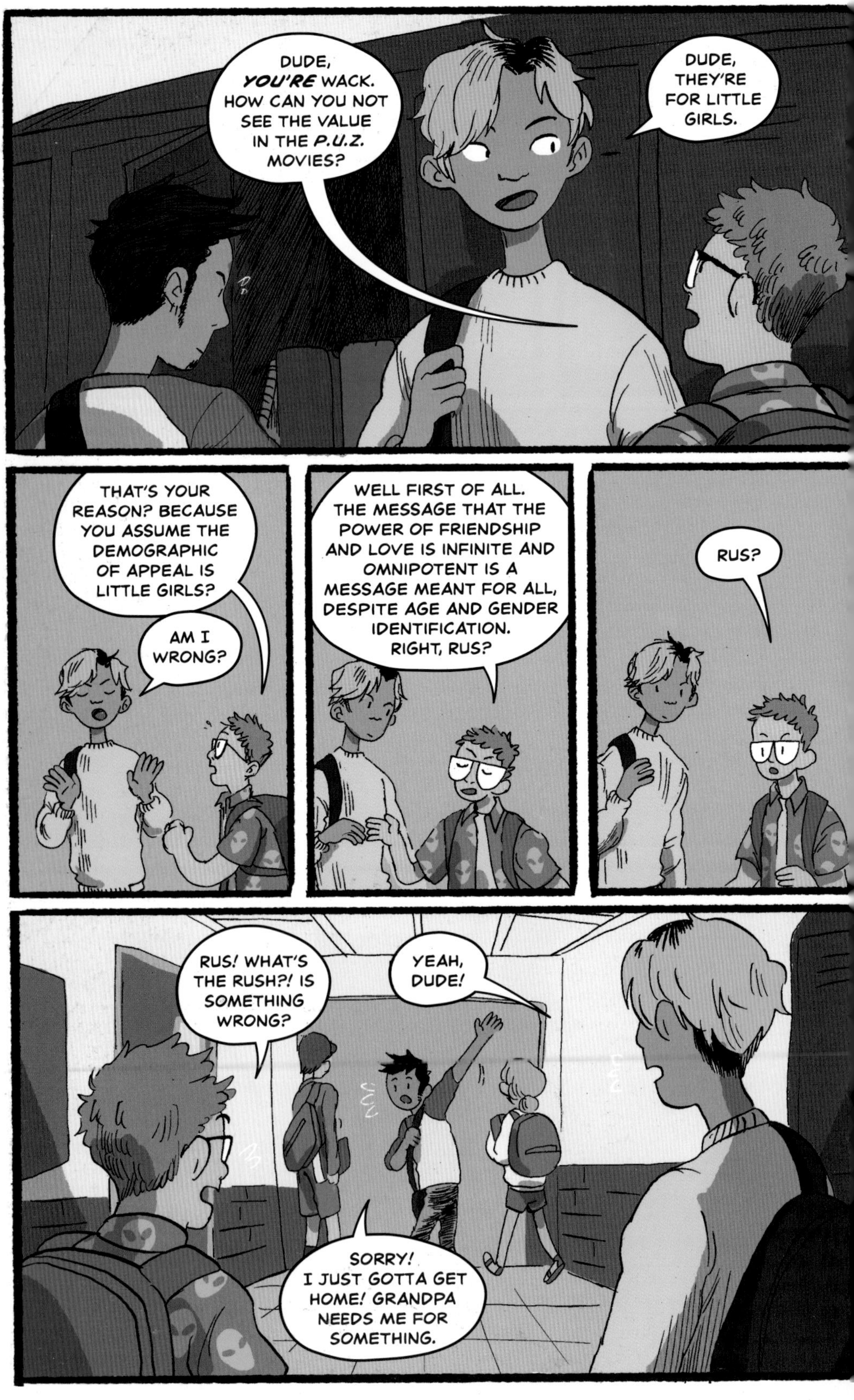
DUDE, *YOU'RE* WACK. HOW CAN YOU NOT SEE THE VALUE IN THE *P.U.Z.* MOVIES?
DUDE, THEY'RE FOR LITTLE GIRLS.
THAT'S YOUR REASON? BECAUSE YOU ASSUME THE DEMOGRAPHIC OF APPEAL IS LITTLE GIRLS?
AM I WRONG?
WELL FIRST OF ALL. THE MESSAGE THAT THE POWER OF FRIENDSHIP AND LOVE IS INFINITE AND OMNIPOTENT IS A MESSAGE MEANT FOR ALL, DESPITE AGE AND GENDER IDENTIFICATION. RIGHT, RUS?
RUS?
RUS! WHAT'S THE RUSH?! IS SOMETHING WRONG?
YEAH, DUDE!
SORRY! I JUST GOTTA GET HOME! GRANDPA NEEDS ME FOR SOMETHING.

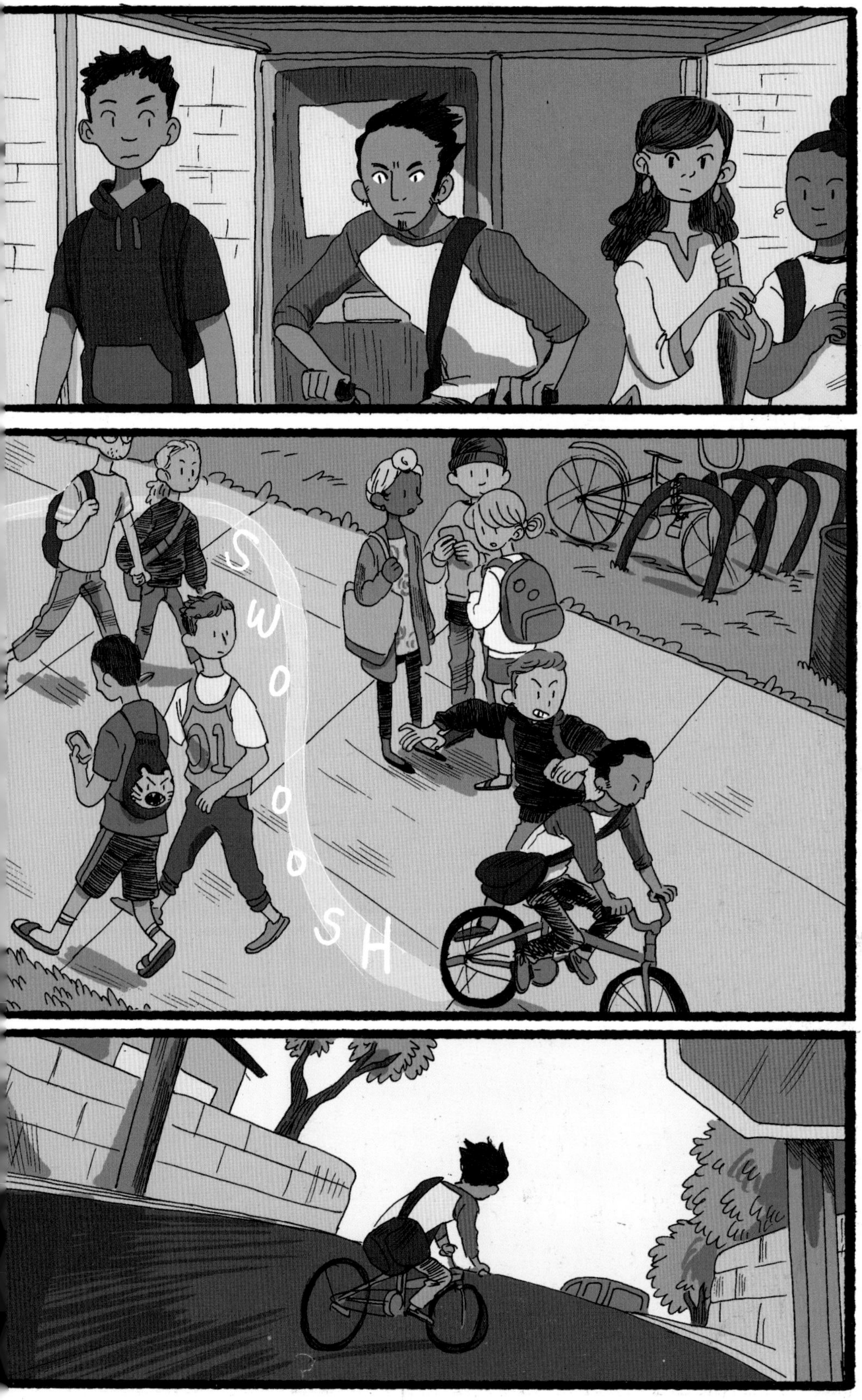
SWOOOOSH

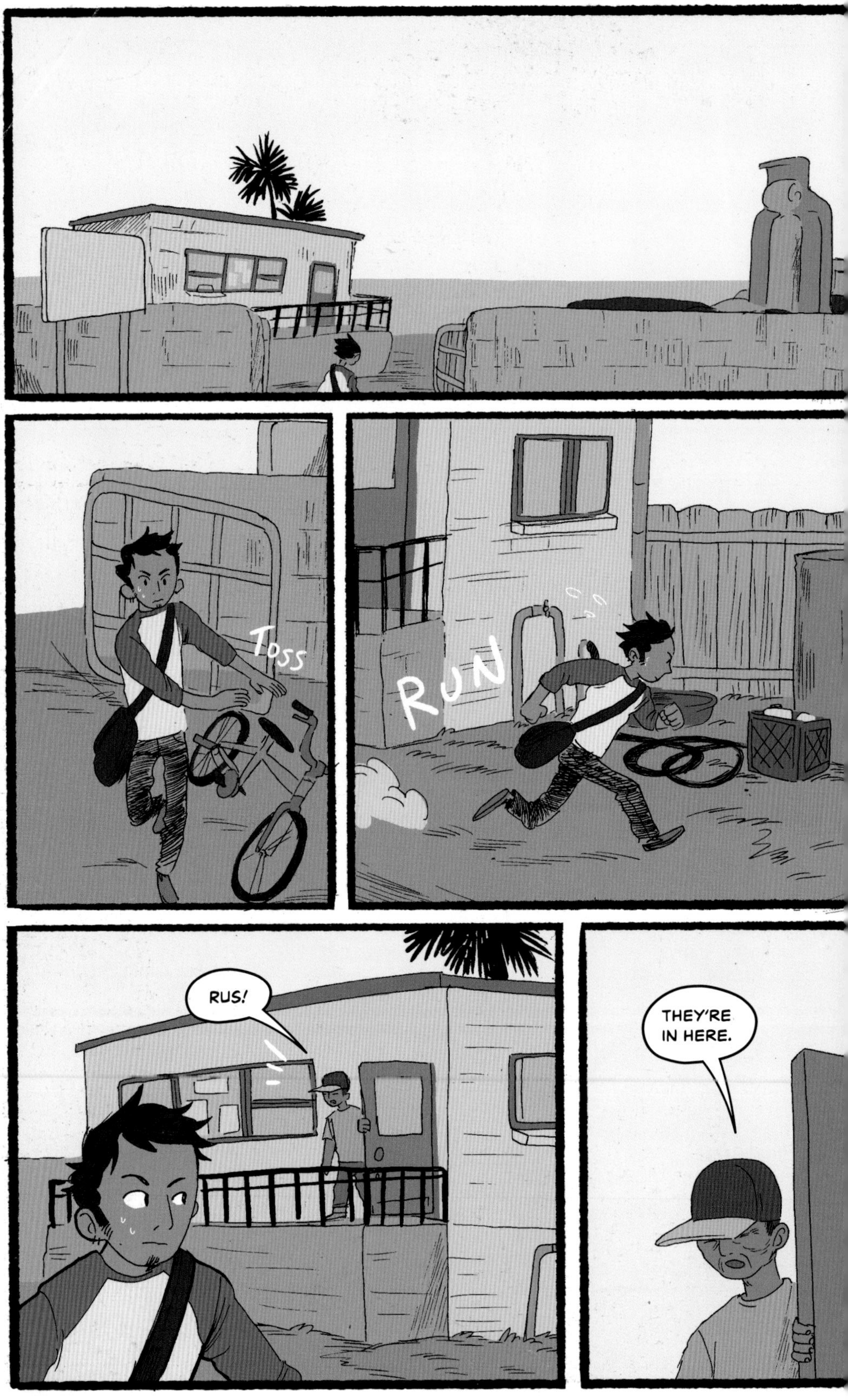
TOSS
RUN
RUS!
THEY'RE IN HERE.

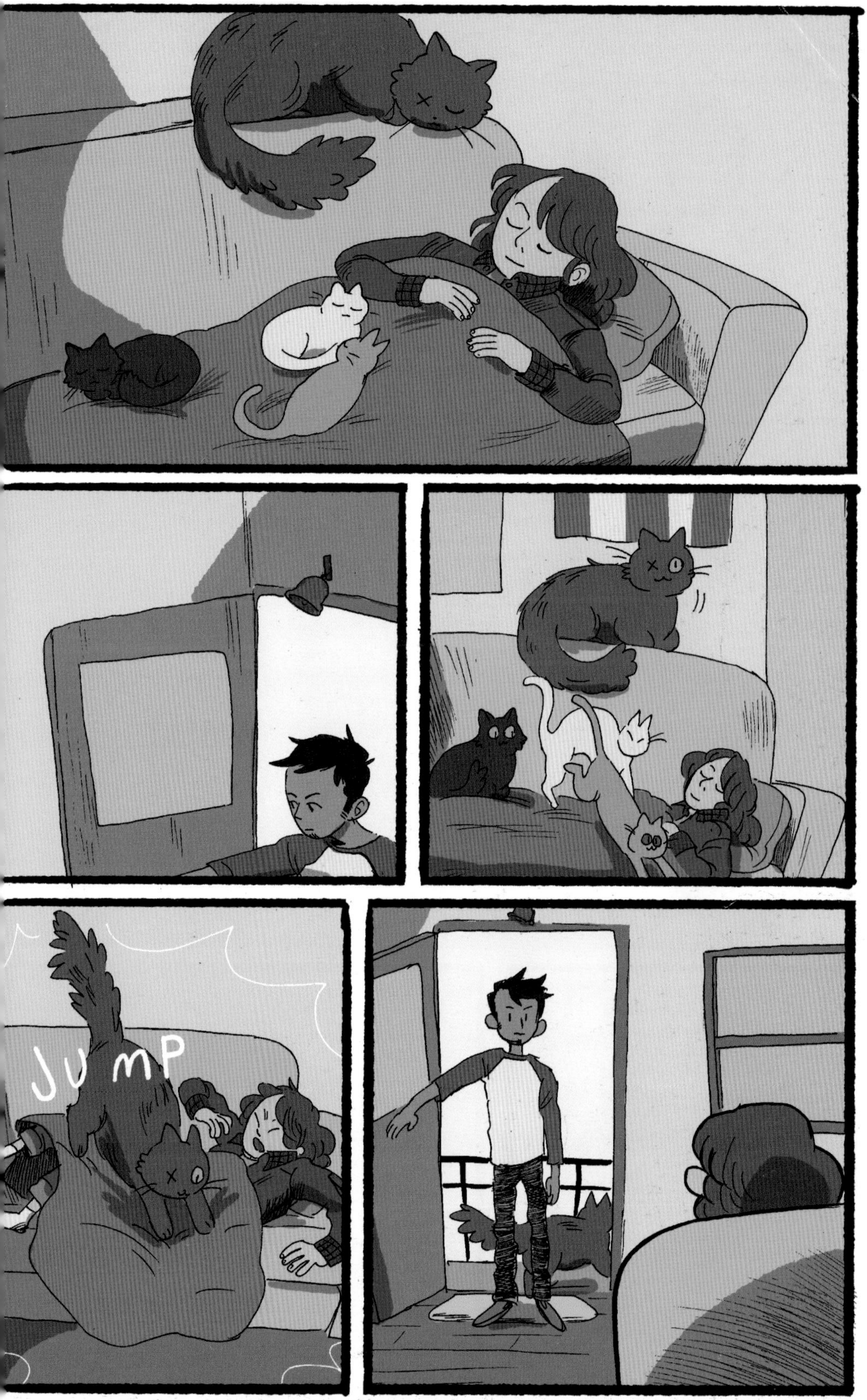
JUMP

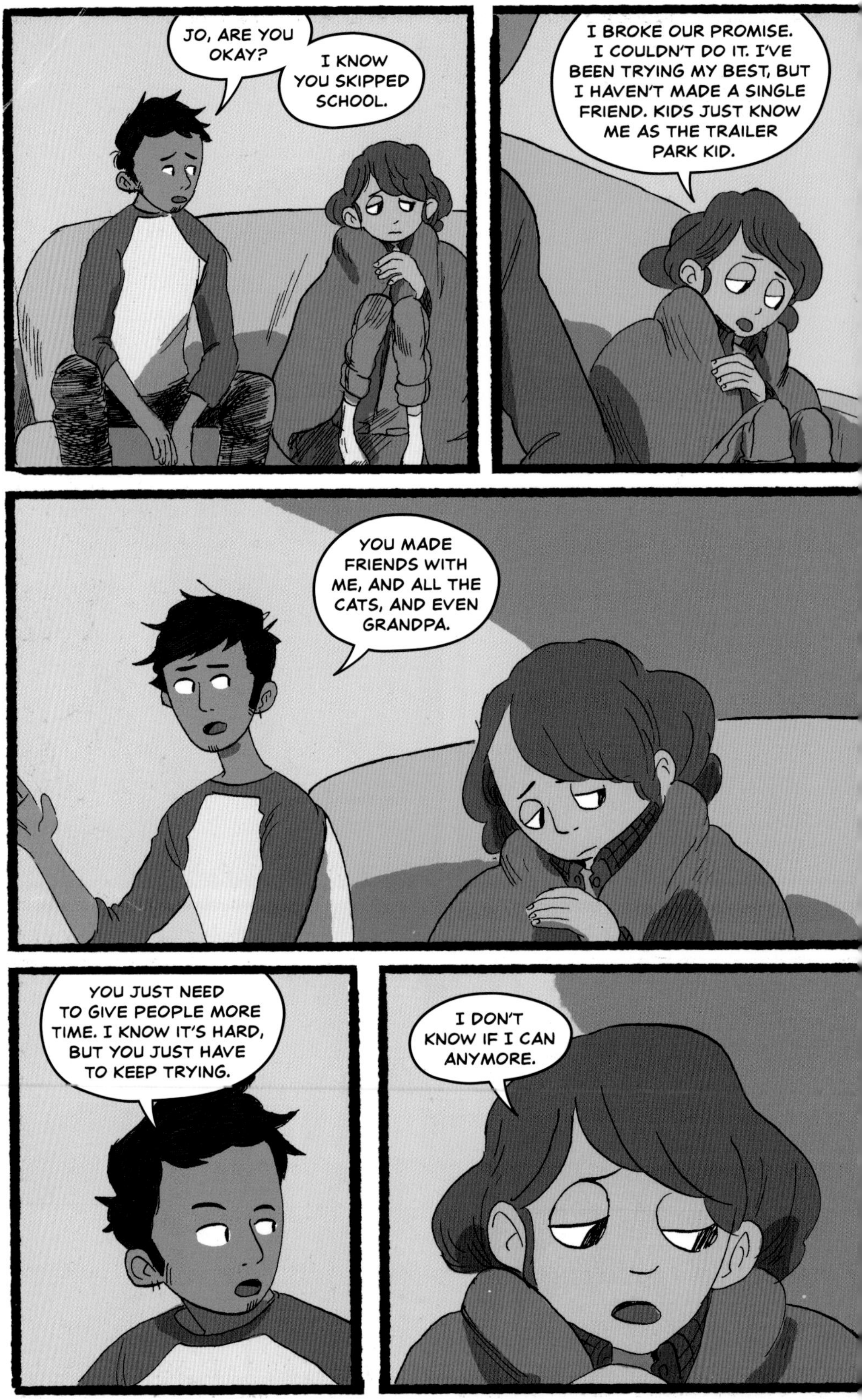

JO, ARE YOU OKAY?
I KNOW YOU SKIPPED SCHOOL.
I BROKE OUR PROMISE. I COULDN'T DO IT. I'VE BEEN TRYING MY BEST, BUT I HAVEN'T MADE A SINGLE FRIEND. KIDS JUST KNOW ME AS THE TRAILER PARK KID.
YOU MADE FRIENDS WITH ME, AND ALL THE CATS, AND EVEN GRANDPA.
YOU JUST NEED TO GIVE PEOPLE MORE TIME. I KNOW IT'S HARD, BUT YOU JUST HAVE TO KEEP TRYING.
I DON'T KNOW IF I CAN ANYMORE.

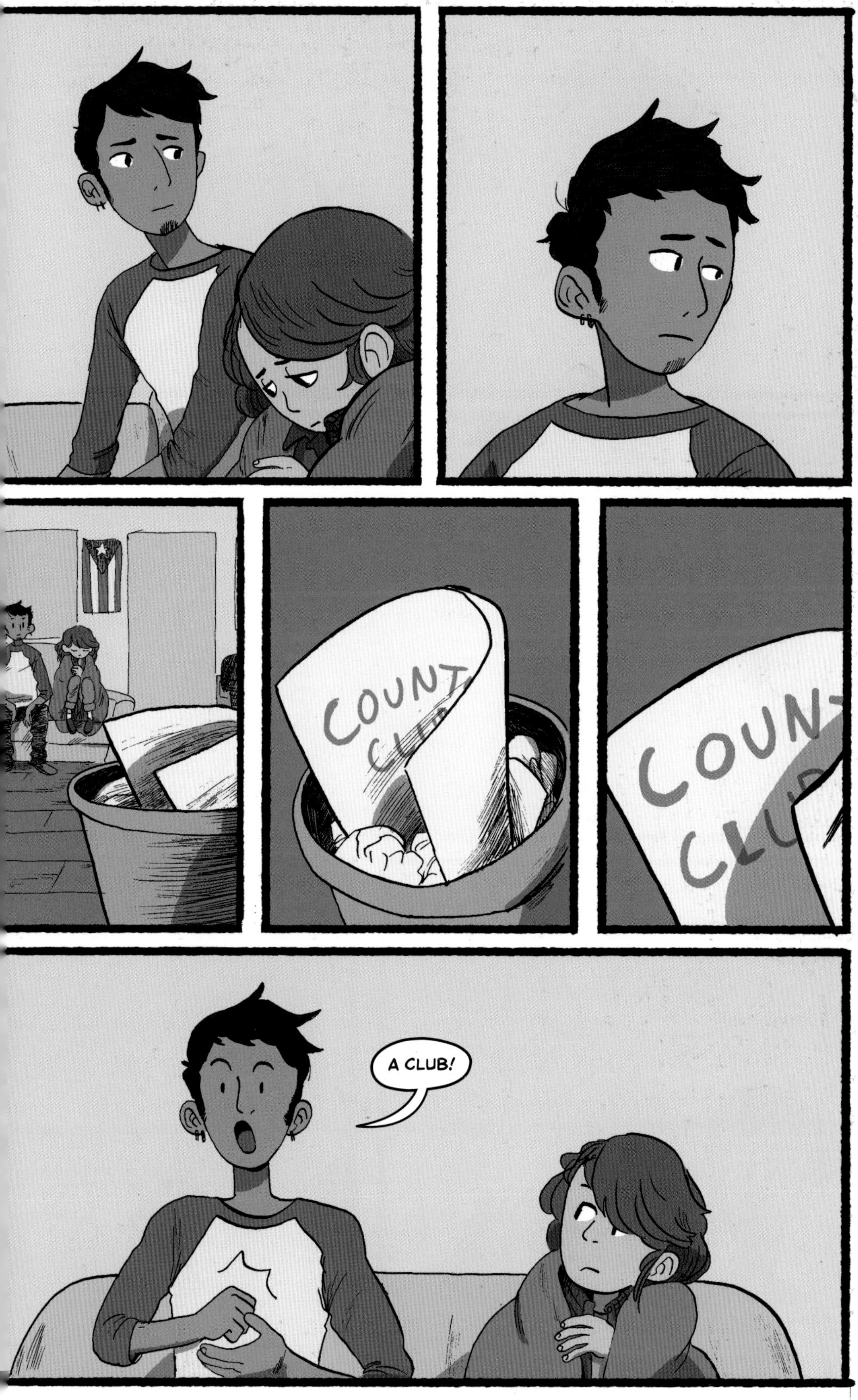
COUNT
CLU
A CLUB!

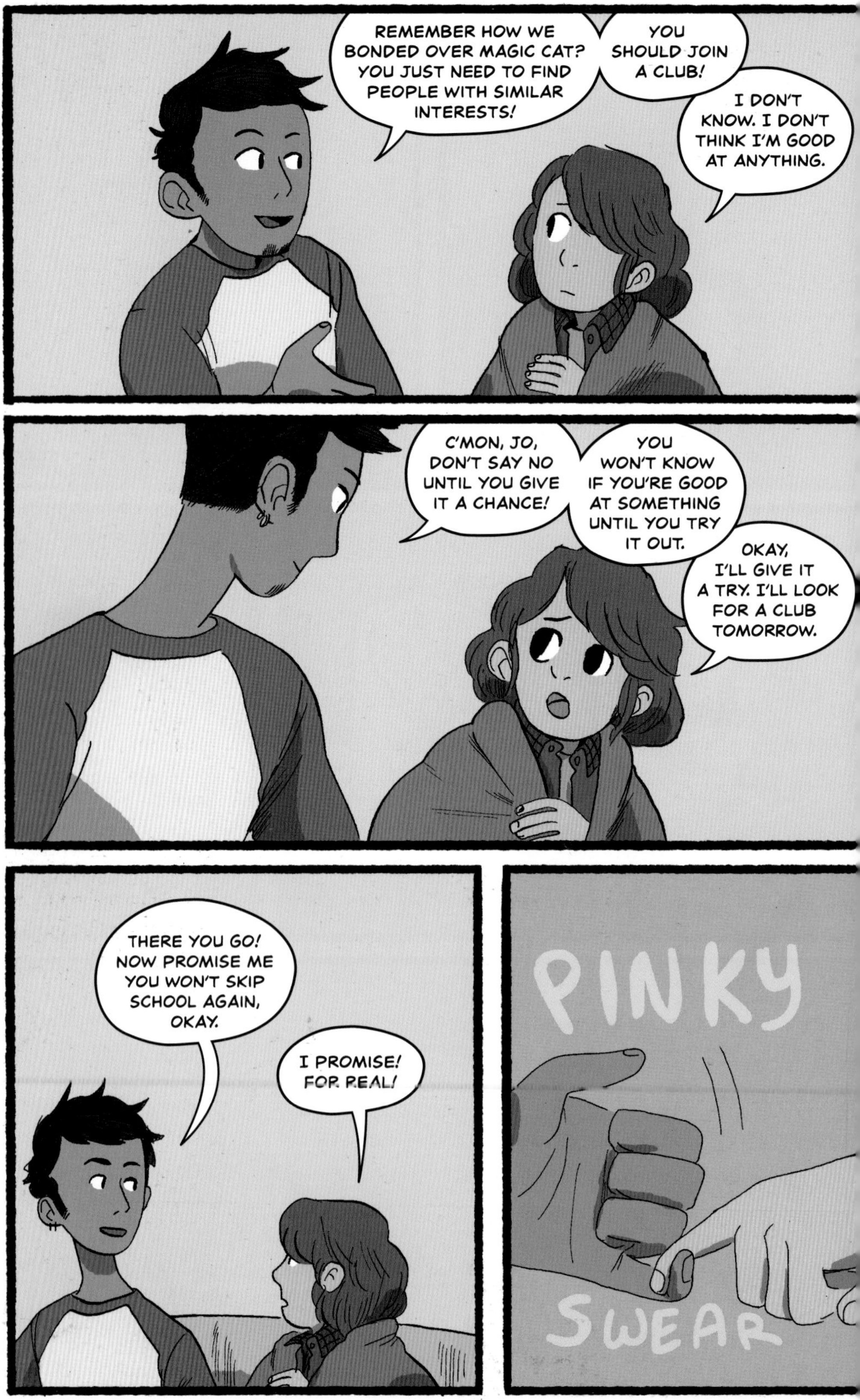
REMEMBER HOW WE BONDED OVER MAGIC CAT? YOU JUST NEED TO FIND PEOPLE WITH SIMILAR INTERESTS!
YOU SHOULD JOIN A CLUB!
I DON'T KNOW. I DON'T THINK I'M GOOD AT ANYTHING.
C'MON, JO, DON'T SAY NO UNTIL YOU GIVE IT A CHANCE!
YOU WON'T KNOW IF YOU'RE GOOD AT SOMETHING UNTIL YOU TRY IT OUT.
OKAY, I'LL GIVE IT A TRY. I'LL LOOK FOR A CLUB TOMORROW.
THERE YOU GO! NOW PROMISE ME YOU WON'T SKIP SCHOOL AGAIN, OKAY.
I PROMISE! FOR REAL!
PINKY
SWEAR

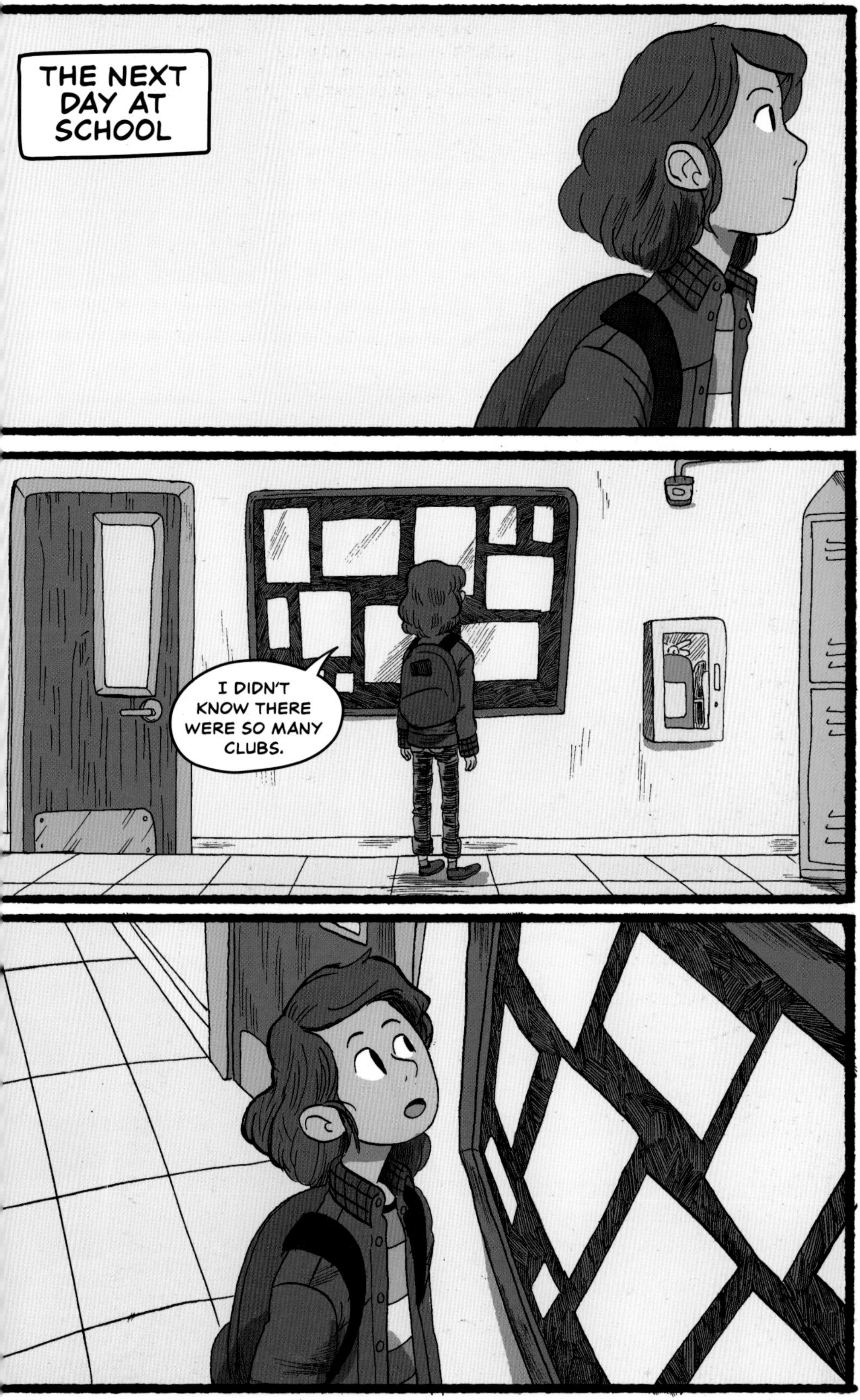
THE NEXT DAY AT SCHOOL
I DIDN'T KNOW THERE WERE SO MANY CLUBS.

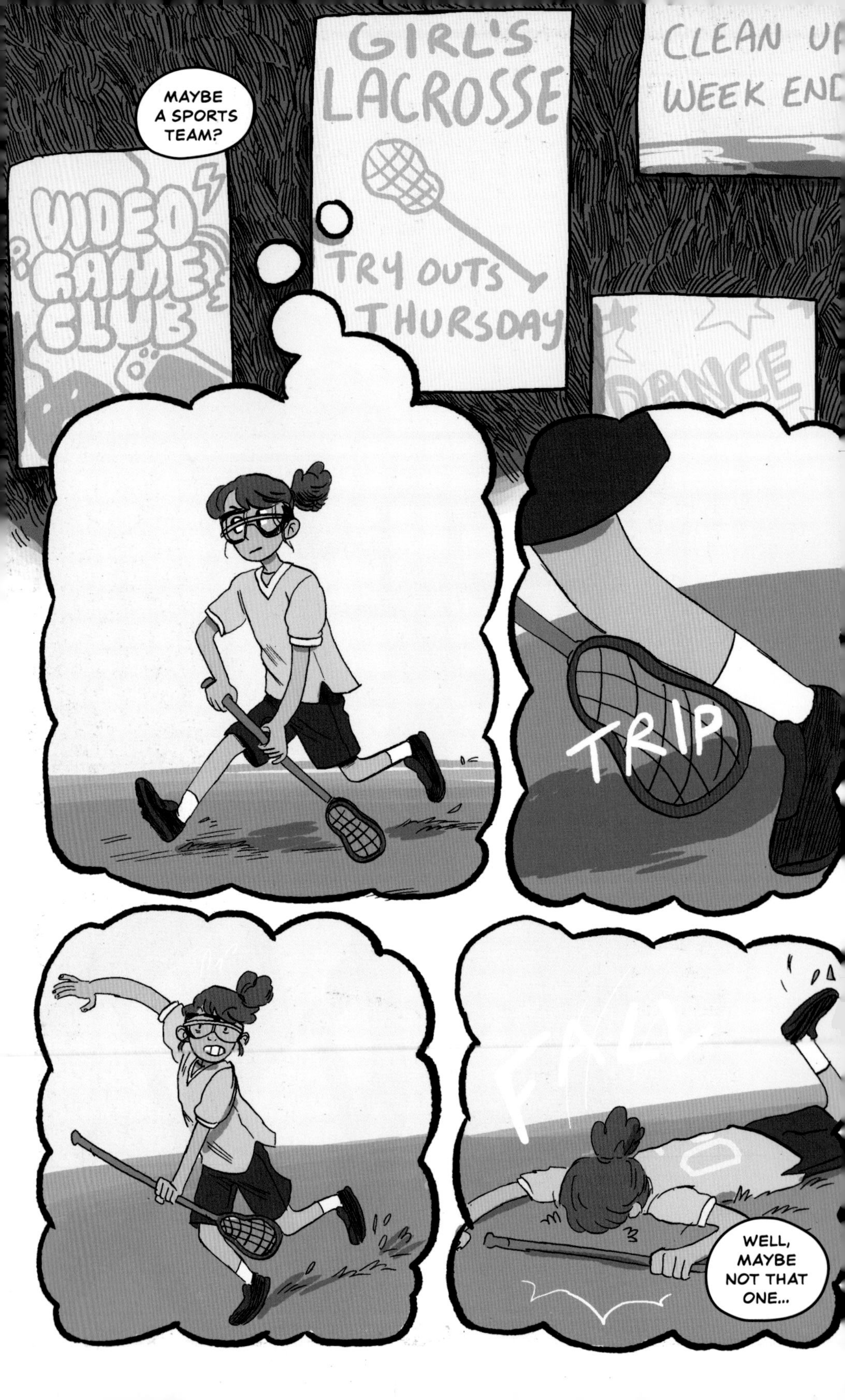
MAYBE A SPORTS TEAM?
VIDEO GAME CLUB
GIRL'S LACROSSE
TRY OUTS THURSDAY
CLEAN UP WEEK END
TRIP
WELL, MAYBE NOT THAT ONE...

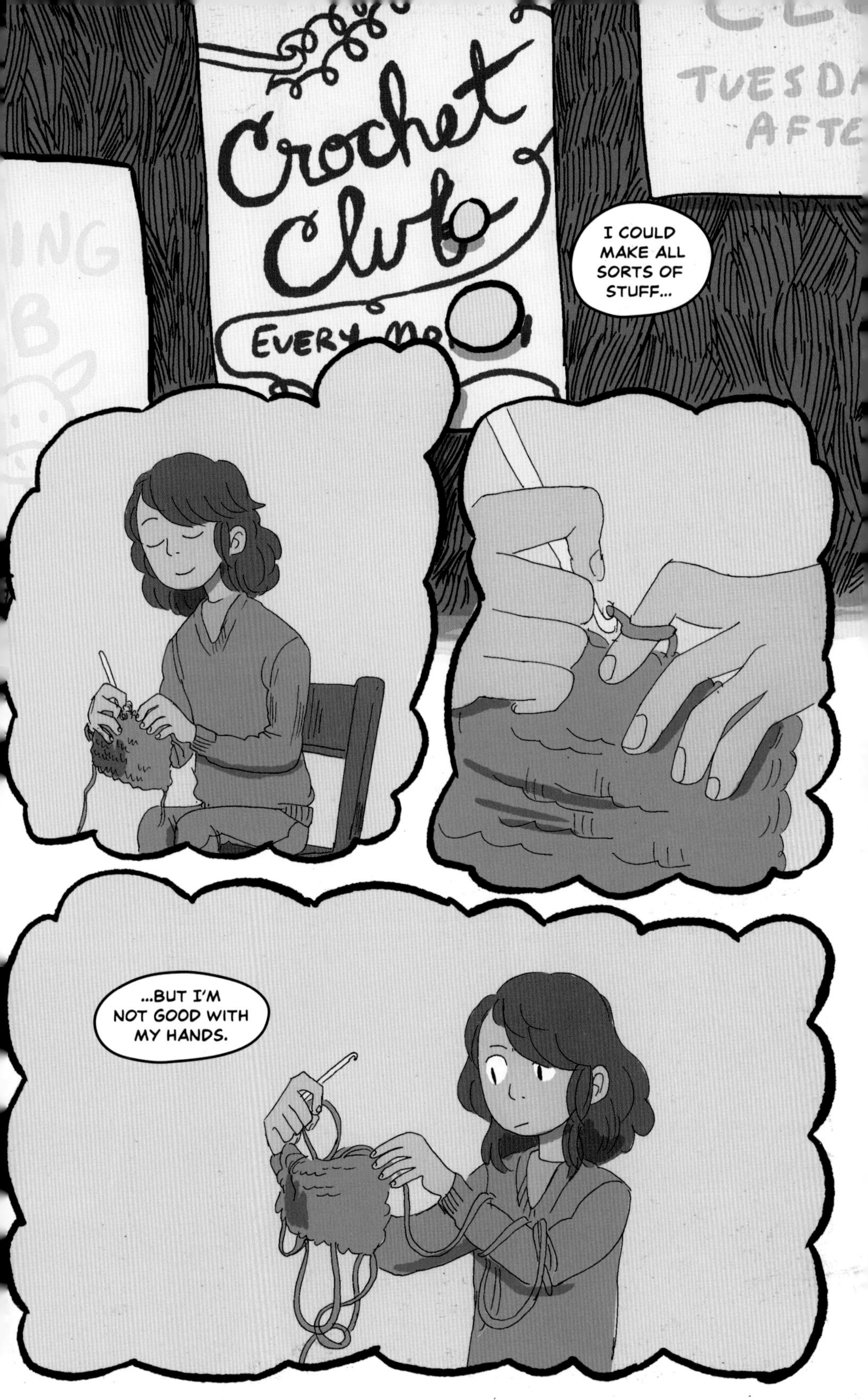
Crochet Club
I COULD MAKE ALL SORTS OF STUFF...
...BUT I'M NOT GOOD WITH MY HANDS.

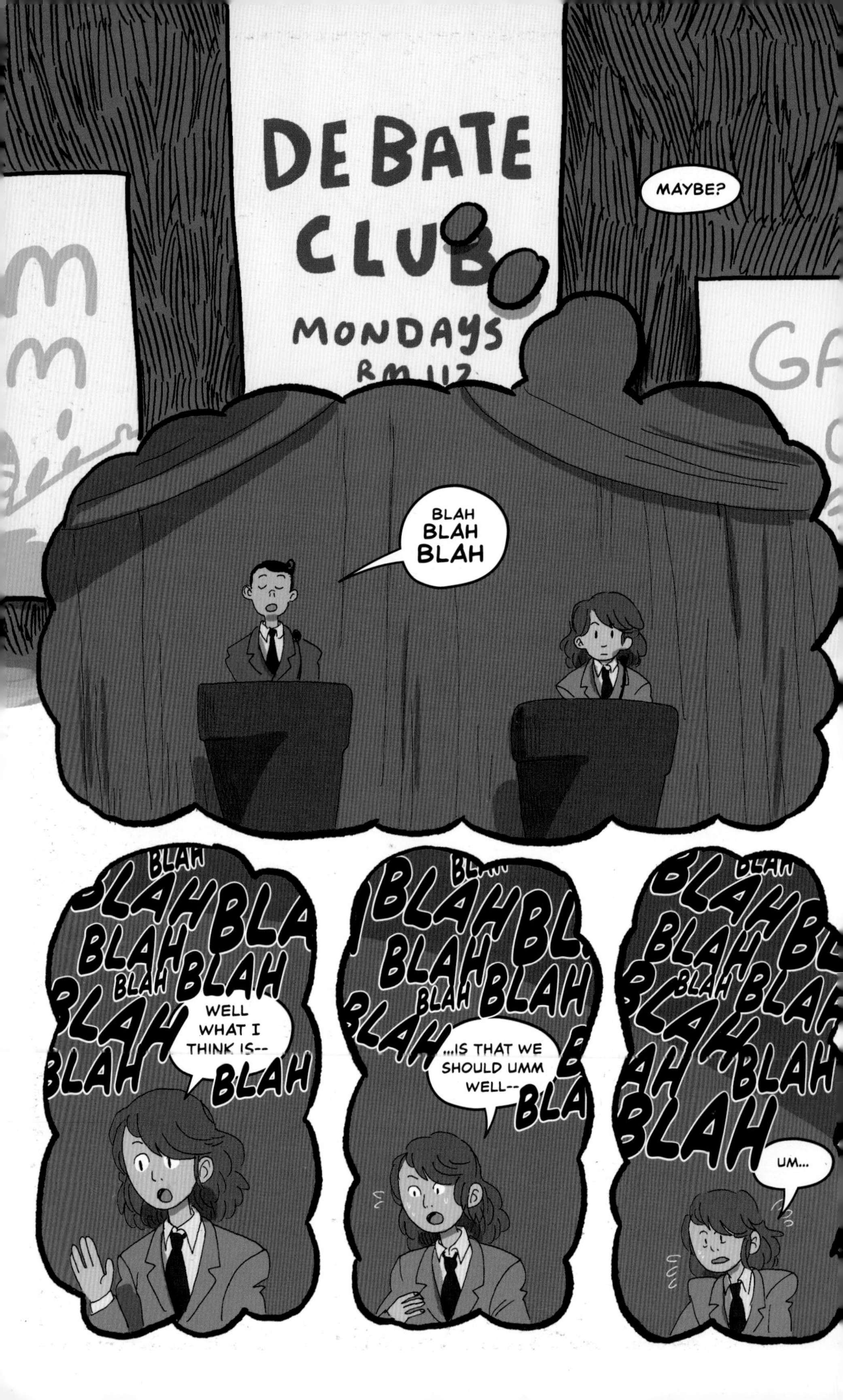
DEBATE CLUB
MONDAYS
RM 112
MAYBE?
BLAH BLAH BLAH
BLAH BLAH BLAH BLAH BLAH BLAH BLAH
WELL WHAT I THINK IS--
BLAH
BLAH BLAH BLAH BLAH BLAH
...IS THAT WE SHOULD UMM WELL--
BLAH BLAH BLAH BLAH BLAH BLAH BLAH
UM...

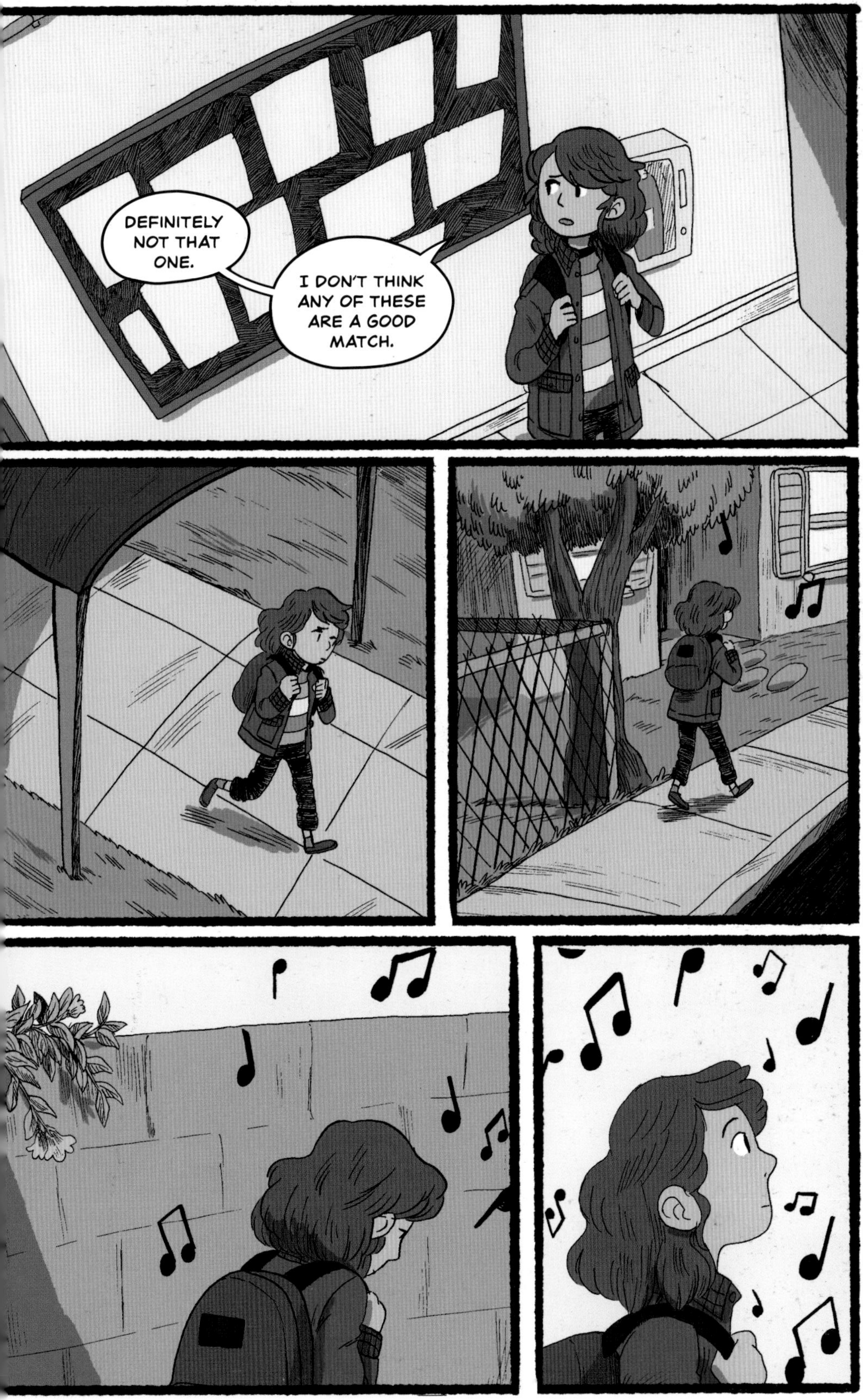
DEFINITELY NOT THAT ONE.
I DON'T THINK ANY OF THESE ARE A GOOD MATCH.

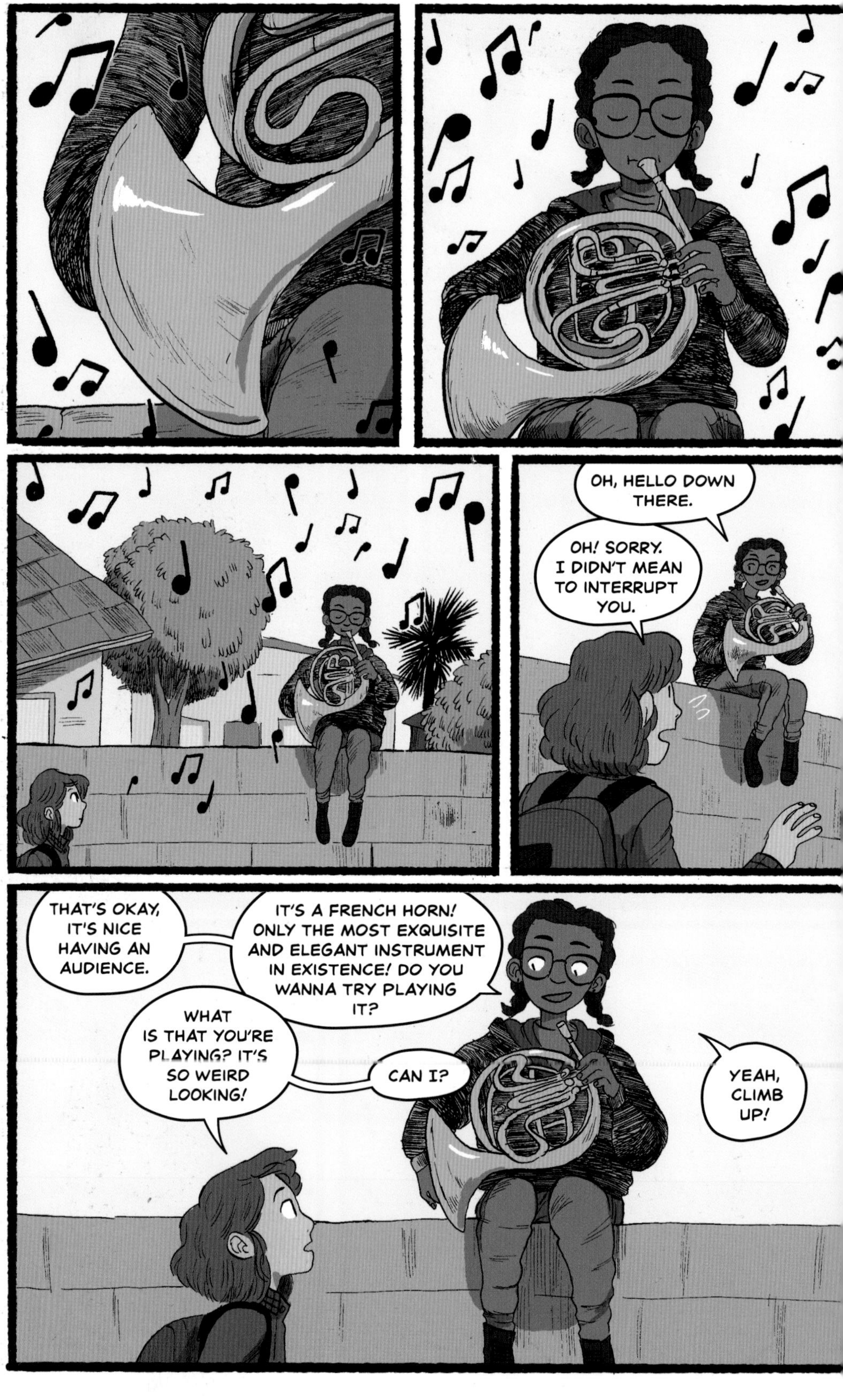
OH, HELLO DOWN THERE.
OH! SORRY. I DIDN'T MEAN TO INTERRUPT YOU.
THAT'S OKAY, IT'S NICE HAVING AN AUDIENCE.
WHAT IS THAT YOU'RE PLAYING? IT'S SO WEIRD LOOKING!
IT'S A FRENCH HORN! ONLY THE MOST EXQUISITE AND ELEGANT INSTRUMENT IN EXISTENCE! DO YOU WANNA TRY PLAYING IT?
CAN I?
YEAH, CLIMB UP!

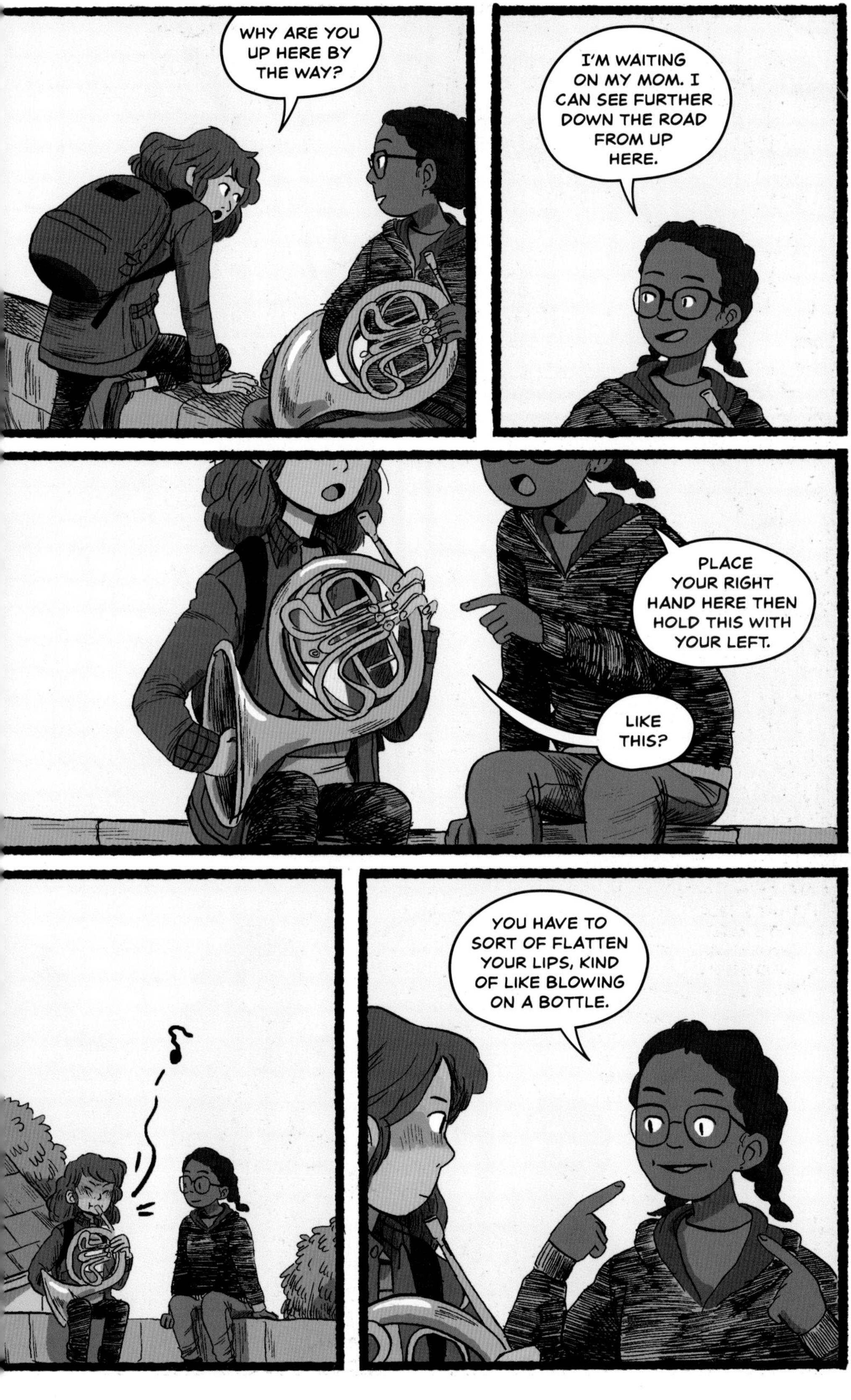

WHY ARE YOU UP HERE BY THE WAY?
I'M WAITING ON MY MOM. I CAN SEE FURTHER DOWN THE ROAD FROM UP HERE.
PLACE YOUR RIGHT HAND HERE THEN HOLD THIS WITH YOUR LEFT.
LIKE THIS?
YOU HAVE TO SORT OF FLATTEN YOUR LIPS, KIND OF LIKE BLOWING ON A BOTTLE.

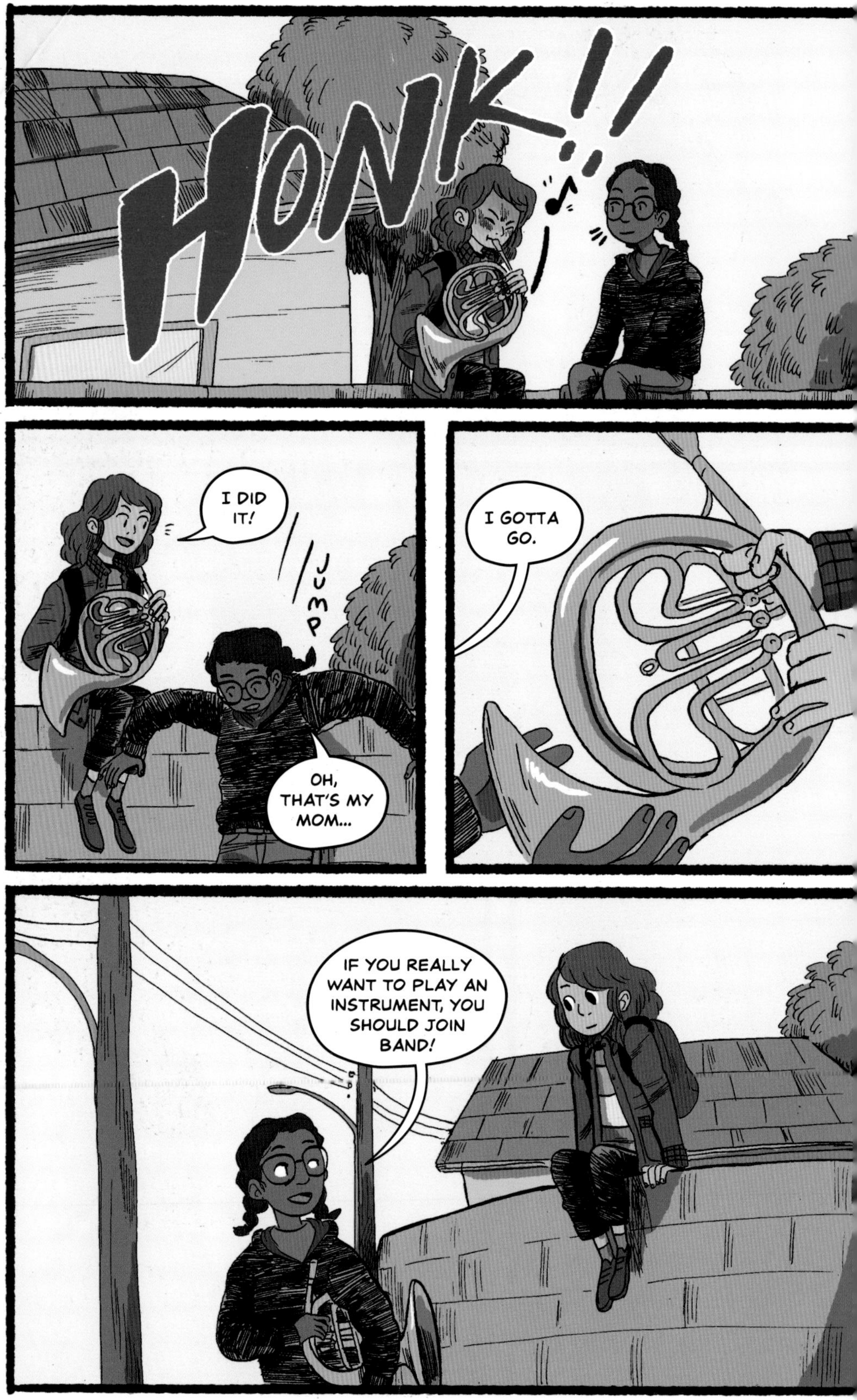
HONK!!
I DID IT!
JUMP
OH, THAT'S MY MOM...
I GOTTA GO.
IF YOU REALLY WANT TO PLAY AN INSTRUMENT, YOU SHOULD JOIN BAND!

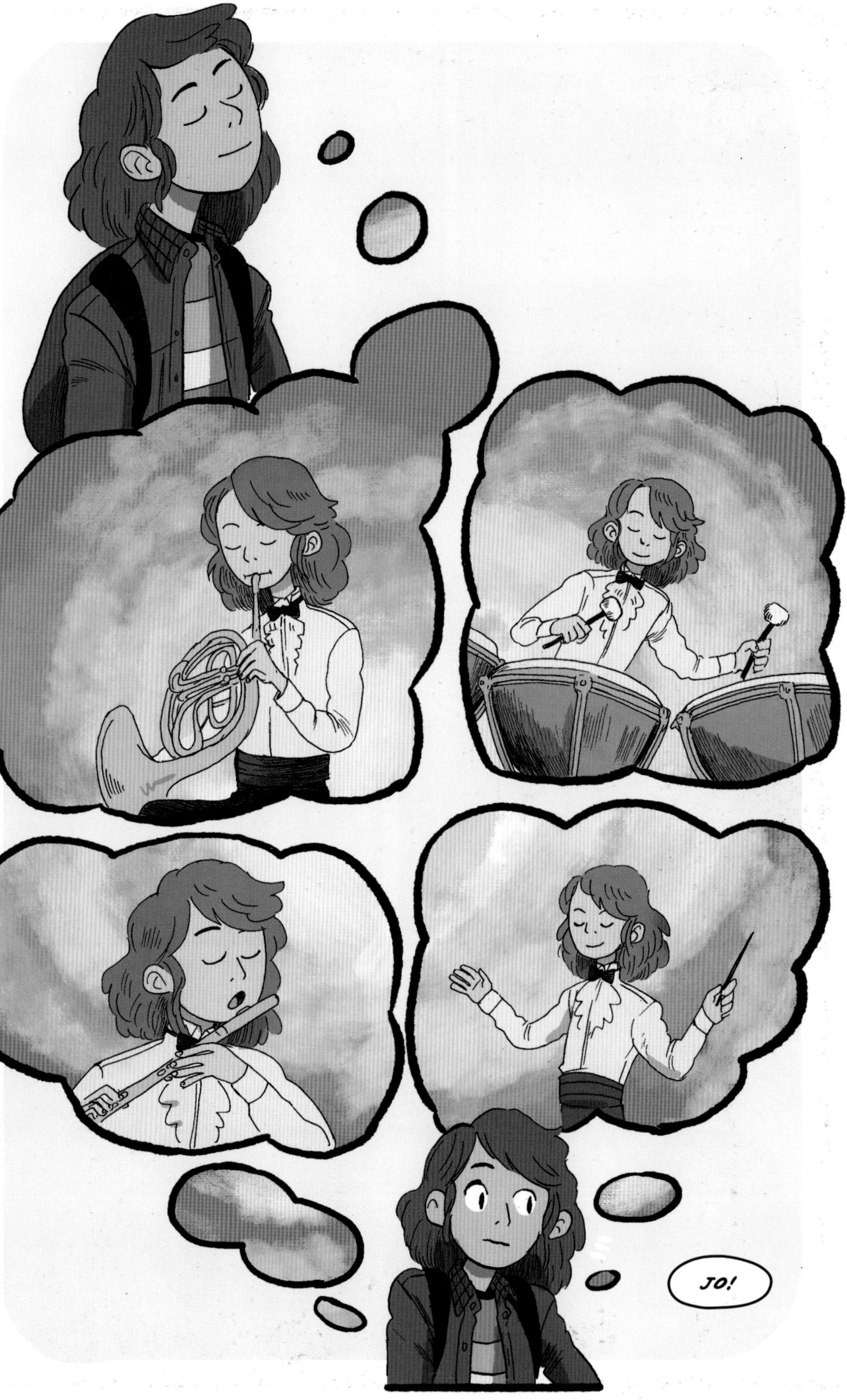
JO!

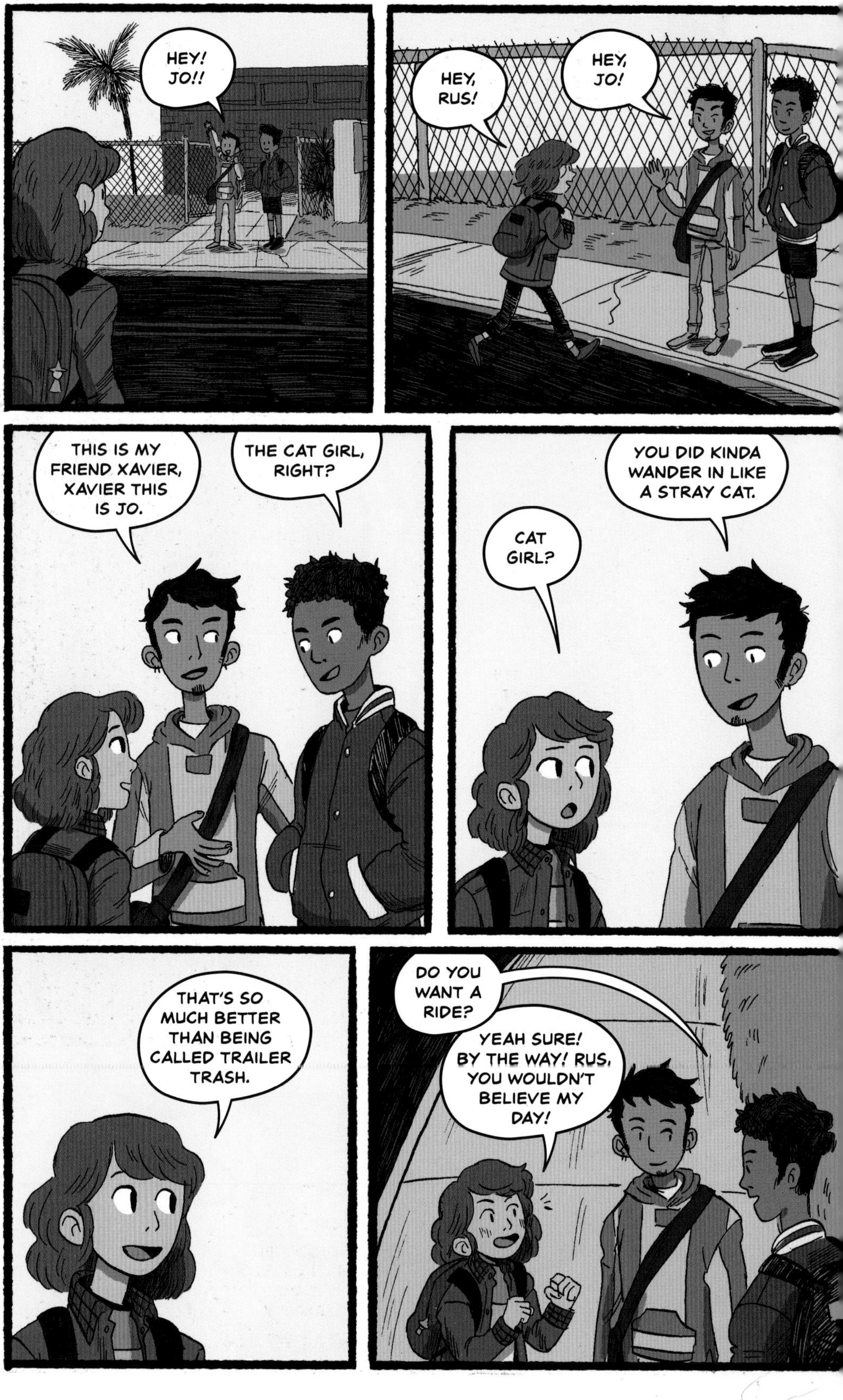
HEY! JO!!
HEY, RUS!
HEY, JO!
THIS IS MY FRIEND XAVIER, XAVIER THIS IS JO.
THE CAT GIRL, RIGHT?
YOU DID KINDA WANDER IN LIKE A STRAY CAT.
CAT GIRL?
THAT'S SO MUCH BETTER THAN BEING CALLED TRAILER TRASH.
DO YOU WANT A RIDE?
YEAH SURE! BY THE WAY! RUS, YOU WOULDN'T BELIEVE MY DAY!

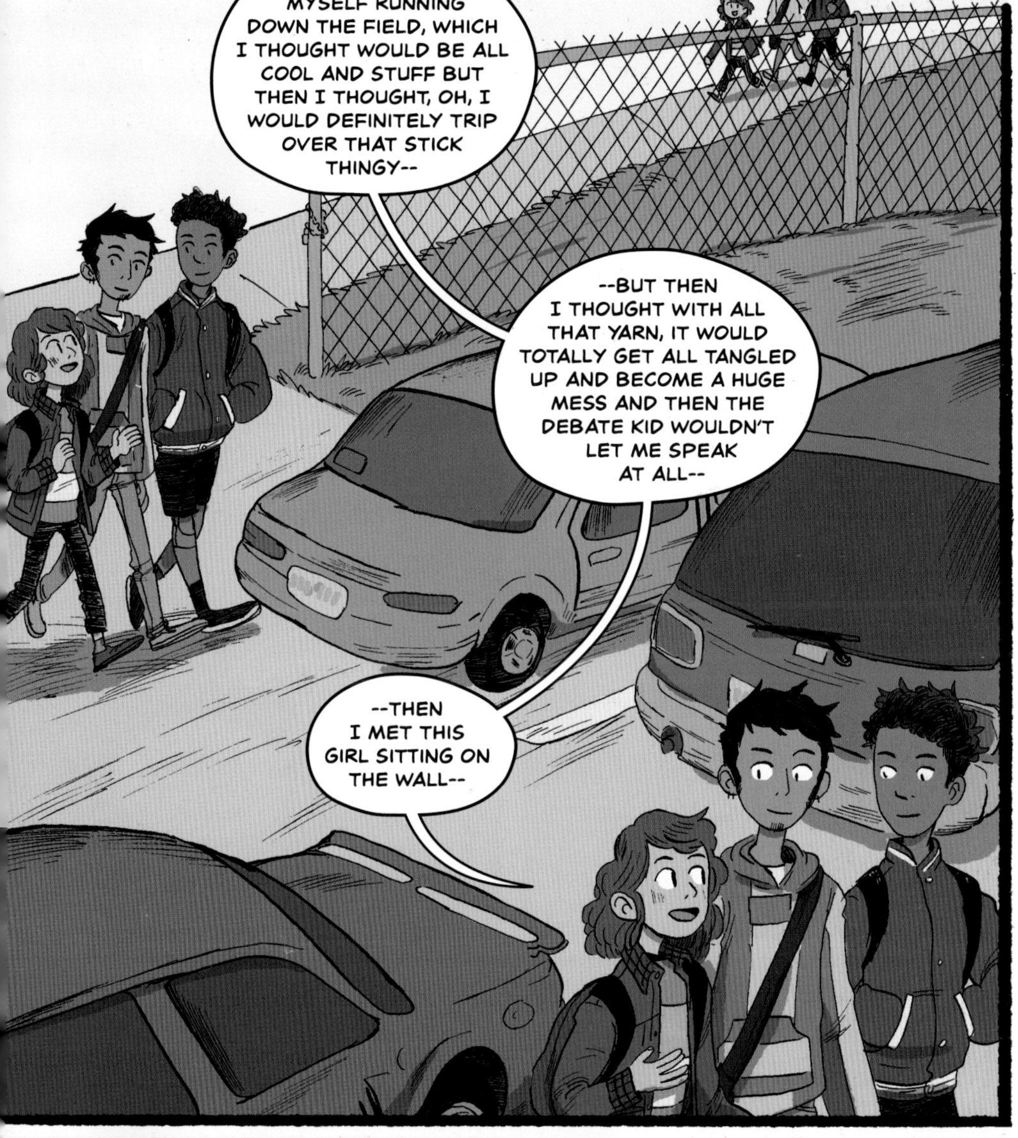
SO I IMAGINED MYSELF RUNNING DOWN THE FIELD, WHICH I THOUGHT WOULD BE ALL COOL AND STUFF BUT THEN I THOUGHT, OH, I WOULD DEFINITELY TRIP OVER THAT STICK THINGY--
--BUT THEN I THOUGHT WITH ALL THAT YARN, IT WOULD TOTALLY GET ALL TANGLED UP AND BECOME A HUGE MESS AND THEN THE DEBATE KID WOULDN'T LET ME SPEAK AT ALL--
--THEN I MET THIS GIRL SITTING ON THE WALL--

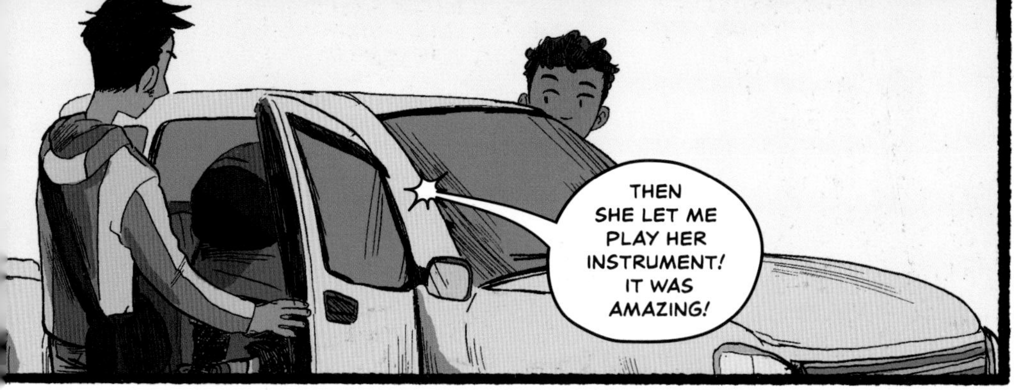
THEN SHE LET ME PLAY HER INSTRUMENT! IT WAS AMAZING!

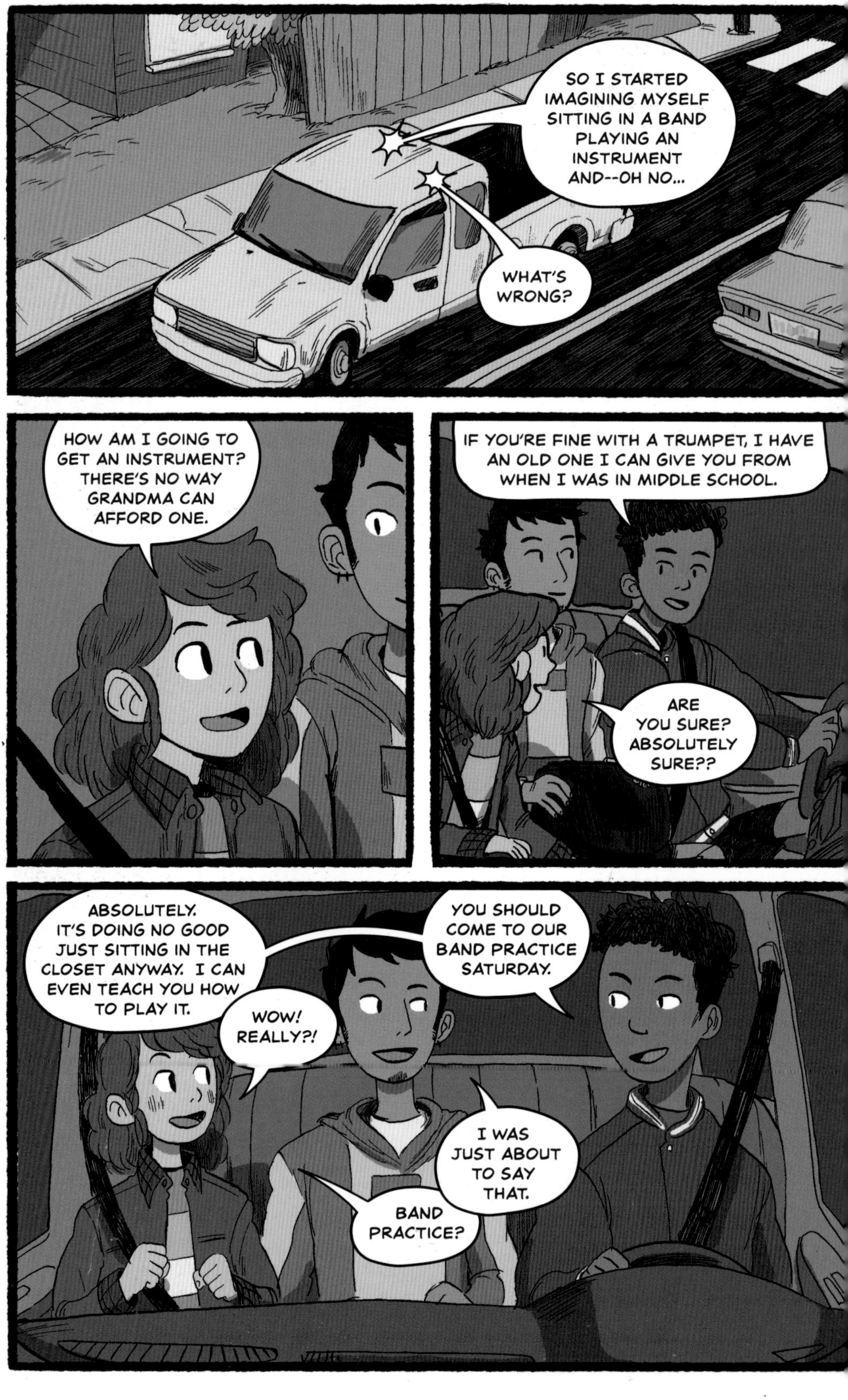
SO I STARTED IMAGINING MYSELF SITTING IN A BAND PLAYING AN INSTRUMENT AND--OH NO...
WHAT'S WRONG?
HOW AM I GOING TO GET AN INSTRUMENT? THERE'S NO WAY GRANDMA CAN AFFORD ONE.
IF YOU'RE FINE WITH A TRUMPET, I HAVE AN OLD ONE I CAN GIVE YOU FROM WHEN I WAS IN MIDDLE SCHOOL.
ARE YOU SURE? ABSOLUTELY SURE??
ABSOLUTELY. IT'S DOING NO GOOD JUST SITTING IN THE CLOSET ANYWAY. I CAN EVEN TEACH YOU HOW TO PLAY IT.
YOU SHOULD COME TO OUR BAND PRACTICE SATURDAY.
WOW! REALLY?!
I WAS JUST ABOUT TO SAY THAT.
BAND PRACTICE?

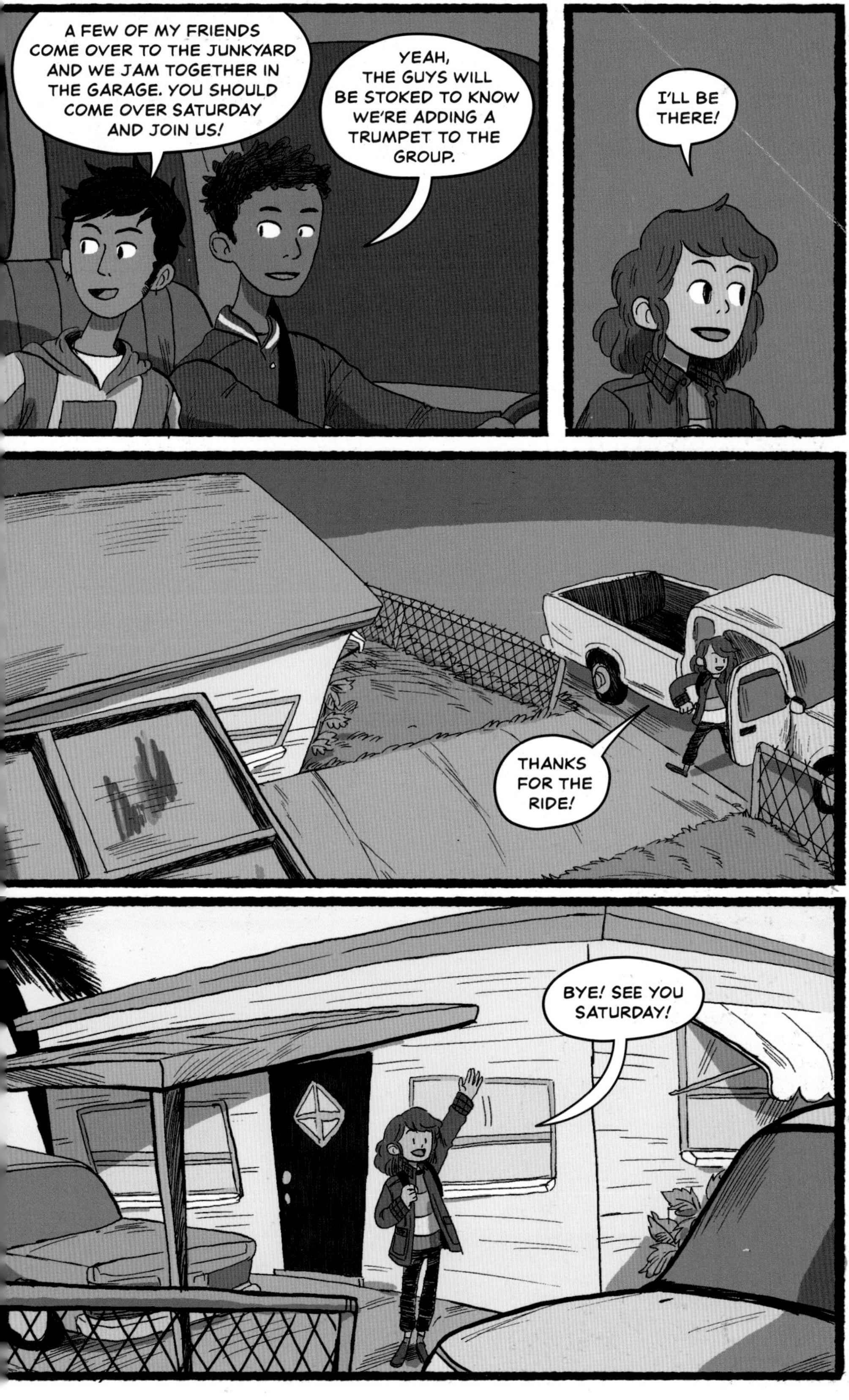
A FEW OF MY FRIENDS COME OVER TO THE JUNKYARD AND WE JAM TOGETHER IN THE GARAGE. YOU SHOULD COME OVER SATURDAY AND JOIN US!
YEAH, THE GUYS WILL BE STOKED TO KNOW WE'RE ADDING A TRUMPET TO THE GROUP.
I'LL BE THERE!
THANKS FOR THE RIDE!
BYE! SEE YOU SATURDAY!

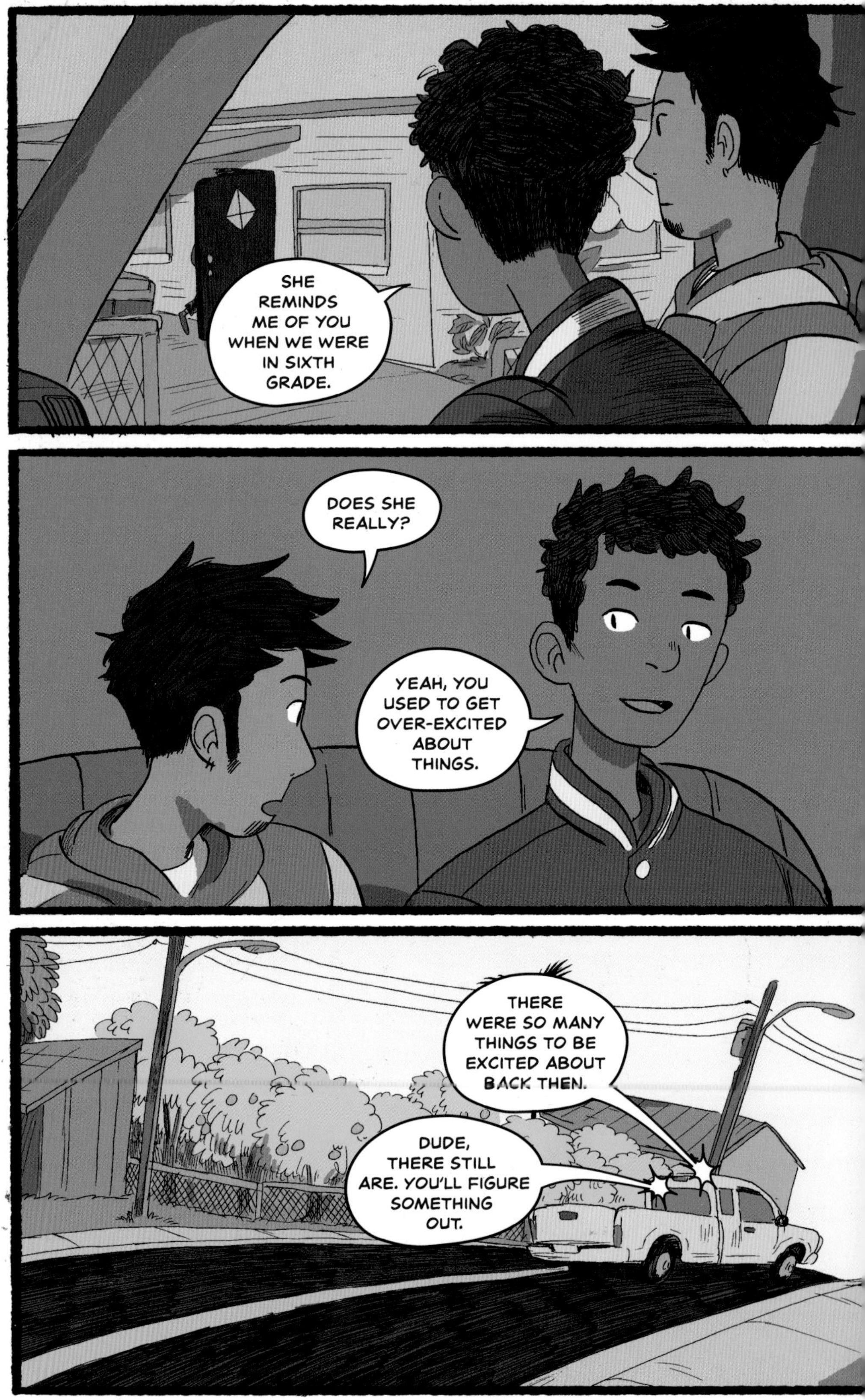
SHE REMINDS ME OF YOU WHEN WE WERE IN SIXTH GRADE.
DOES SHE REALLY?
YEAH, YOU USED TO GET OVER-EXCITED ABOUT THINGS.
THERE WERE SO MANY THINGS TO BE EXCITED ABOUT BACK THEN.
DUDE, THERE STILL ARE. YOU'LL FIGURE SOMETHING OUT.

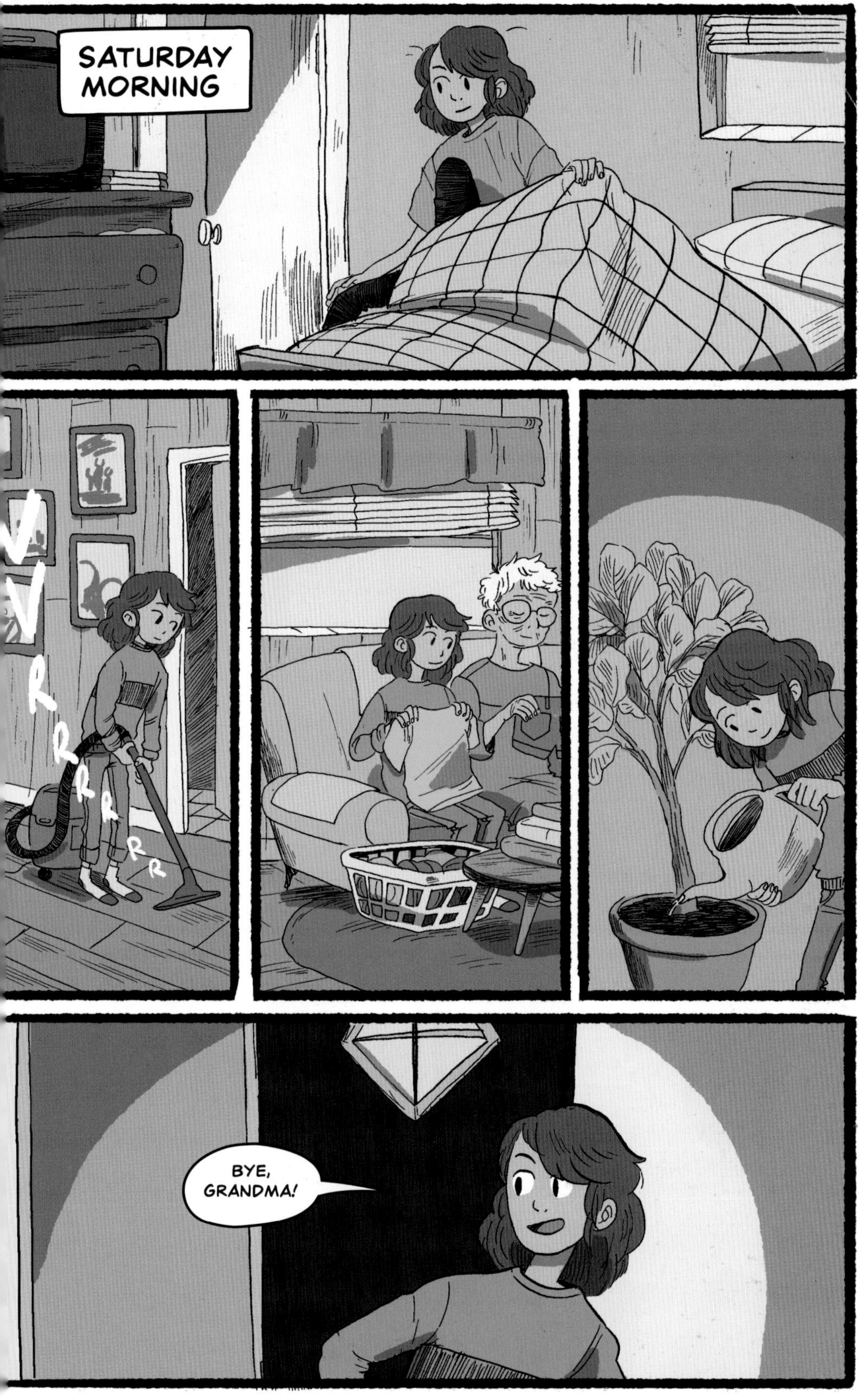
SATURDAY MORNING
VVRRRRRR
BYE, GRANDMA!

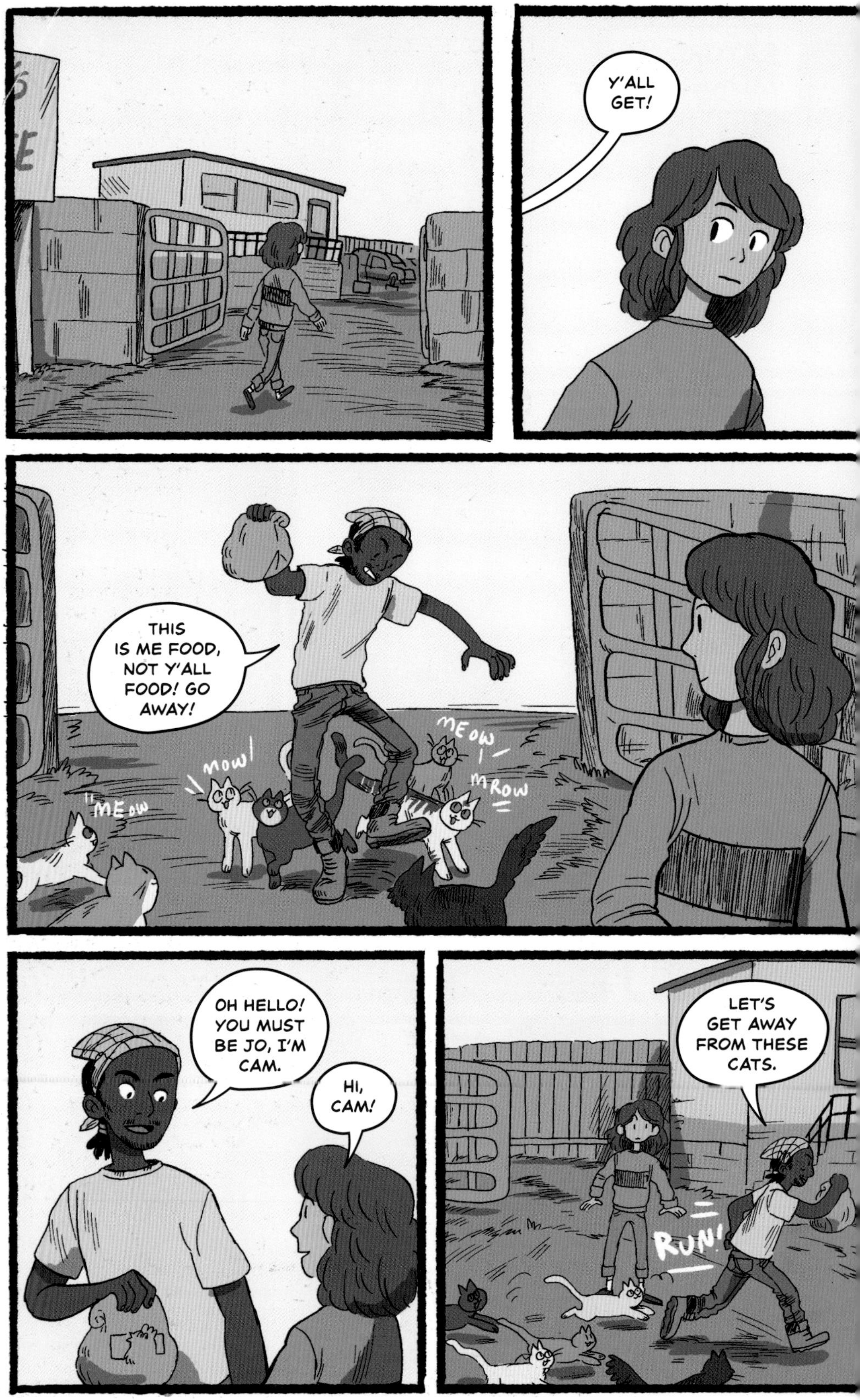
Y'ALL GET!
THIS IS ME FOOD, NOT Y'ALL FOOD! GO AWAY!
MEOW
MOW!
MEOW!
MROW
OH HELLO! YOU MUST BE JO, I'M CAM.
HI, CAM!
LET'S GET AWAY FROM THESE CATS.
RUN!

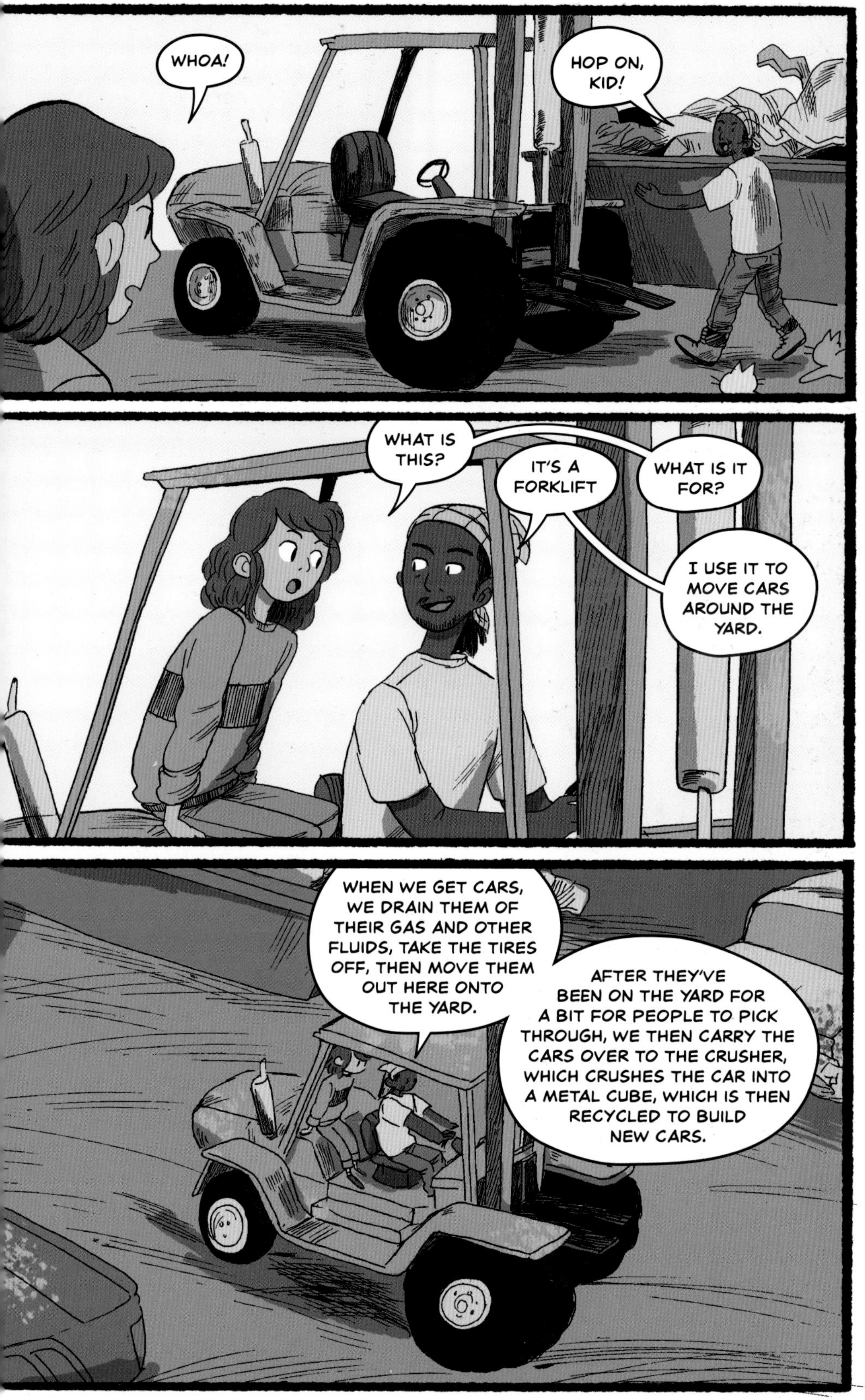
WHOA!
HOP ON, KID!
WHAT IS THIS?
IT'S A FORKLIFT
WHAT IS IT FOR?
I USE IT TO MOVE CARS AROUND THE YARD.
WHEN WE GET CARS, WE DRAIN THEM OF THEIR GAS AND OTHER FLUIDS, TAKE THE TIRES OFF, THEN MOVE THEM OUT HERE ONTO THE YARD.
AFTER THEY'VE BEEN ON THE YARD FOR A BIT FOR PEOPLE TO PICK THROUGH, WE THEN CARRY THE CARS OVER TO THE CRUSHER, WHICH CRUSHES THE CAR INTO A METAL CUBE, WHICH IS THEN RECYCLED TO BUILD NEW CARS.

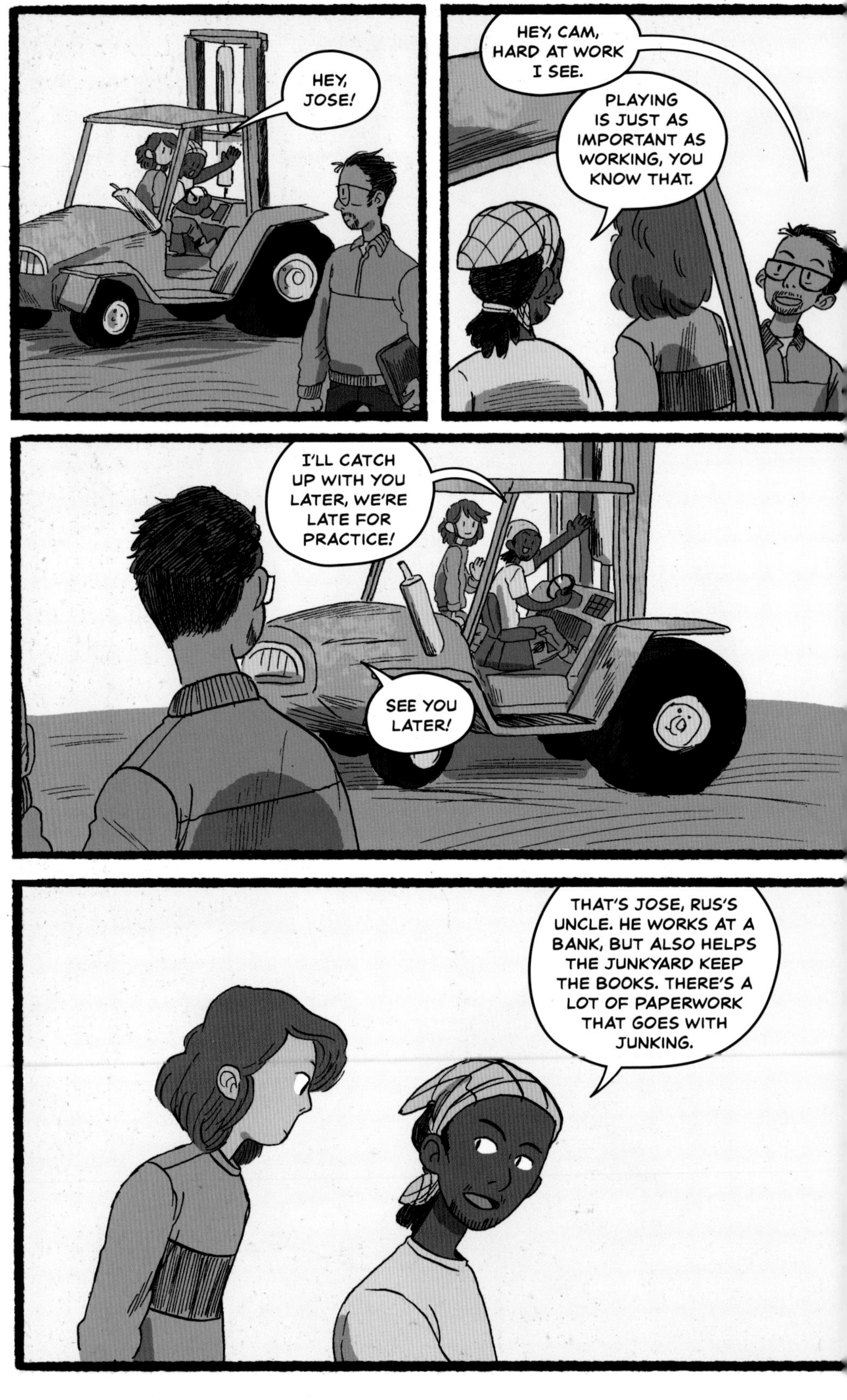

HEY, JOSE!
HEY, CAM, HARD AT WORK I SEE.
PLAYING IS JUST AS IMPORTANT AS WORKING, YOU KNOW THAT.
I'LL CATCH UP WITH YOU LATER, WE'RE LATE FOR PRACTICE!
SEE YOU LATER!
THAT'S JOSE, RUS'S UNCLE. HE WORKS AT A BANK, BUT ALSO HELPS THE JUNKYARD KEEP THE BOOKS. THERE'S A LOT OF PAPERWORK THAT GOES WITH JUNKING.

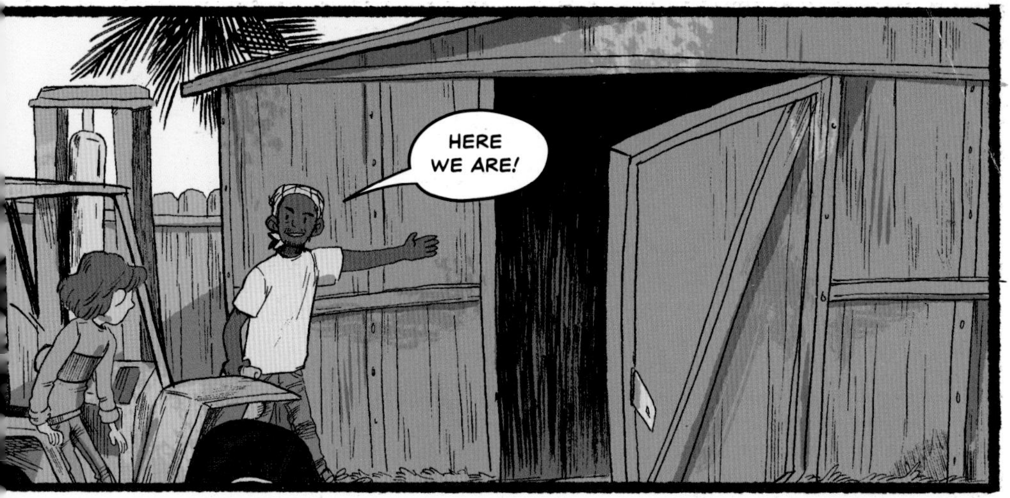
HERE WE ARE!

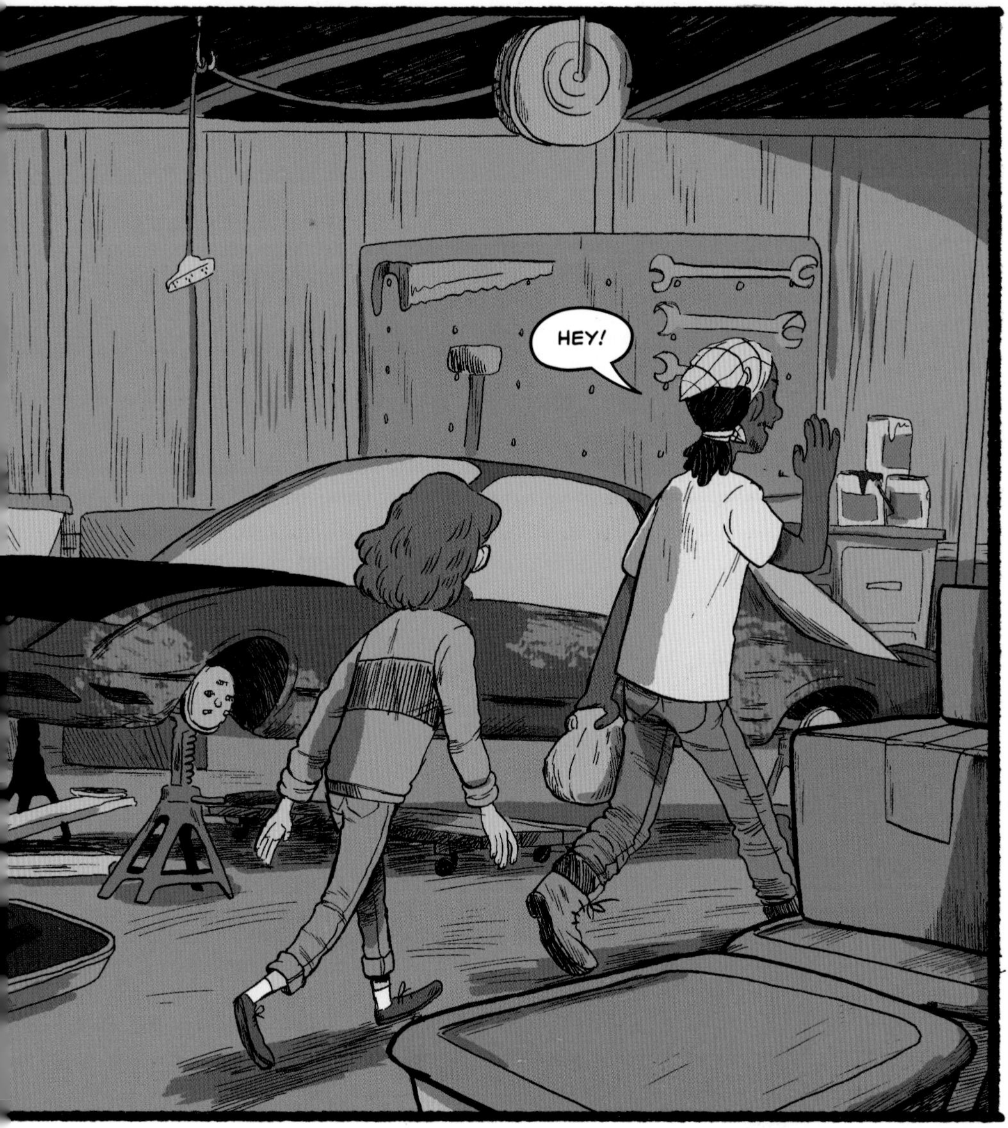
HEY!

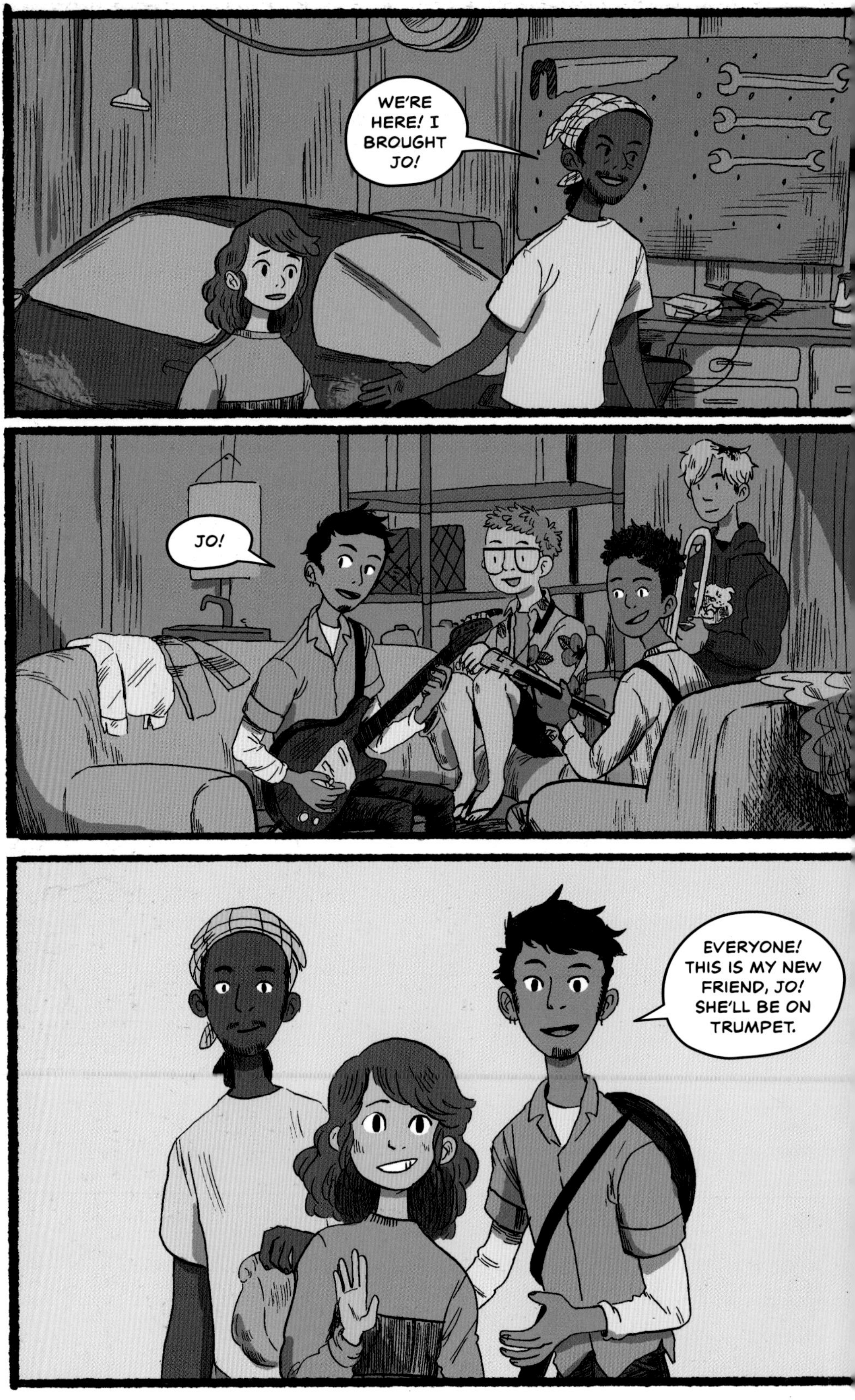
WE'RE HERE! I BROUGHT JO!
JO!
EVERYONE! THIS IS MY NEW FRIEND, JO! SHE'LL BE ON TRUMPET.

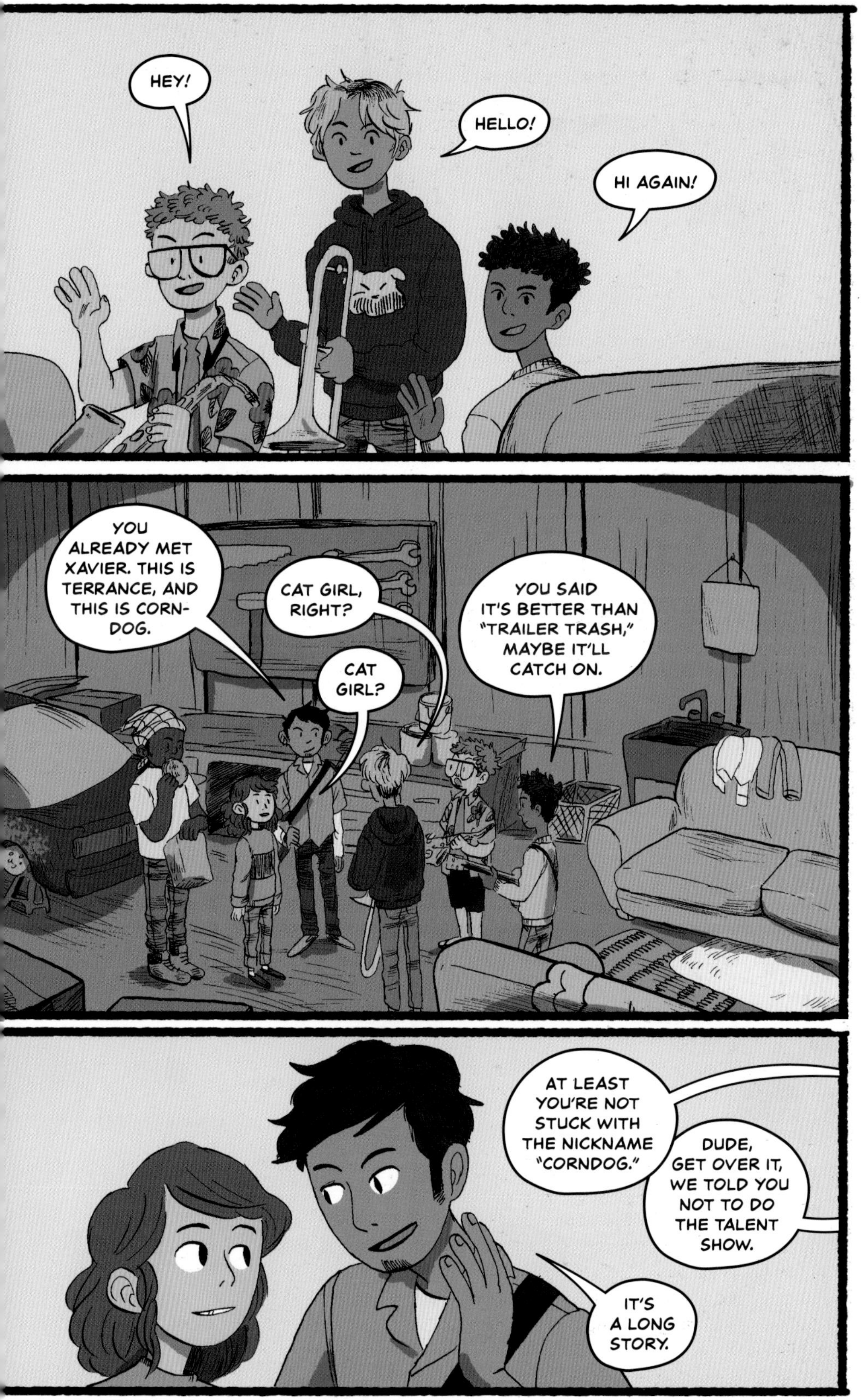
HEY!
HELLO!
HI AGAIN!
YOU ALREADY MET XAVIER. THIS IS TERRANCE, AND THIS IS CORN-DOG.
CAT GIRL, RIGHT?
CAT GIRL?
YOU SAID IT'S BETTER THAN "TRAILER TRASH," MAYBE IT'LL CATCH ON.
AT LEAST YOU'RE NOT STUCK WITH THE NICKNAME "CORNDOG."
DUDE, GET OVER IT, WE TOLD YOU NOT TO DO THE TALENT SHOW.
IT'S A LONG STORY.

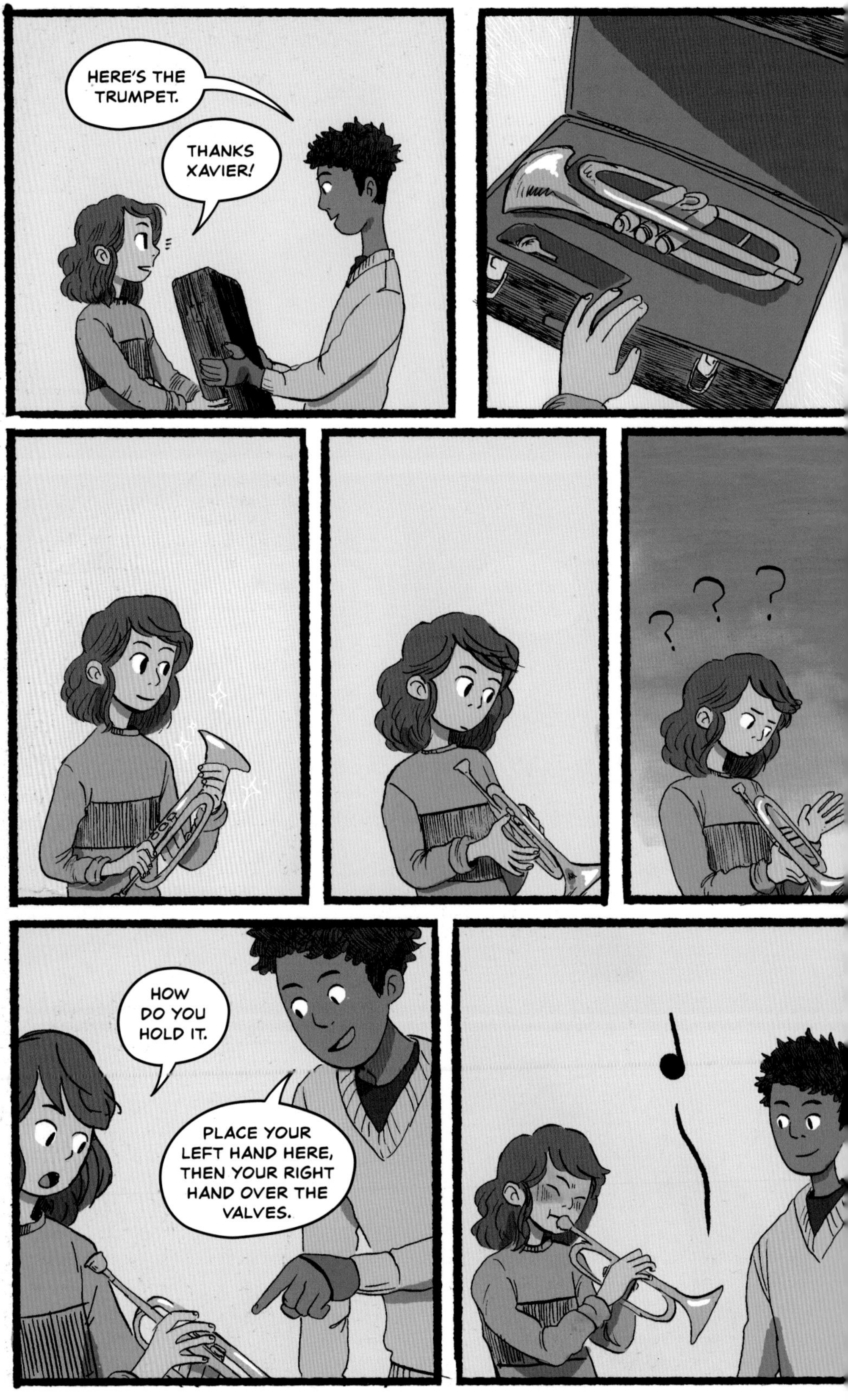
HERE'S THE TRUMPET.
THANKS XAVIER!
HOW DO YOU HOLD IT.
PLACE YOUR LEFT HAND HERE, THEN YOUR RIGHT HAND OVER THE VALVES.

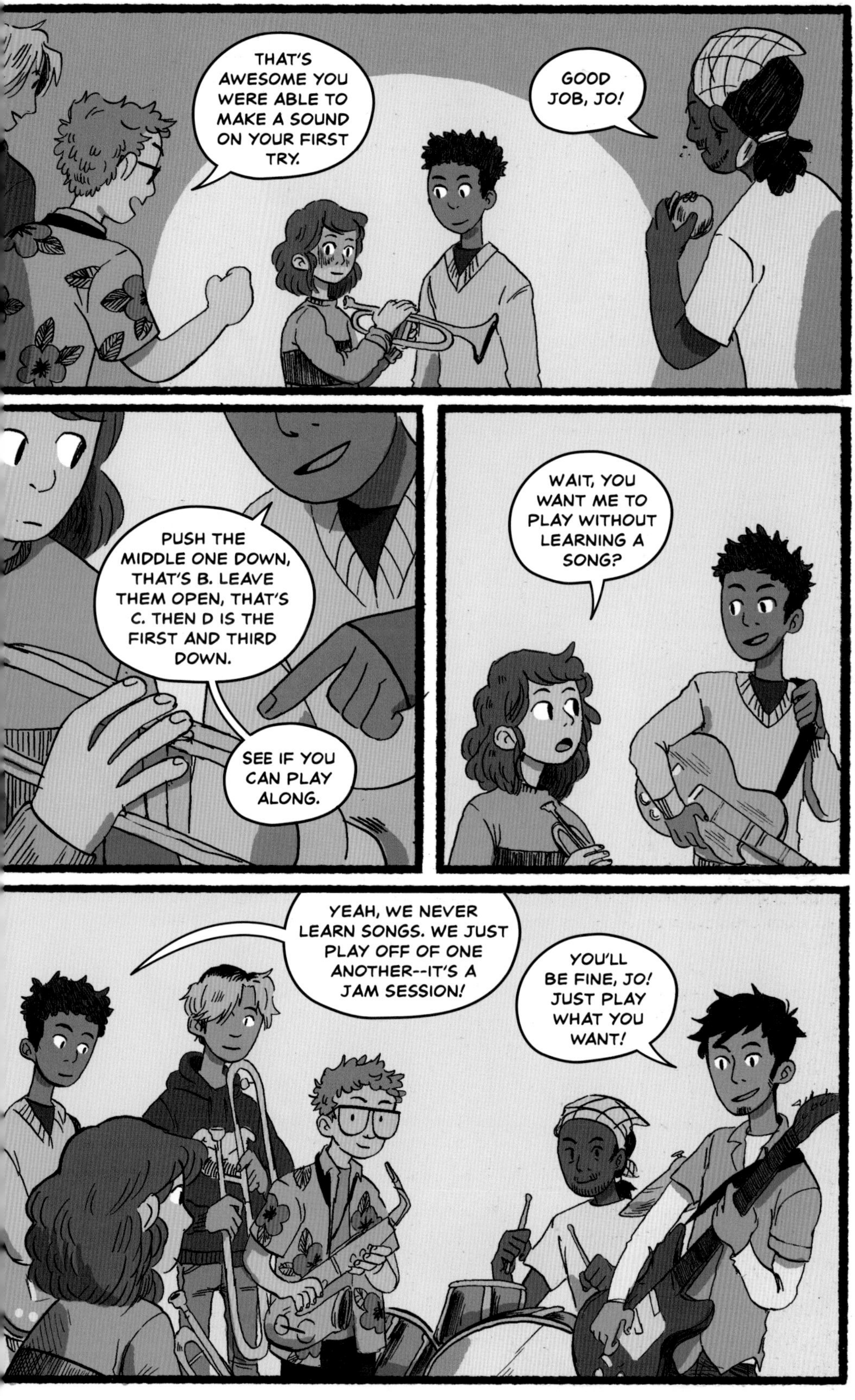
THAT'S AWESOME YOU WERE ABLE TO MAKE A SOUND ON YOUR FIRST TRY.
GOOD JOB, JO!
PUSH THE MIDDLE ONE DOWN, THAT'S B. LEAVE THEM OPEN, THAT'S C. THEN D IS THE FIRST AND THIRD DOWN.
SEE IF YOU CAN PLAY ALONG.
WAIT, YOU WANT ME TO PLAY WITHOUT LEARNING A SONG?
YEAH, WE NEVER LEARN SONGS. WE JUST PLAY OFF OF ONE ANOTHER--IT'S A JAM SESSION!
YOU'LL BE FINE, JO! JUST PLAY WHAT YOU WANT!

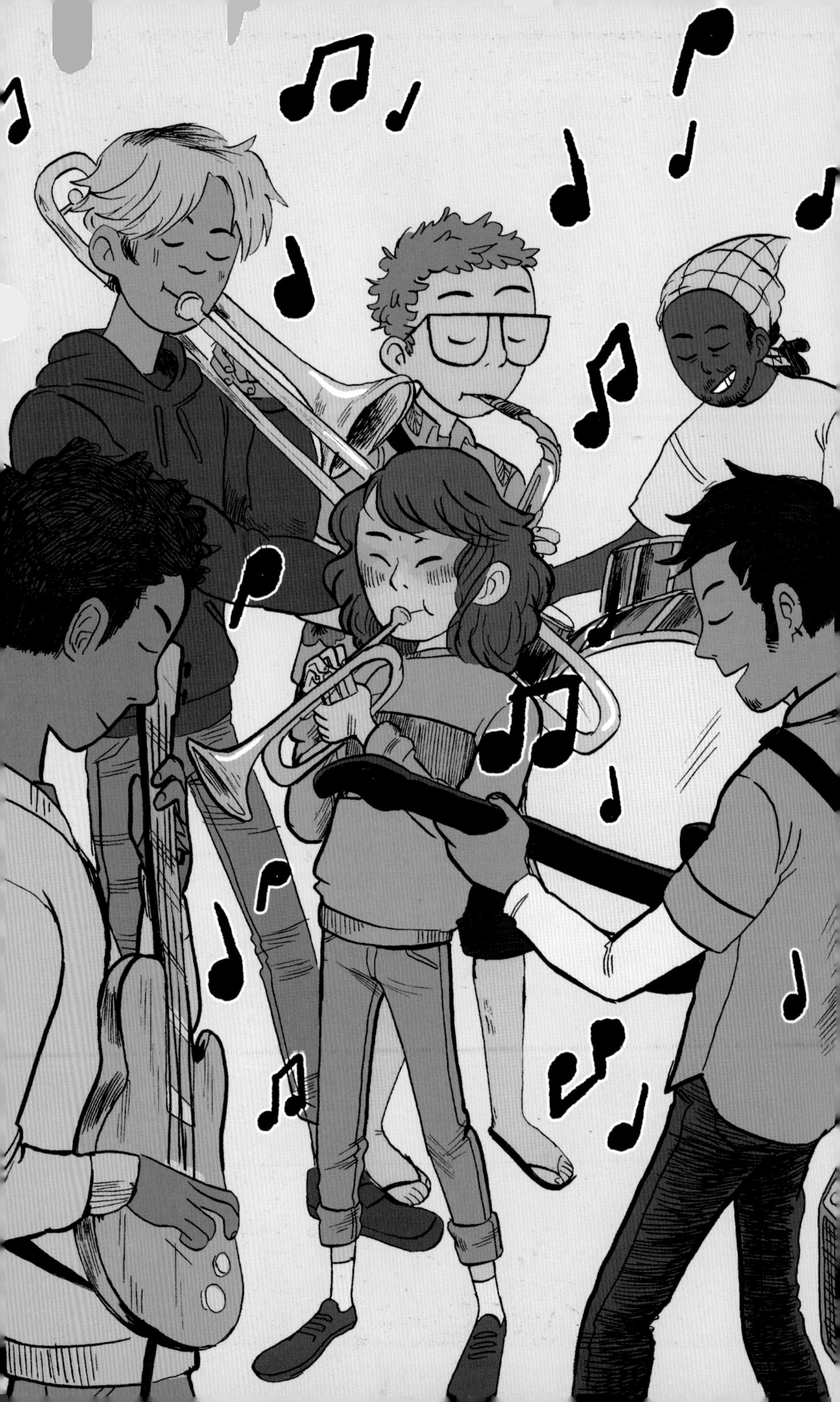

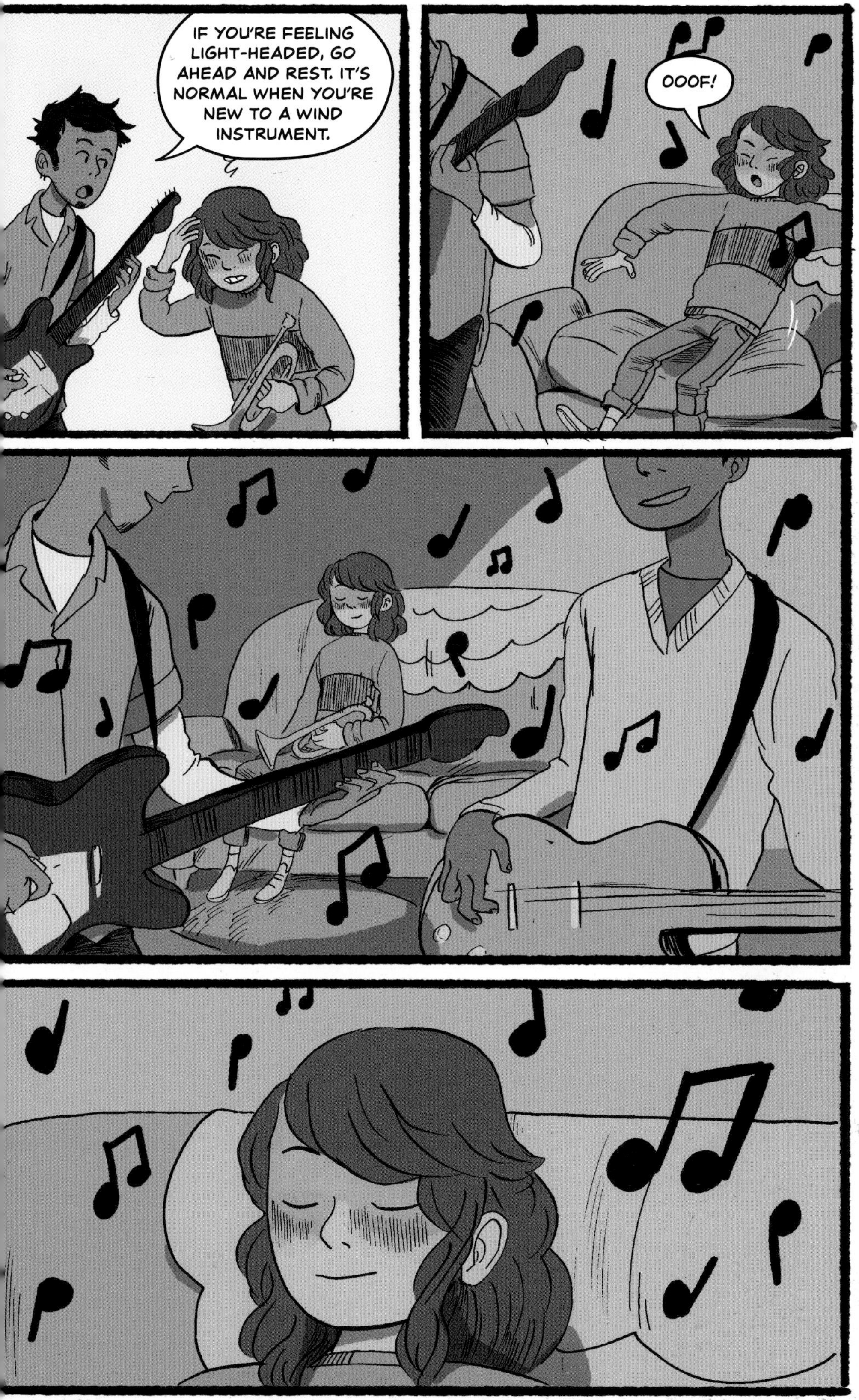
IF YOU'RE FEELING LIGHT-HEADED, GO AHEAD AND REST. IT'S NORMAL WHEN YOU'RE NEW TO A WIND INSTRUMENT.
OOOF!

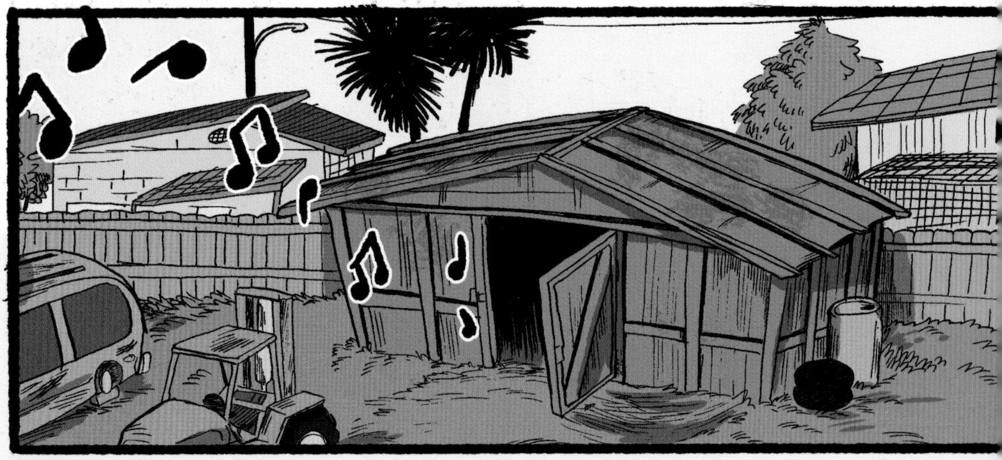

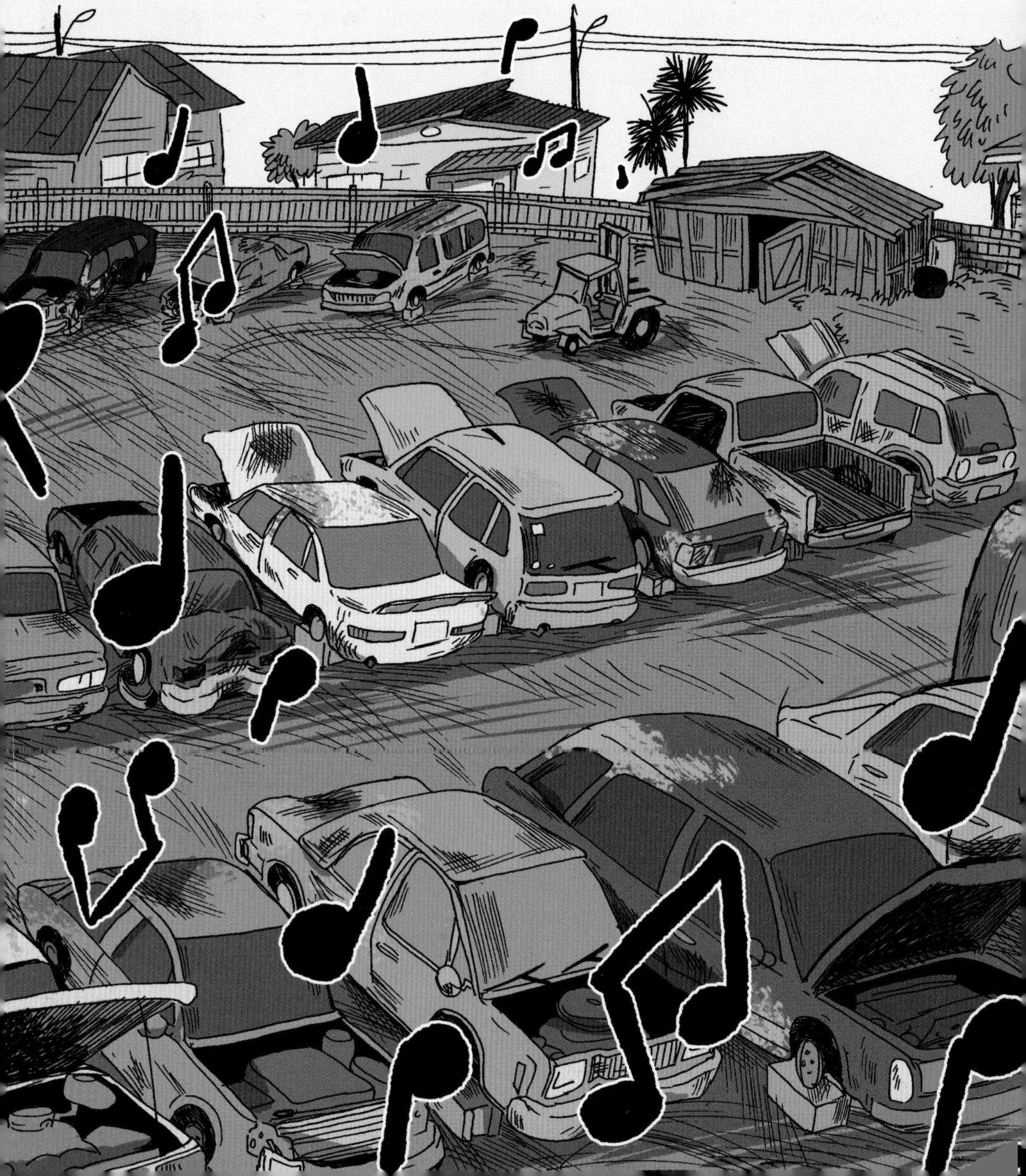

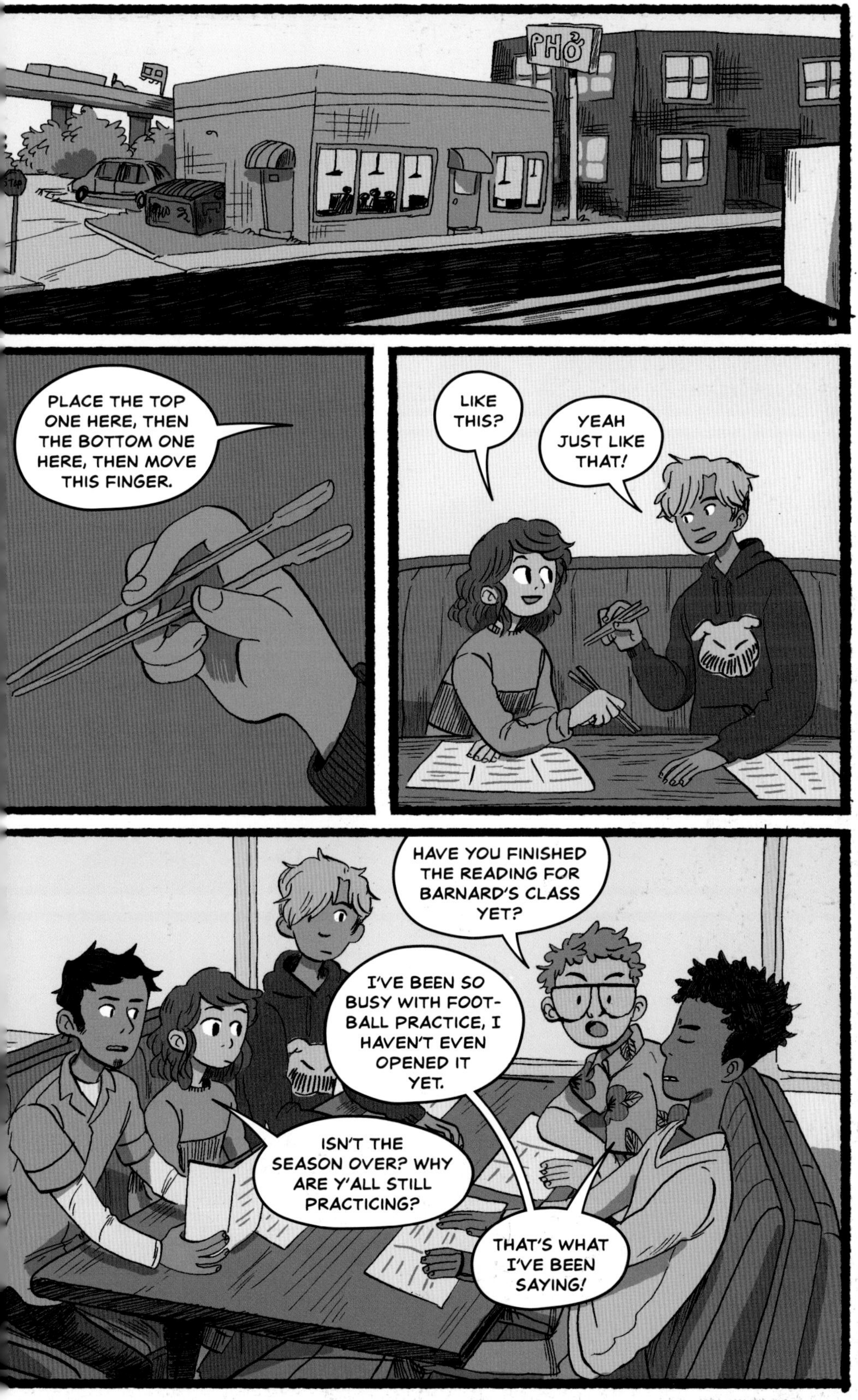
PHỞ
PLACE THE TOP ONE HERE, THEN THE BOTTOM ONE HERE, THEN MOVE THIS FINGER.
LIKE THIS?
YEAH JUST LIKE THAT!
HAVE YOU FINISHED THE READING FOR BARNARD'S CLASS YET?
I'VE BEEN SO BUSY WITH FOOT-BALL PRACTICE, I HAVEN'T EVEN OPENED IT YET.
ISN'T THE SEASON OVER? WHY ARE Y'ALL STILL PRACTICING?
THAT'S WHAT I'VE BEEN SAYING!

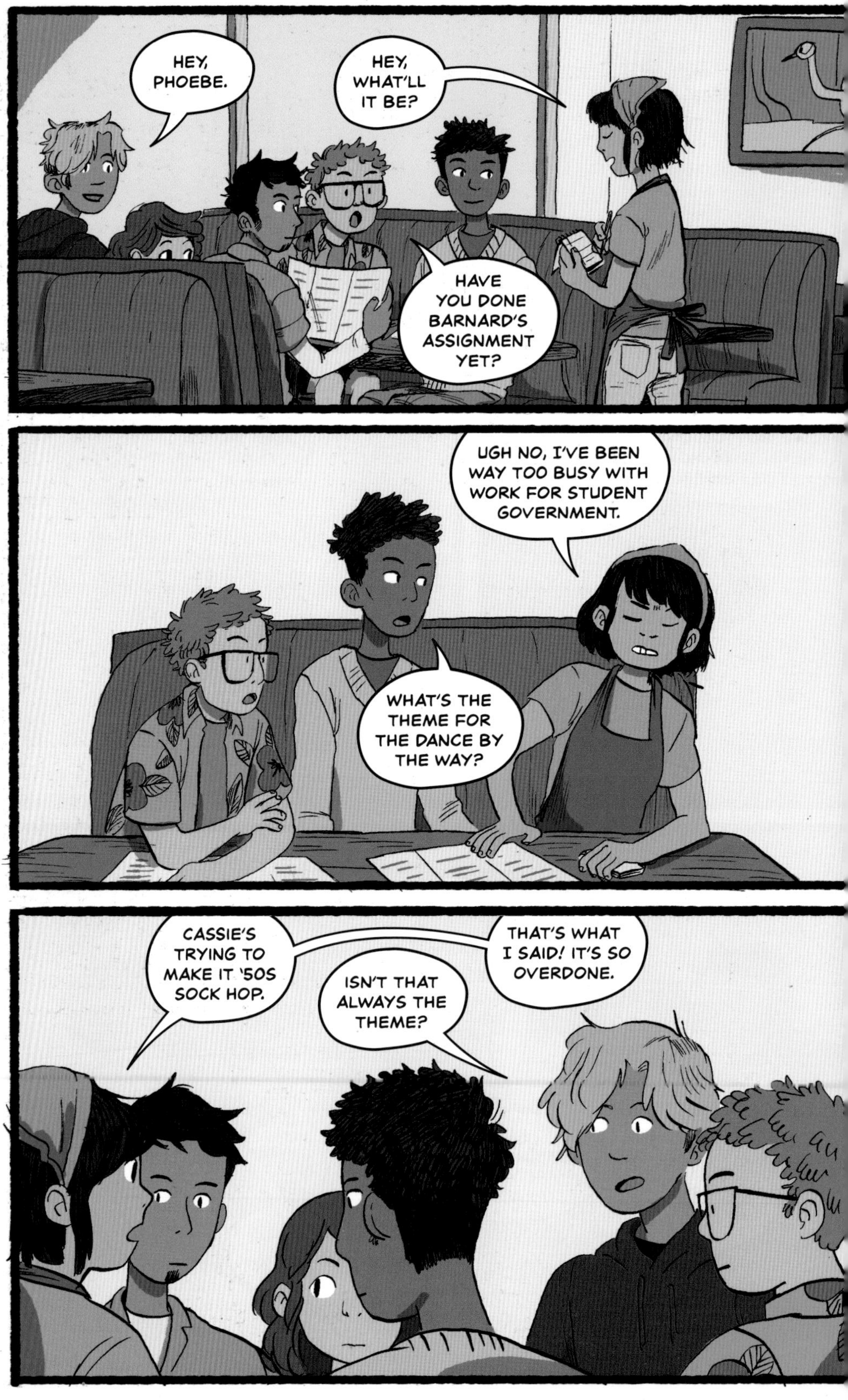
HEY, PHOEBE.
HEY, WHAT'LL IT BE?
HAVE YOU DONE BARNARD'S ASSIGNMENT YET?
UGH NO, I'VE BEEN WAY TOO BUSY WITH WORK FOR STUDENT GOVERNMENT.
WHAT'S THE THEME FOR THE DANCE BY THE WAY?
CASSIE'S TRYING TO MAKE IT '50S SOCK HOP.
ISN'T THAT ALWAYS THE THEME?
THAT'S WHAT I SAID! IT'S SO OVERDONE.

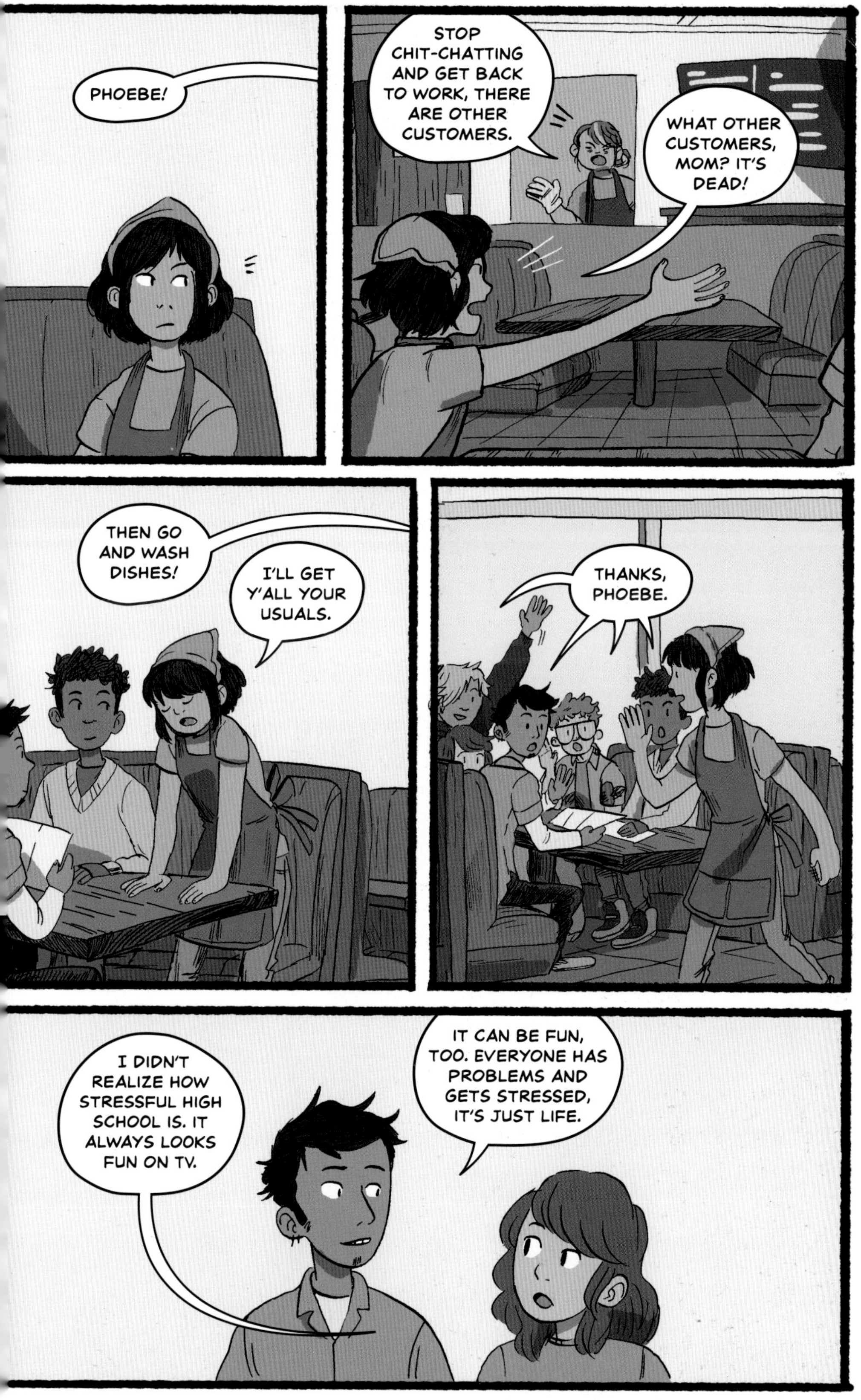
PHOEBE!
STOP CHIT-CHATTING AND GET BACK TO WORK, THERE ARE OTHER CUSTOMERS.
WHAT OTHER CUSTOMERS, MOM? IT'S DEAD!
THEN GO AND WASH DISHES!
I'LL GET Y'ALL YOUR USUALS.
THANKS, PHOEBE.
I DIDN'T REALIZE HOW STRESSFUL HIGH SCHOOL IS. IT ALWAYS LOOKS FUN ON TV.
IT CAN BE FUN, TOO. EVERYONE HAS PROBLEMS AND GETS STRESSED, IT'S JUST LIFE.

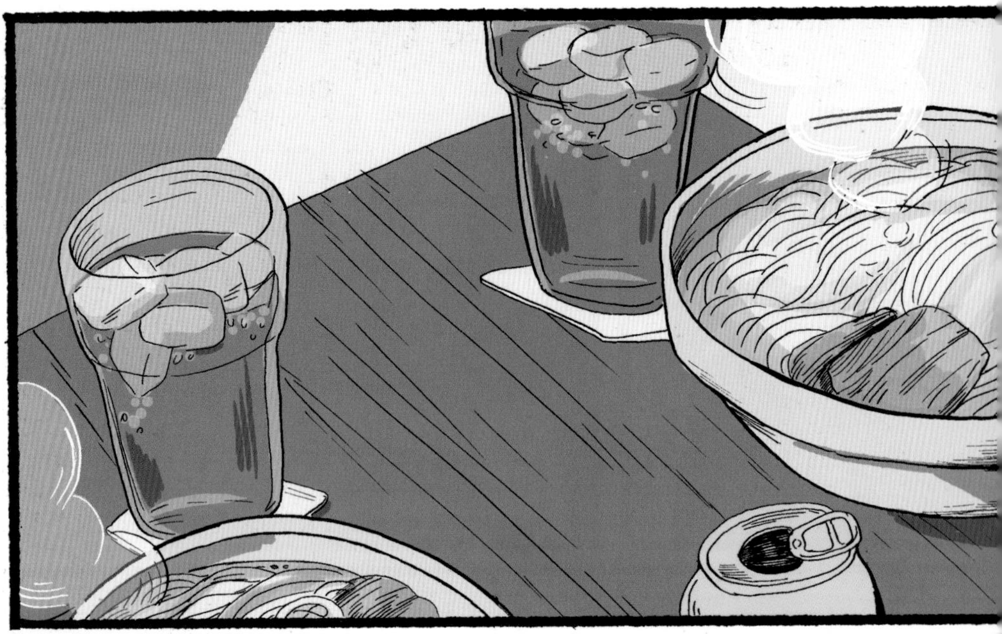

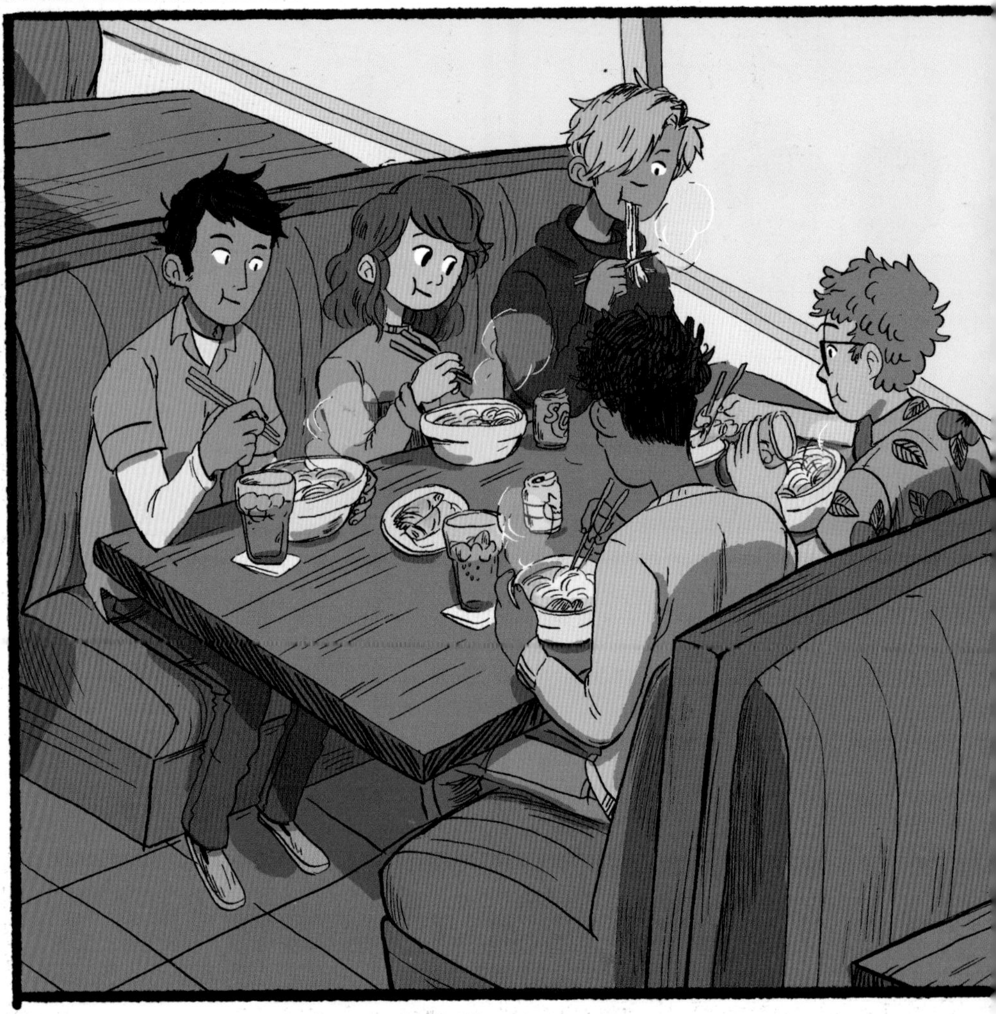

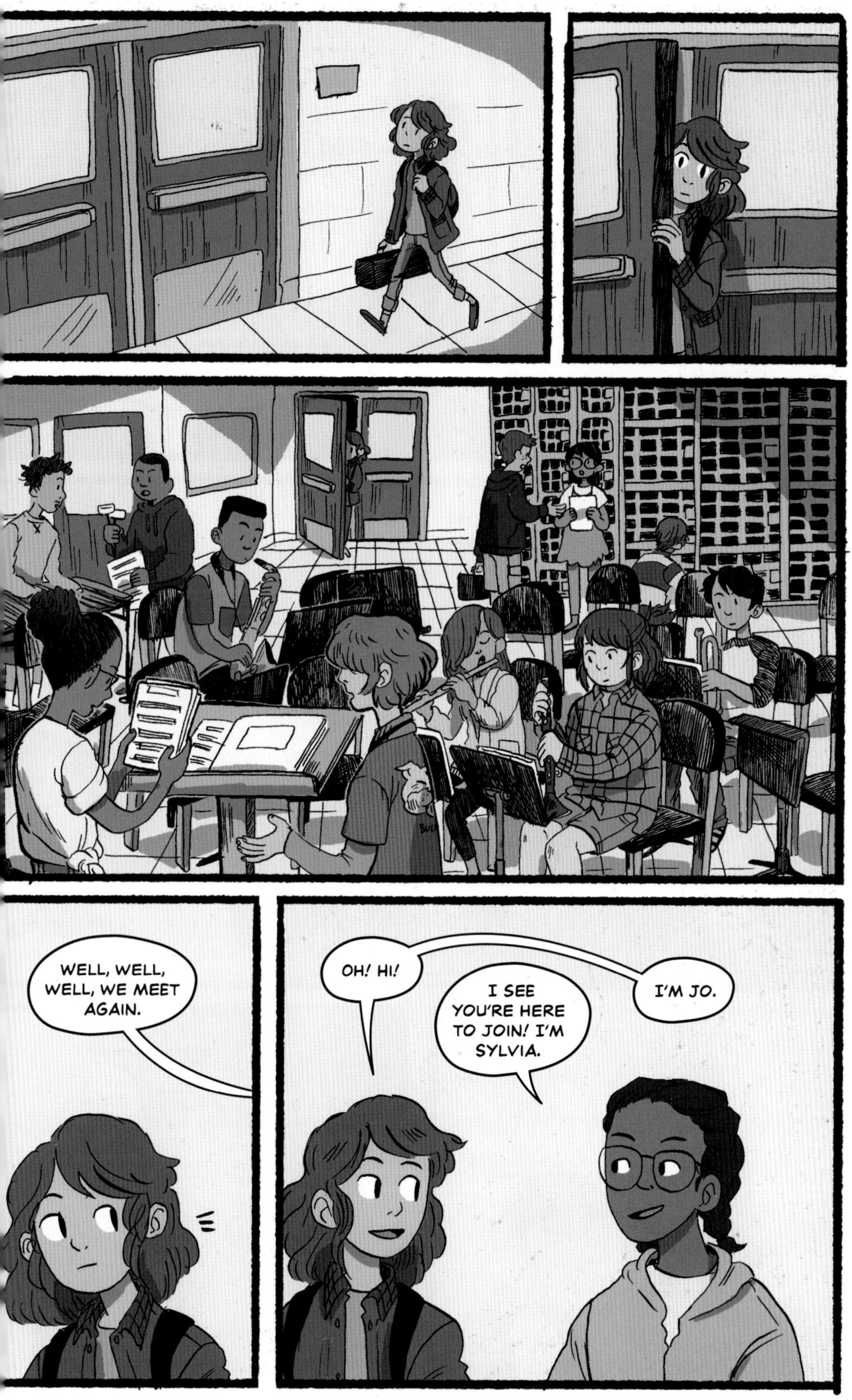
WELL, WELL, WELL, WE MEET AGAIN.
OH! HI!
I SEE YOU'RE HERE TO JOIN! I'M SYLVIA.
I'M JO.

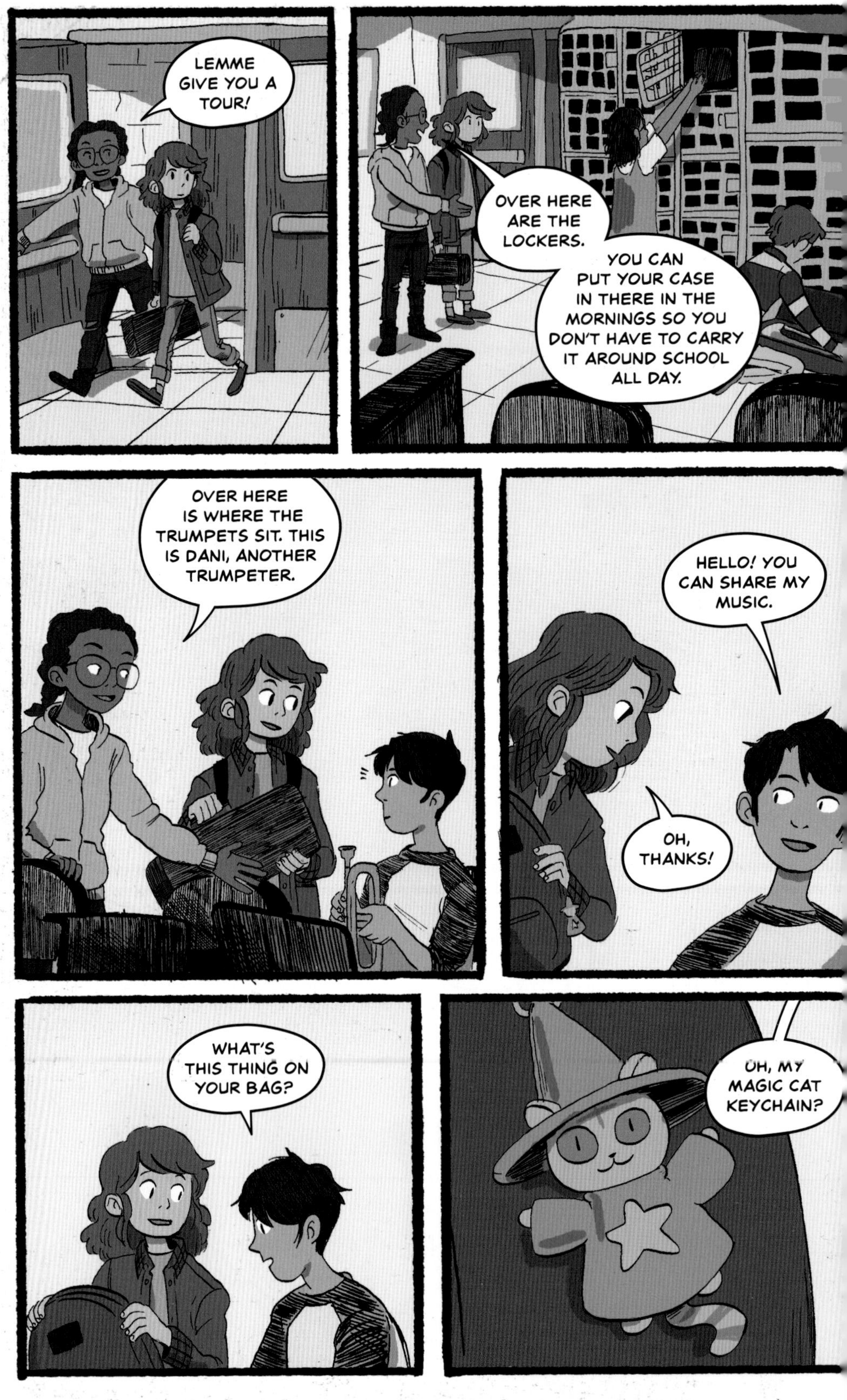
LEMME GIVE YOU A TOUR!
OVER HERE ARE THE LOCKERS.
YOU CAN PUT YOUR CASE IN THERE IN THE MORNINGS SO YOU DON'T HAVE TO CARRY IT AROUND SCHOOL ALL DAY.
OVER HERE IS WHERE THE TRUMPETS SIT. THIS IS DANI, ANOTHER TRUMPETER.
HELLO! YOU CAN SHARE MY MUSIC.
OH, THANKS!
WHAT'S THIS THING ON YOUR BAG?
OH, MY MAGIC CAT KEYCHAIN?

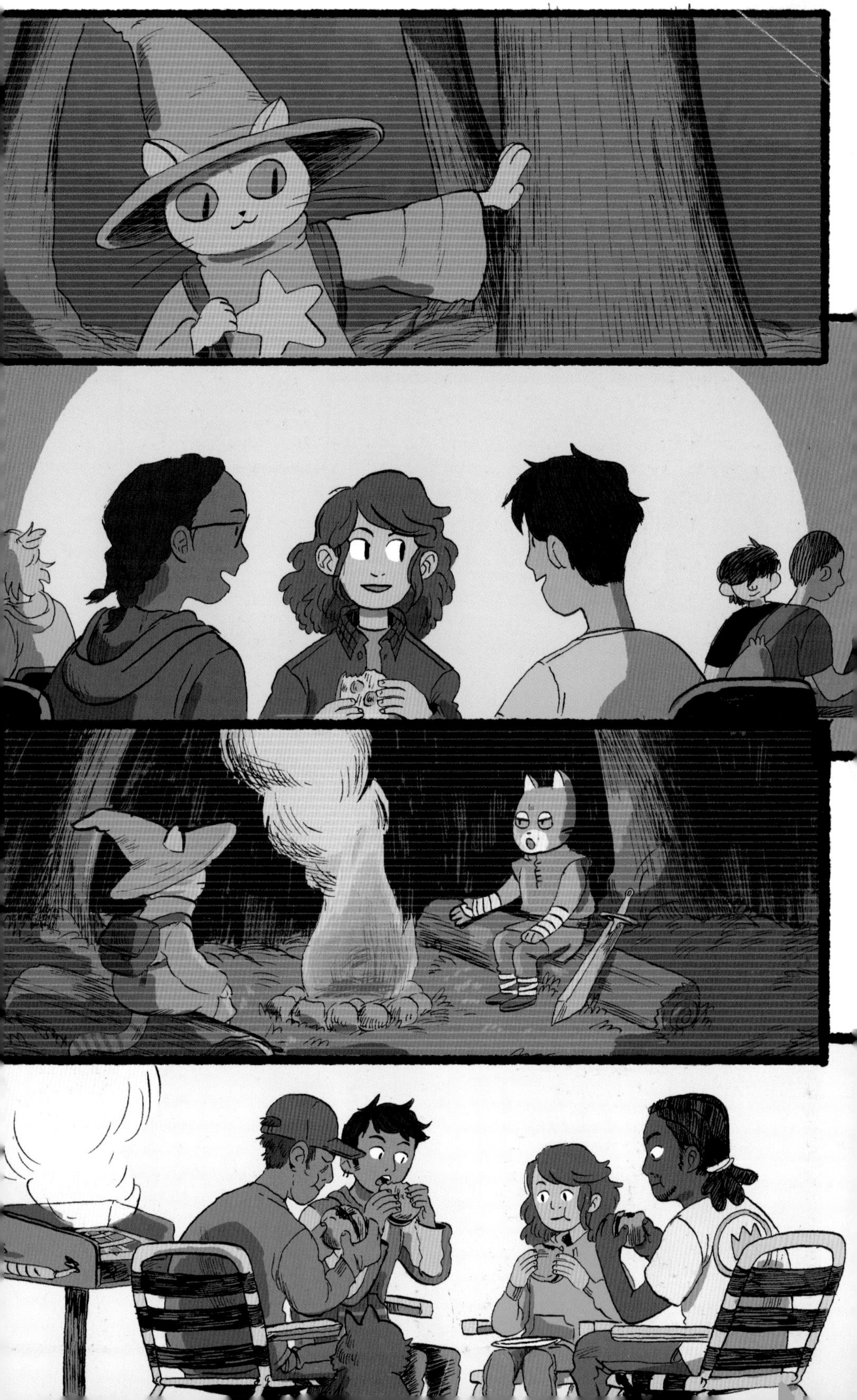

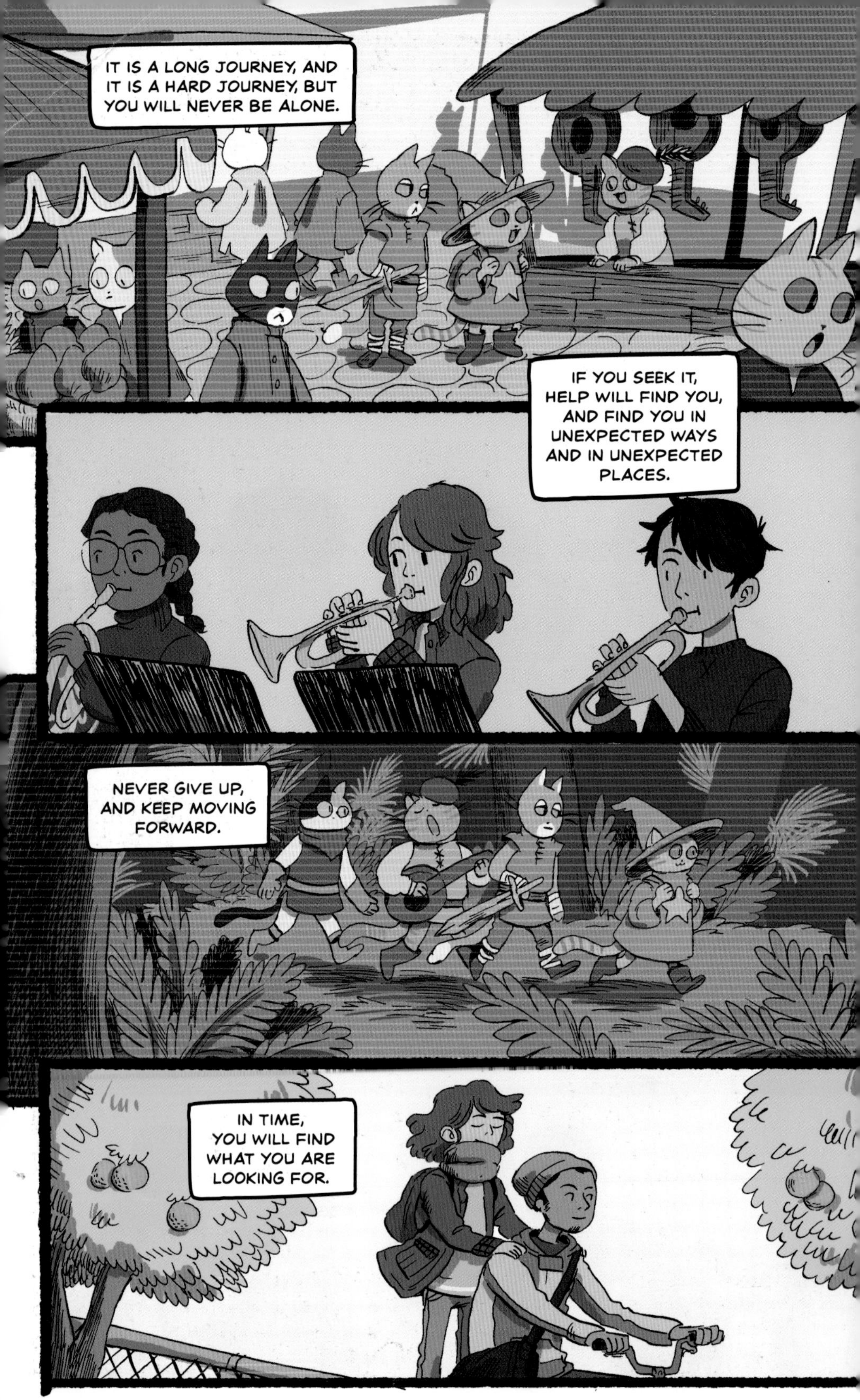

IT IS A LONG JOURNEY, AND IT IS A HARD JOURNEY, BUT YOU WILL NEVER BE ALONE.
IF YOU SEEK IT, HELP WILL FIND YOU, AND FIND YOU IN UNEXPECTED WAYS AND IN UNEXPECTED PLACES.
NEVER GIVE UP, AND KEEP MOVING FORWARD.
IN TIME, YOU WILL FIND WHAT YOU ARE LOOKING FOR.

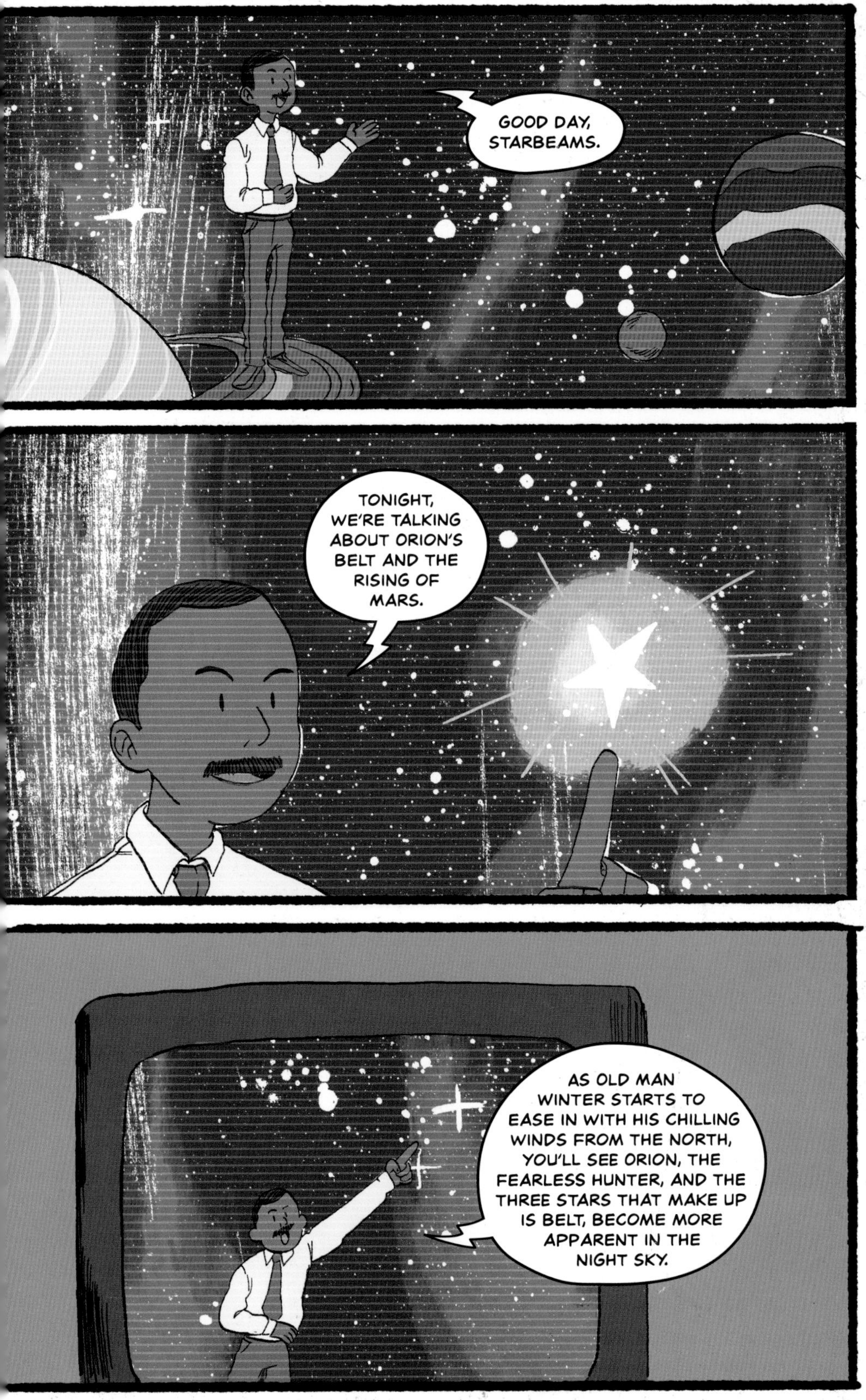
GOOD DAY, STARBEAMS.
TONIGHT, WE'RE TALKING ABOUT ORION'S BELT AND THE RISING OF MARS.
AS OLD MAN WINTER STARTS TO EASE IN WITH HIS CHILLING WINDS FROM THE NORTH, YOU'LL SEE ORION, THE FEARLESS HUNTER, AND THE THREE STARS THAT MAKE UP IS BELT, BECOME MORE APPARENT IN THE NIGHT SKY.

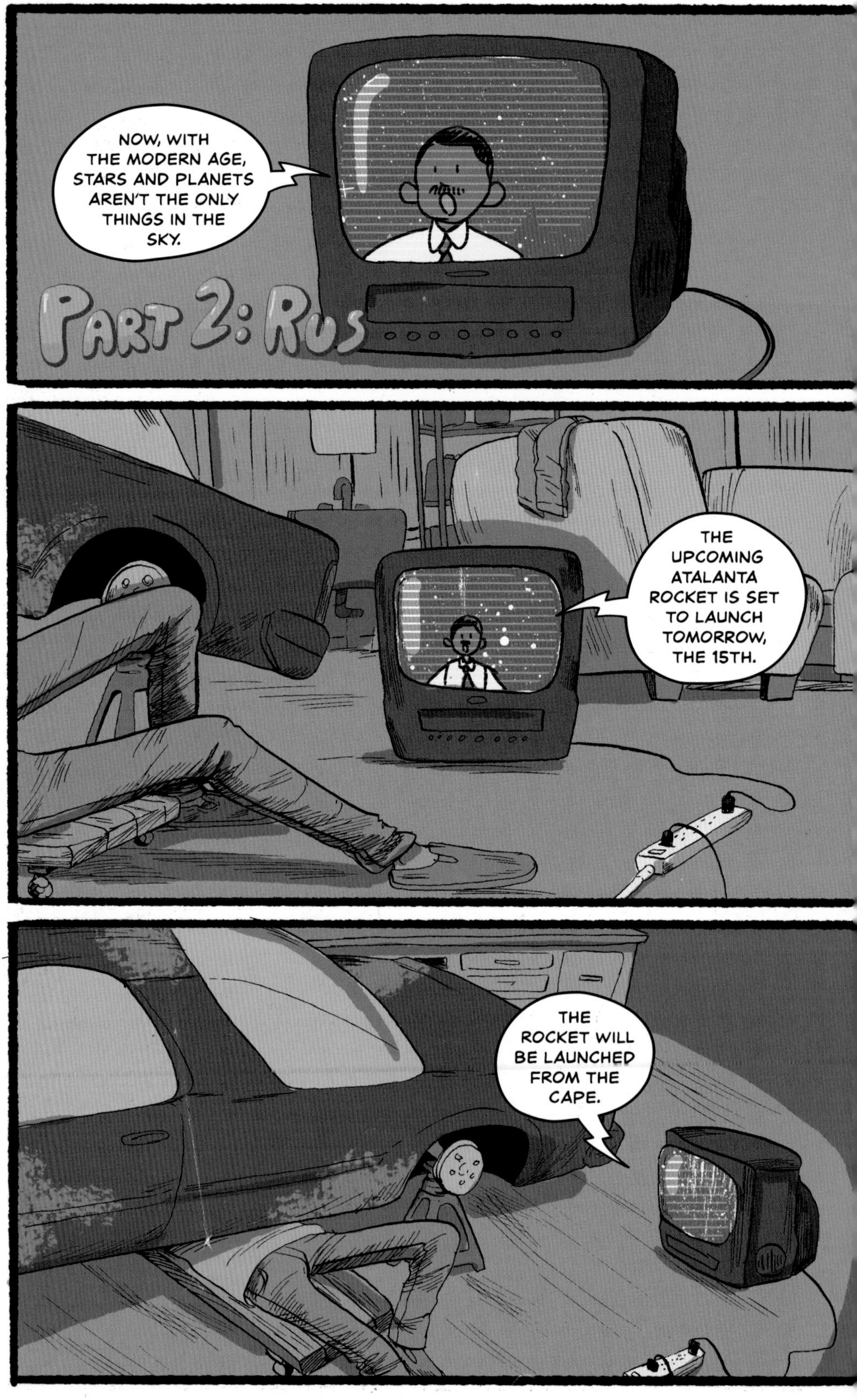
NOW, WITH THE MODERN AGE, STARS AND PLANETS AREN'T THE ONLY THINGS IN THE SKY.
PART 2: RUS
THE UPCOMING ATALANTA ROCKET IS SET TO LAUNCH TOMORROW, THE 15TH.
THE ROCKET WILL BE LAUNCHED FROM THE CAPE.

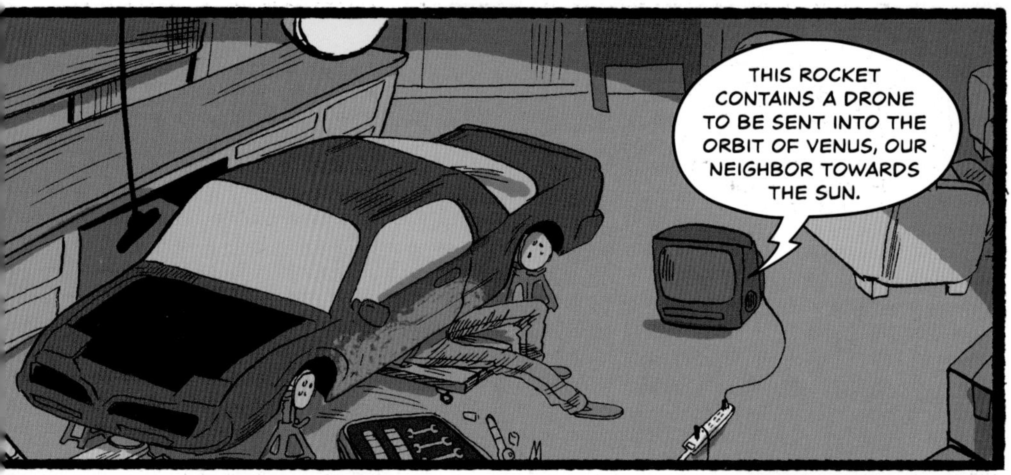
THIS ROCKET CONTAINS A DRONE TO BE SENT INTO THE ORBIT OF VENUS, OUR NEIGHBOR TOWARDS THE SUN.

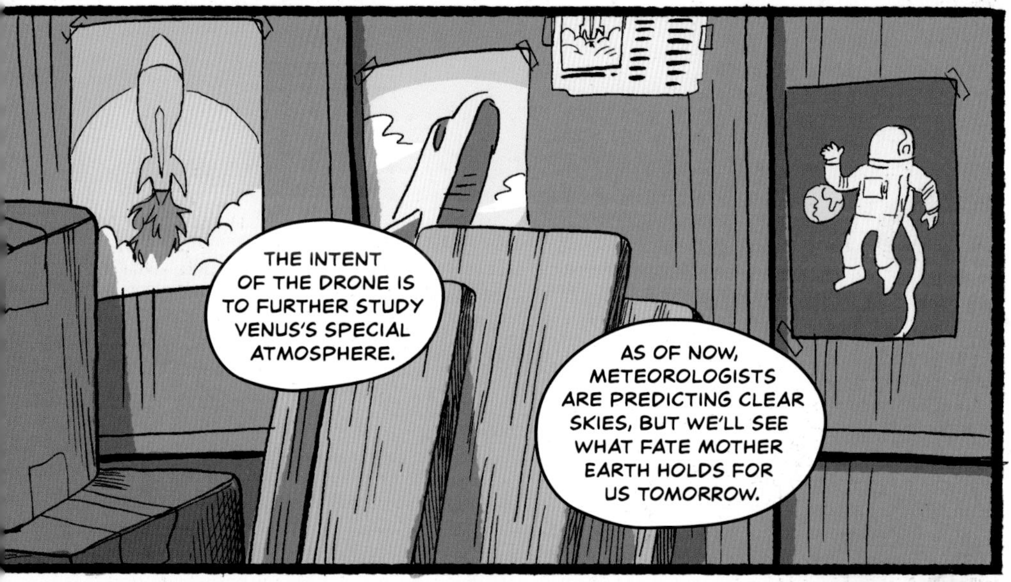
THE INTENT OF THE DRONE IS TO FURTHER STUDY VENUS'S SPECIAL ATMOSPHERE.
AS OF NOW, METEOROLOGISTS ARE PREDICTING CLEAR SKIES, BUT WE'LL SEE WHAT FATE MOTHER EARTH HOLDS FOR US TOMORROW.

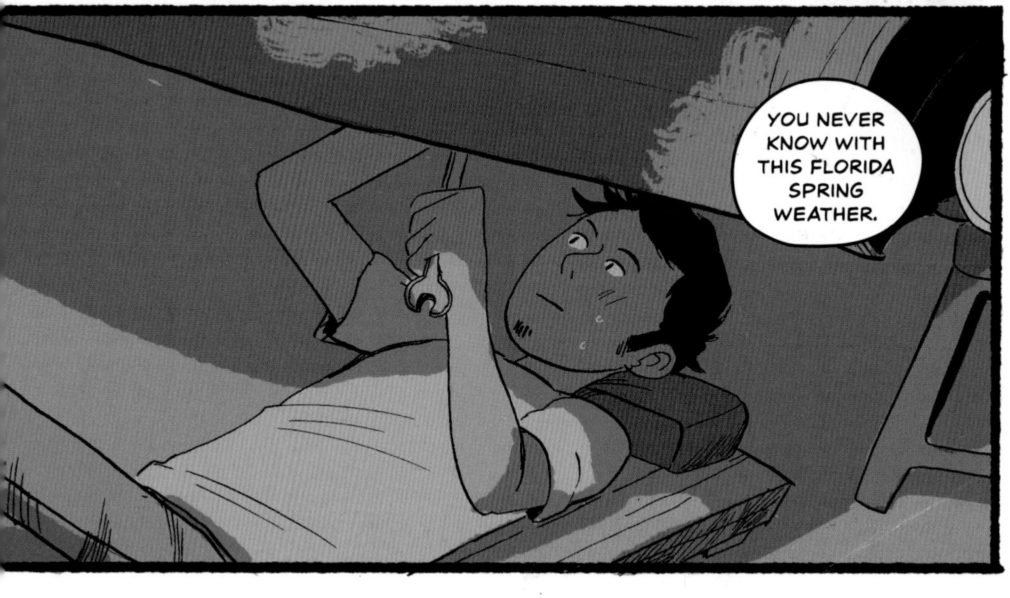
YOU NEVER KNOW WITH THIS FLORIDA SPRING WEATHER.

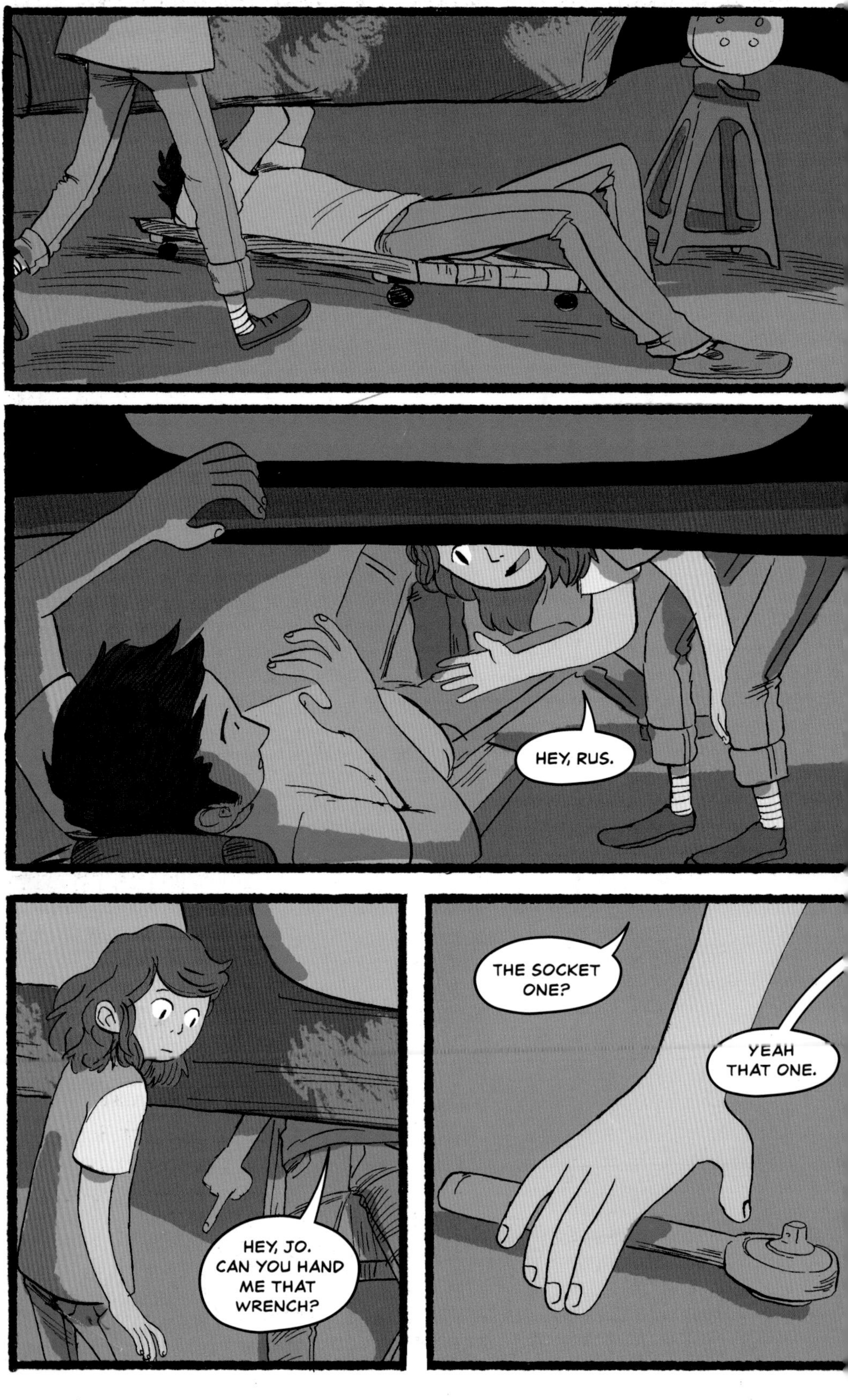
HEY, RUS.
HEY, JO. CAN YOU HAND ME THAT WRENCH?
THE SOCKET ONE?
YEAH THAT ONE.

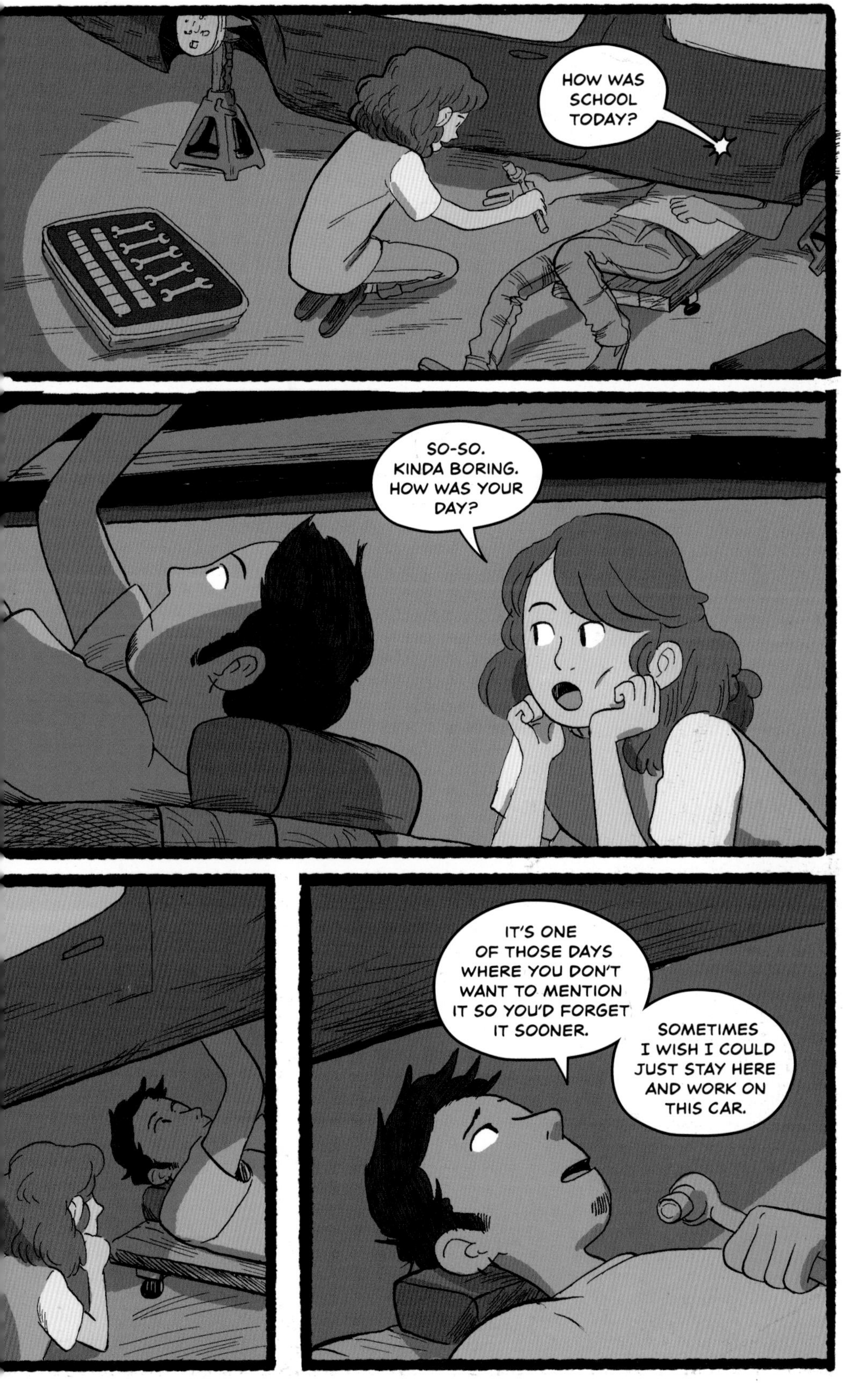
HOW WAS SCHOOL TODAY?
SO-SO. KINDA BORING. HOW WAS YOUR DAY?
IT'S ONE OF THOSE DAYS WHERE YOU DON'T WANT TO MENTION IT SO YOU'D FORGET IT SOONER.
SOMETIMES I WISH I COULD JUST STAY HERE AND WORK ON THIS CAR.

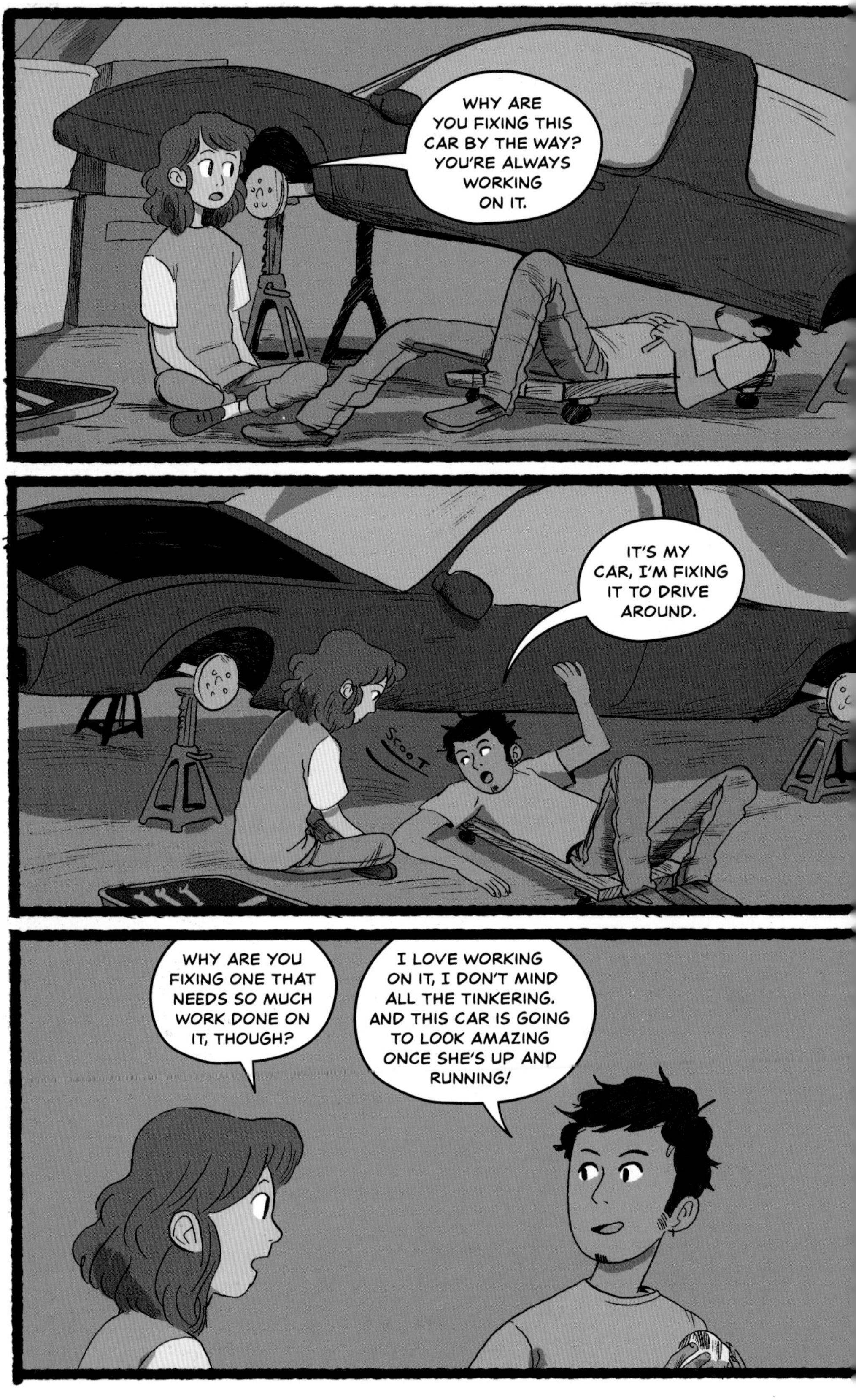
WHY ARE YOU FIXING THIS CAR BY THE WAY? YOU'RE ALWAYS WORKING ON IT.
IT'S MY CAR, I'M FIXING IT TO DRIVE AROUND.
SCOOT
WHY ARE YOU FIXING ONE THAT NEEDS SO MUCH WORK DONE ON IT, THOUGH?
I LOVE WORKING ON IT, I DON'T MIND ALL THE TINKERING. AND THIS CAR IS GOING TO LOOK AMAZING ONCE SHE'S UP AND RUNNING!

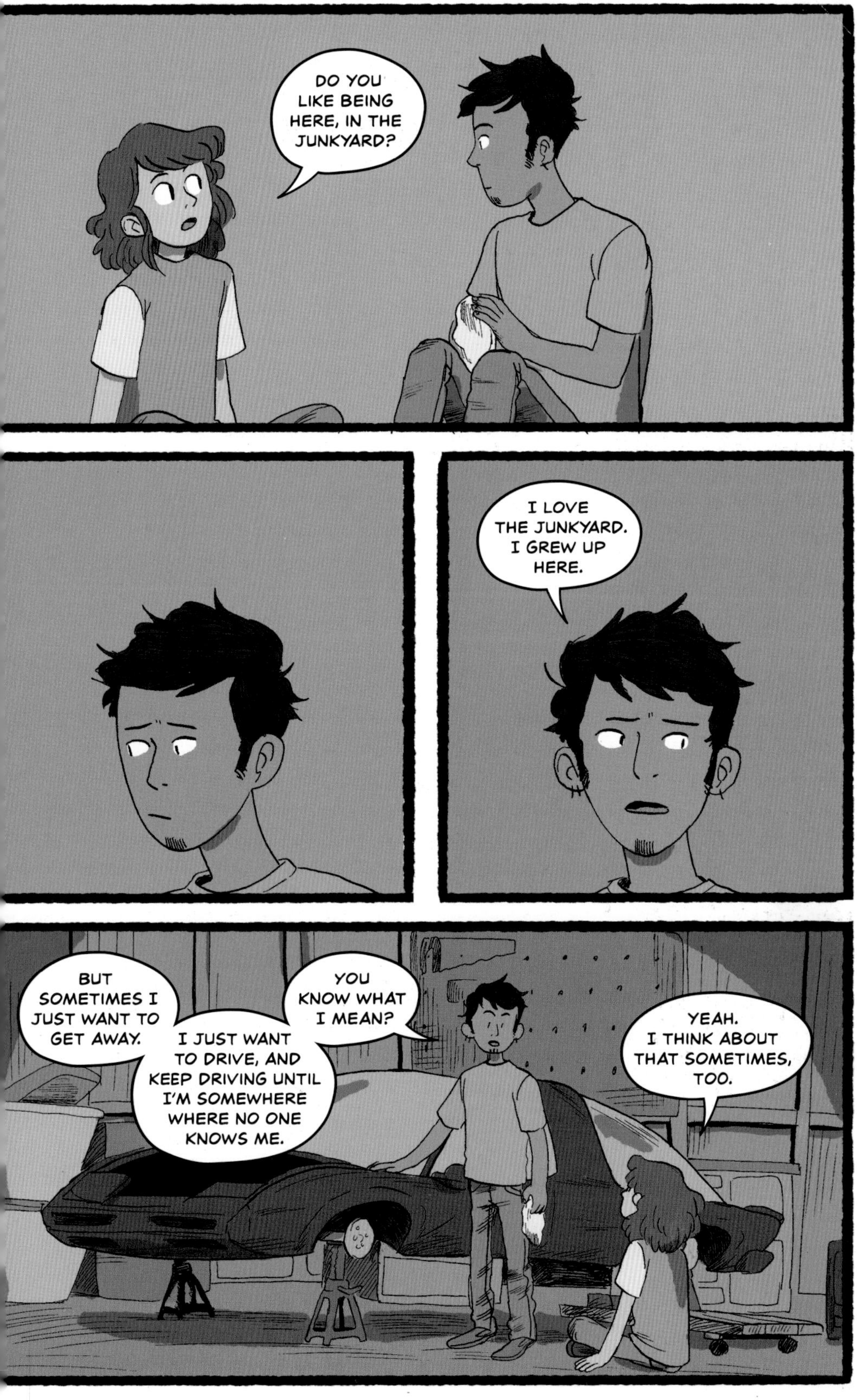
DO YOU LIKE BEING HERE, IN THE JUNKYARD?
I LOVE THE JUNKYARD. I GREW UP HERE.
BUT SOMETIMES I JUST WANT TO GET AWAY.
I JUST WANT TO DRIVE, AND KEEP DRIVING UNTIL I'M SOMEWHERE WHERE NO ONE KNOWS ME.
YOU KNOW WHAT I MEAN?
YEAH. I THINK ABOUT THAT SOMETIMES, TOO.

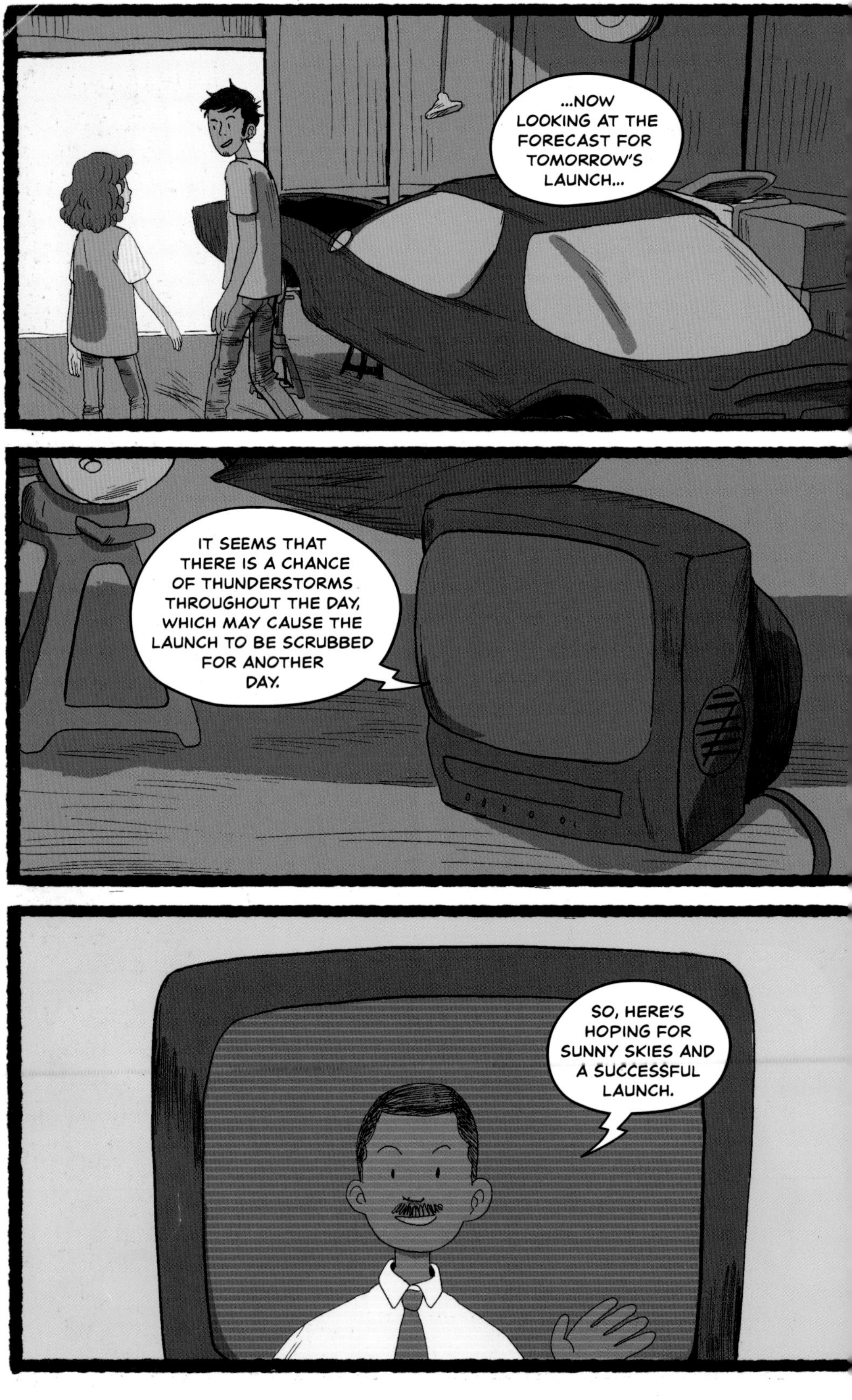
...NOW LOOKING AT THE FORECAST FOR TOMORROW'S LAUNCH...
IT SEEMS THAT THERE IS A CHANCE OF THUNDERSTORMS THROUGHOUT THE DAY, WHICH MAY CAUSE THE LAUNCH TO BE SCRUBBED FOR ANOTHER DAY.
SO, HERE'S HOPING FOR SUNNY SKIES AND A SUCCESSFUL LAUNCH.

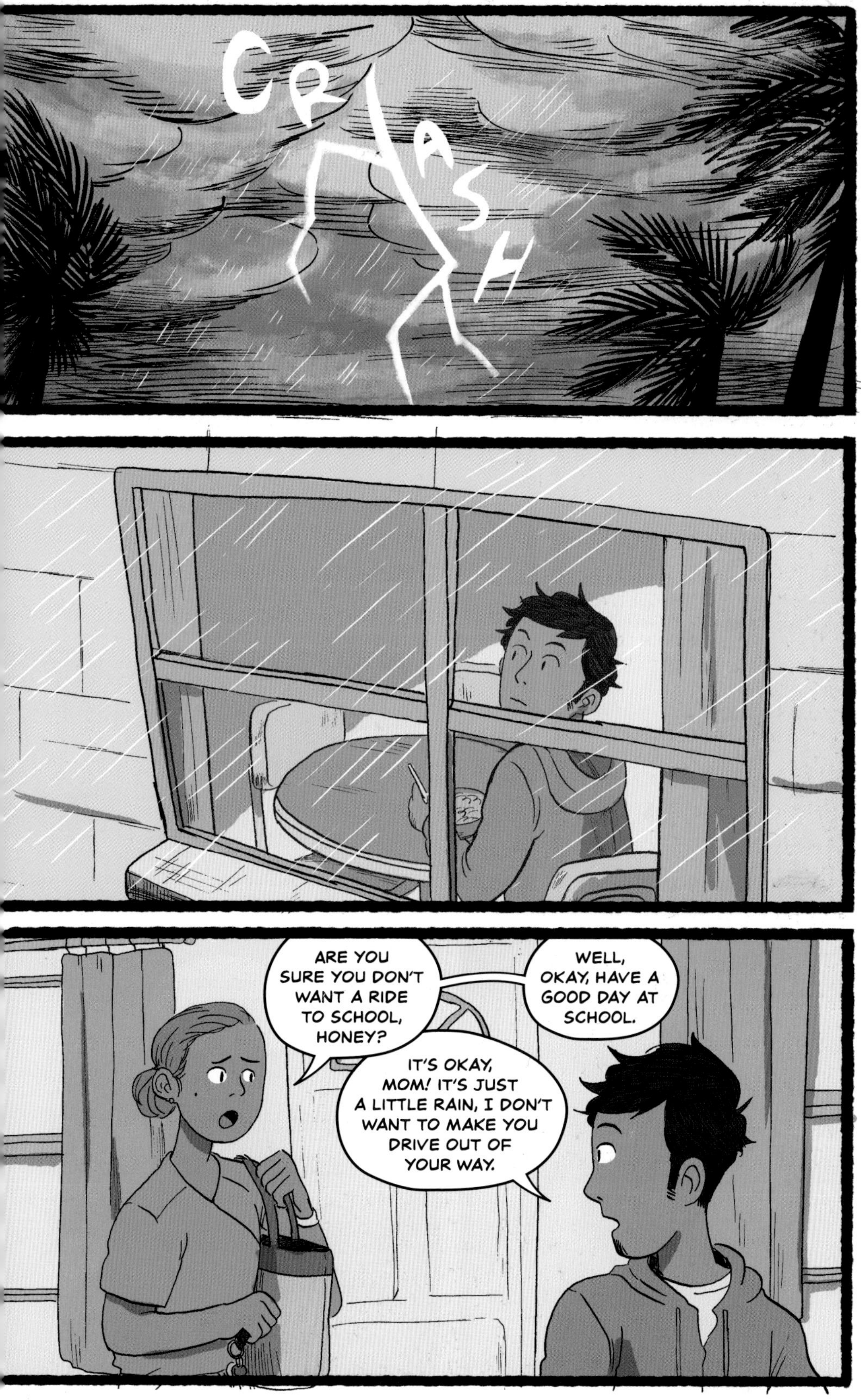
CRASH
ARE YOU SURE YOU DON'T WANT A RIDE TO SCHOOL, HONEY?
IT'S OKAY, MOM! IT'S JUST A LITTLE RAIN, I DON'T WANT TO MAKE YOU DRIVE OUT OF YOUR WAY.
WELL, OKAY, HAVE A GOOD DAY AT SCHOOL.

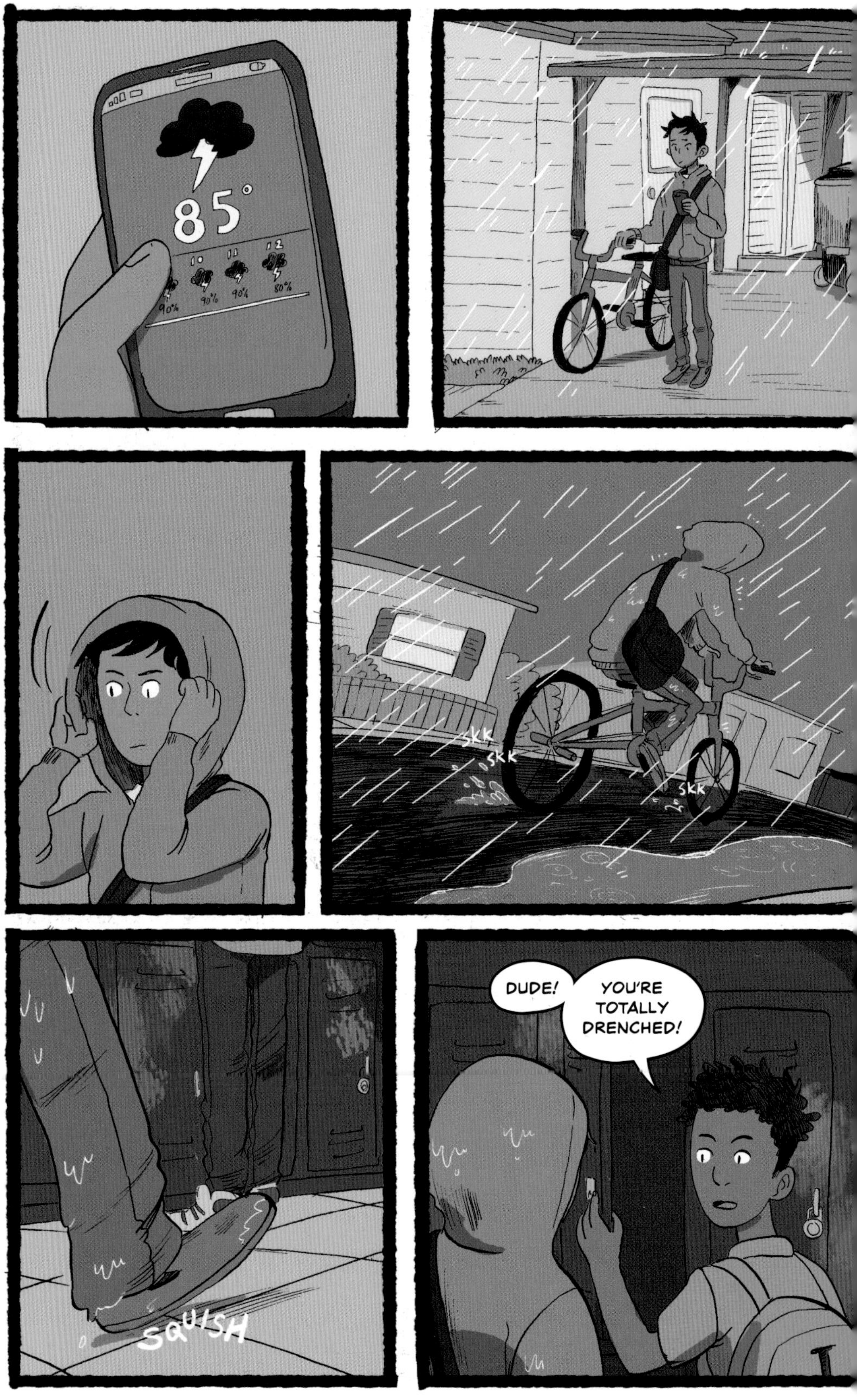
85°
SKK
SKK
SKK
SQUISH
DUDE!
YOU'RE TOTALLY DRENCHED!

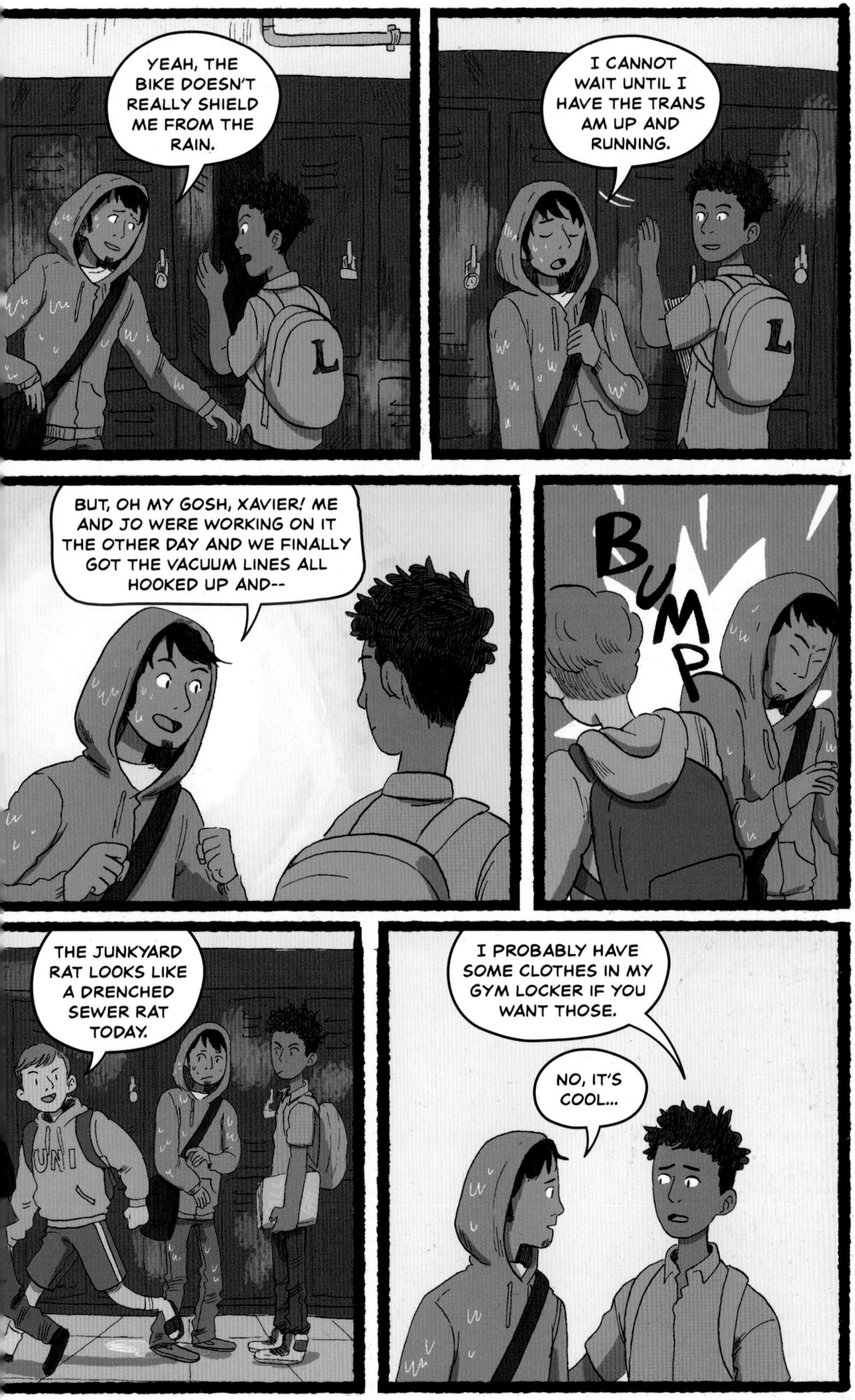
YEAH, THE BIKE DOESN'T REALLY SHIELD ME FROM THE RAIN.
I CANNOT WAIT UNTIL I HAVE THE TRANS AM UP AND RUNNING.
BUT, OH MY GOSH, XAVIER! ME AND JO WERE WORKING ON IT THE OTHER DAY AND WE FINALLY GOT THE VACUUM LINES ALL HOOKED UP AND--
BUMP
THE JUNKYARD RAT LOOKS LIKE A DRENCHED SEWER RAT TODAY.
UNI
I PROBABLY HAVE SOME CLOTHES IN MY GYM LOCKER IF YOU WANT THOSE.
NO, IT'S COOL...

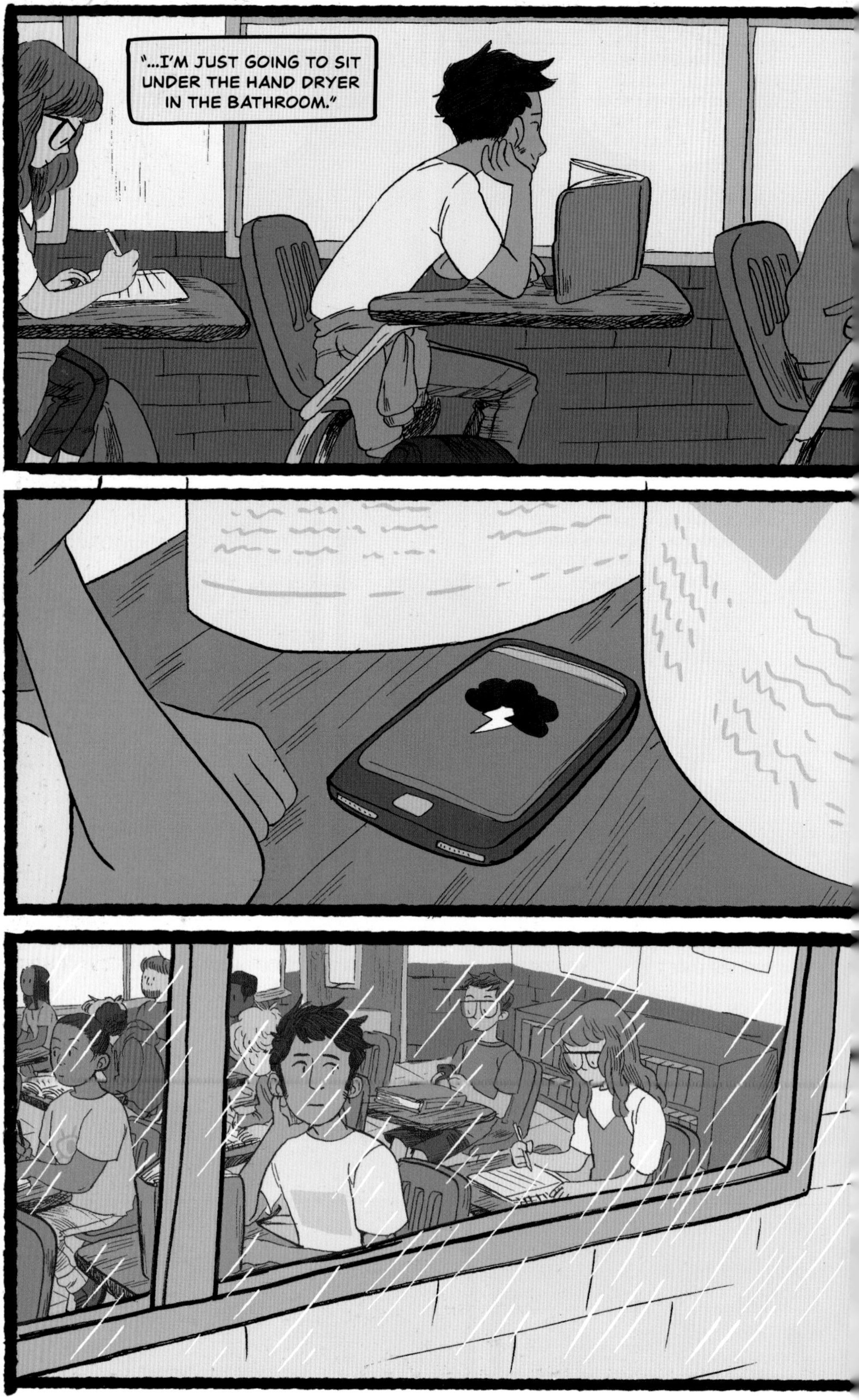
"...I'M JUST GOING TO SIT UNDER THE HAND DRYER IN THE BATHROOM."

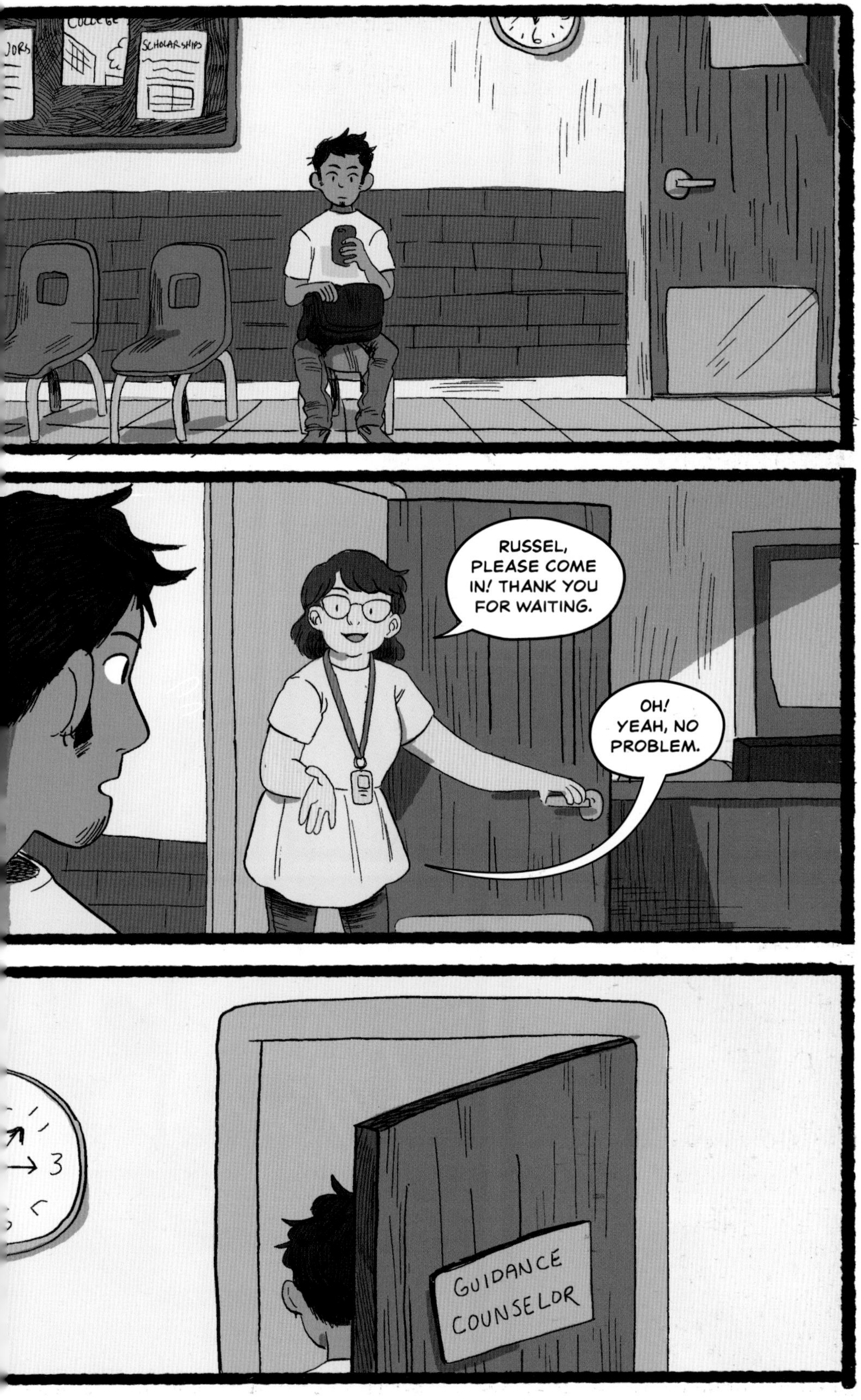
JOBS
COLLEGE
SCHOLARSHIPS
RUSSEL, PLEASE COME IN! THANK YOU FOR WAITING.
OH! YEAH, NO PROBLEM.
3
GUIDANCE COUNSELOR

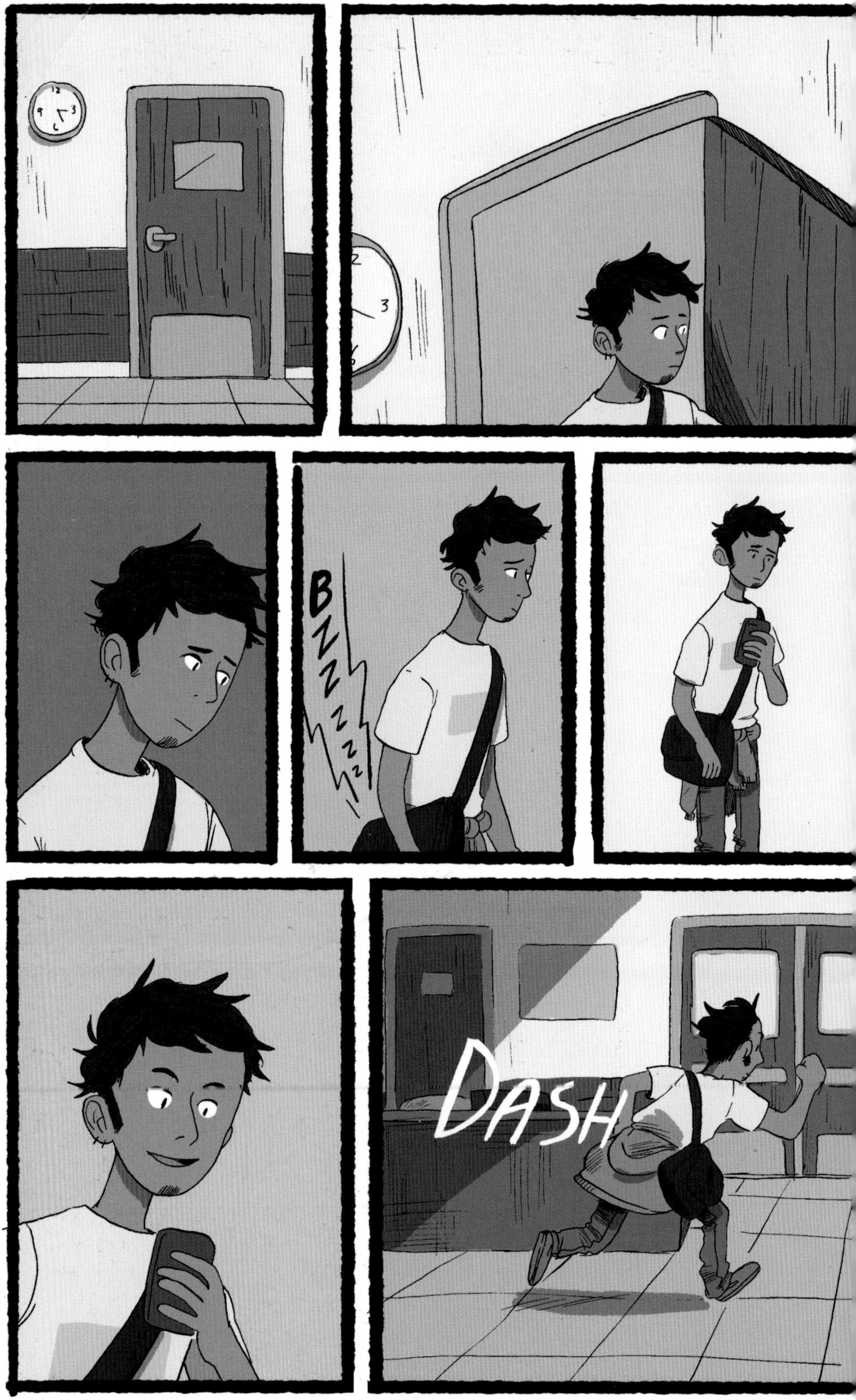
BZZZZZZ
DASH

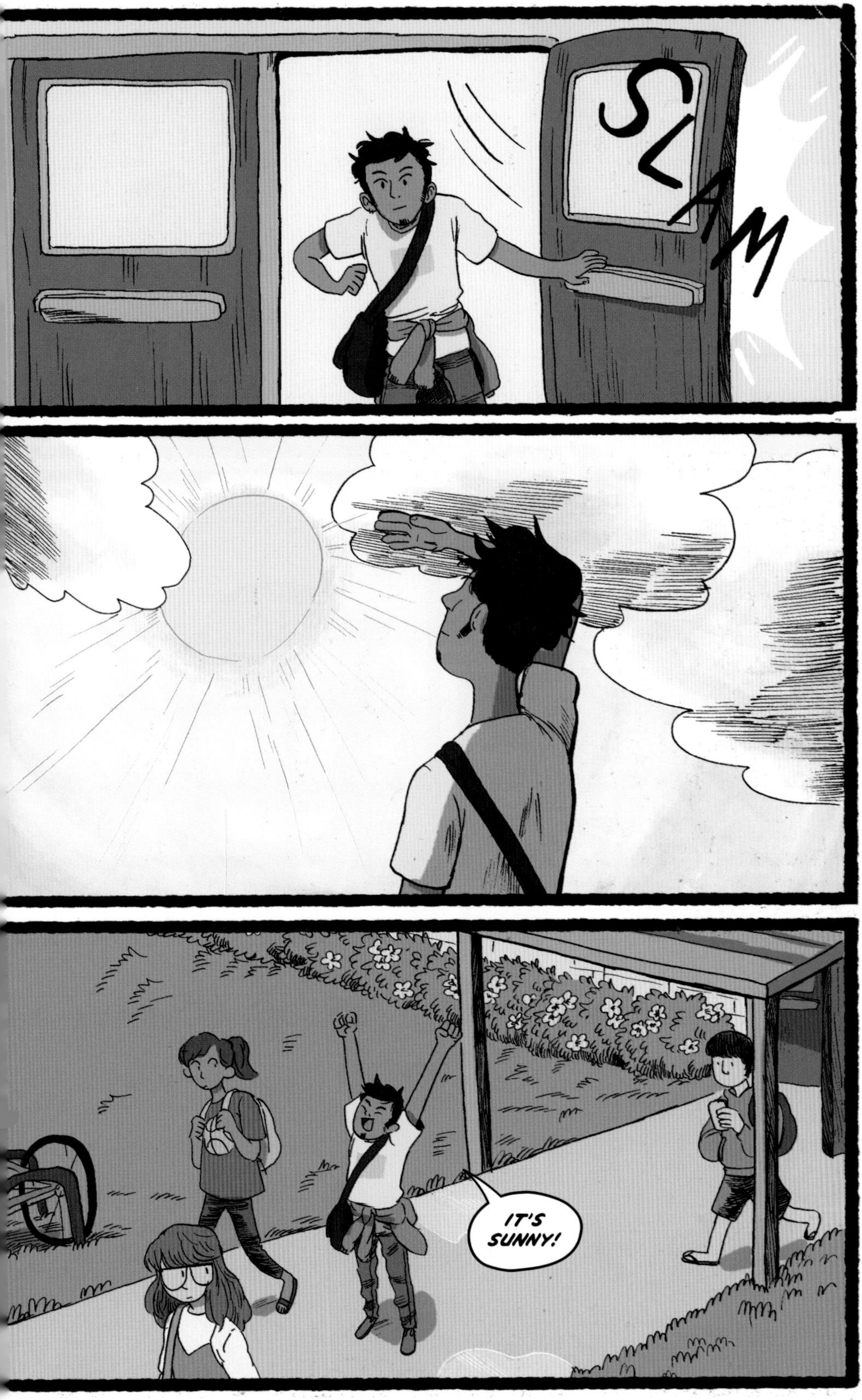
SLAM
IT'S SUNNY!

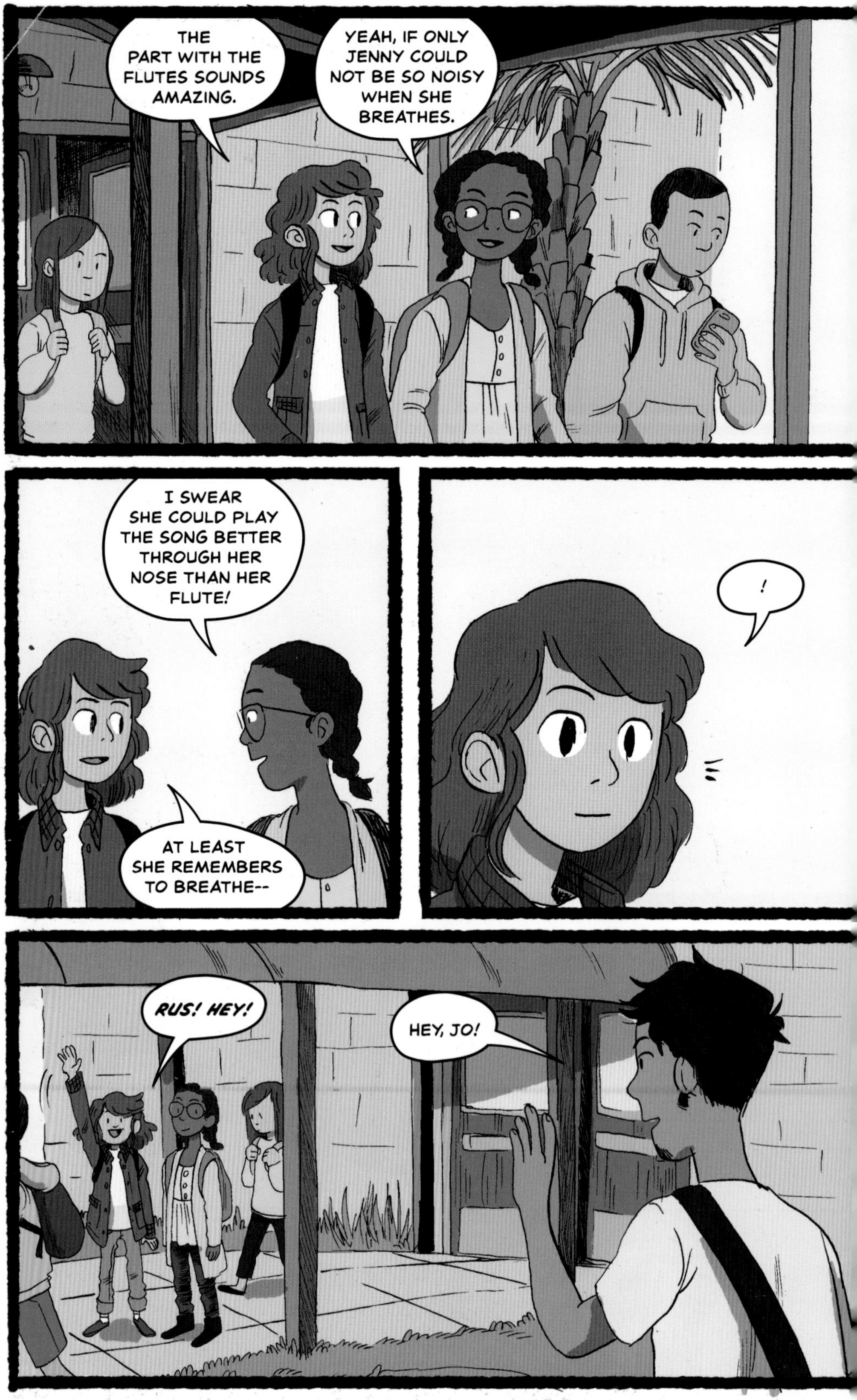
THE PART WITH THE FLUTES SOUNDS AMAZING.
YEAH, IF ONLY JENNY COULD NOT BE SO NOISY WHEN SHE BREATHES.
I SWEAR SHE COULD PLAY THE SONG BETTER THROUGH HER NOSE THAN HER FLUTE!
AT LEAST SHE REMEMBERS TO BREATHE--
!
RUS! HEY!
HEY, JO!

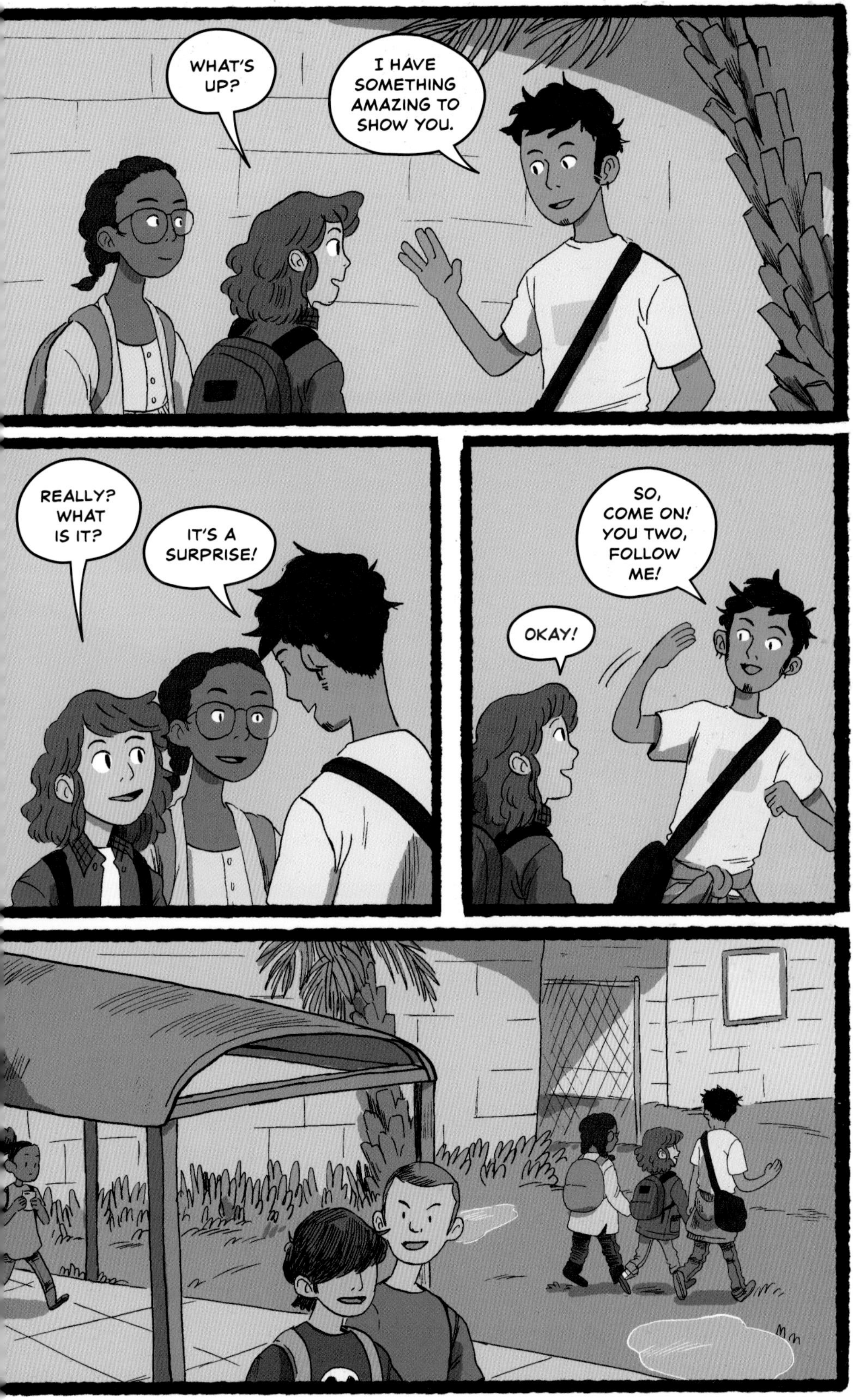
WHAT'S UP?
I HAVE SOMETHING AMAZING TO SHOW YOU.
REALLY? WHAT IS IT?
IT'S A SURPRISE!
SO, COME ON! YOU TWO, FOLLOW ME!
OKAY!

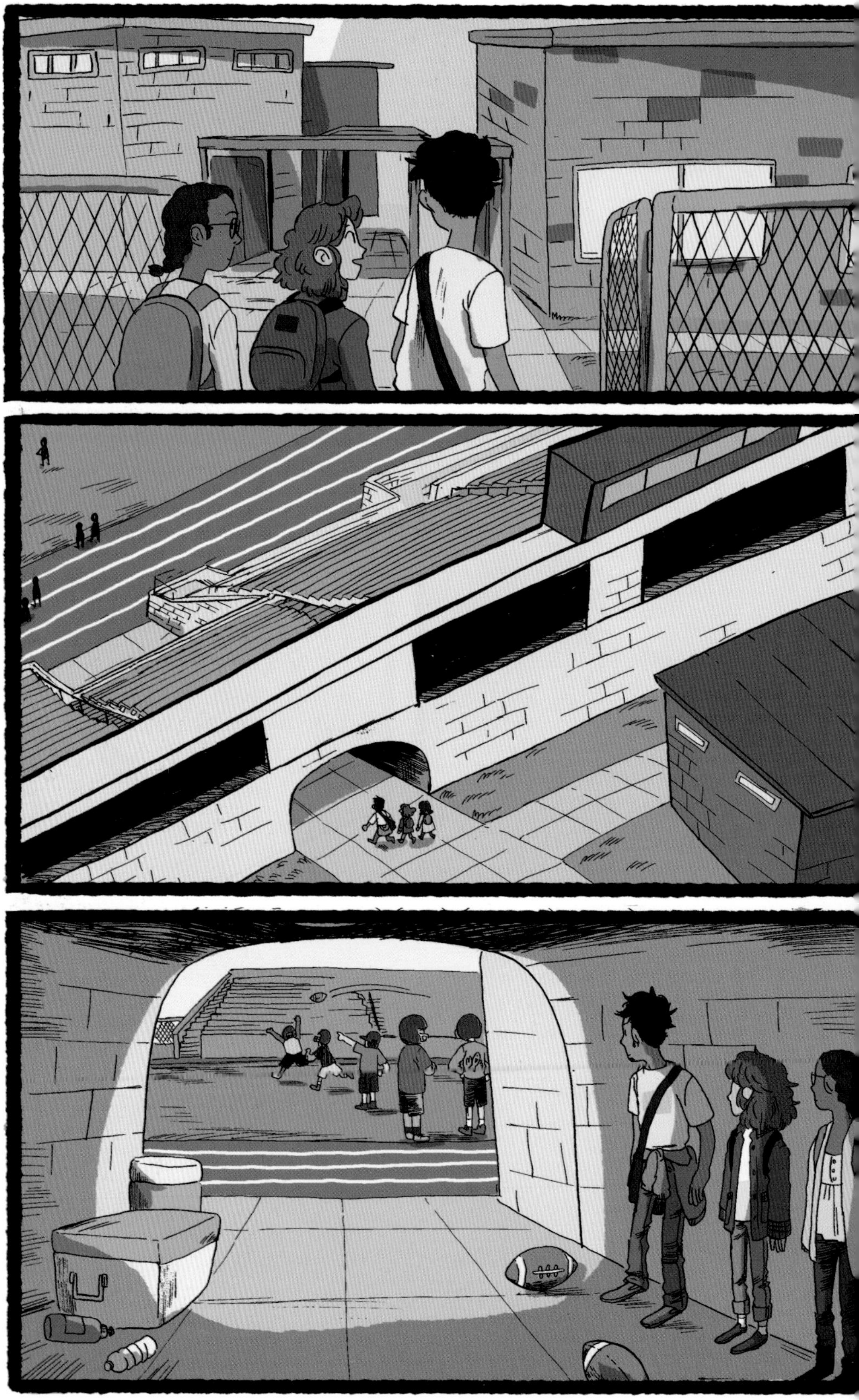

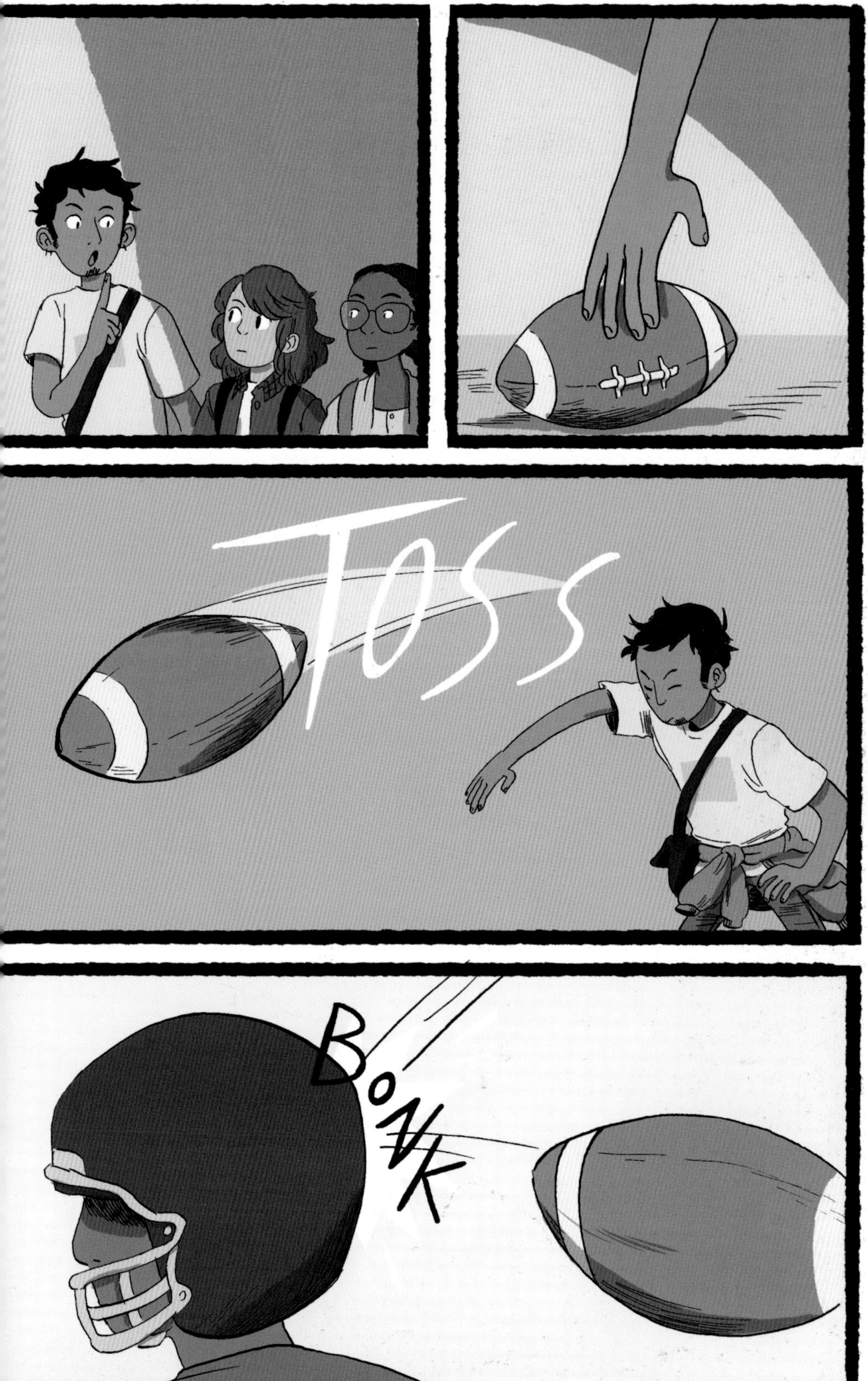
TOSS
BONK

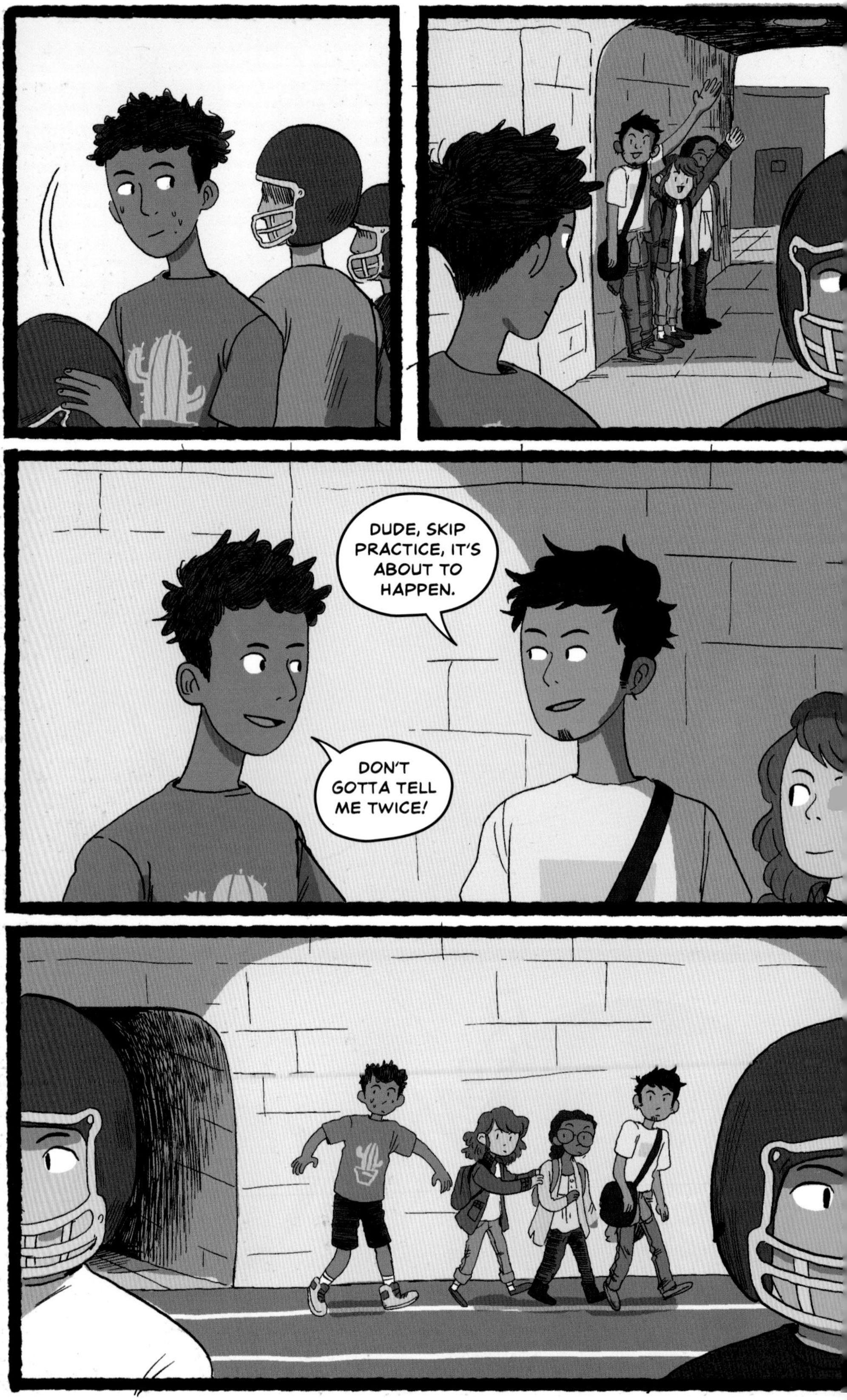
DUDE, SKIP PRACTICE, IT'S ABOUT TO HAPPEN.
DON'T GOTTA TELL ME TWICE!

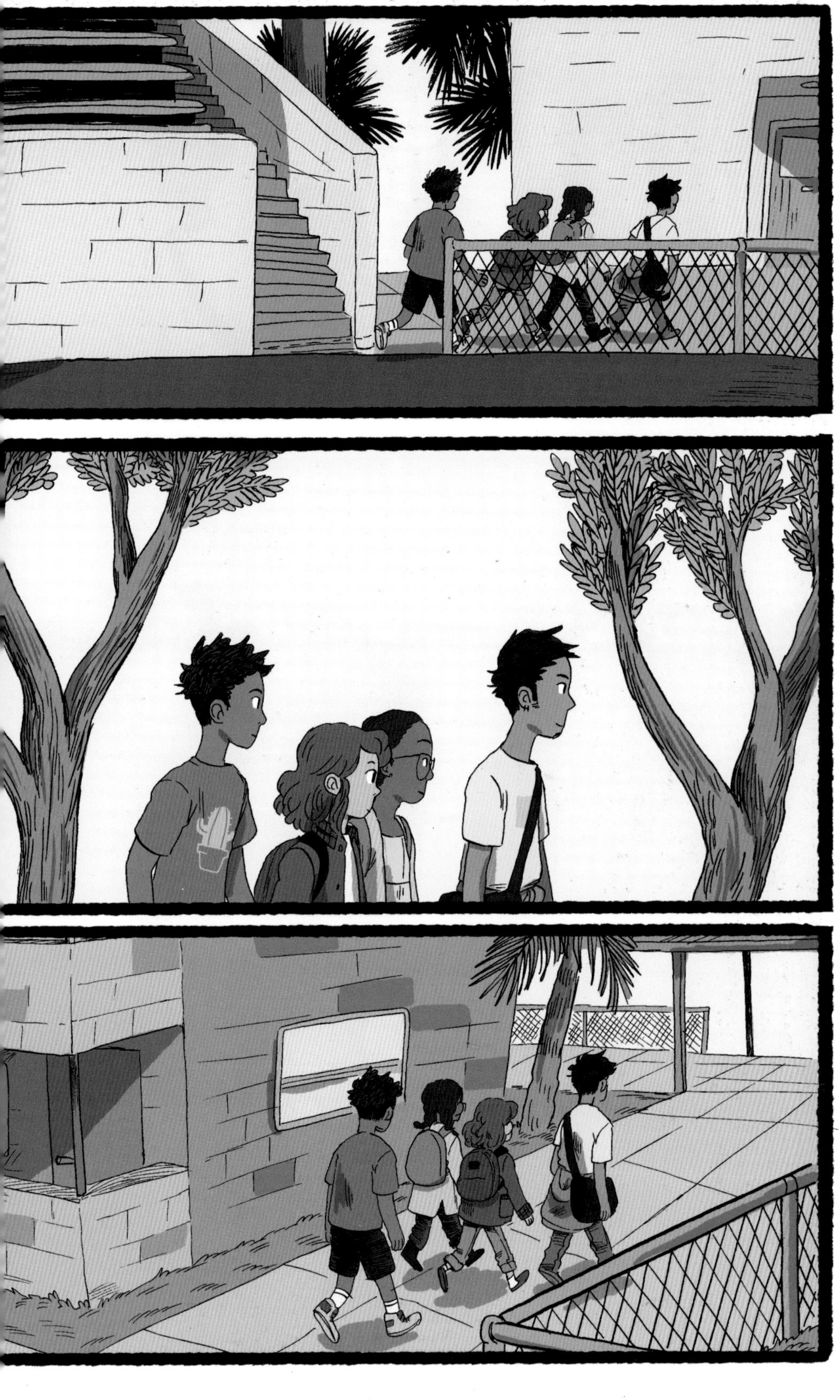

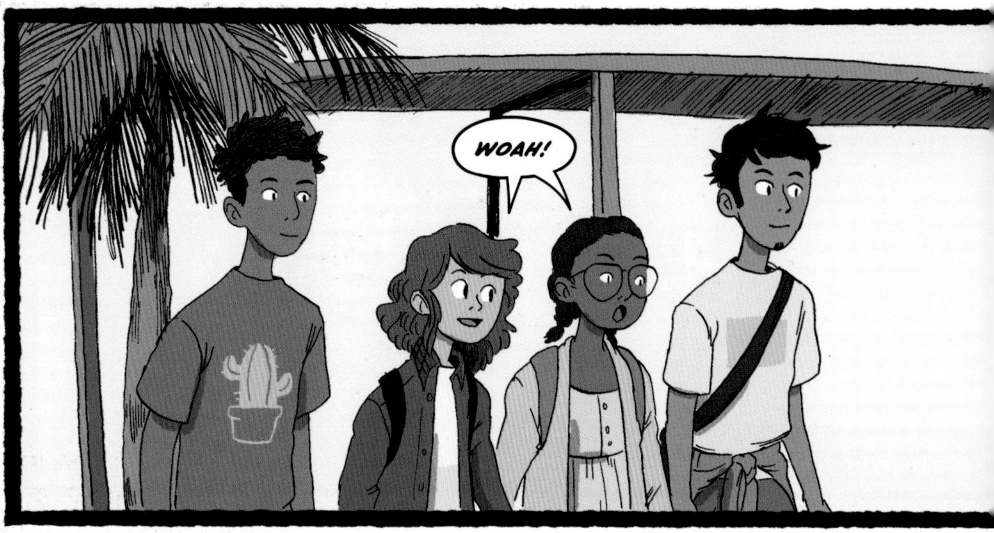
WOAH!

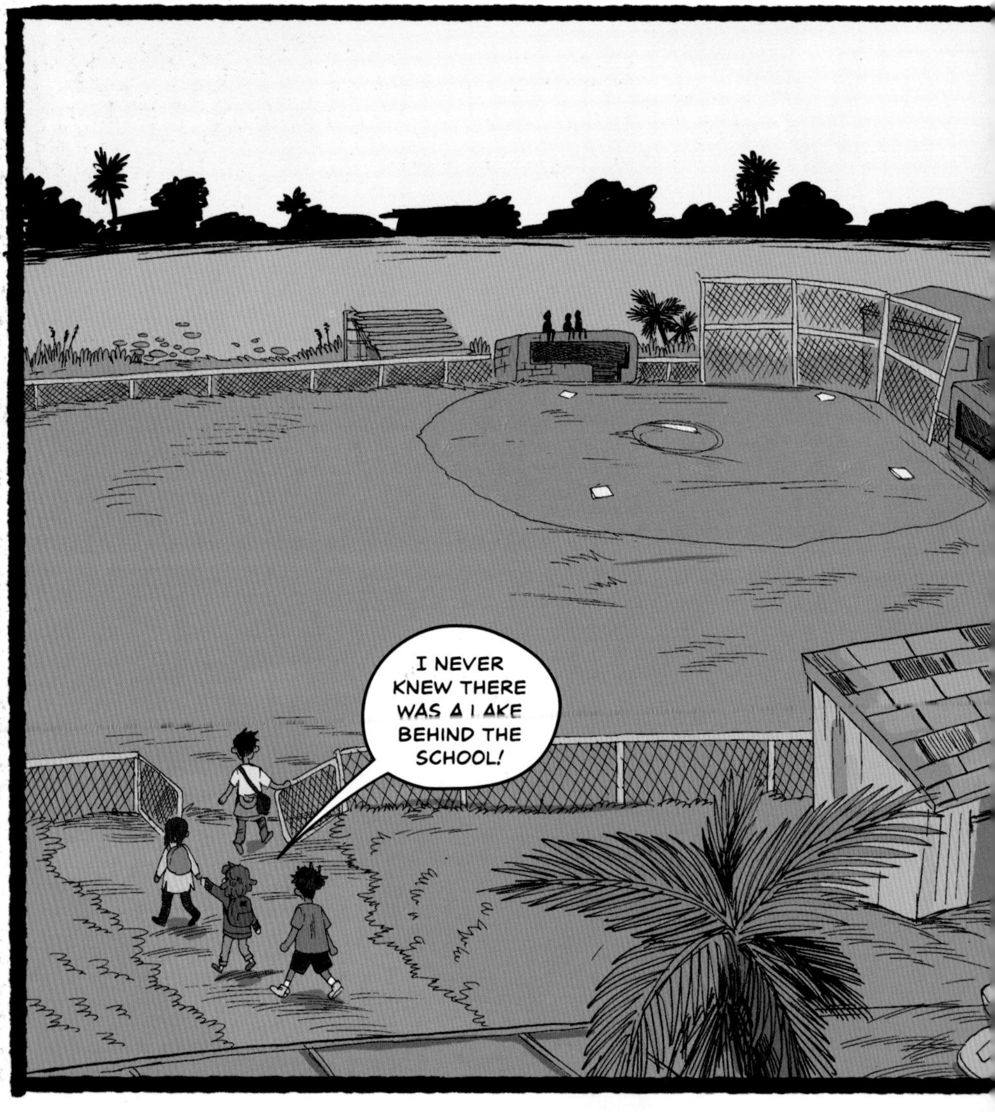
I NEVER KNEW THERE WAS A LAKE BEHIND THE SCHOOL!

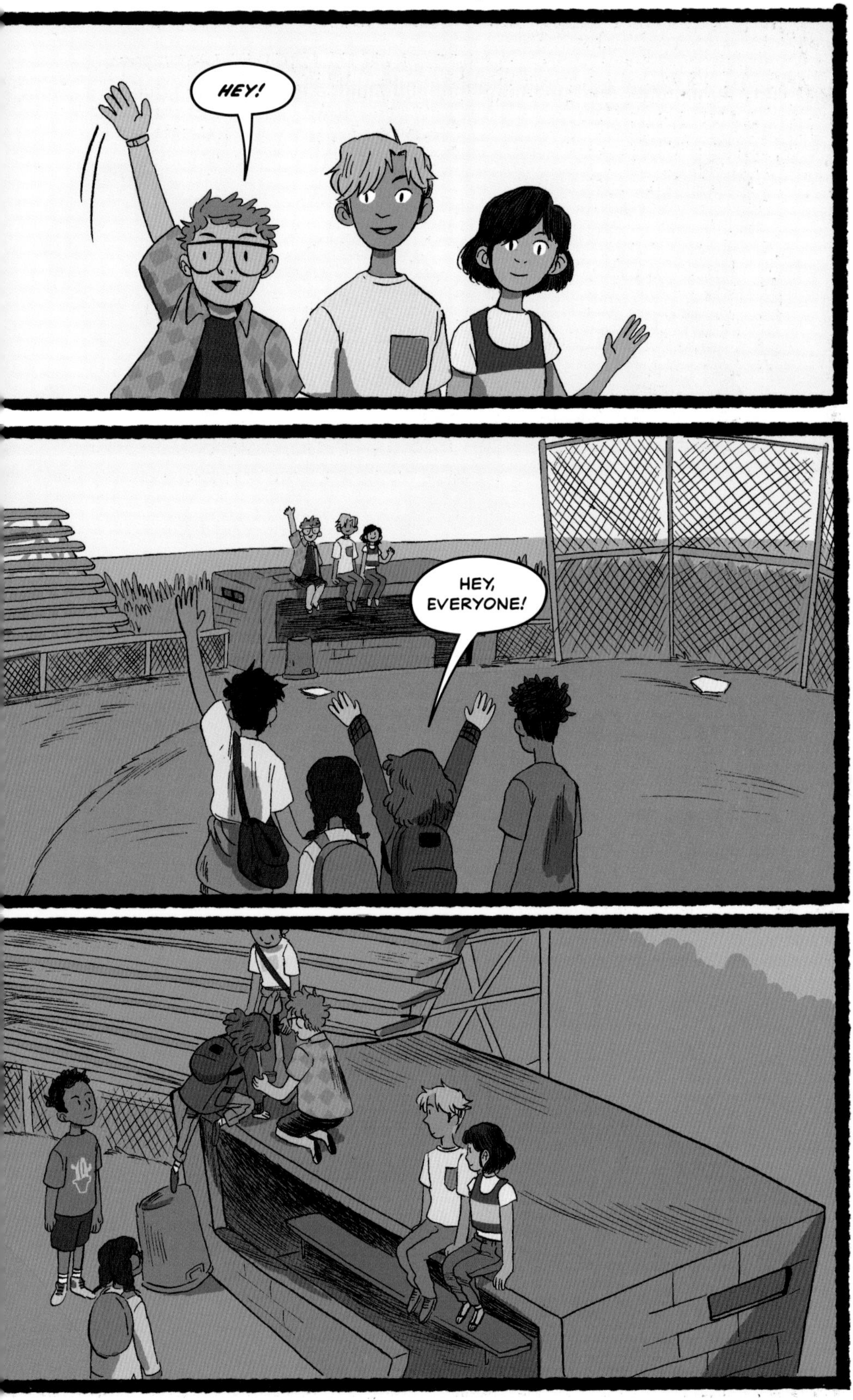
HEY!
HEY, EVERYONE!

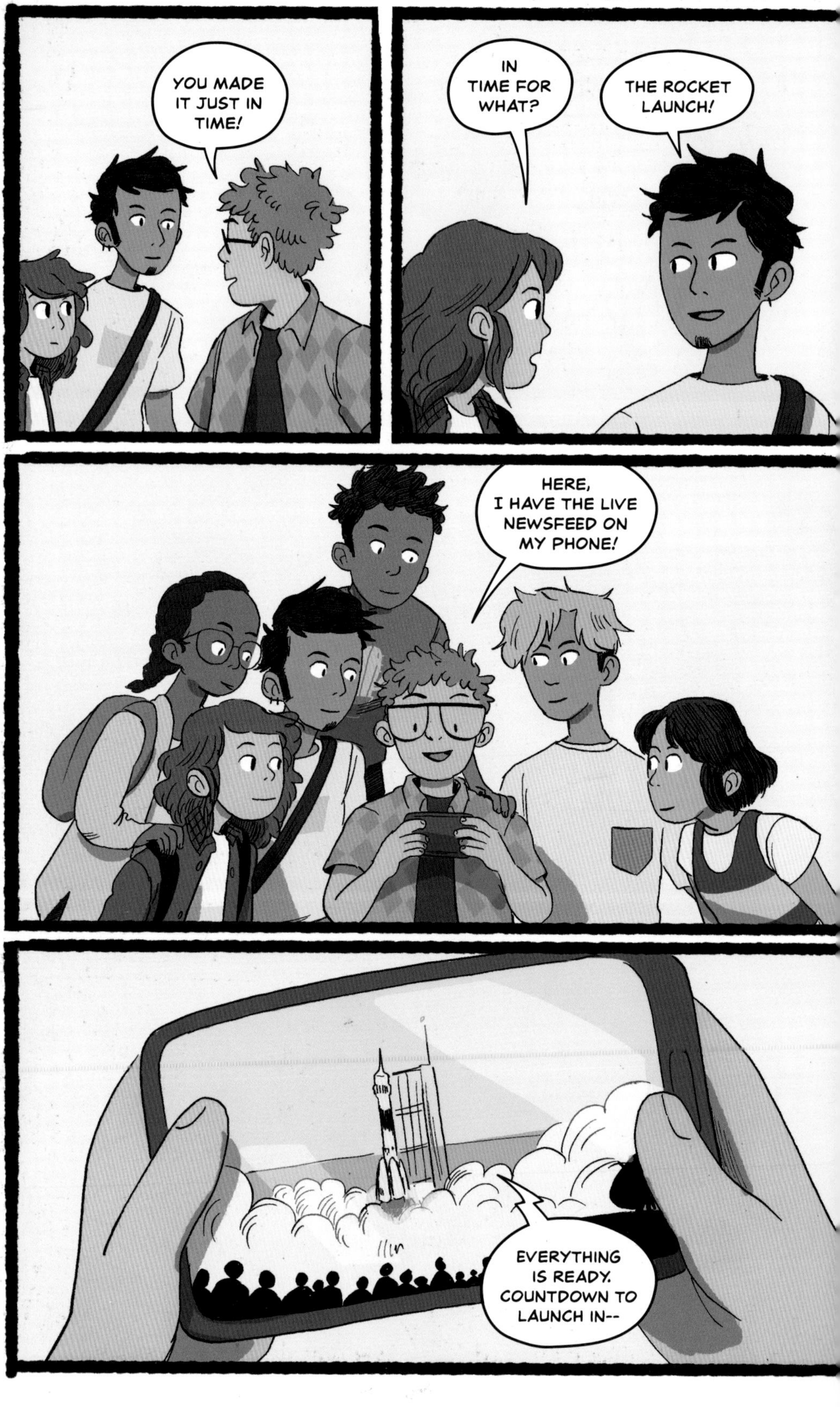
YOU MADE IT JUST IN TIME!
IN TIME FOR WHAT?
THE ROCKET LAUNCH!
HERE, I HAVE THE LIVE NEWSFEED ON MY PHONE!
EVERYTHING IS READY. COUNTDOWN TO LAUNCH IN--

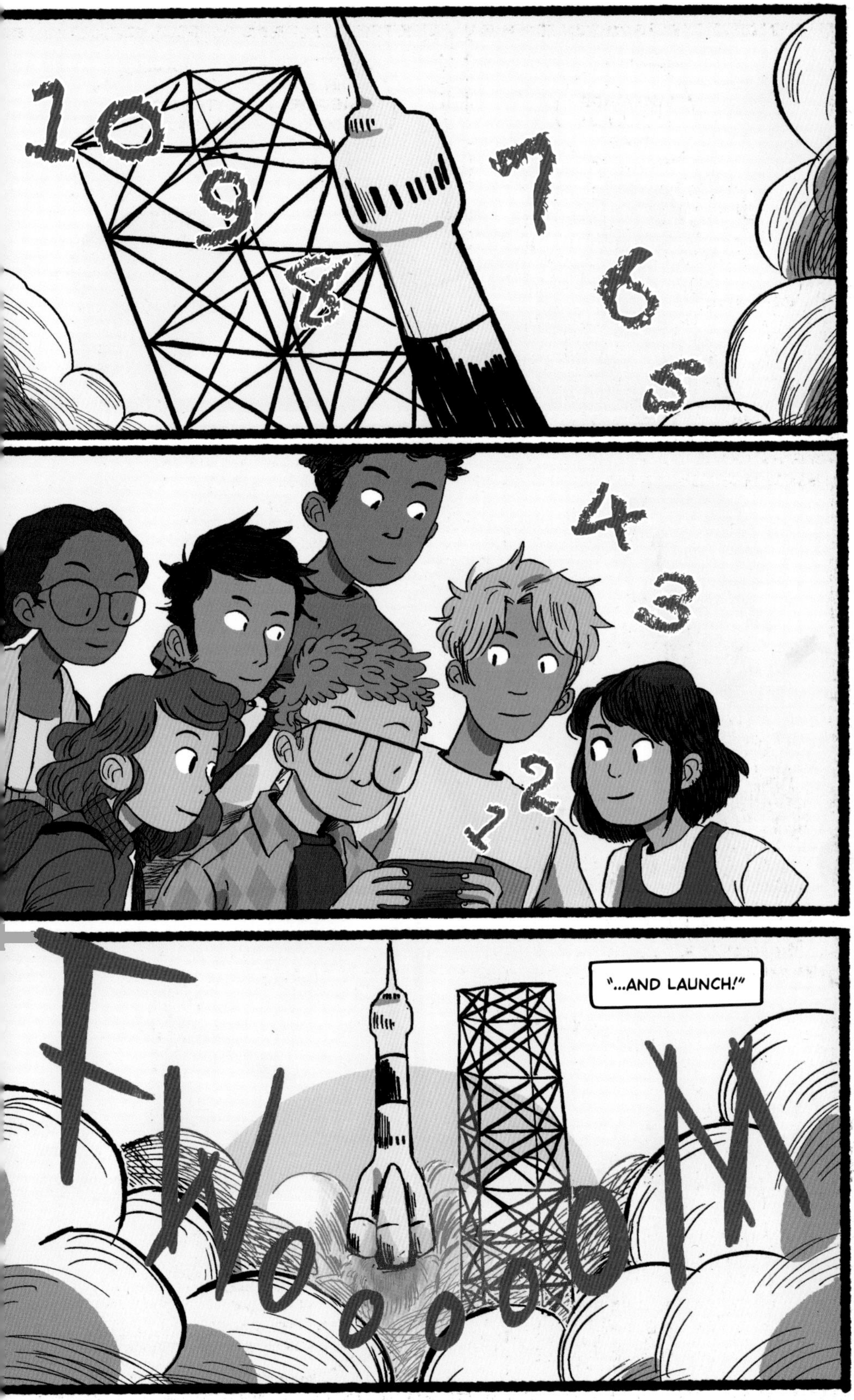
10
9
8
7
6
5
4
3
2
1
"...AND LAUNCH!"
FWOOOOOOM

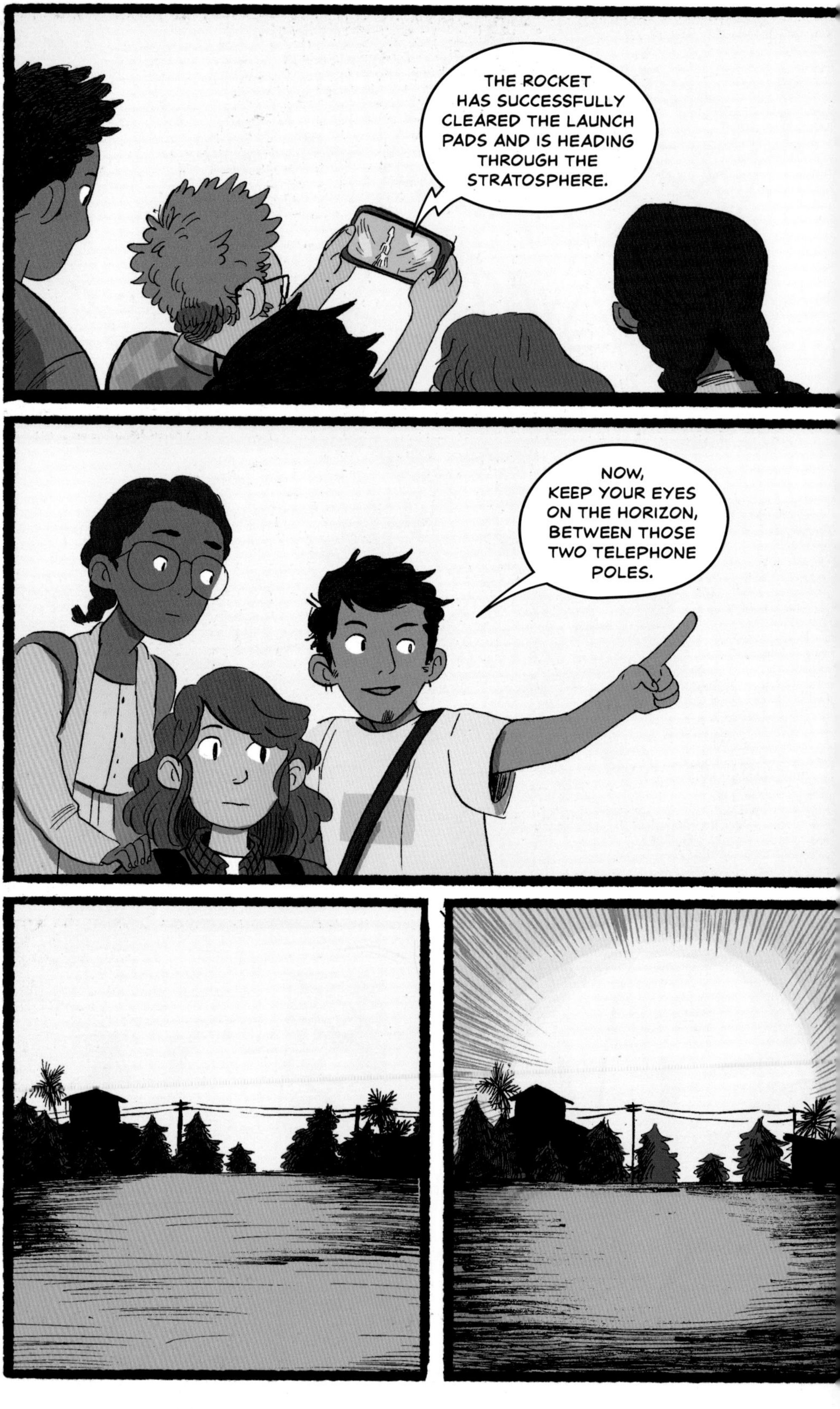
THE ROCKET HAS SUCCESSFULLY CLEARED THE LAUNCH PADS AND IS HEADING THROUGH THE STRATOSPHERE.
NOW, KEEP YOUR EYES ON THE HORIZON, BETWEEN THOSE TWO TELEPHONE POLES.

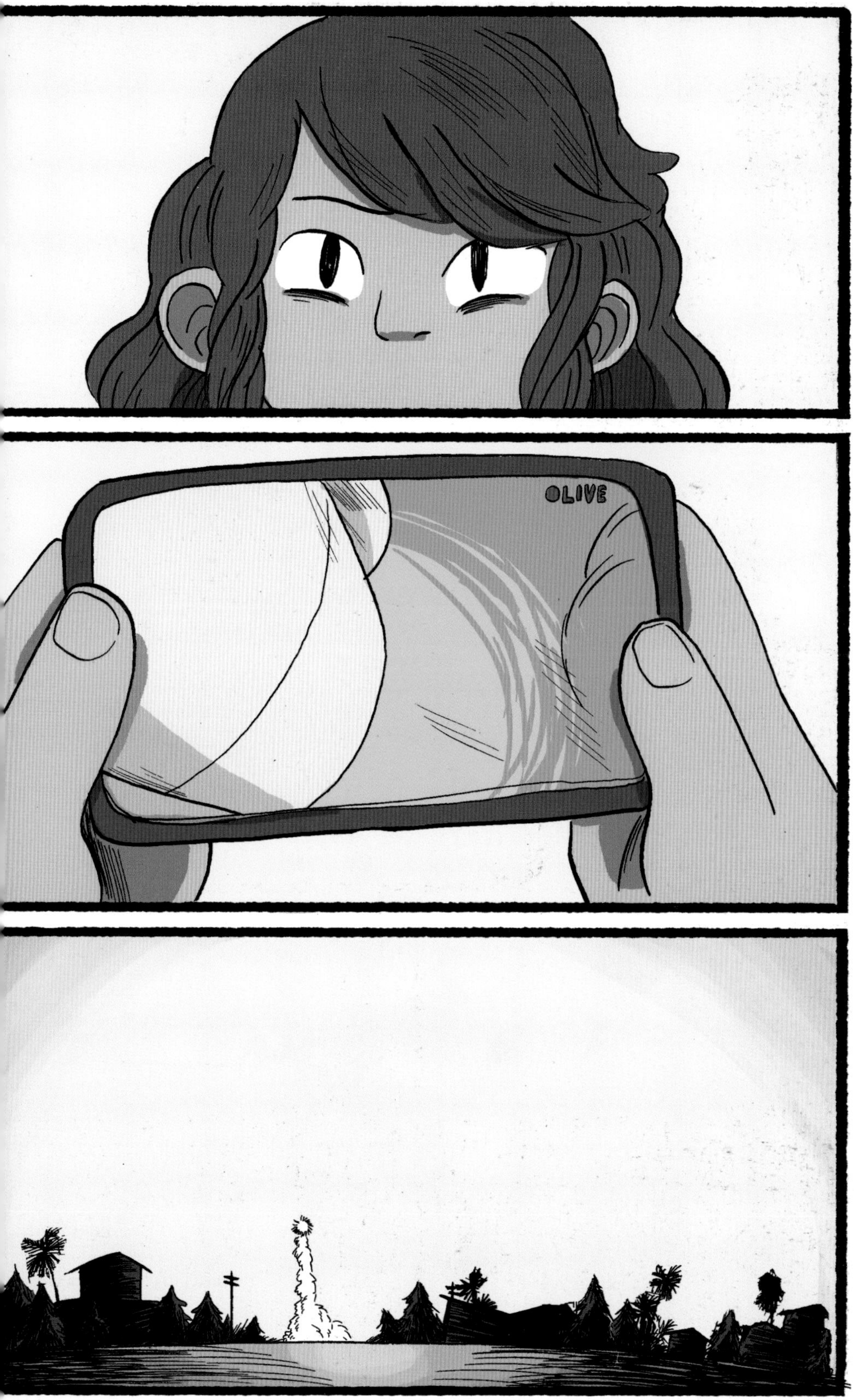
OLIVE

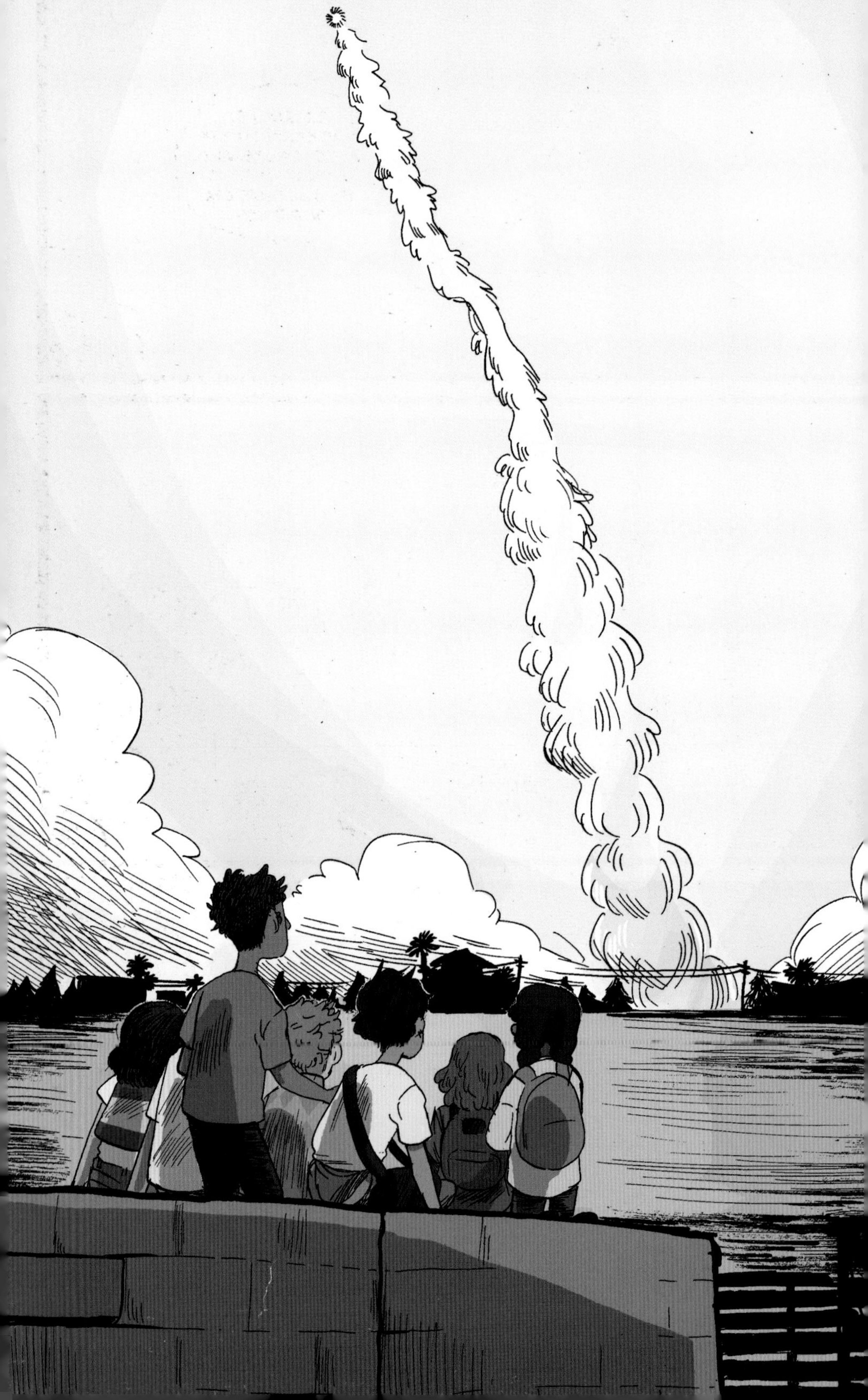

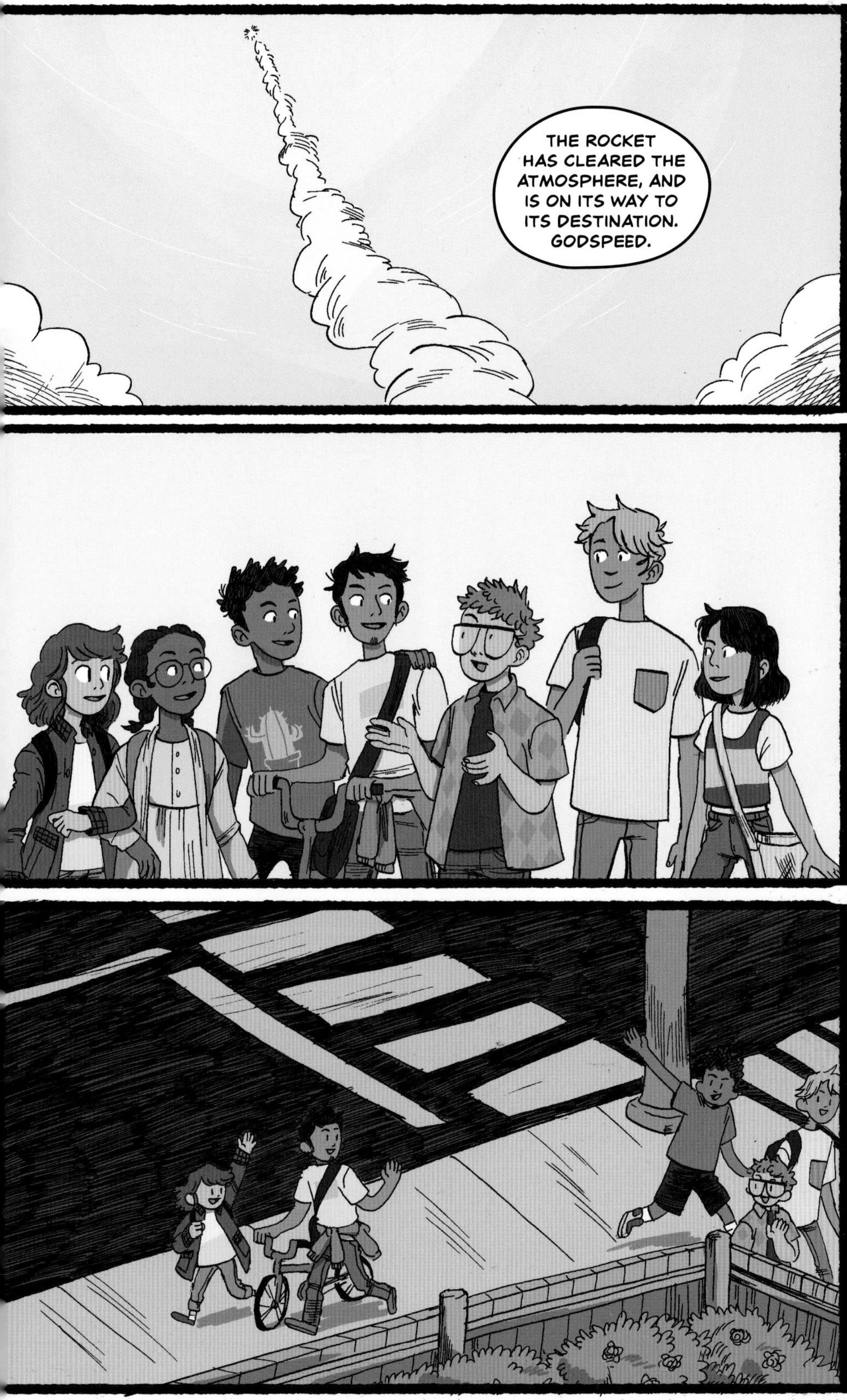
THE ROCKET HAS CLEARED THE ATMOSPHERE, AND IS ON ITS WAY TO ITS DESTINATION. GODSPEED.

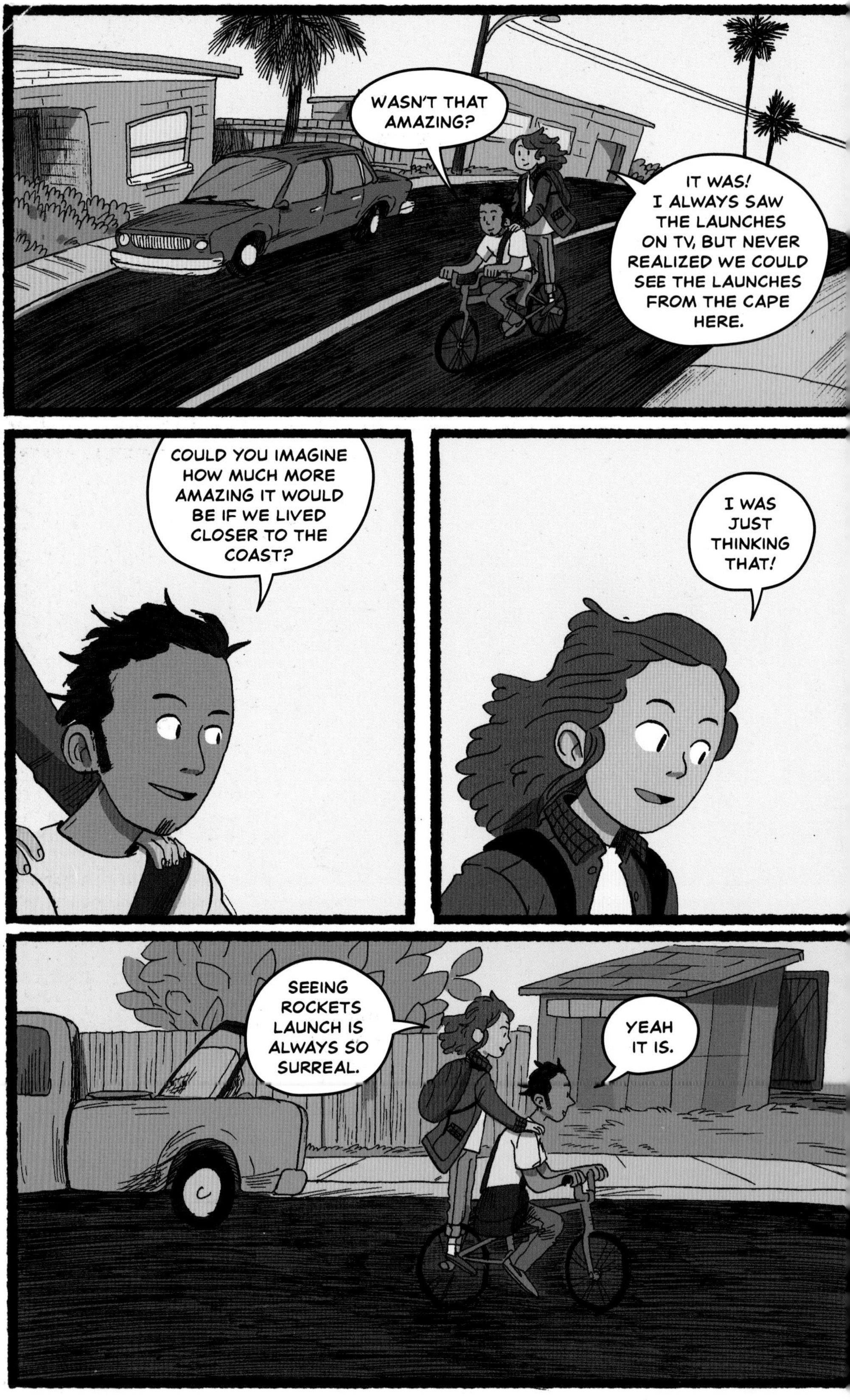
WASN'T THAT AMAZING?
IT WAS! I ALWAYS SAW THE LAUNCHES ON TV, BUT NEVER REALIZED WE COULD SEE THE LAUNCHES FROM THE CAPE HERE.
COULD YOU IMAGINE HOW MUCH MORE AMAZING IT WOULD BE IF WE LIVED CLOSER TO THE COAST?
I WAS JUST THINKING THAT!
SEEING ROCKETS LAUNCH IS ALWAYS SO SURREAL.
YEAH IT IS.

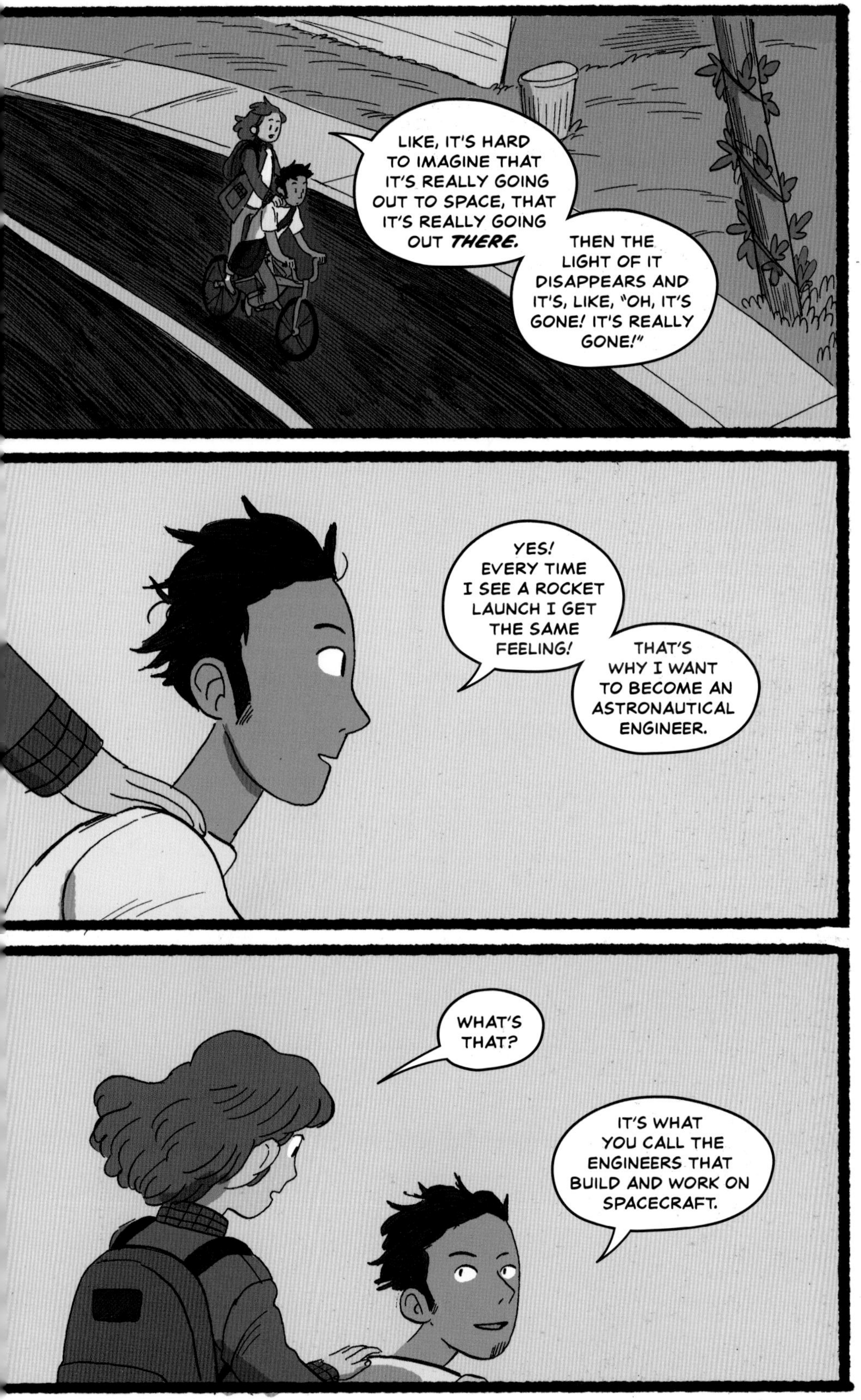
LIKE, IT'S HARD TO IMAGINE THAT IT'S REALLY GOING OUT TO SPACE, THAT IT'S REALLY GOING OUT *THERE.*
THEN THE LIGHT OF IT DISAPPEARS AND IT'S, LIKE, "OH, IT'S GONE! IT'S REALLY GONE!"
YES! EVERY TIME I SEE A ROCKET LAUNCH I GET THE SAME FEELING!
THAT'S WHY I WANT TO BECOME AN ASTRONAUTICAL ENGINEER.
WHAT'S THAT?
IT'S WHAT YOU CALL THE ENGINEERS THAT BUILD AND WORK ON SPACECRAFT.

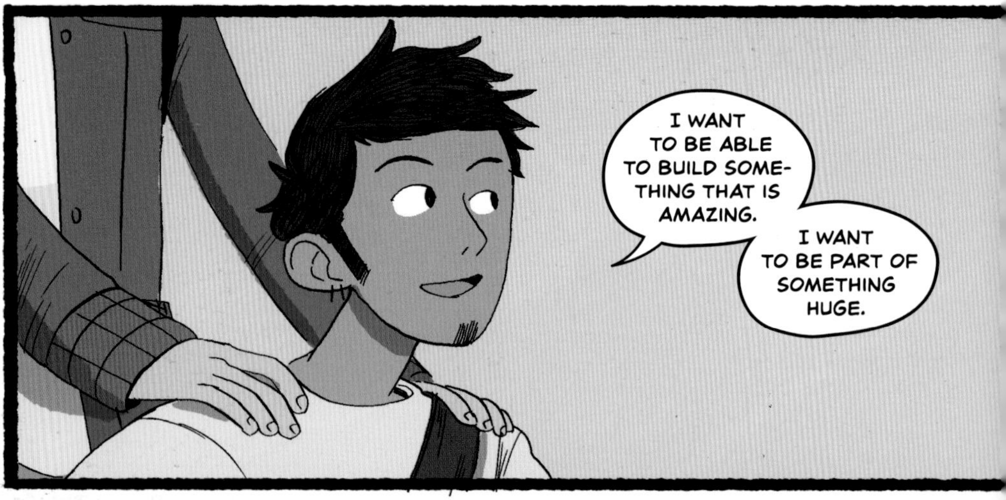
I WANT TO BE ABLE TO BUILD SOME-THING THAT IS AMAZING.
I WANT TO BE PART OF SOMETHING HUGE.

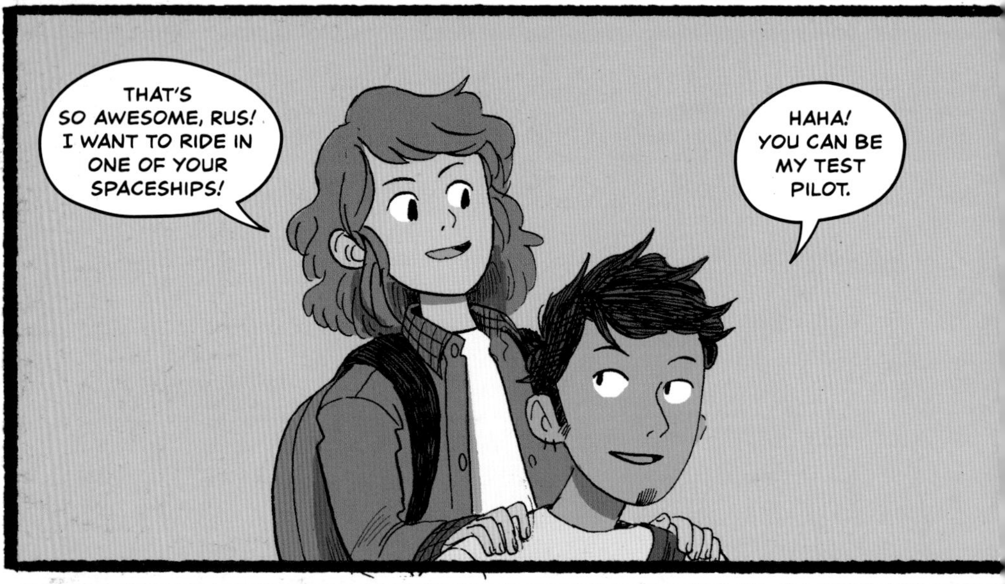
THAT'S SO AWESOME, RUS! I WANT TO RIDE IN ONE OF YOUR SPACESHIPS!
HAHA! YOU CAN BE MY TEST PILOT.

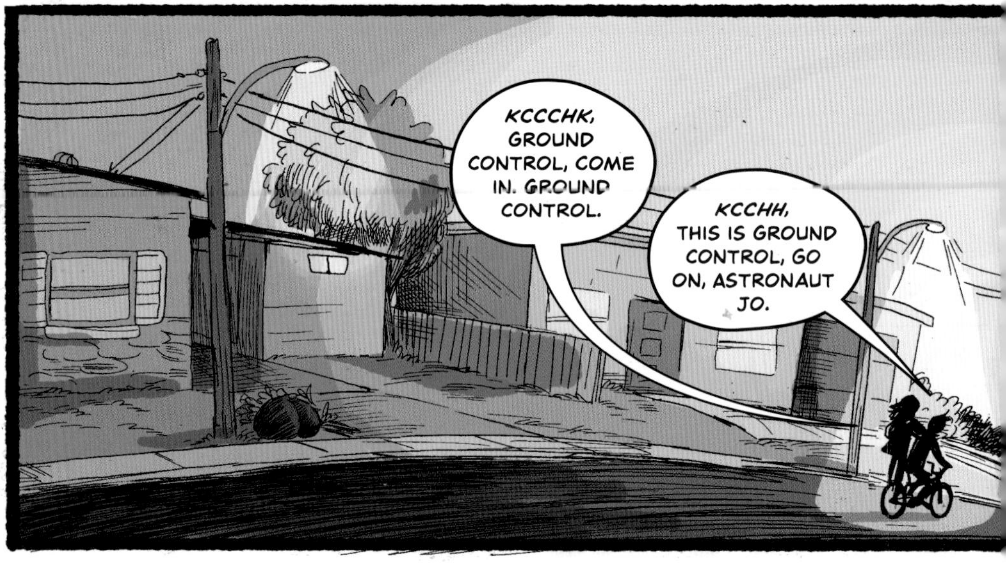
KCCCHK, GROUND CONTROL, COME IN. GROUND CONTROL.
KCCHH, THIS IS GROUND CONTROL, GO ON, ASTRONAUT JO.

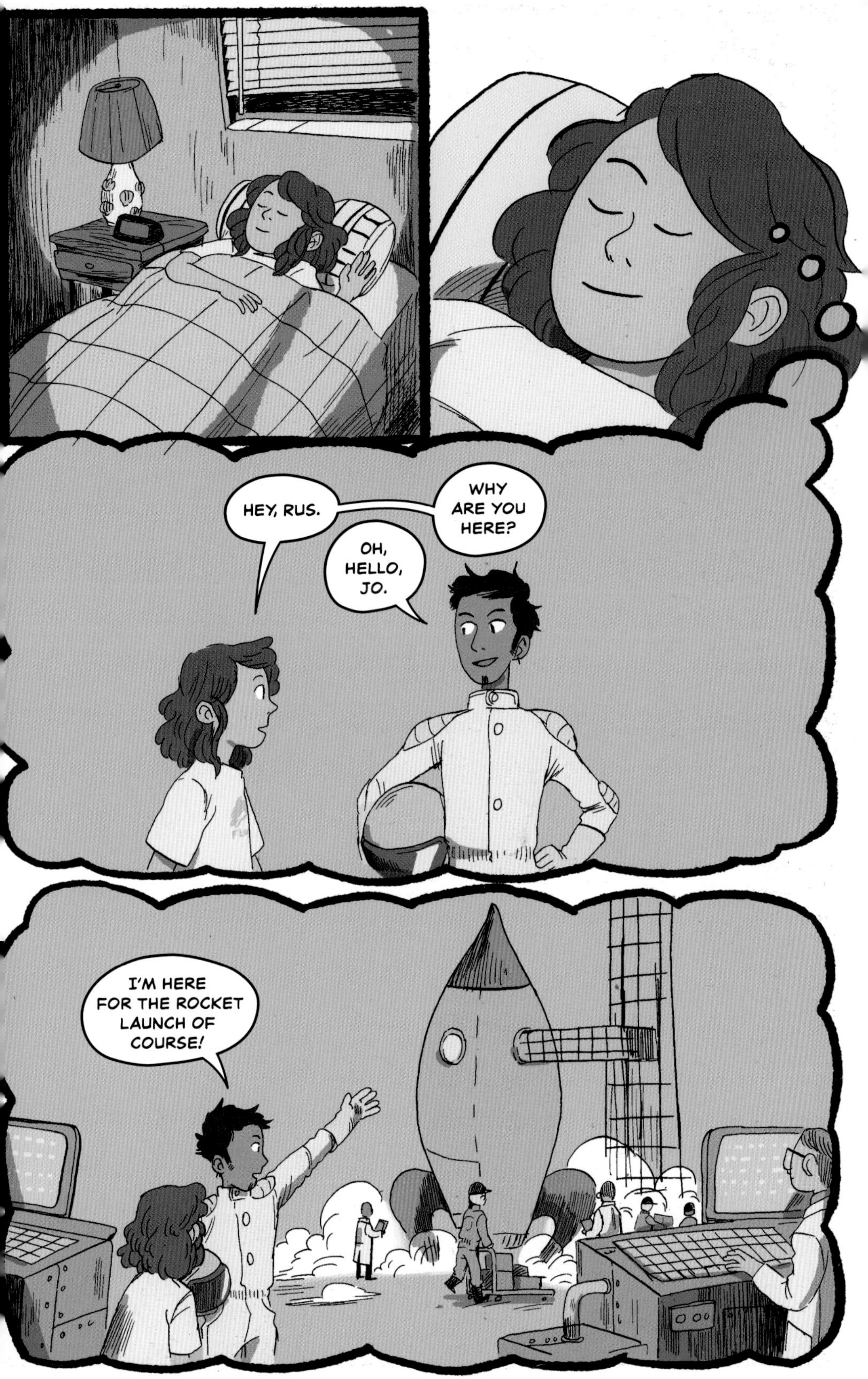

HEY, RUS.
WHY ARE YOU HERE?
OH, HELLO, JO.
I'M HERE FOR THE ROCKET LAUNCH OF COURSE!

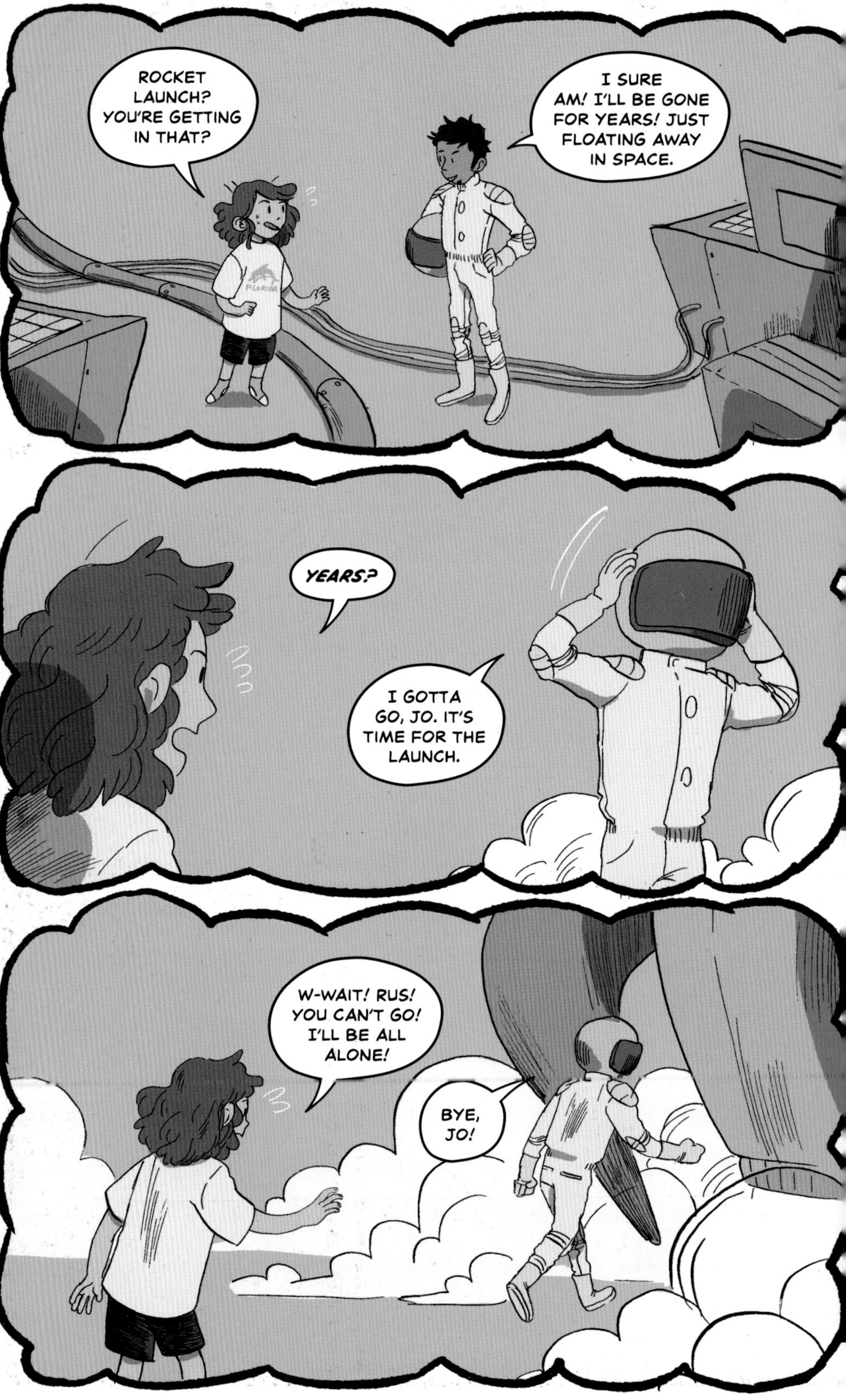
ROCKET LAUNCH? YOU'RE GETTING IN THAT?
I SURE AM! I'LL BE GONE FOR YEARS! JUST FLOATING AWAY IN SPACE.
YEARS?
I GOTTA GO, JO. IT'S TIME FOR THE LAUNCH.
W-WAIT! RUS! YOU CAN'T GO! I'LL BE ALL ALONE!
BYE, JO!

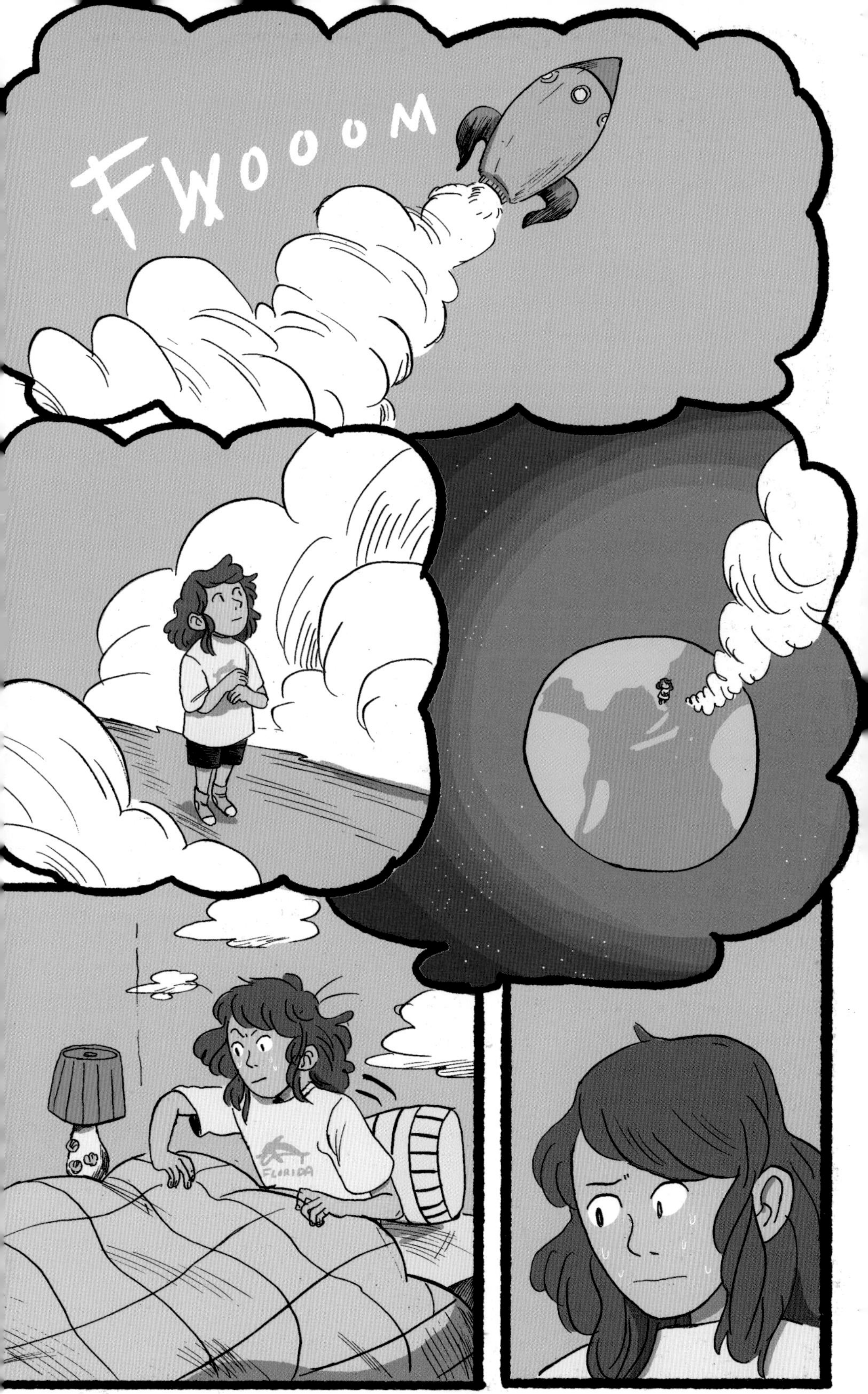
FWOOOM
FLORIDA

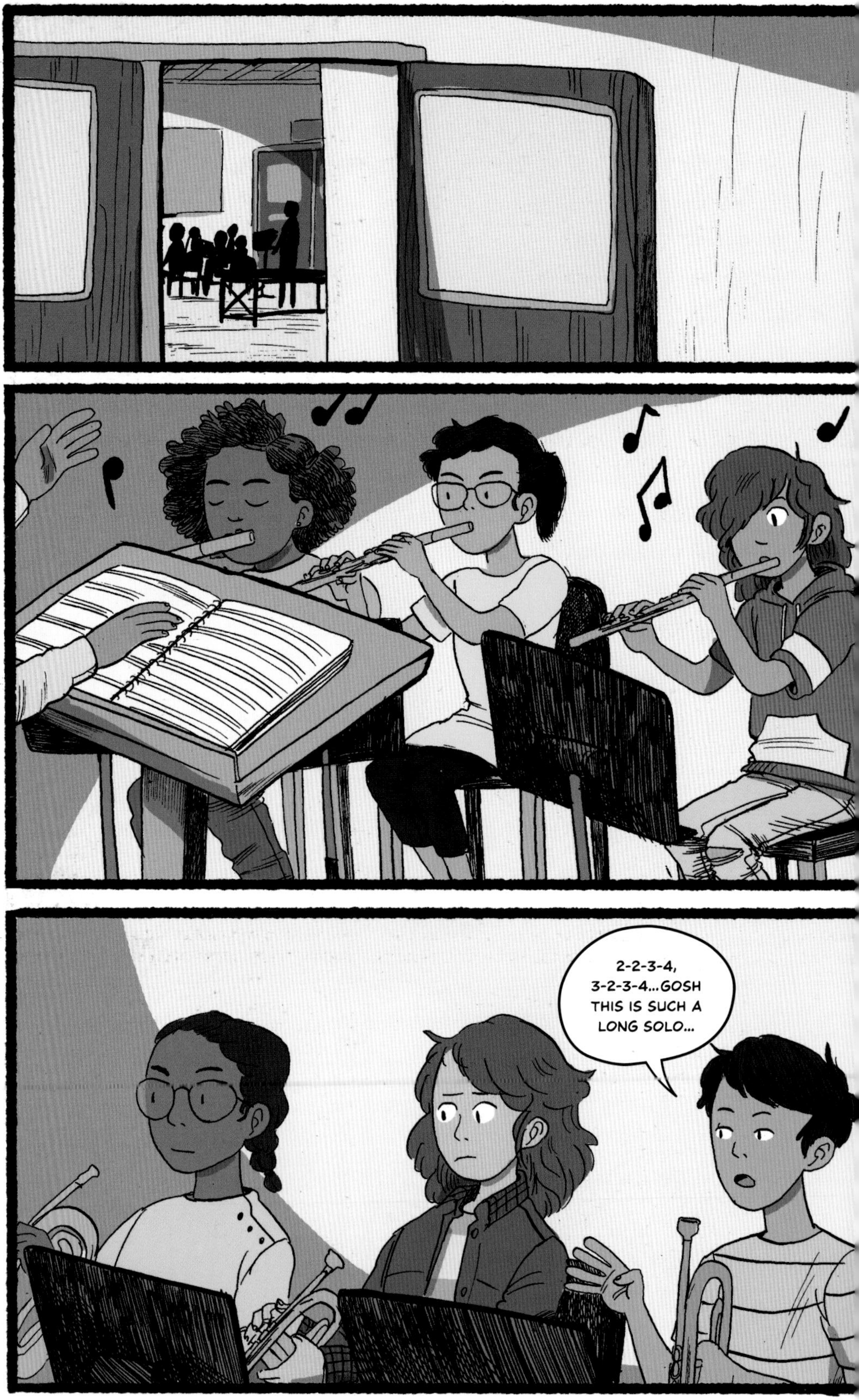
2-2-3-4, 3-2-3-4...GOSH THIS IS SUCH A LONG SOLO...

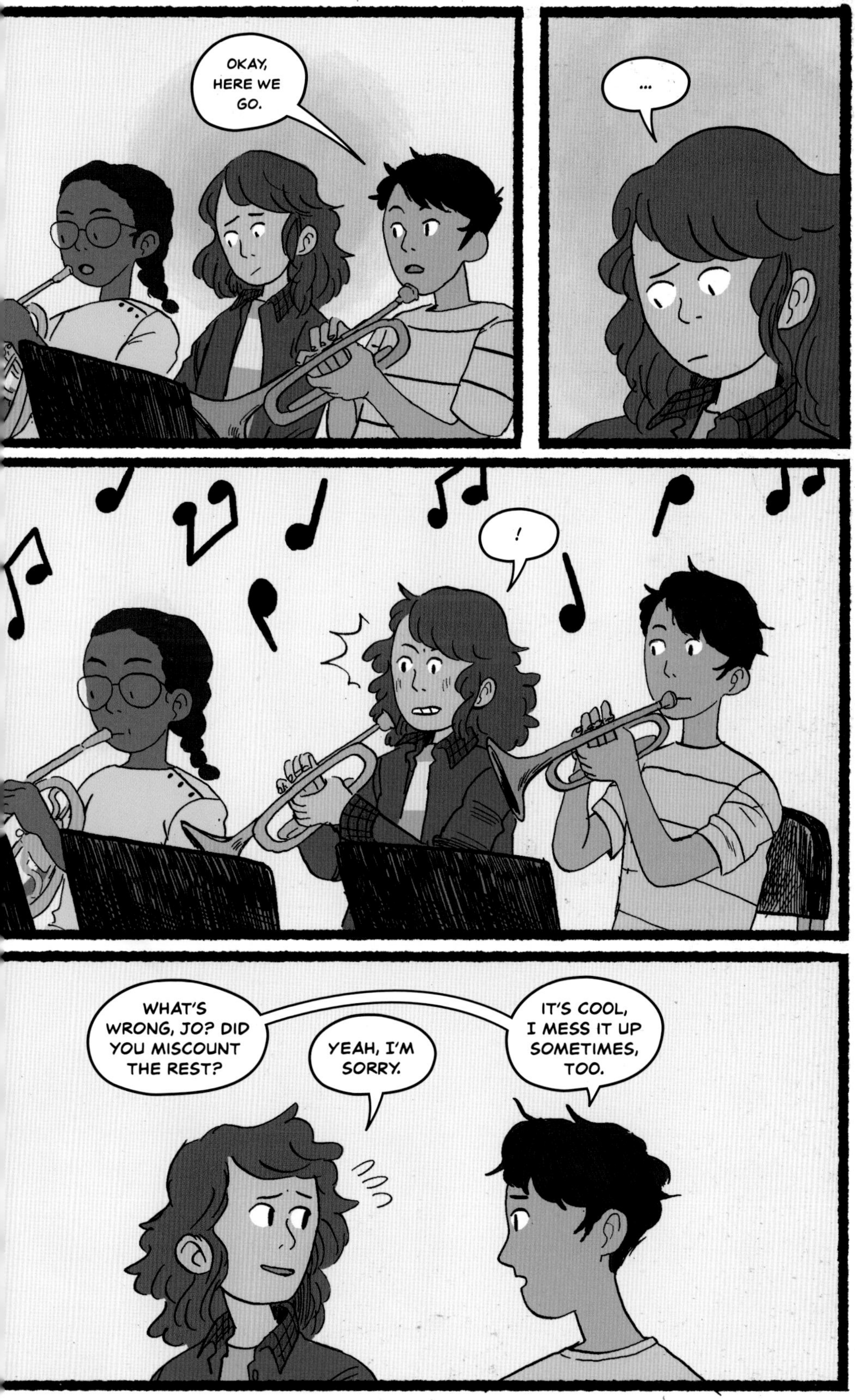
OKAY, HERE WE GO.
...
!
WHAT'S WRONG, JO? DID YOU MISCOUNT THE REST?
YEAH, I'M SORRY.
IT'S COOL, I MESS IT UP SOMETIMES, TOO.

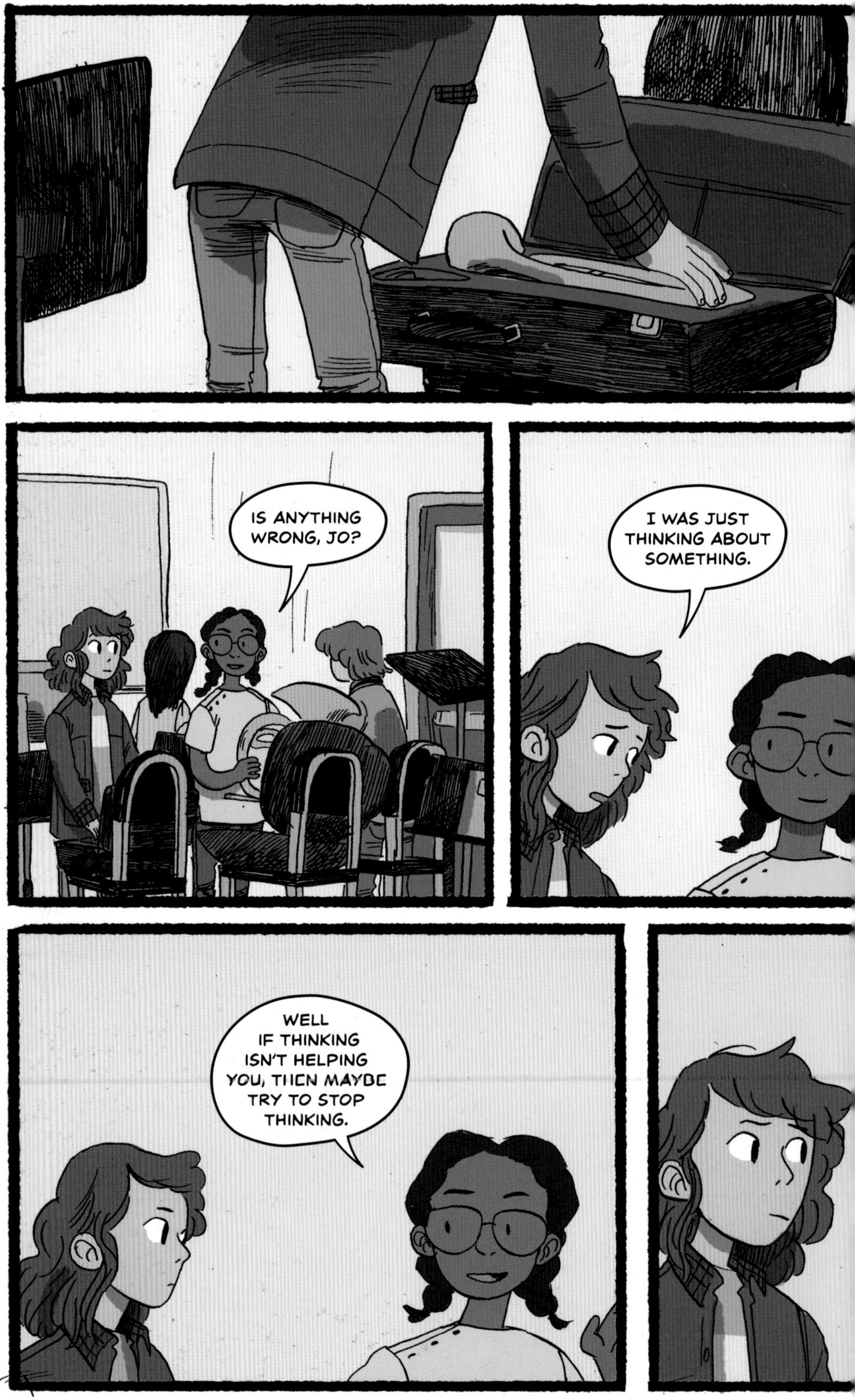
IS ANYTHING WRONG, JO?
I WAS JUST THINKING ABOUT SOMETHING.
WELL IF THINKING ISN'T HELPING YOU, THEN MAYBE TRY TO STOP THINKING.

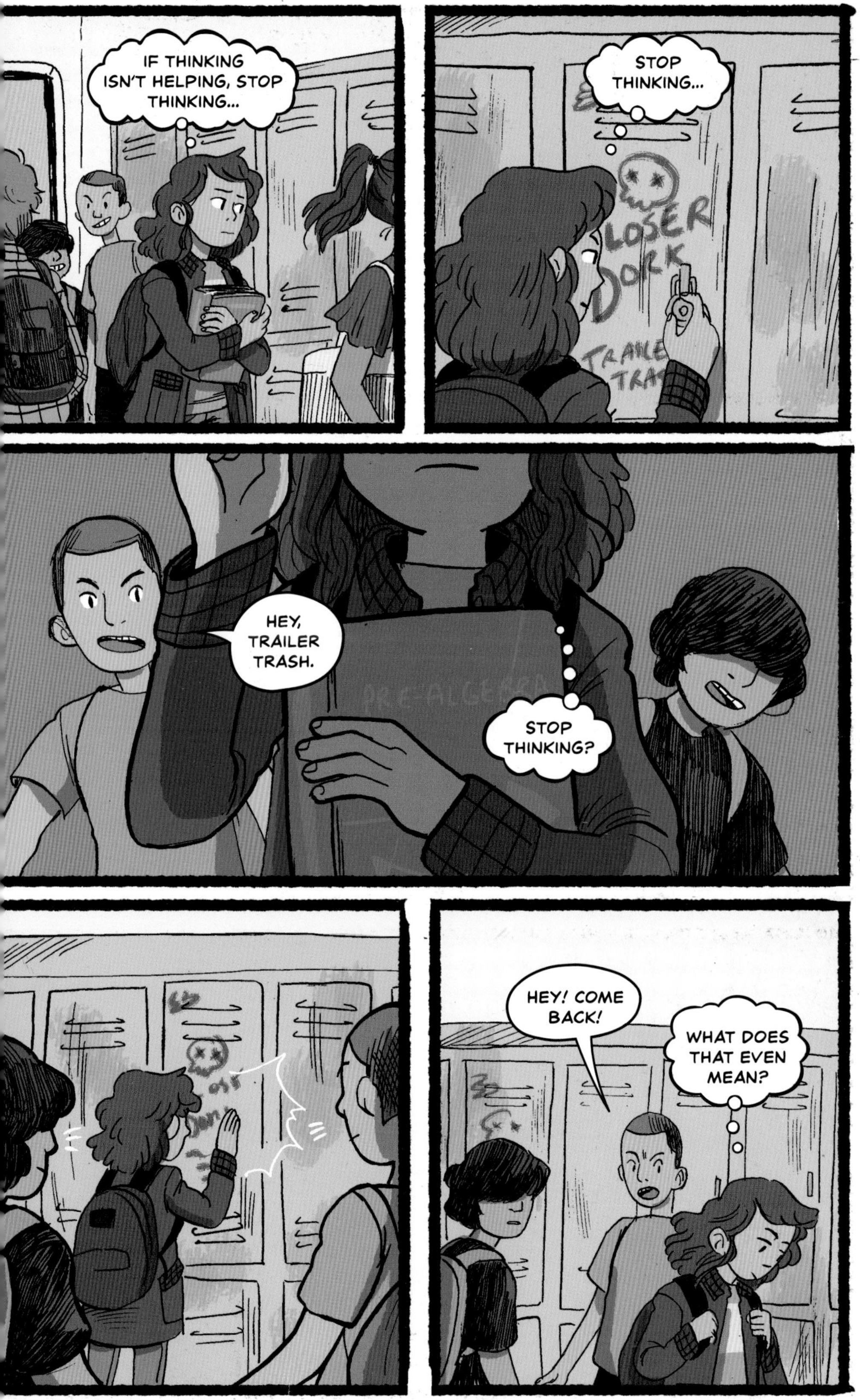
IF THINKING ISN'T HELPING, STOP THINKING...
STOP THINKING...
LOSER
DORK
HEY, TRAILER TRASH.
STOP THINKING?
HEY! COME BACK!
WHAT DOES THAT EVEN MEAN?

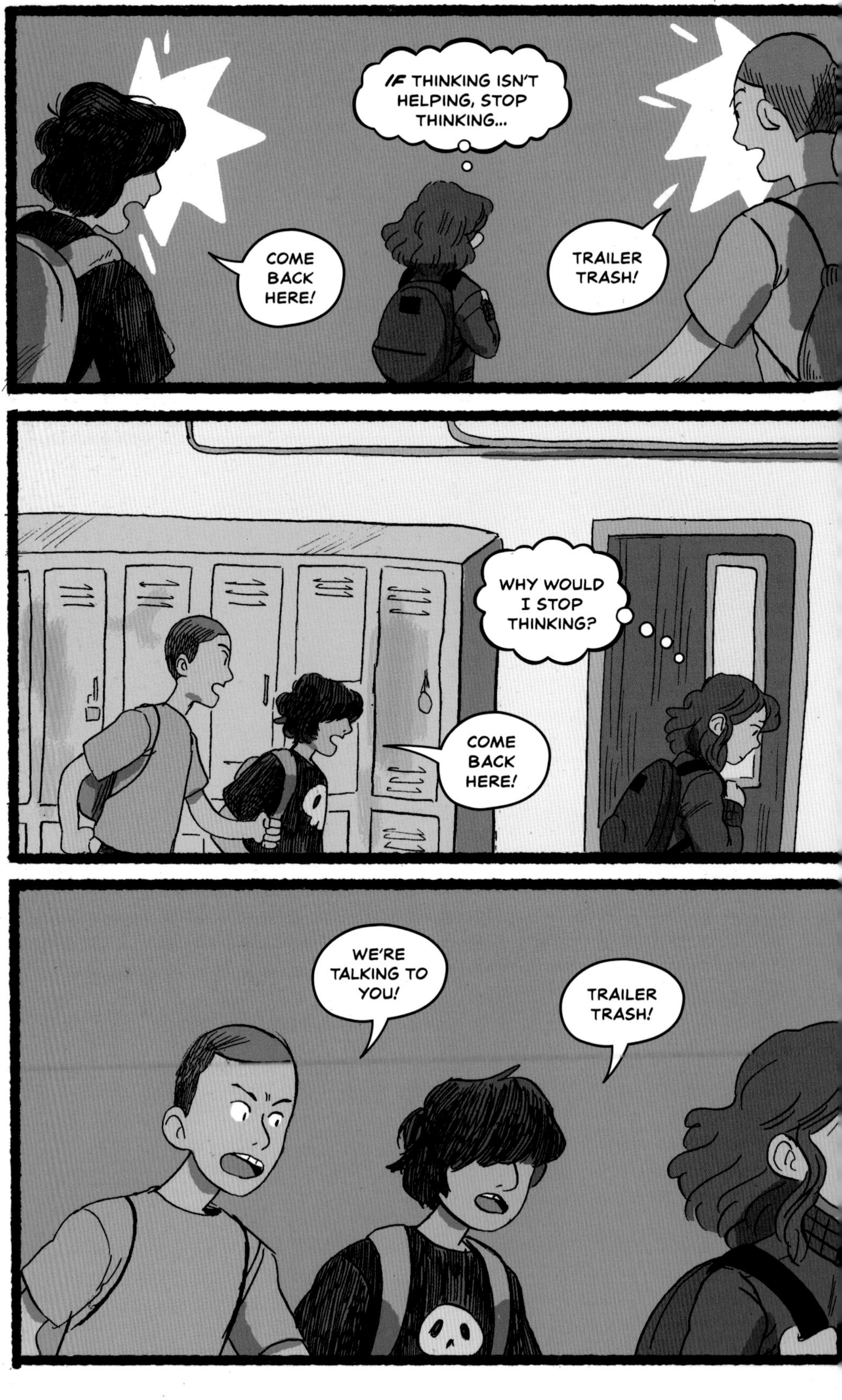
IF THINKING ISN'T HELPING, STOP THINKING...
COME BACK HERE!
TRAILER TRASH!
WHY WOULD I STOP THINKING?
COME BACK HERE!
WE'RE TALKING TO YOU!
TRAILER TRASH!

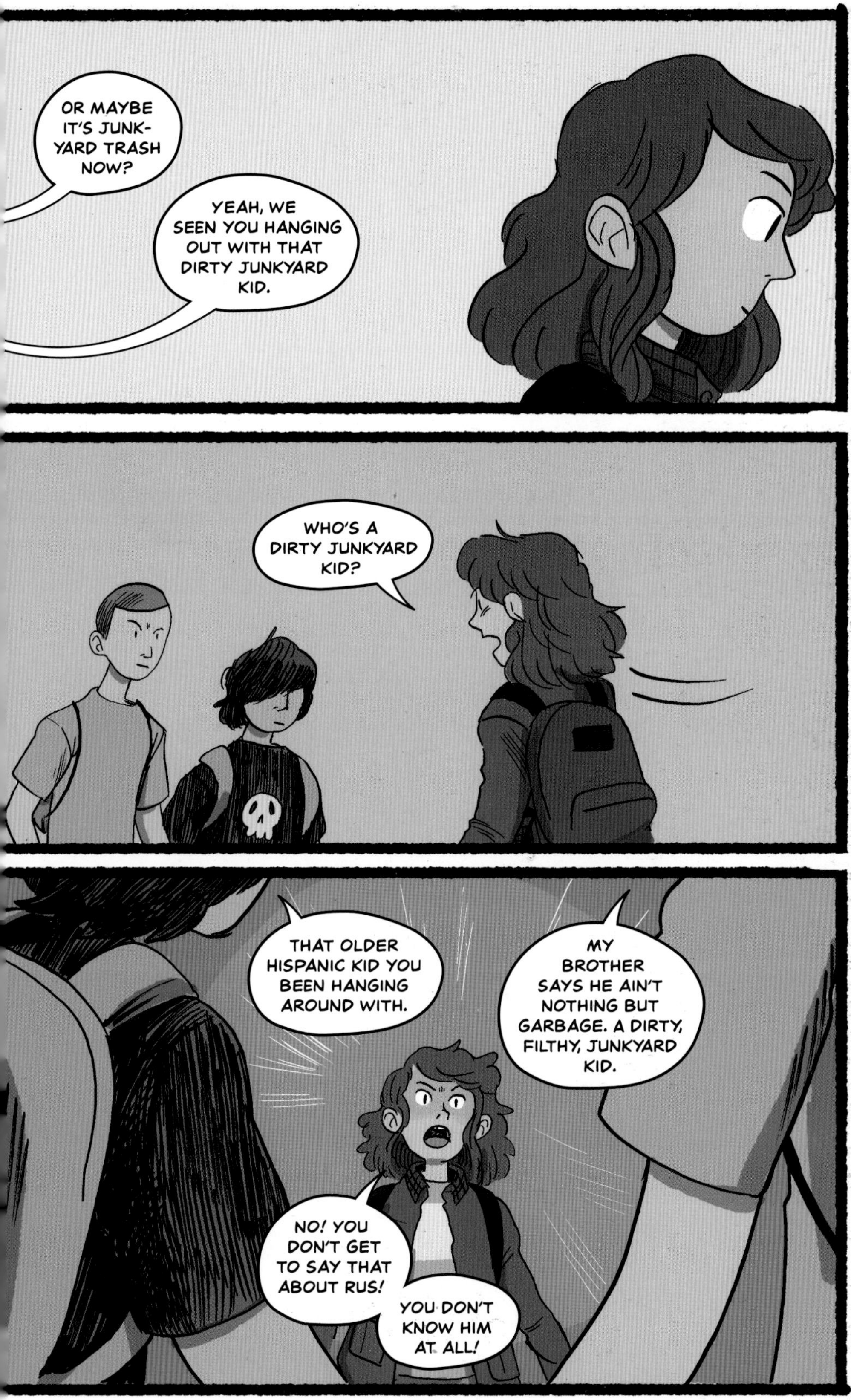
OR MAYBE IT'S JUNK-YARD TRASH NOW?
YEAH, WE SEEN YOU HANGING OUT WITH THAT DIRTY JUNKYARD KID.
WHO'S A DIRTY JUNKYARD KID?
THAT OLDER HISPANIC KID YOU BEEN HANGING AROUND WITH.
MY BROTHER SAYS HE AIN'T NOTHING BUT GARBAGE. A DIRTY, FILTHY, JUNKYARD KID.
NO! YOU DON'T GET TO SAY THAT ABOUT RUS!
YOU DON'T KNOW HIM AT ALL!

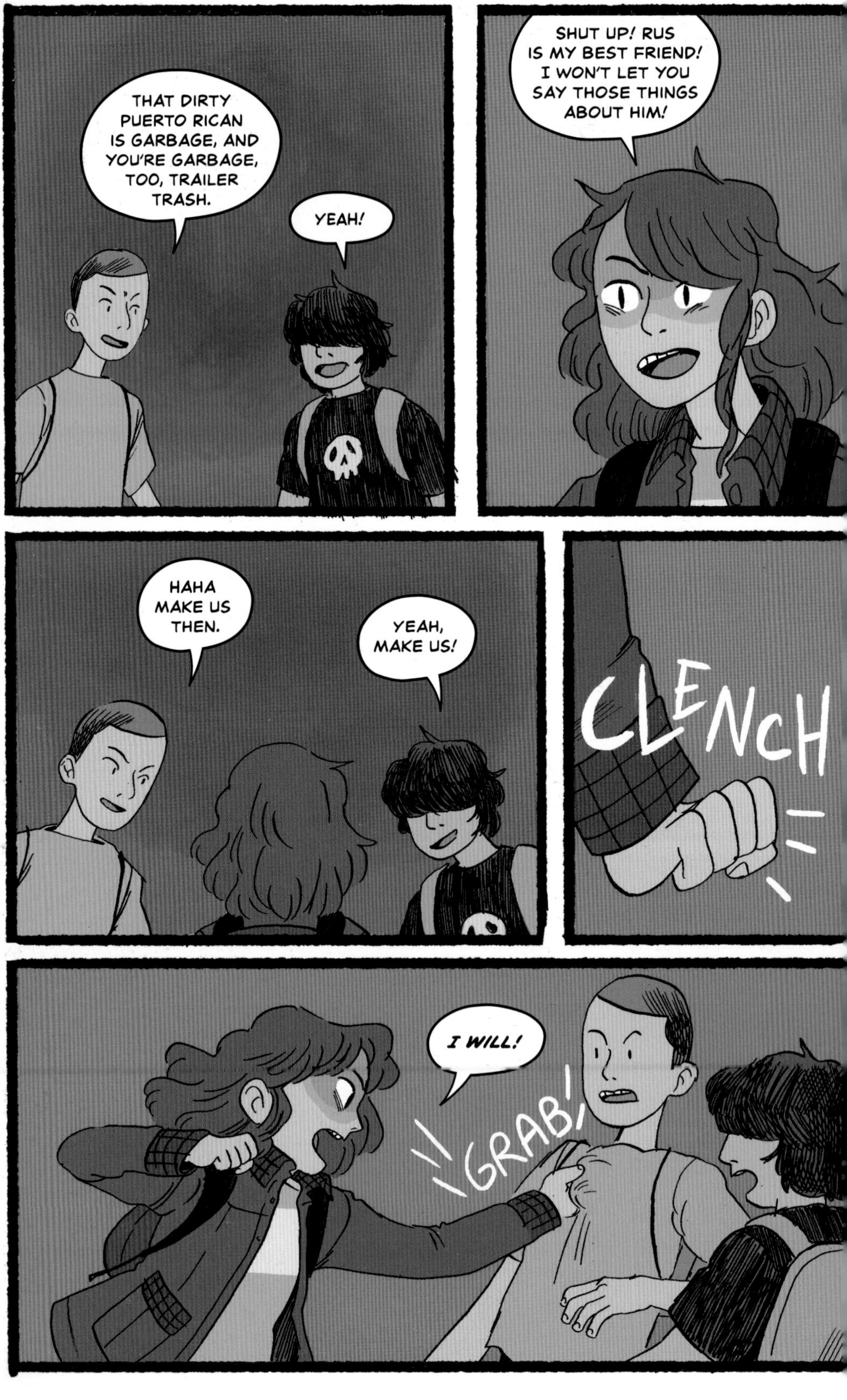
THAT DIRTY PUERTO RICAN IS GARBAGE, AND YOU'RE GARBAGE, TOO, TRAILER TRASH.
YEAH!
SHUT UP! RUS IS MY BEST FRIEND! I WON'T LET YOU SAY THOSE THINGS ABOUT HIM!
HAHA MAKE US THEN.
YEAH, MAKE US!
CLENCH
I WILL!
GRAB!

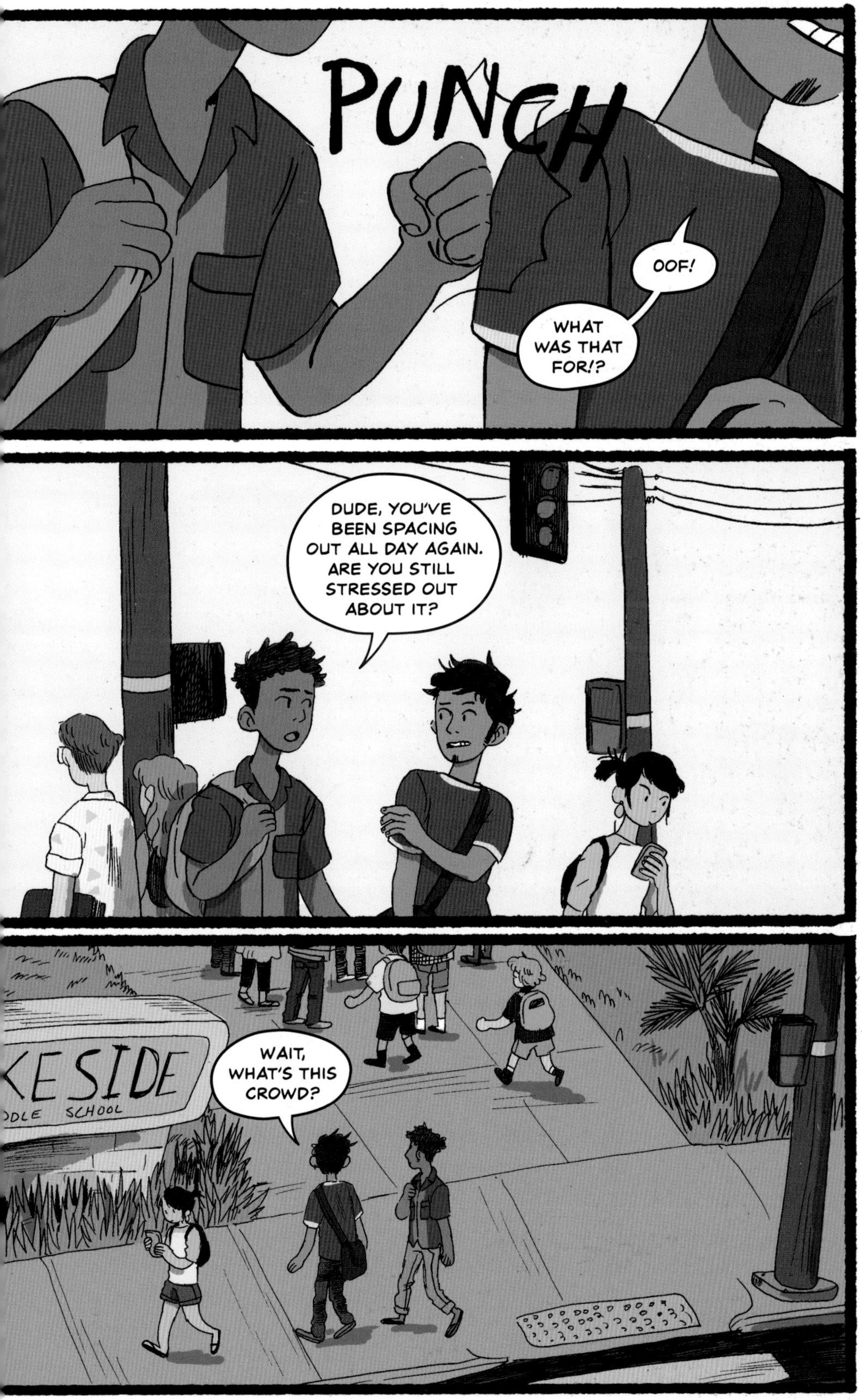
PUNCH
OOF!
WHAT WAS THAT FOR!?
DUDE, YOU'VE BEEN SPACING OUT ALL DAY AGAIN. ARE YOU STILL STRESSED OUT ABOUT IT?
KESIDE
DDLE SCHOOL
WAIT, WHAT'S THIS CROWD?

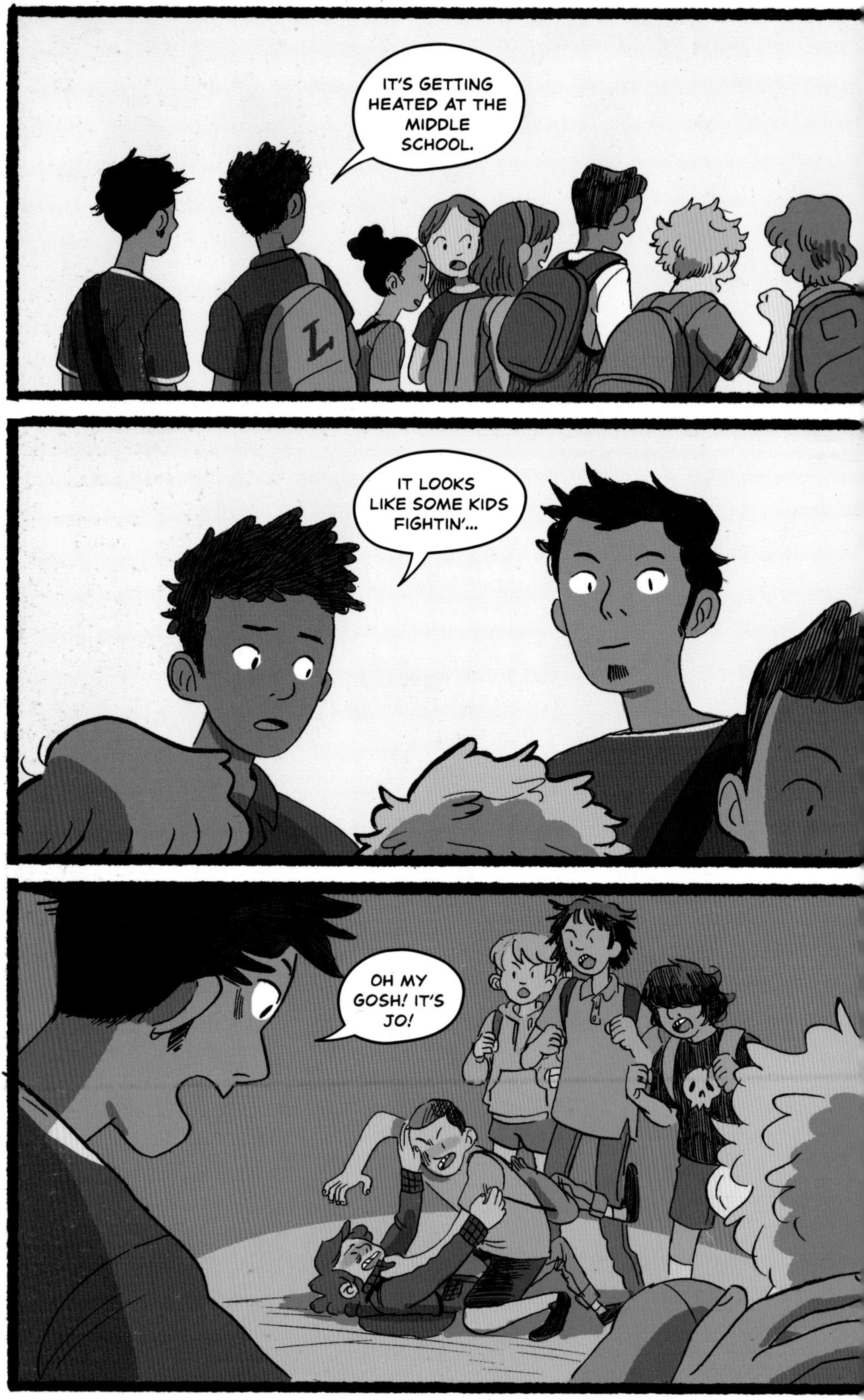
IT'S GETTING HEATED AT THE MIDDLE SCHOOL.
IT LOOKS LIKE SOME KIDS FIGHTIN'...
OH MY GOSH! IT'S JO!

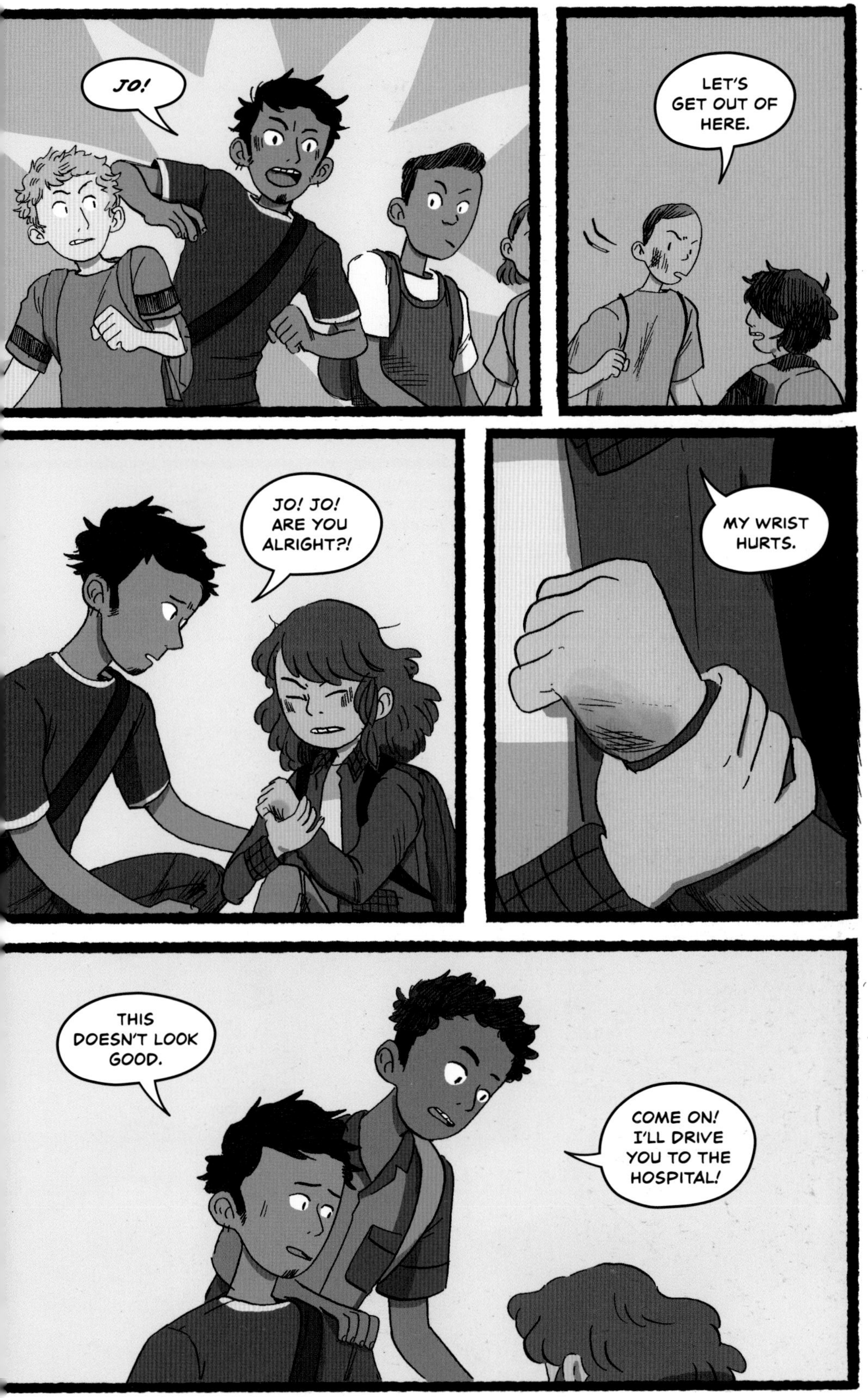
JO!
LET'S GET OUT OF HERE.
JO! JO! ARE YOU ALRIGHT?!
MY WRIST HURTS.
THIS DOESN'T LOOK GOOD.
COME ON! I'LL DRIVE YOU TO THE HOSPITAL!

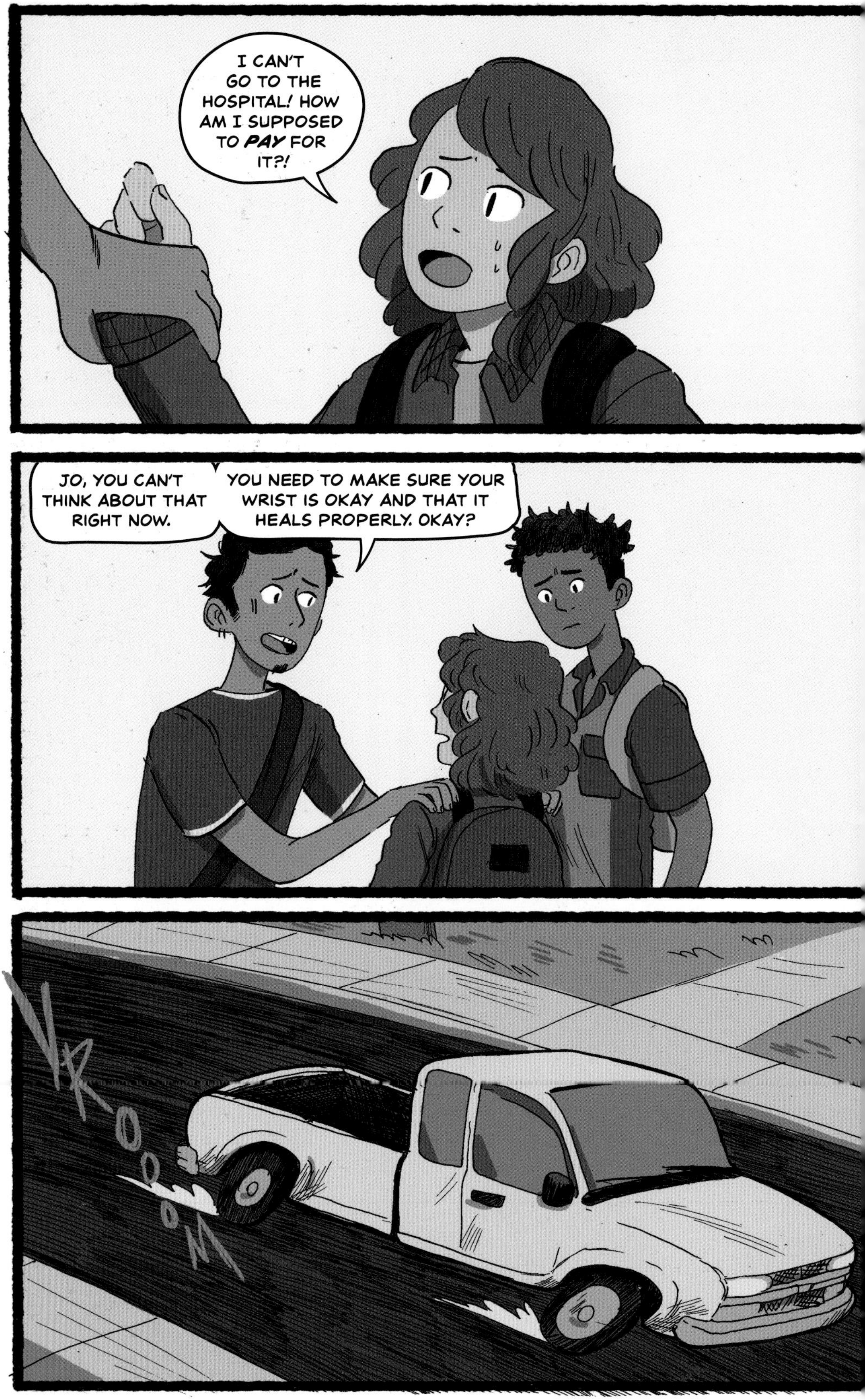
I CAN'T GO TO THE HOSPITAL! HOW AM I SUPPOSED TO *PAY* FOR IT?!
JO, YOU CAN'T THINK ABOUT THAT RIGHT NOW.
YOU NEED TO MAKE SURE YOUR WRIST IS OKAY AND THAT IT HEALS PROPERLY. OKAY?
VROOOOM

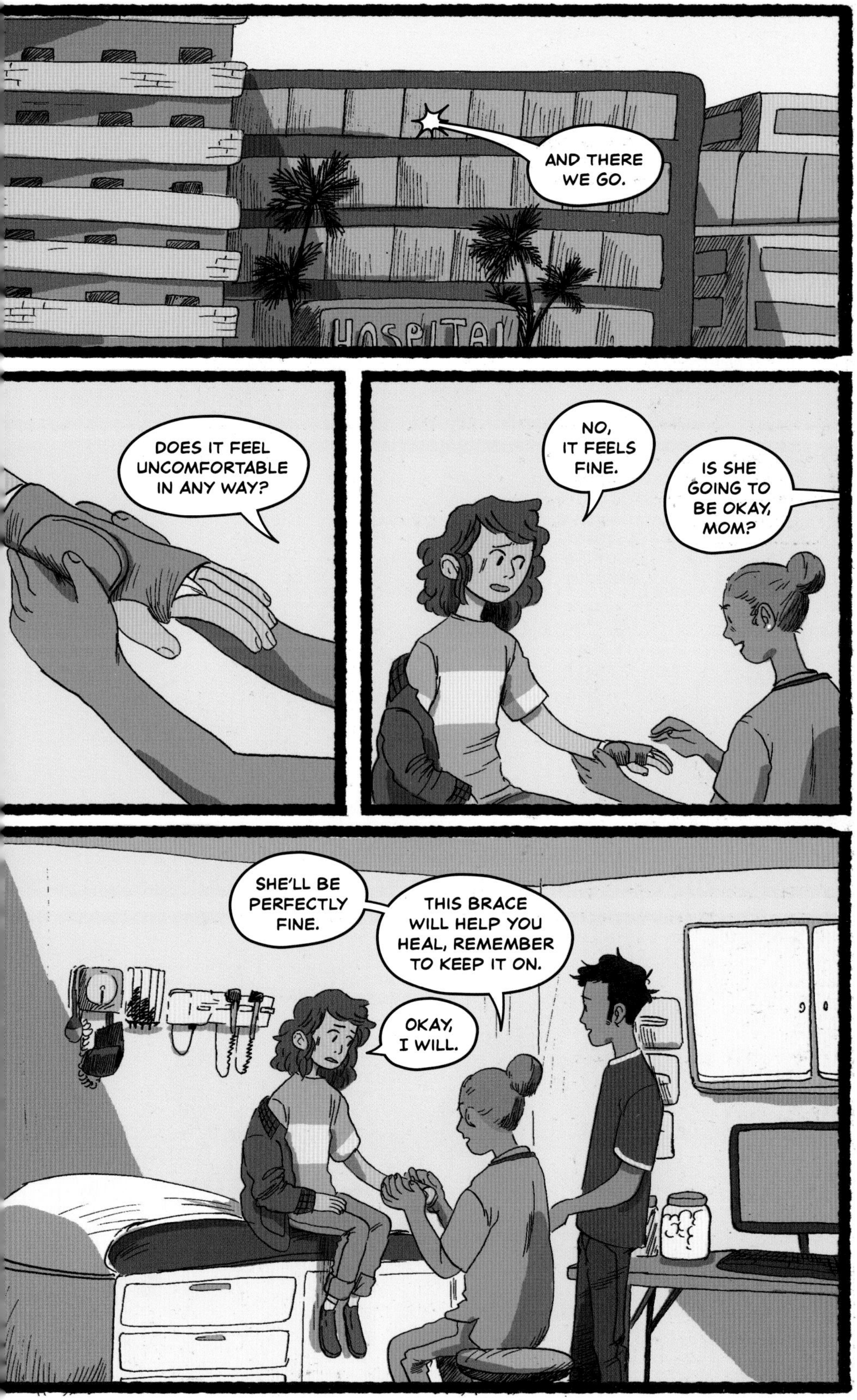
AND THERE WE GO.
HOSPITAL
DOES IT FEEL UNCOMFORTABLE IN ANY WAY?
NO, IT FEELS FINE.
IS SHE GOING TO BE OKAY, MOM?
SHE'LL BE PERFECTLY FINE.
THIS BRACE WILL HELP YOU HEAL, REMEMBER TO KEEP IT ON.
OKAY, I WILL.

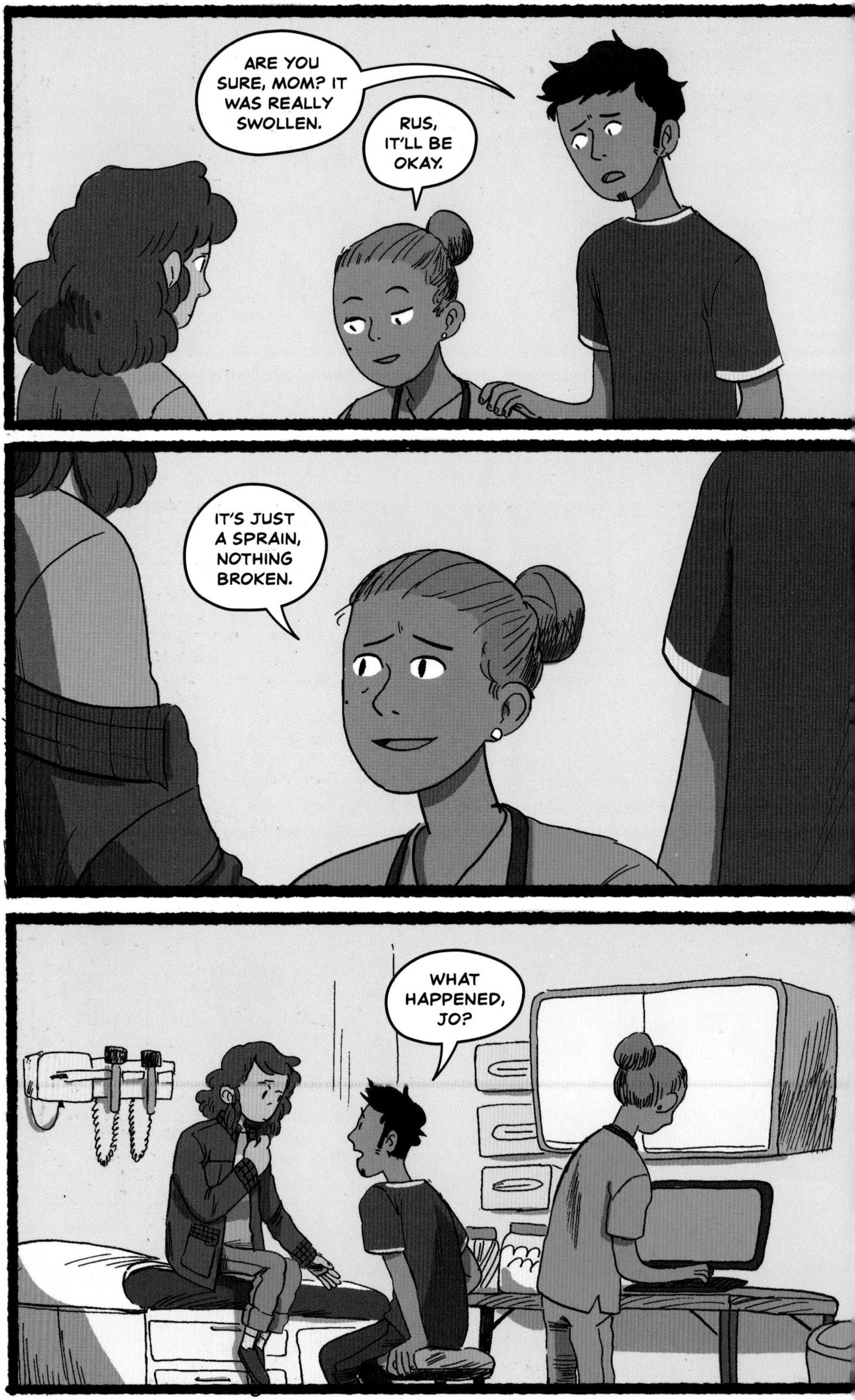
ARE YOU SURE, MOM? IT WAS REALLY SWOLLEN.
RUS, IT'LL BE OKAY.
IT'S JUST A SPRAIN, NOTHING BROKEN.
WHAT HAPPENED, JO?

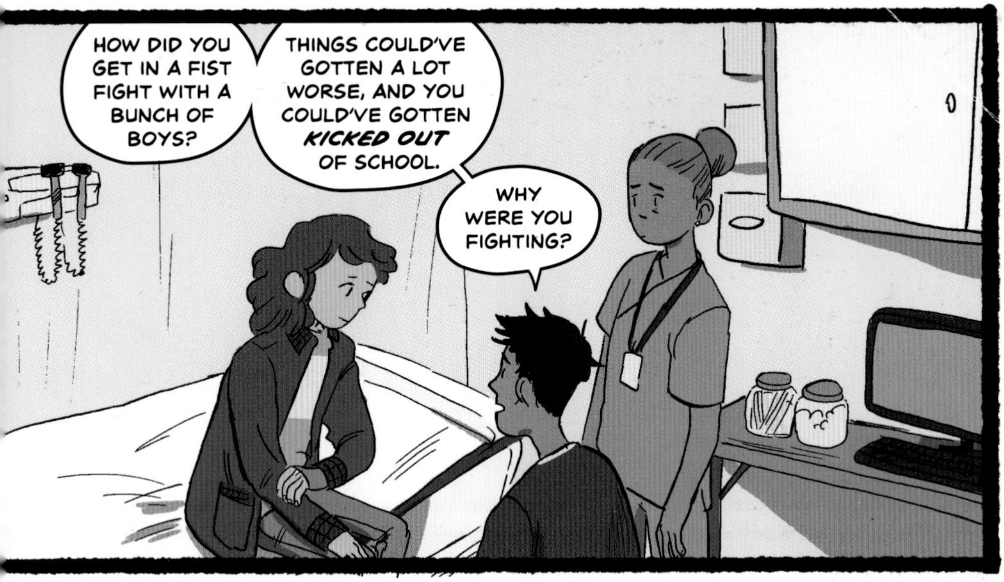
HOW DID YOU GET IN A FIST FIGHT WITH A BUNCH OF BOYS?
THINGS COULD'VE GOTTEN A LOT WORSE, AND YOU COULD'VE GOTTEN *KICKED OUT* OF SCHOOL.
WHY WERE YOU FIGHTING?

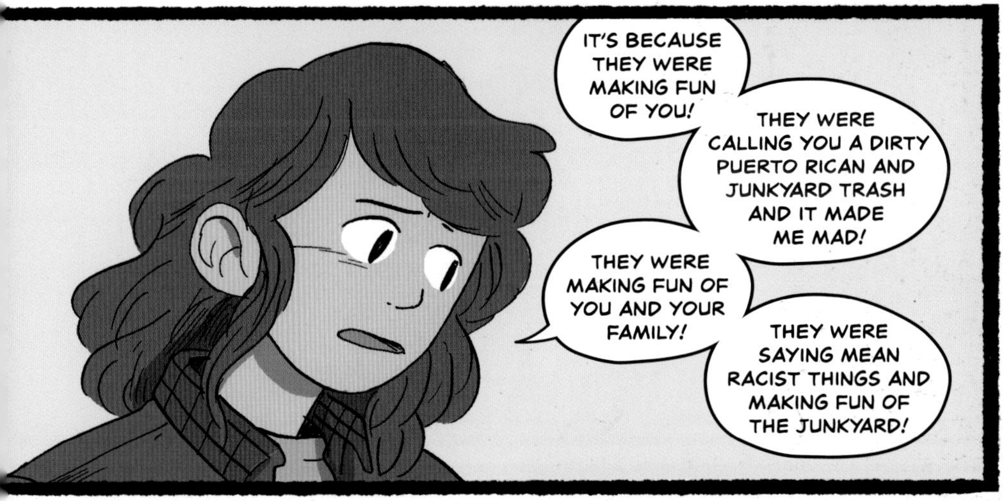
IT'S BECAUSE THEY WERE MAKING FUN OF YOU!
THEY WERE CALLING YOU A DIRTY PUERTO RICAN AND JUNKYARD TRASH AND IT MADE ME MAD!
THEY WERE MAKING FUN OF YOU AND YOUR FAMILY!
THEY WERE SAYING MEAN RACIST THINGS AND MAKING FUN OF THE JUNKYARD!

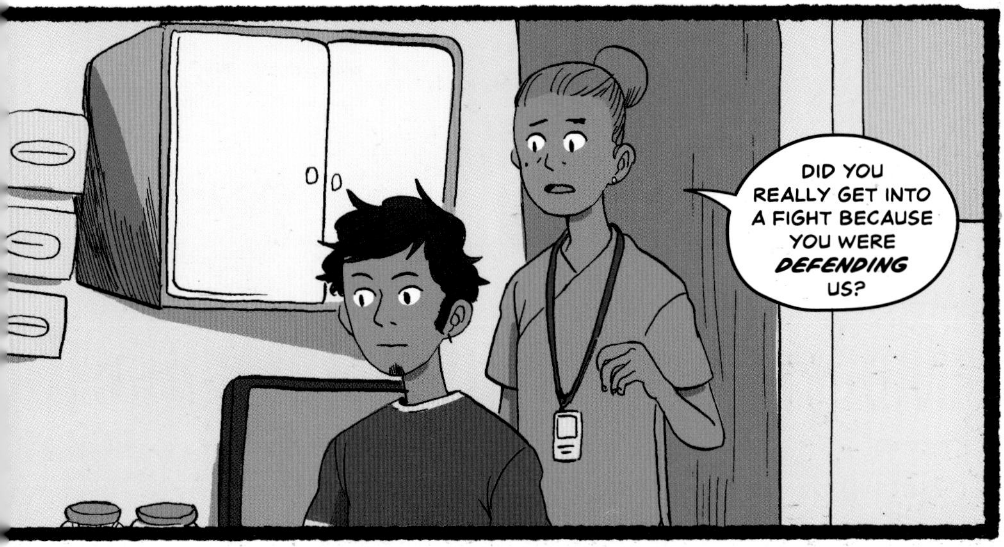
DID YOU REALLY GET INTO A FIGHT BECAUSE YOU WERE *DEFENDING* US?

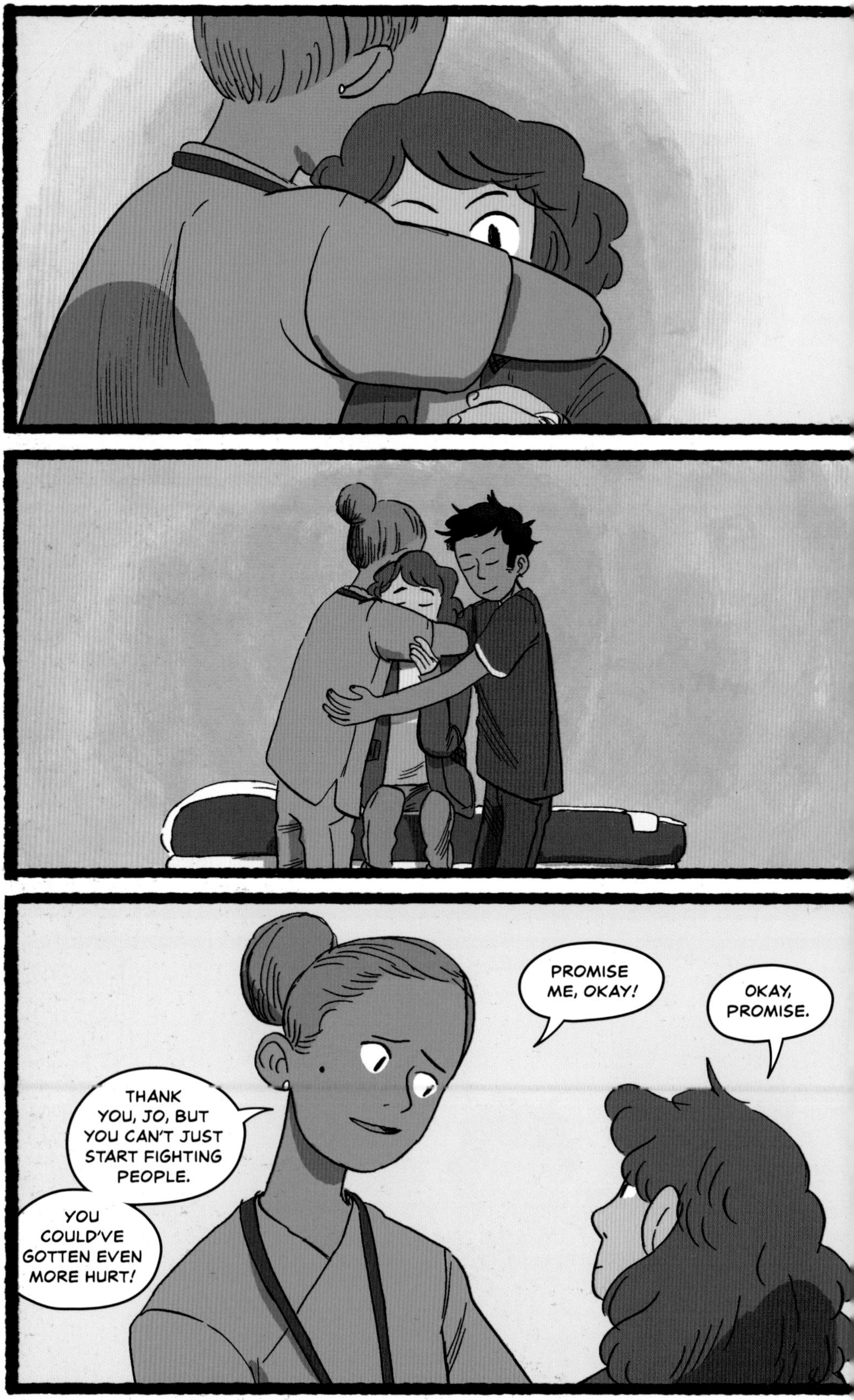
THANK YOU, JO, BUT YOU CAN'T JUST START FIGHTING PEOPLE.
YOU COULD'VE GOTTEN EVEN MORE HURT!
PROMISE ME, OKAY!
OKAY, PROMISE.

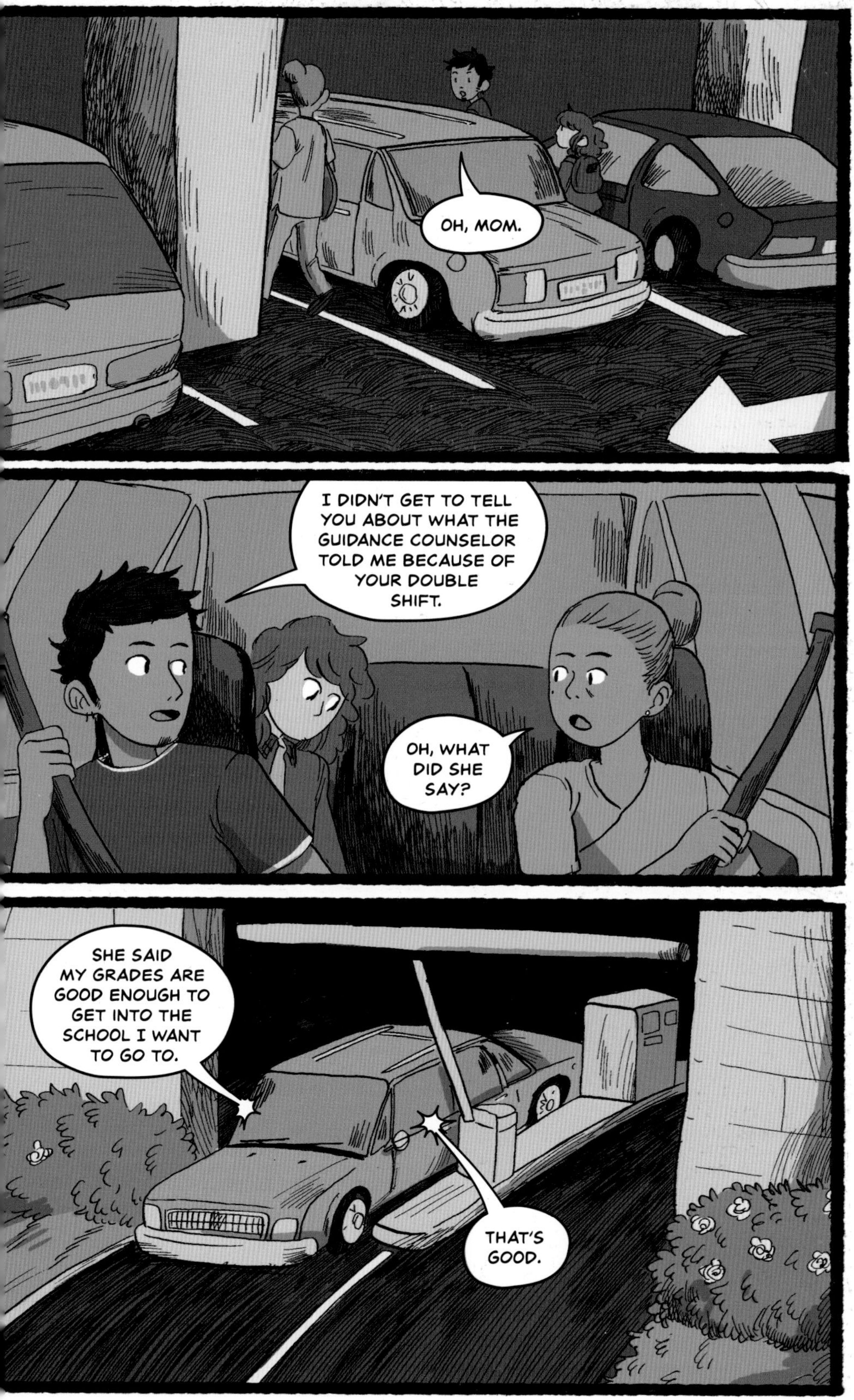
OH, MOM.
I DIDN'T GET TO TELL YOU ABOUT WHAT THE GUIDANCE COUNSELOR TOLD ME BECAUSE OF YOUR DOUBLE SHIFT.
OH, WHAT DID SHE SAY?
SHE SAID MY GRADES ARE GOOD ENOUGH TO GET INTO THE SCHOOL I WANT TO GO TO.
THAT'S GOOD.

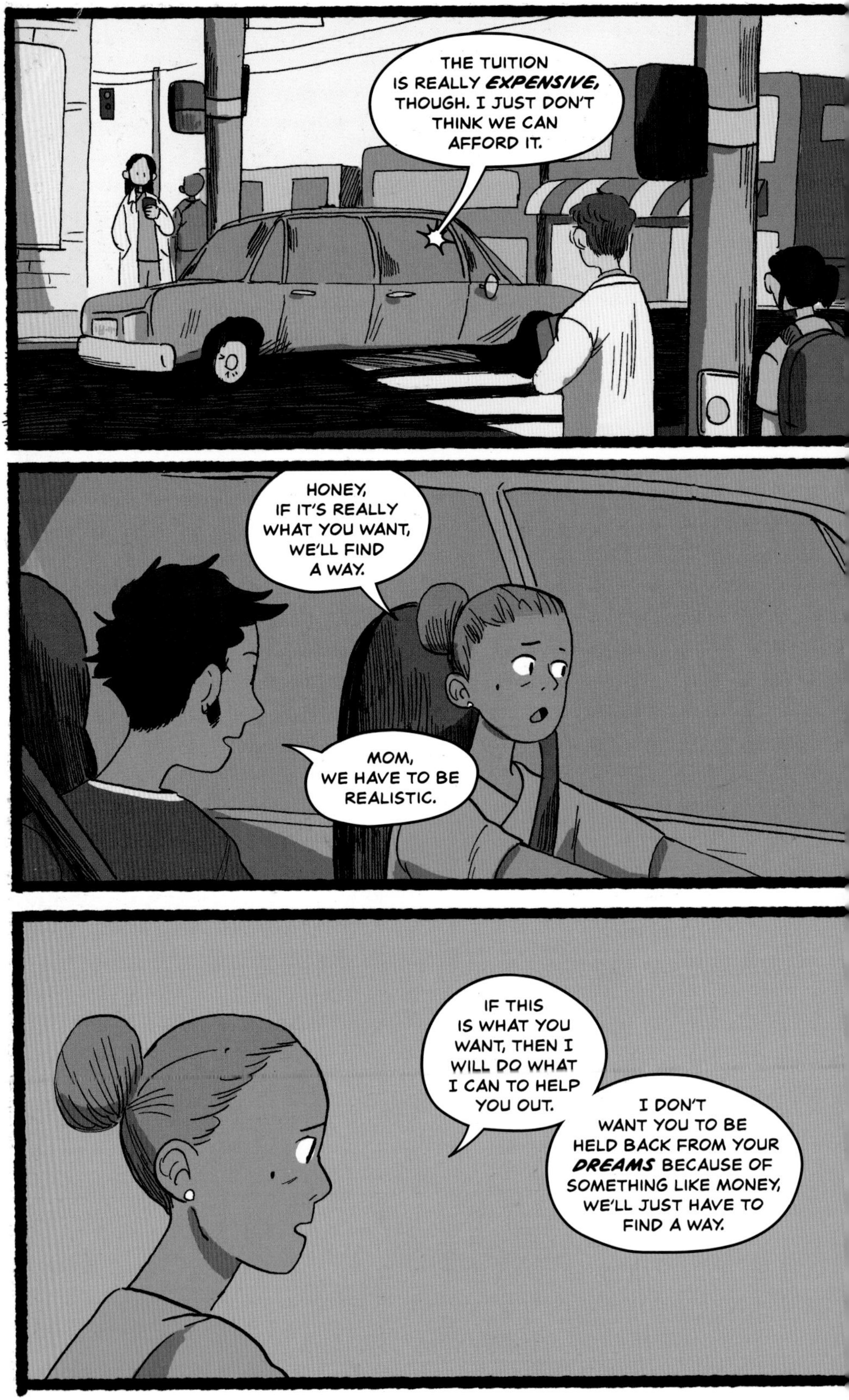
THE TUITION IS REALLY *EXPENSIVE,* THOUGH. I JUST DON'T THINK WE CAN AFFORD IT.
HONEY, IF IT'S REALLY WHAT YOU WANT, WE'LL FIND A WAY.
MOM, WE HAVE TO BE REALISTIC.
IF THIS IS WHAT YOU WANT, THEN I WILL DO WHAT I CAN TO HELP YOU OUT.
I DON'T WANT YOU TO BE HELD BACK FROM YOUR *DREAMS* BECAUSE OF SOMETHING LIKE MONEY, WE'LL JUST HAVE TO FIND A WAY.

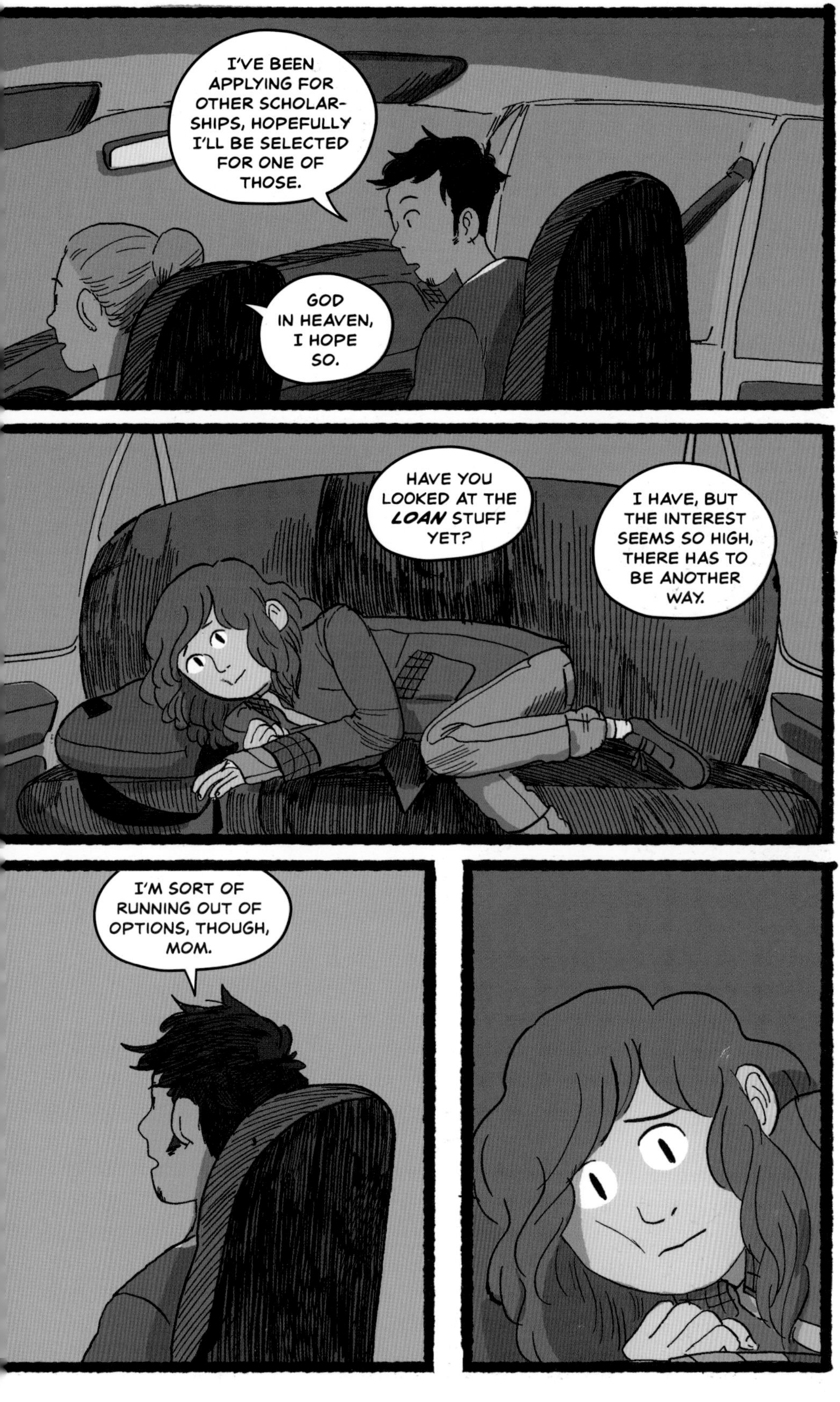
I'VE BEEN APPLYING FOR OTHER SCHOLAR-SHIPS, HOPEFULLY I'LL BE SELECTED FOR ONE OF THOSE.
GOD IN HEAVEN, I HOPE SO.
HAVE YOU LOOKED AT THE *LOAN* STUFF YET?
I HAVE, BUT THE INTEREST SEEMS SO HIGH, THERE HAS TO BE ANOTHER WAY.
I'M SORT OF RUNNING OUT OF OPTIONS, THOUGH, MOM.

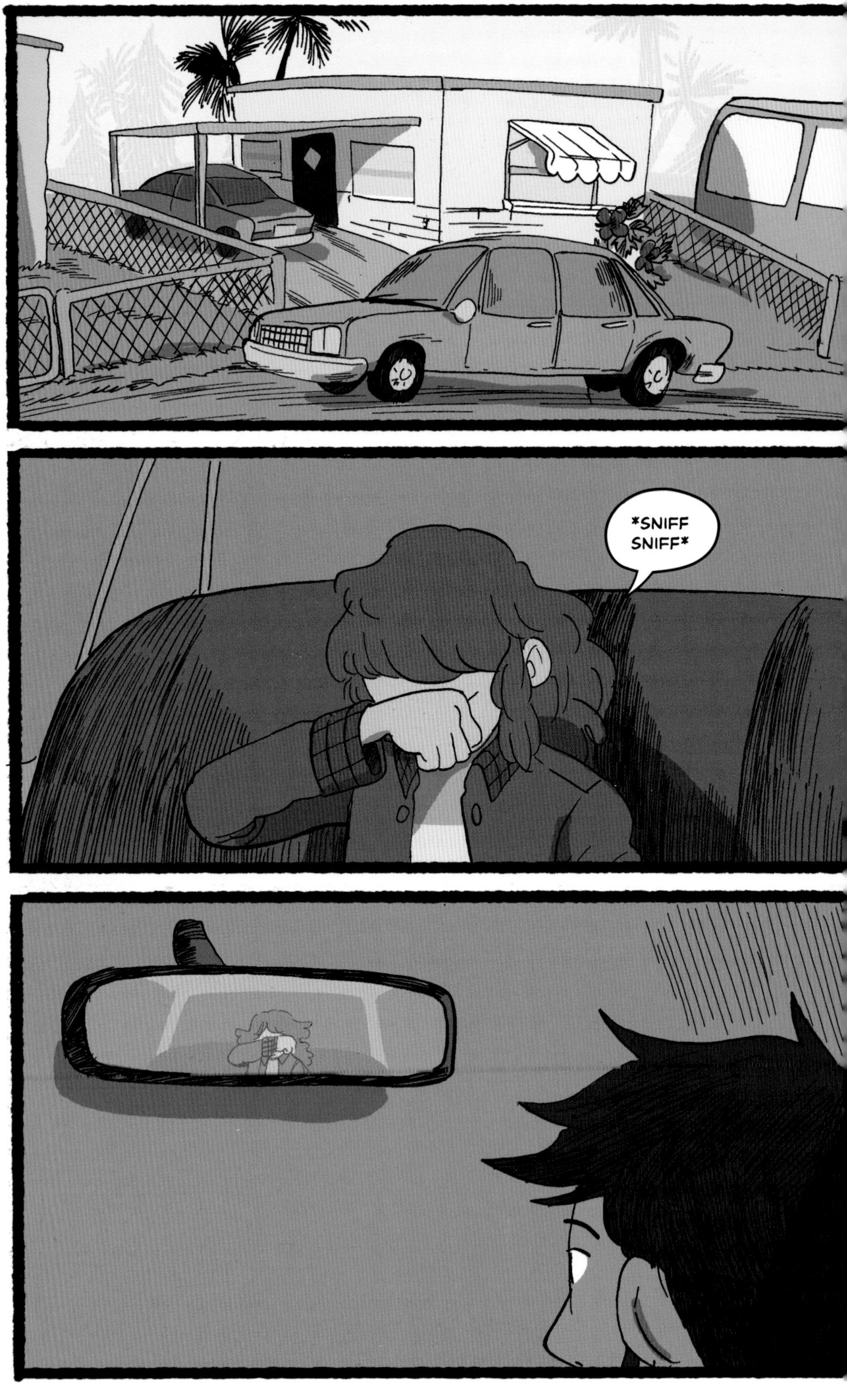
SNIFF SNIFF

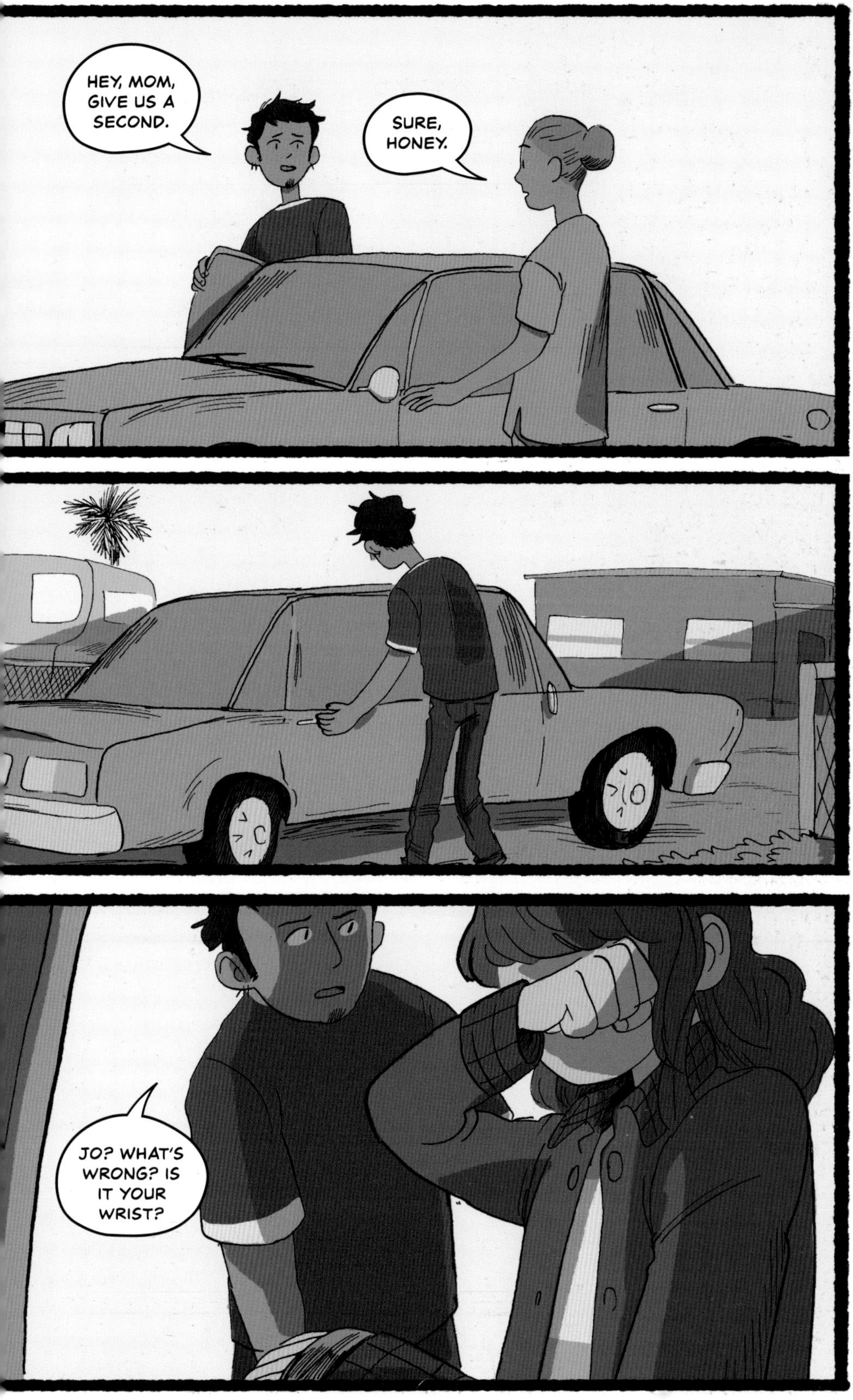
HEY, MOM, GIVE US A SECOND.
SURE, HONEY.
JO? WHAT'S WRONG? IS IT YOUR WRIST?

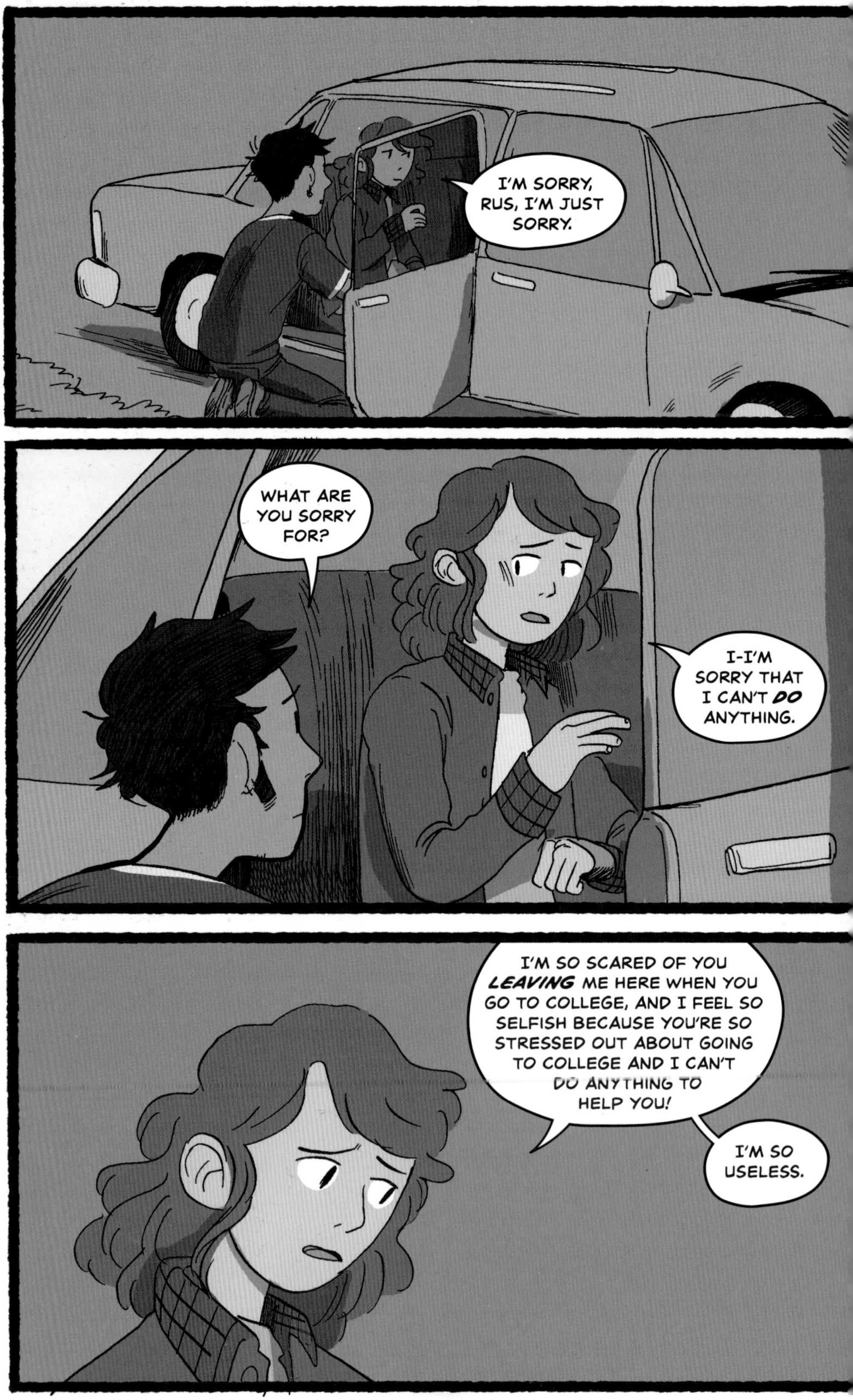
I'M SORRY, RUS, I'M JUST SORRY.
WHAT ARE YOU SORRY FOR?
I-I'M SORRY THAT I CAN'T *DO* ANYTHING.
I'M SO SCARED OF YOU *LEAVING* ME HERE WHEN YOU GO TO COLLEGE, AND I FEEL SO SELFISH BECAUSE YOU'RE SO STRESSED OUT ABOUT GOING TO COLLEGE AND I CAN'T DO ANYTHING TO HELP YOU!
I'M SO USELESS.

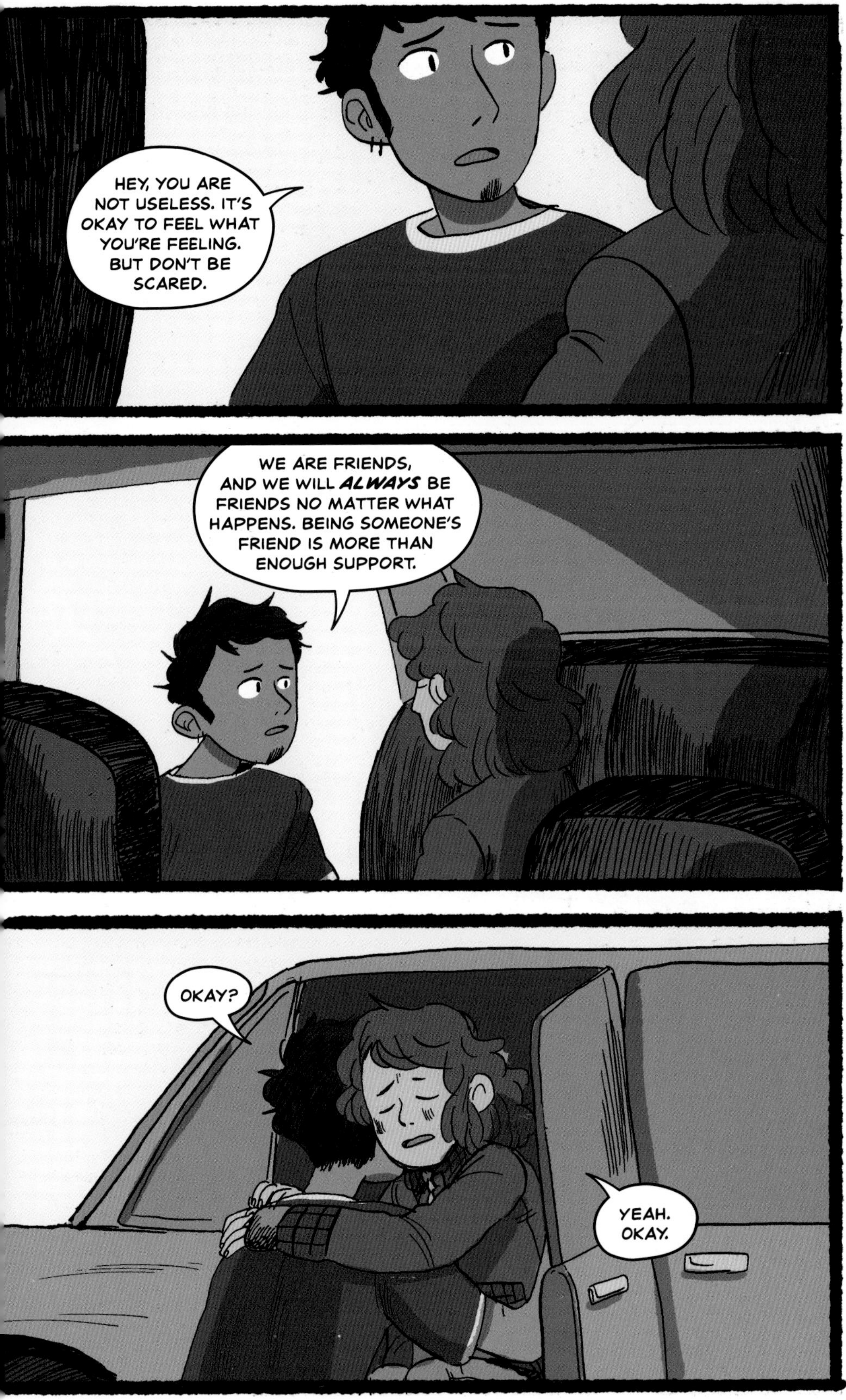
HEY, YOU ARE NOT USELESS. IT'S OKAY TO FEEL WHAT YOU'RE FEELING. BUT DON'T BE SCARED.
WE ARE FRIENDS, AND WE WILL *ALWAYS* BE FRIENDS NO MATTER WHAT HAPPENS. BEING SOMEONE'S FRIEND IS MORE THAN ENOUGH SUPPORT.
OKAY?
YEAH. OKAY.

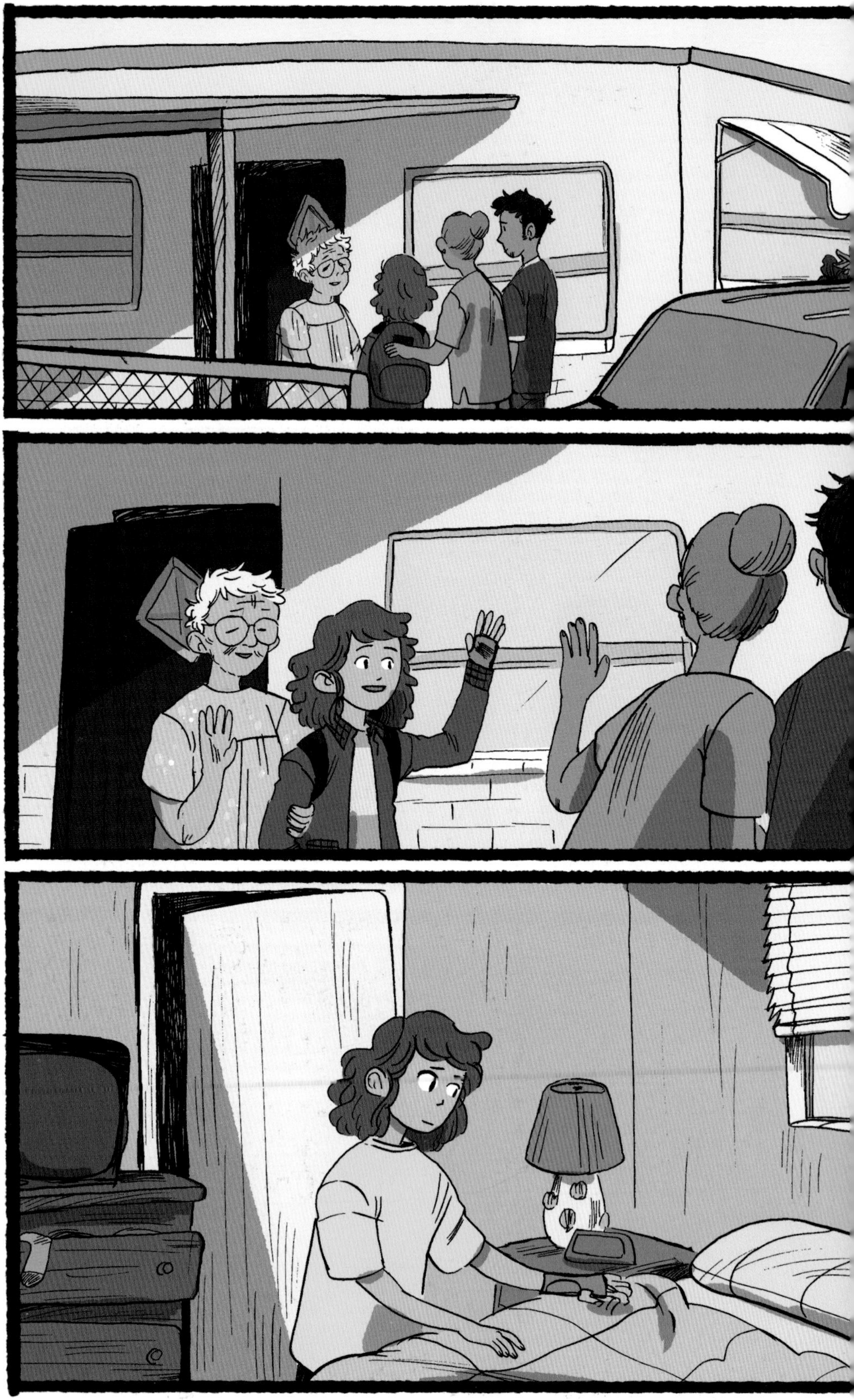

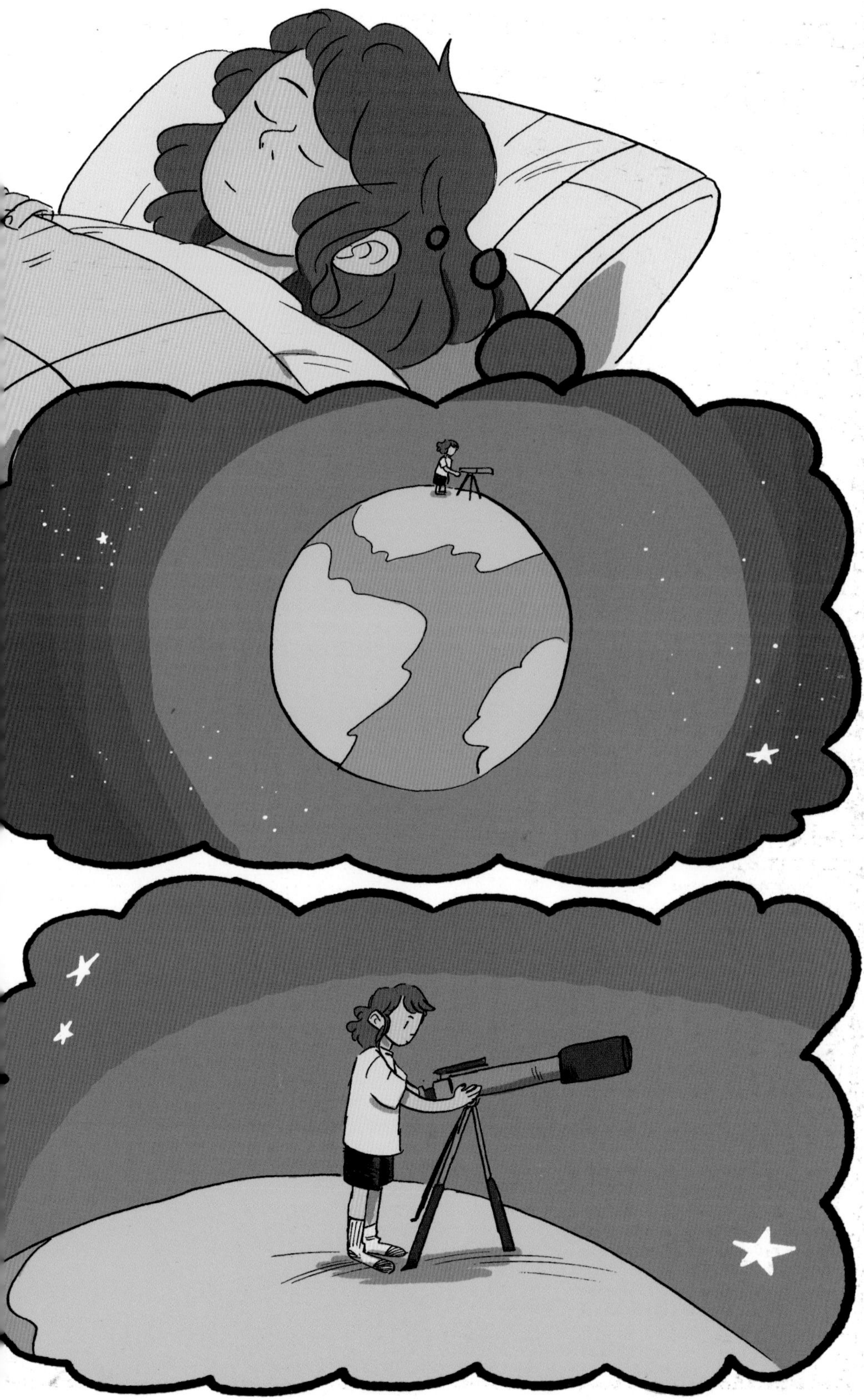

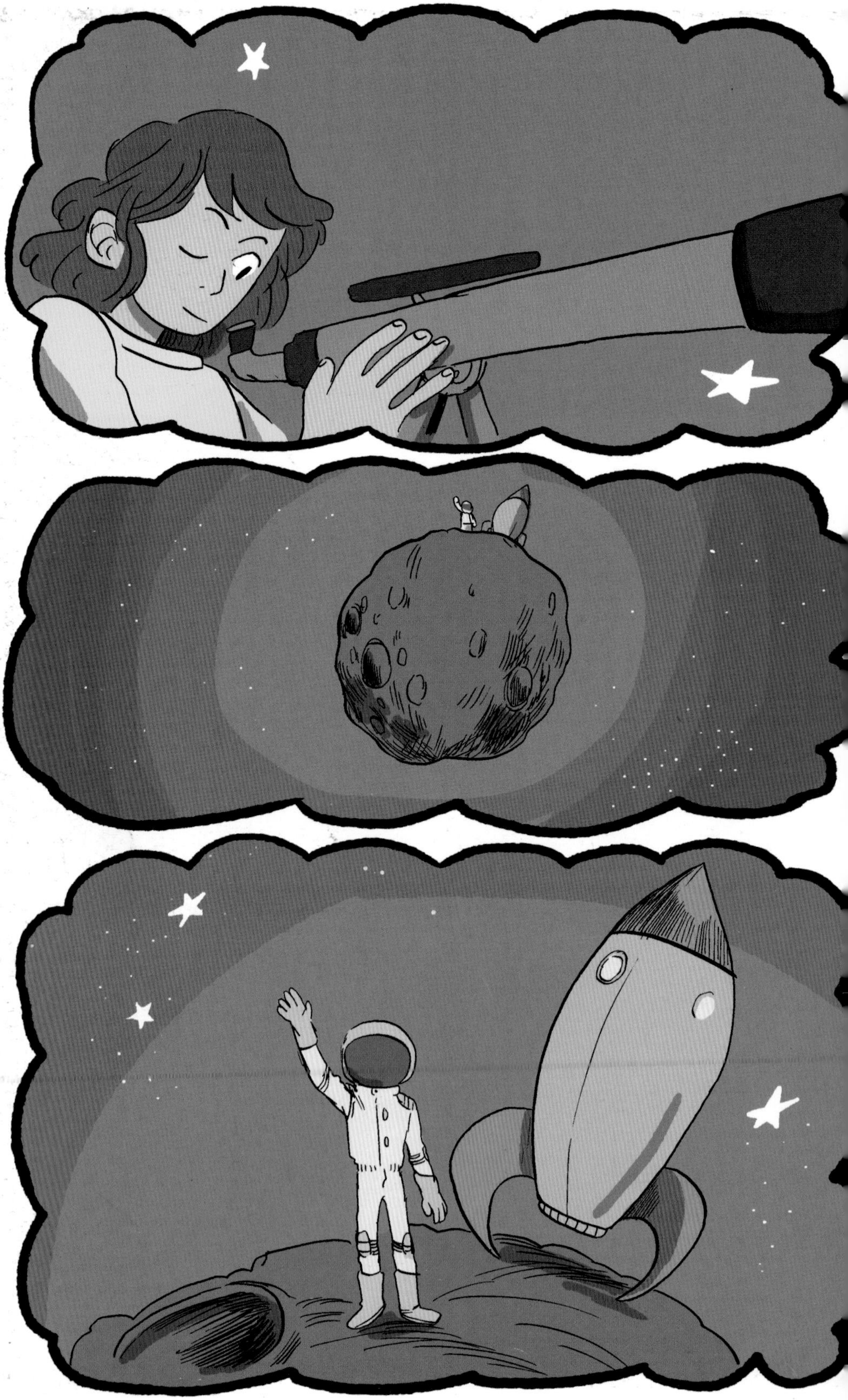

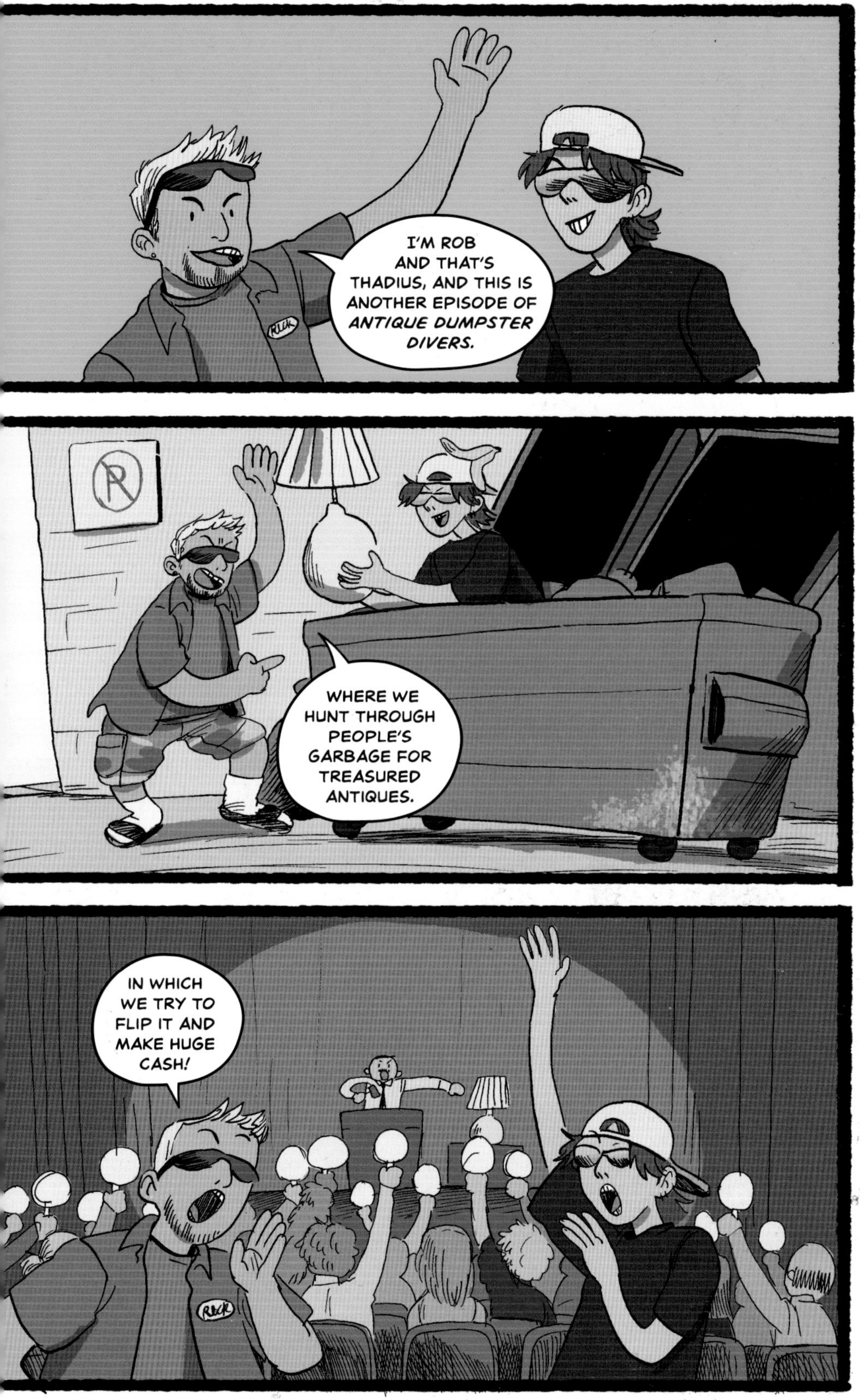
I'M ROB AND THAT'S THADIUS, AND THIS IS ANOTHER EPISODE OF *ANTIQUE DUMPSTER DIVERS.*
WHERE WE HUNT THROUGH PEOPLE'S GARBAGE FOR TREASURED ANTIQUES.
IN WHICH WE TRY TO FLIP IT AND MAKE HUGE CASH!

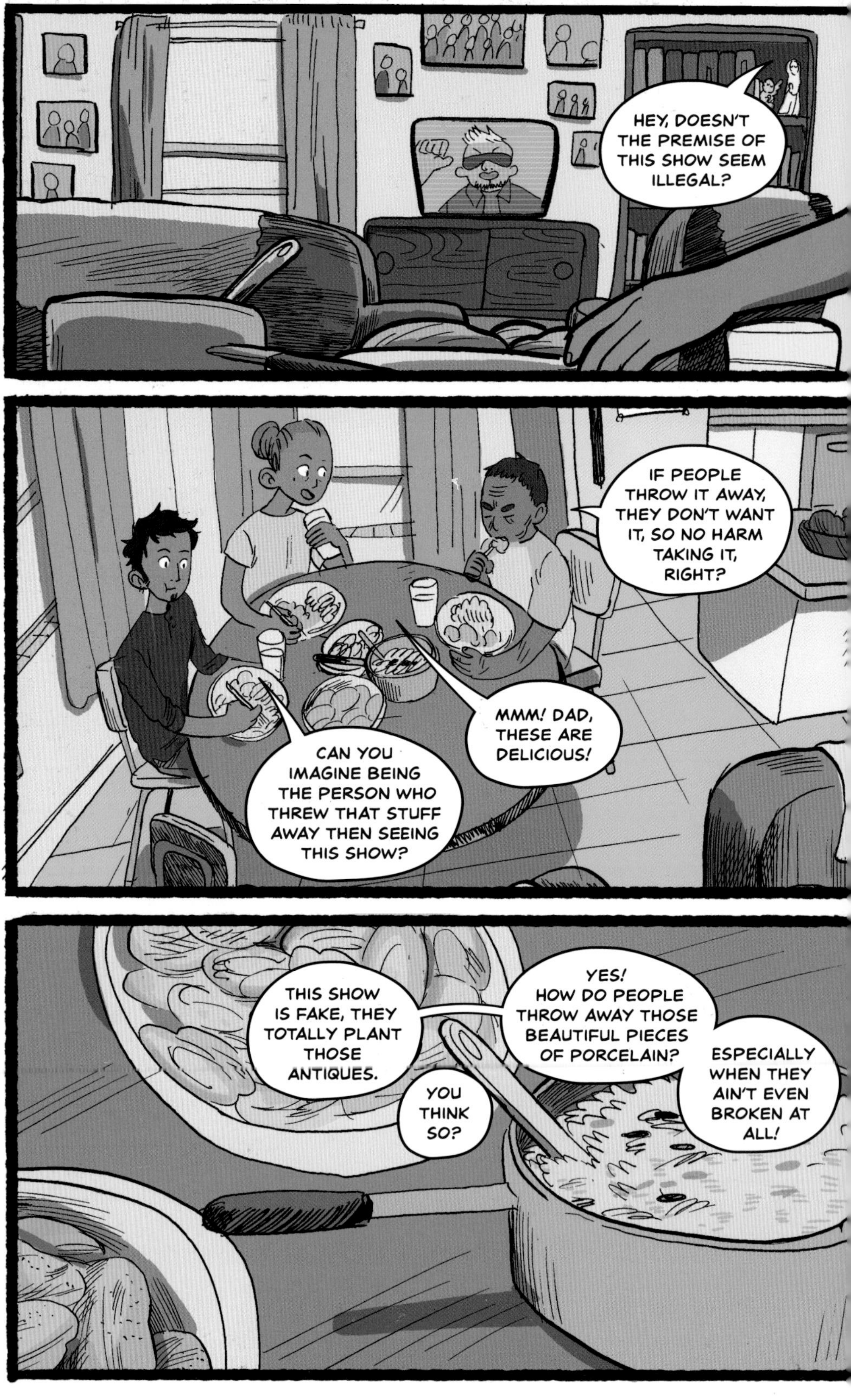
HEY, DOESN'T THE PREMISE OF THIS SHOW SEEM ILLEGAL?
IF PEOPLE THROW IT AWAY, THEY DON'T WANT IT, SO NO HARM TAKING IT, RIGHT?
MMM! DAD, THESE ARE DELICIOUS!
CAN YOU IMAGINE BEING THE PERSON WHO THREW THAT STUFF AWAY THEN SEEING THIS SHOW?
THIS SHOW IS FAKE, THEY TOTALLY PLANT THOSE ANTIQUES.
YES! HOW DO PEOPLE THROW AWAY THOSE BEAUTIFUL PIECES OF PORCELAIN?
YOU THINK SO?
ESPECIALLY WHEN THEY AIN'T EVEN BROKEN AT ALL!

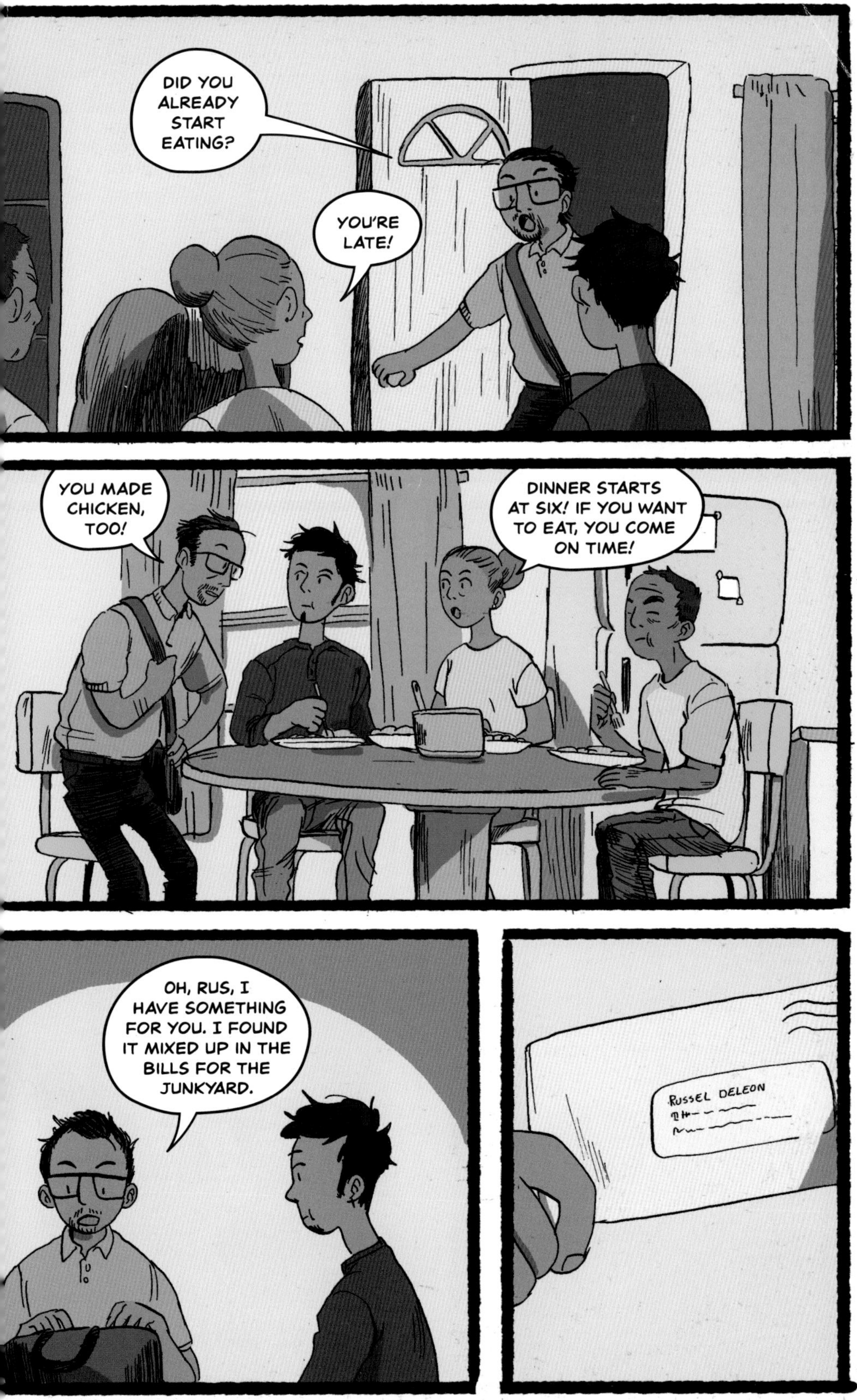
DID YOU ALREADY START EATING?
YOU'RE LATE!
YOU MADE CHICKEN, TOO!
DINNER STARTS AT SIX! IF YOU WANT TO EAT, YOU COME ON TIME!
OH, RUS, I HAVE SOMETHING FOR YOU. I FOUND IT MIXED UP IN THE BILLS FOR THE JUNKYARD.
RUSSEL DELEON

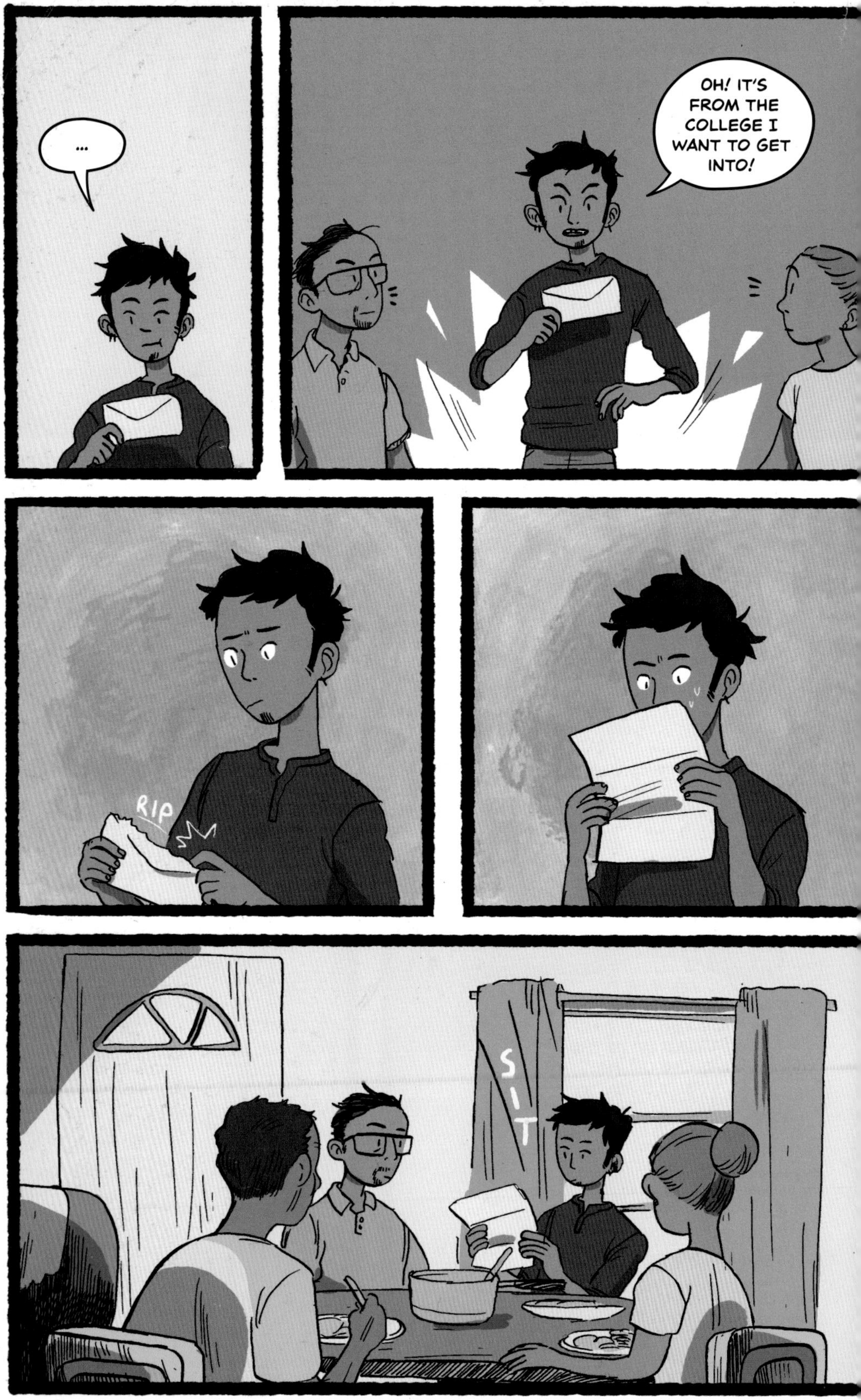
...
OH! IT'S FROM THE COLLEGE I WANT TO GET INTO!
RIP
SIT

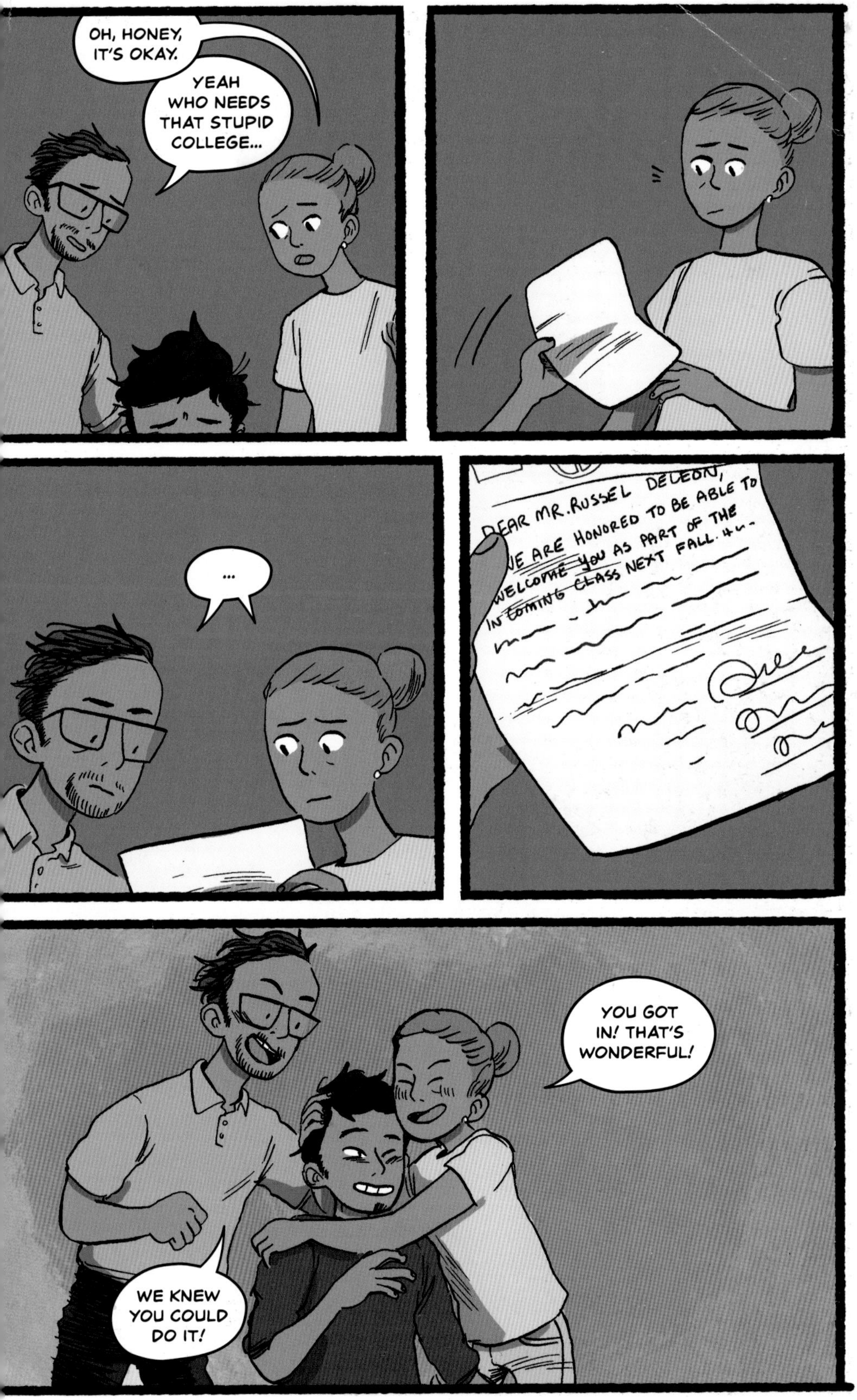
OH, HONEY, IT'S OKAY.
YEAH WHO NEEDS THAT STUPID COLLEGE...
...
DEAR MR. RUSSEL DELEON,
WE ARE HONORED TO BE ABLE TO WELCOME YOU AS PART OF THE INCOMING CLASS NEXT FALL.
YOU GOT IN! THAT'S WONDERFUL!
WE KNEW YOU COULD DO IT!

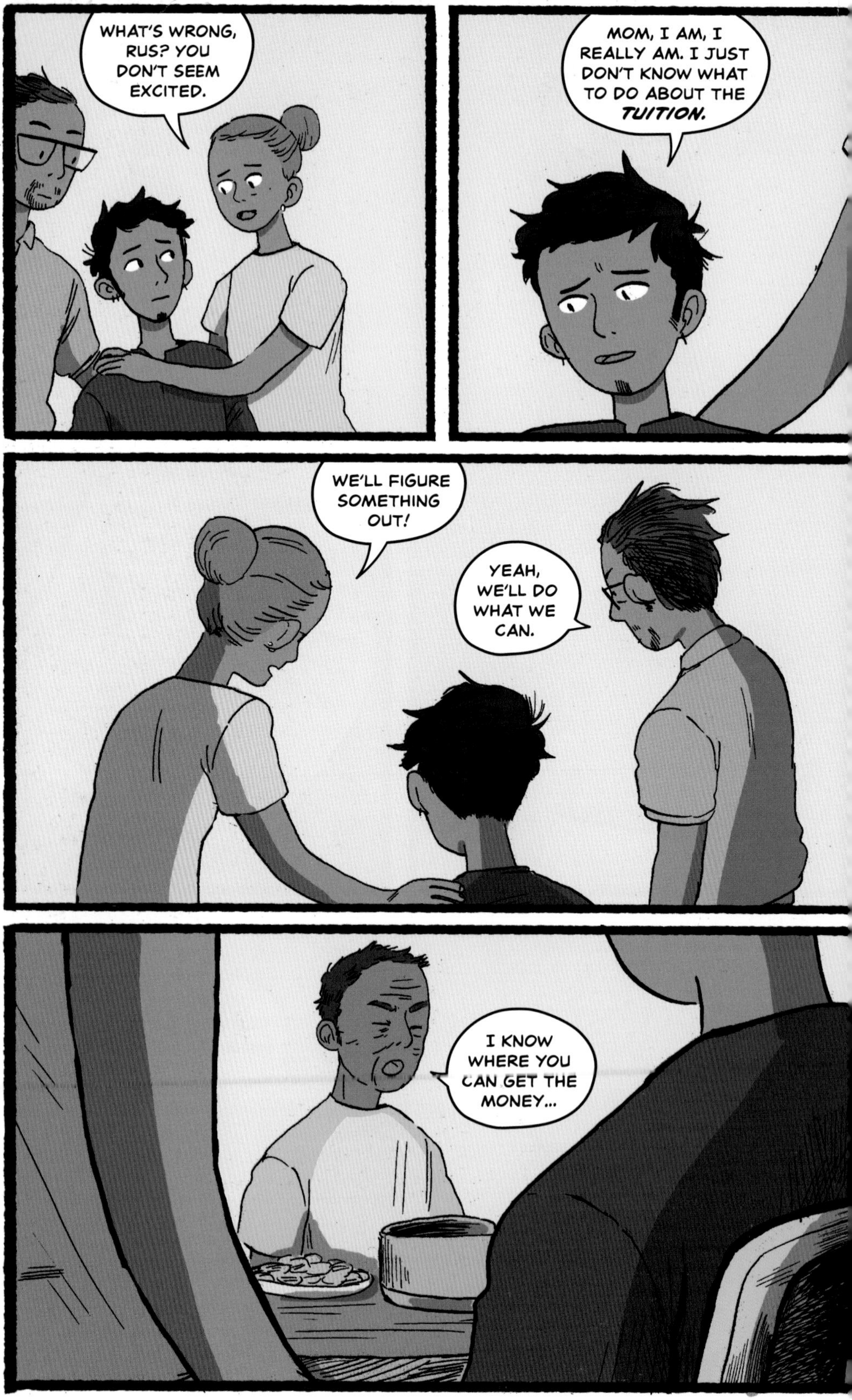
WHAT'S WRONG, RUS? YOU DON'T SEEM EXCITED.
MOM, I AM, I REALLY AM. I JUST DON'T KNOW WHAT TO DO ABOUT THE *TUITION.*
WE'LL FIGURE SOMETHING OUT!
YEAH, WE'LL DO WHAT WE CAN.
I KNOW WHERE YOU CAN GET THE MONEY...

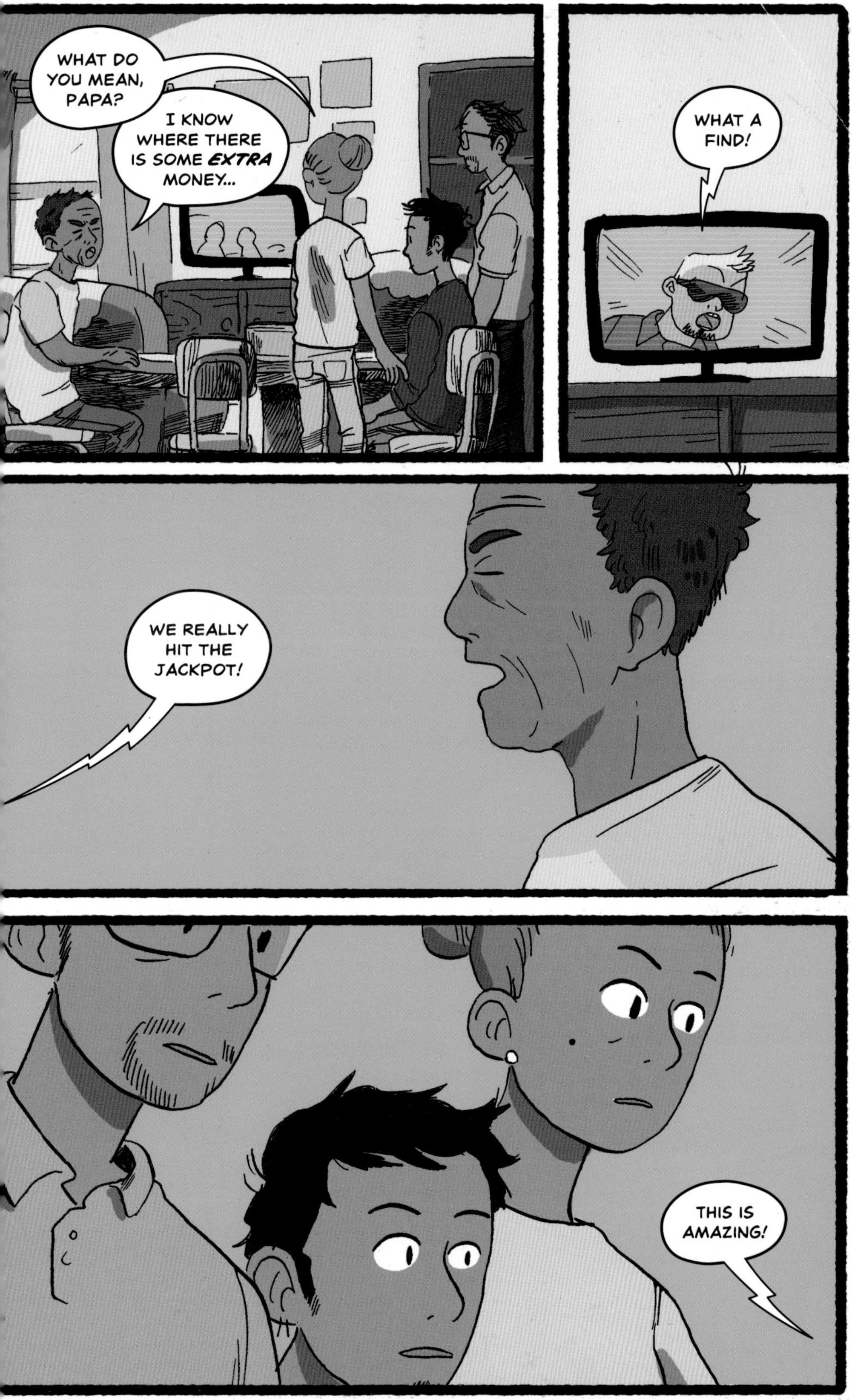

WHAT DO YOU MEAN, PAPA?
I KNOW WHERE THERE IS SOME EXTRA MONEY...
WHAT A FIND!
WE REALLY HIT THE JACKPOT!
THIS IS AMAZING!

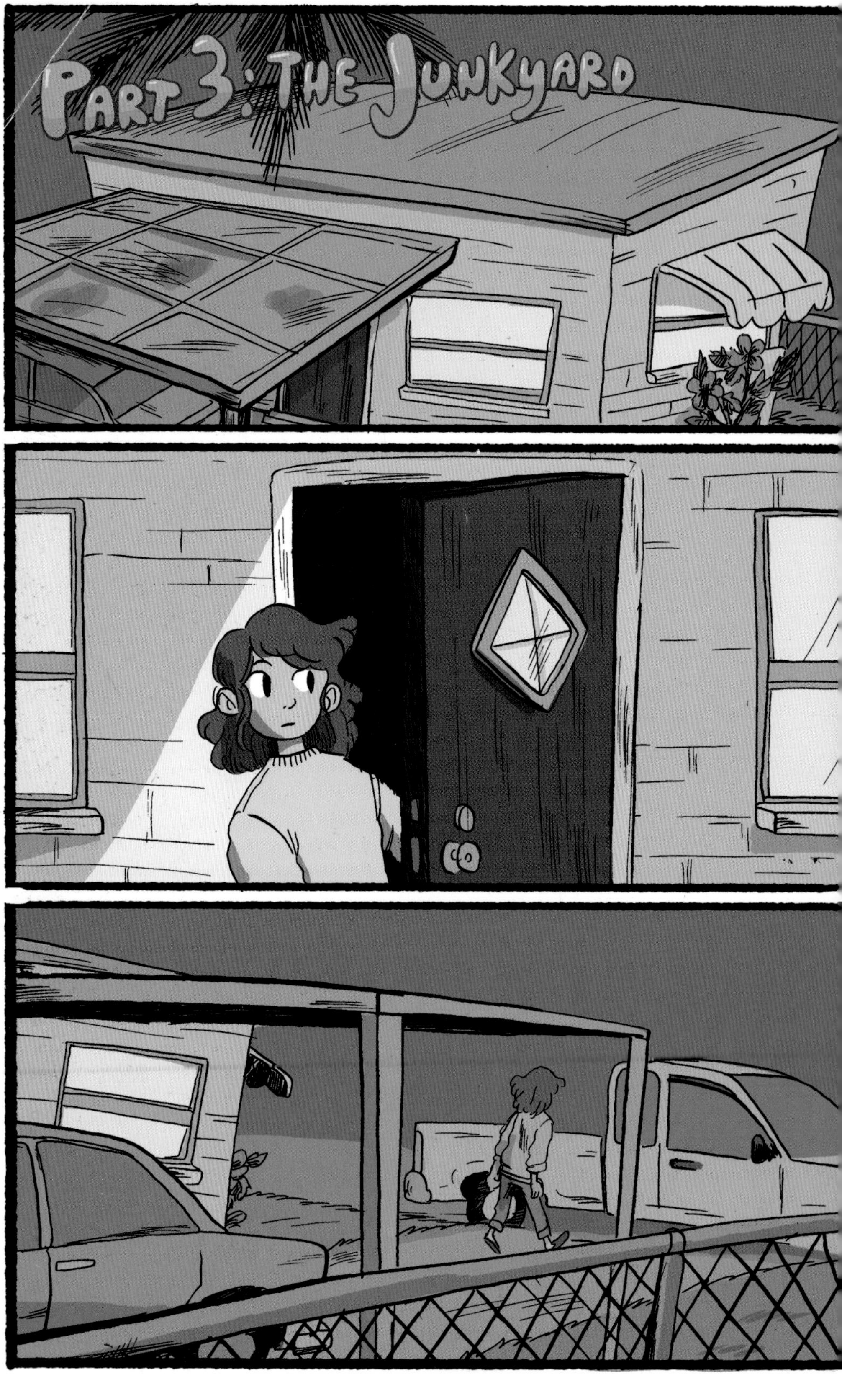
Part 3: The Junkyard

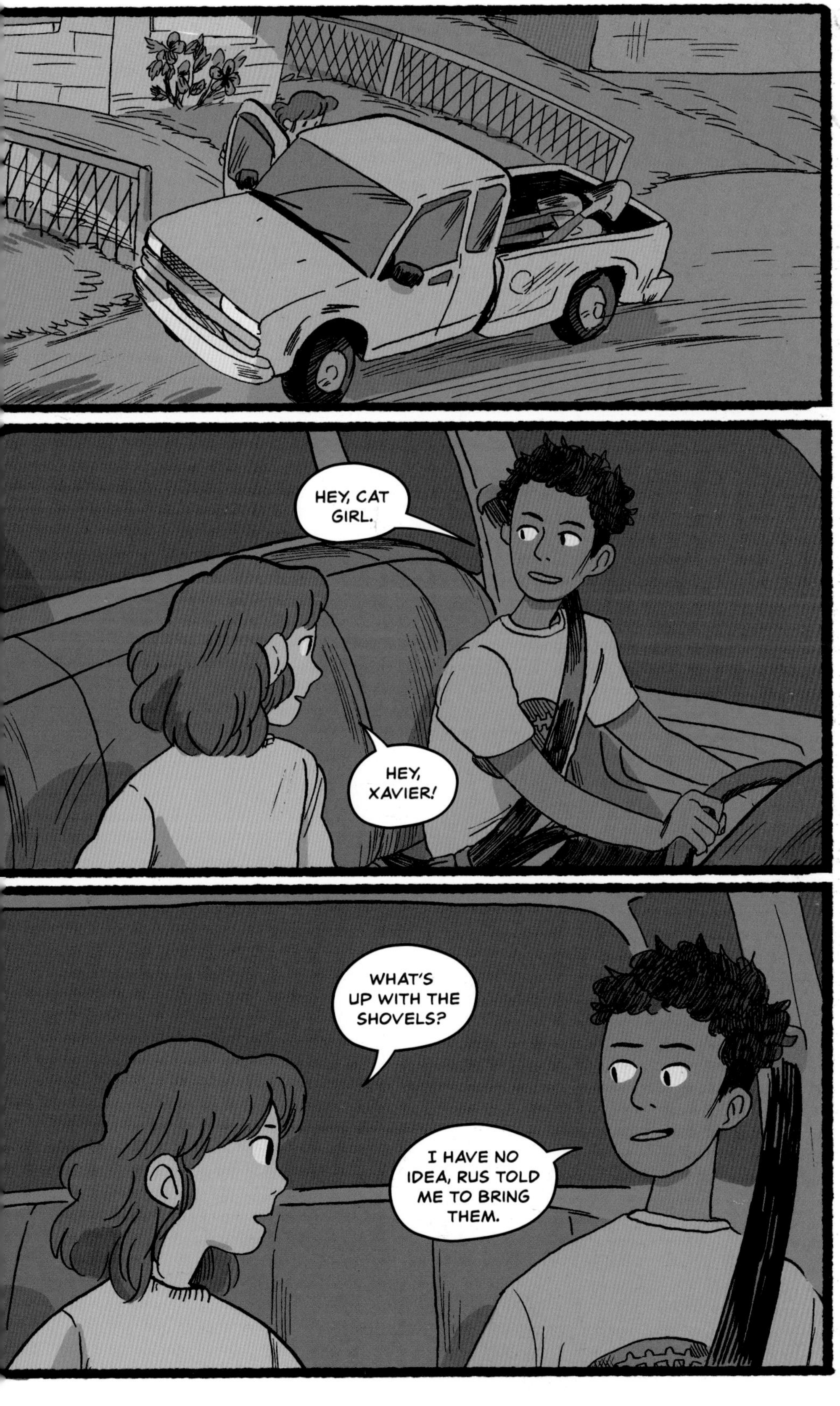
HEY, CAT GIRL.
HEY, XAVIER!
WHAT'S UP WITH THE SHOVELS?
I HAVE NO IDEA, RUS TOLD ME TO BRING THEM.

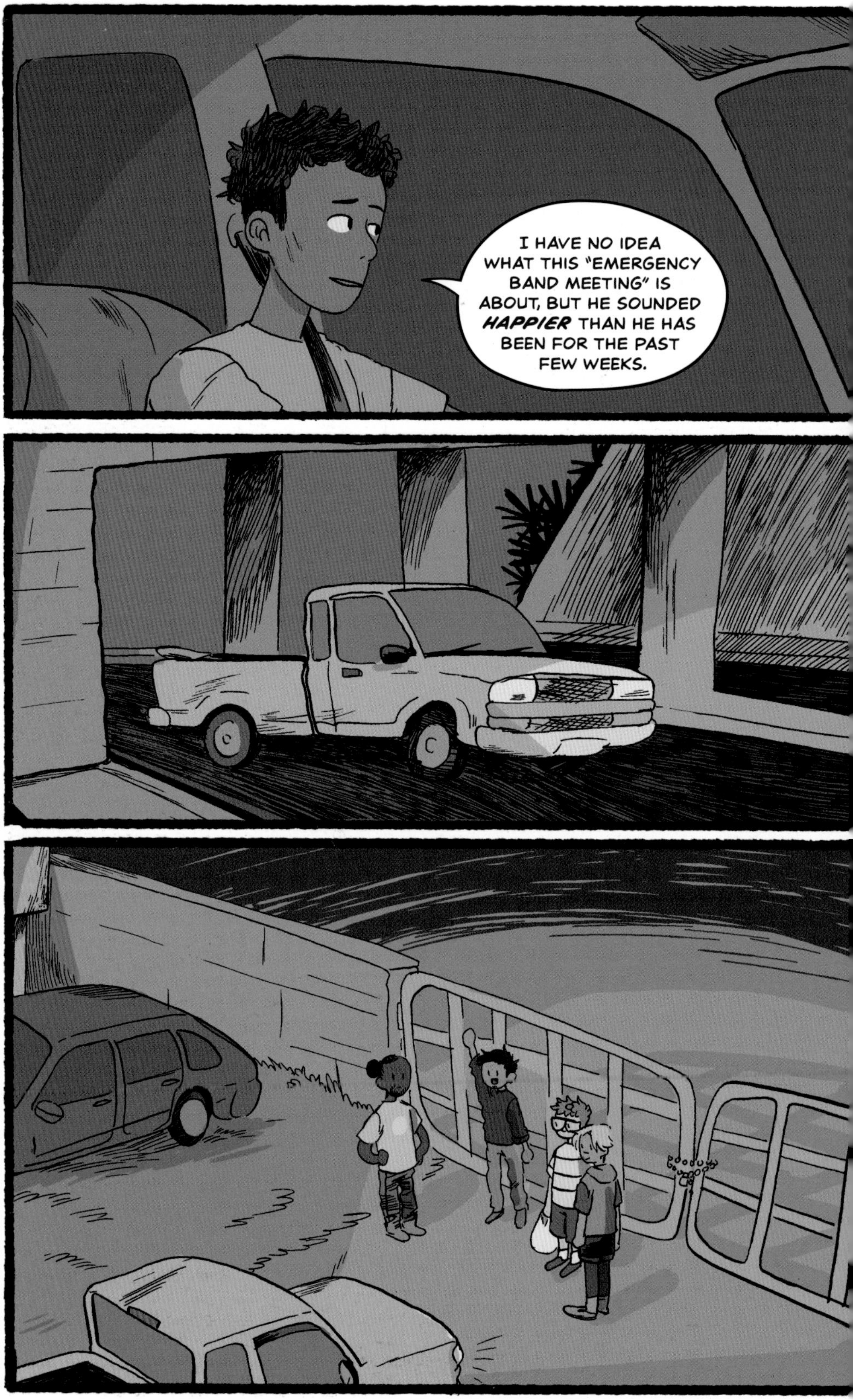
I HAVE NO IDEA WHAT THIS "EMERGENCY BAND MEETING" IS ABOUT, BUT HE SOUNDED *HAPPIER* THAN HE HAS BEEN FOR THE PAST FEW WEEKS.

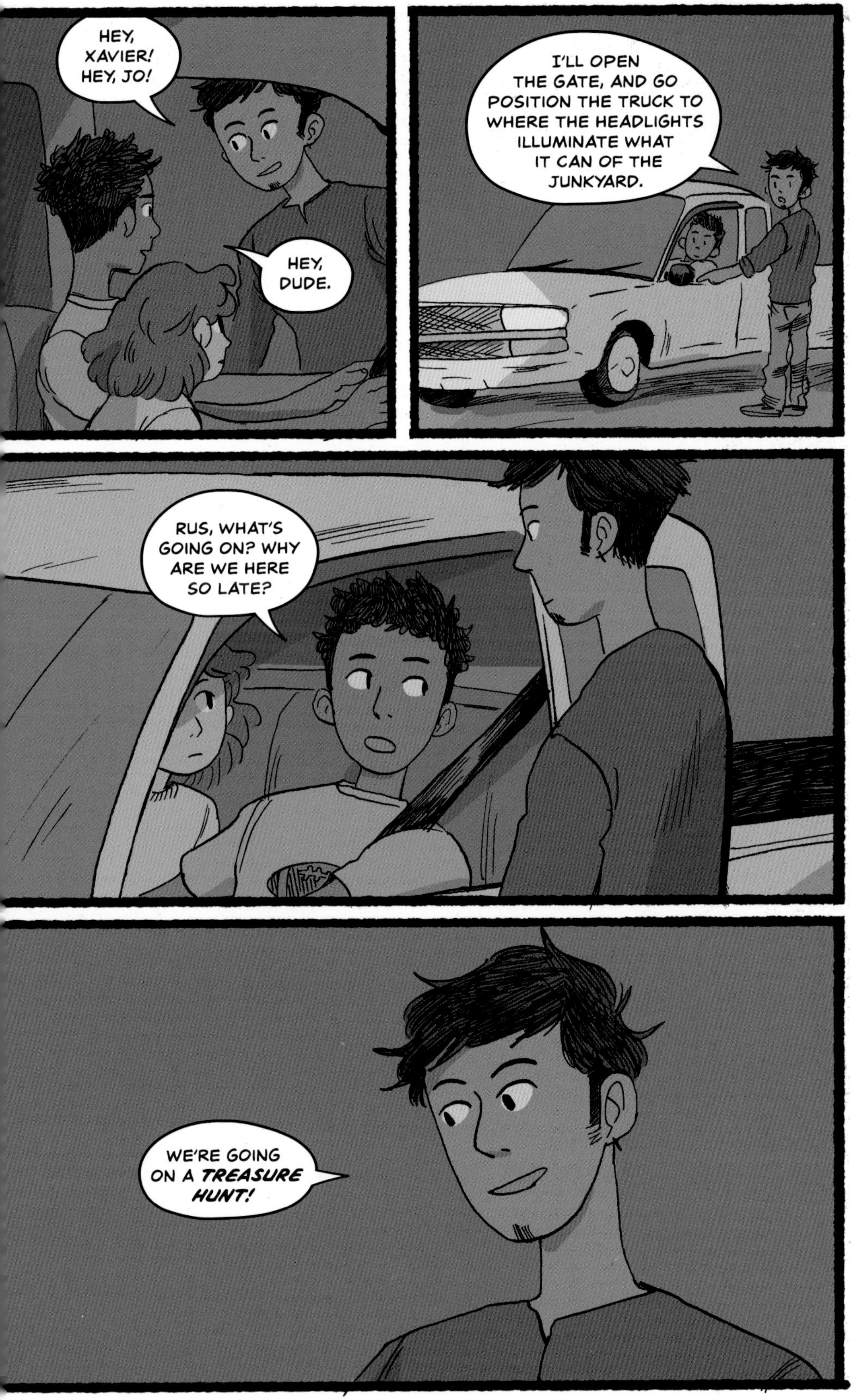
HEY, XAVIER! HEY, JO!
HEY, DUDE.
I'LL OPEN THE GATE, AND GO POSITION THE TRUCK TO WHERE THE HEADLIGHTS ILLUMINATE WHAT IT CAN OF THE JUNKYARD.
RUS, WHAT'S GOING ON? WHY ARE WE HERE SO LATE?
WE'RE GOING ON A *TREASURE HUNT!*

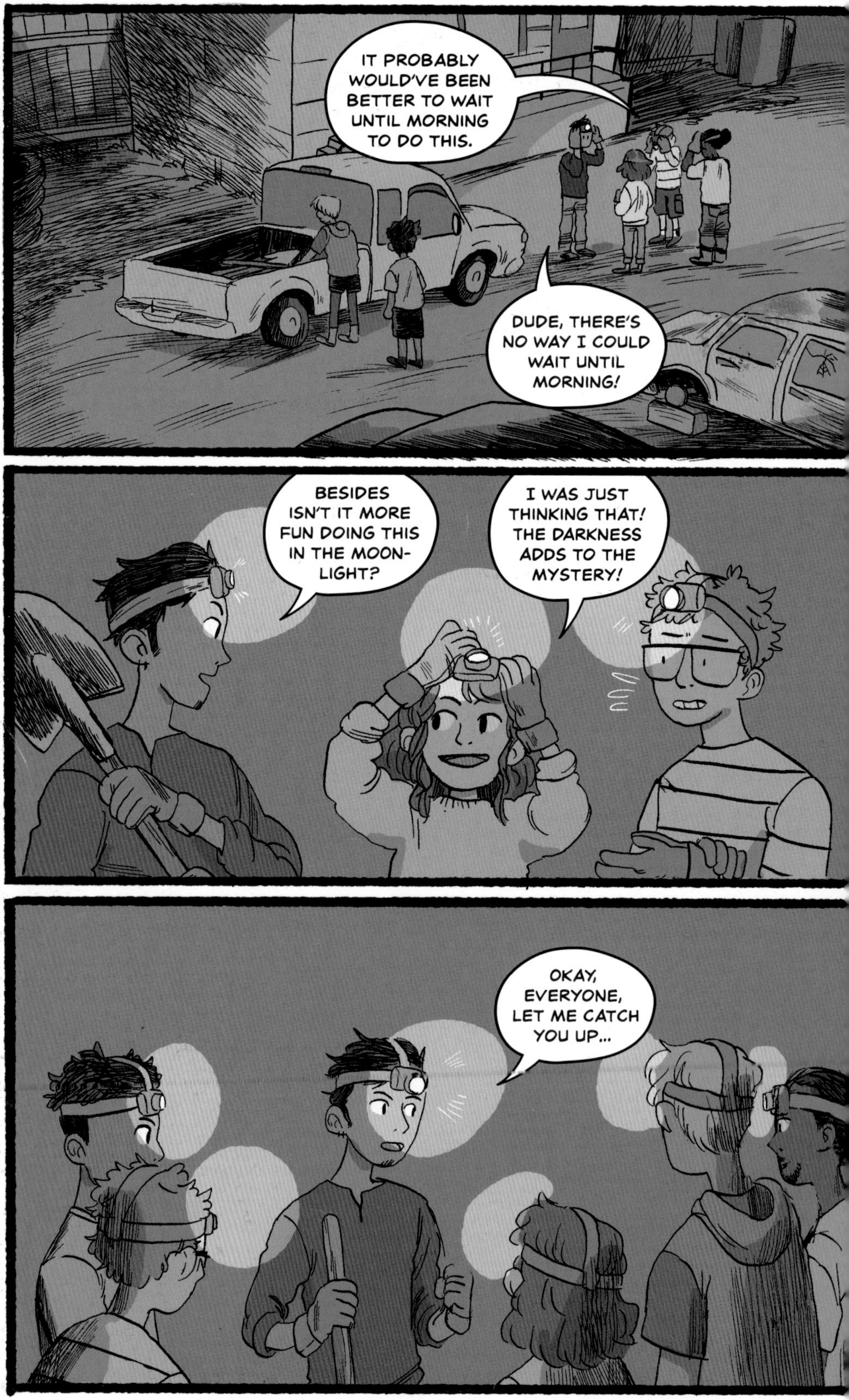
IT PROBABLY WOULD'VE BEEN BETTER TO WAIT UNTIL MORNING TO DO THIS.
DUDE, THERE'S NO WAY I COULD WAIT UNTIL MORNING!
BESIDES ISN'T IT MORE FUN DOING THIS IN THE MOON-LIGHT?
I WAS JUST THINKING THAT! THE DARKNESS ADDS TO THE MYSTERY!
OKAY, EVERYONE, LET ME CATCH YOU UP...

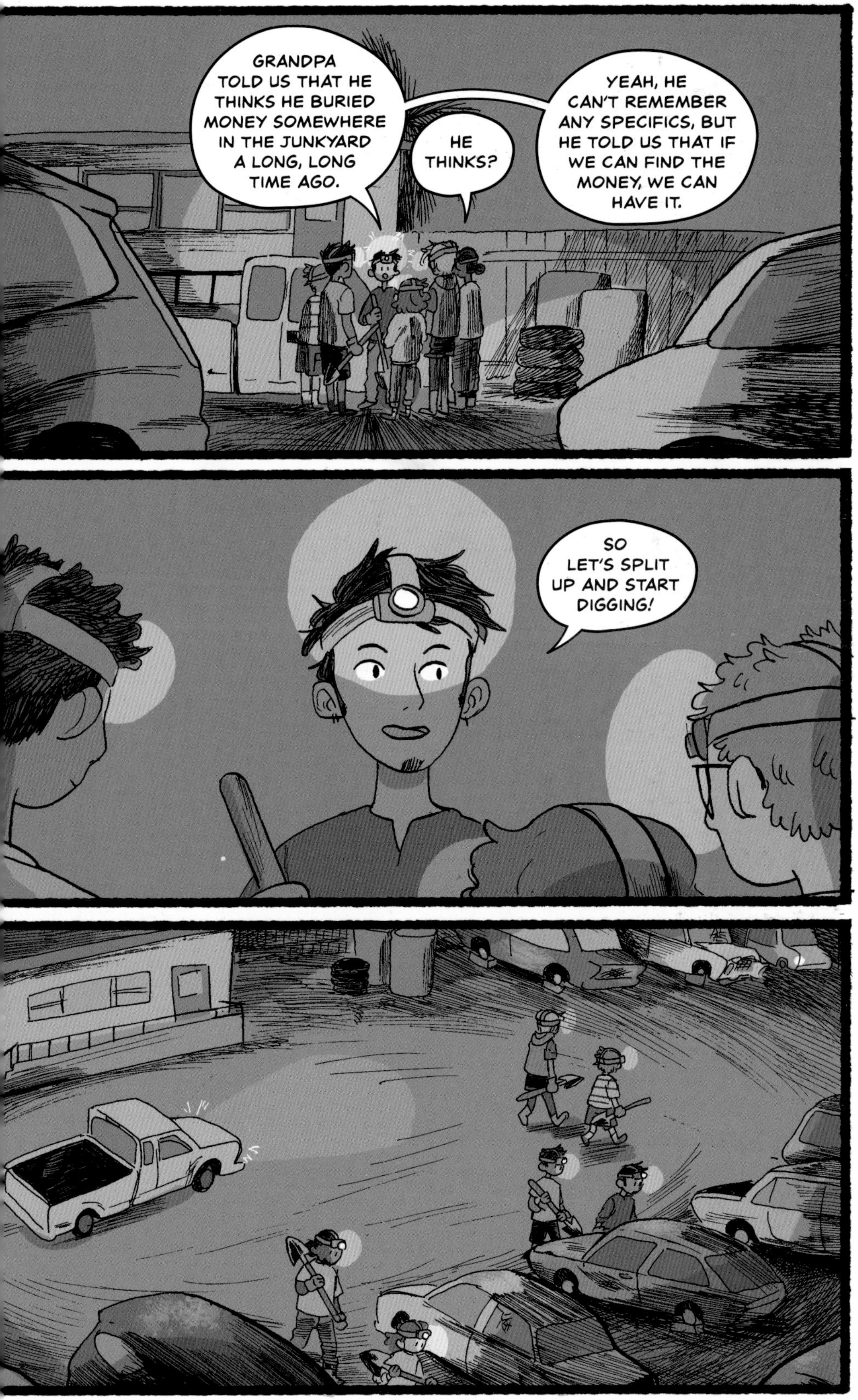
GRANDPA TOLD US THAT HE THINKS HE BURIED MONEY SOMEWHERE IN THE JUNKYARD A LONG, LONG TIME AGO.
HE THINKS?
YEAH, HE CAN'T REMEMBER ANY SPECIFICS, BUT HE TOLD US THAT IF WE CAN FIND THE MONEY, WE CAN HAVE IT.
SO LET'S SPLIT UP AND START DIGGING!

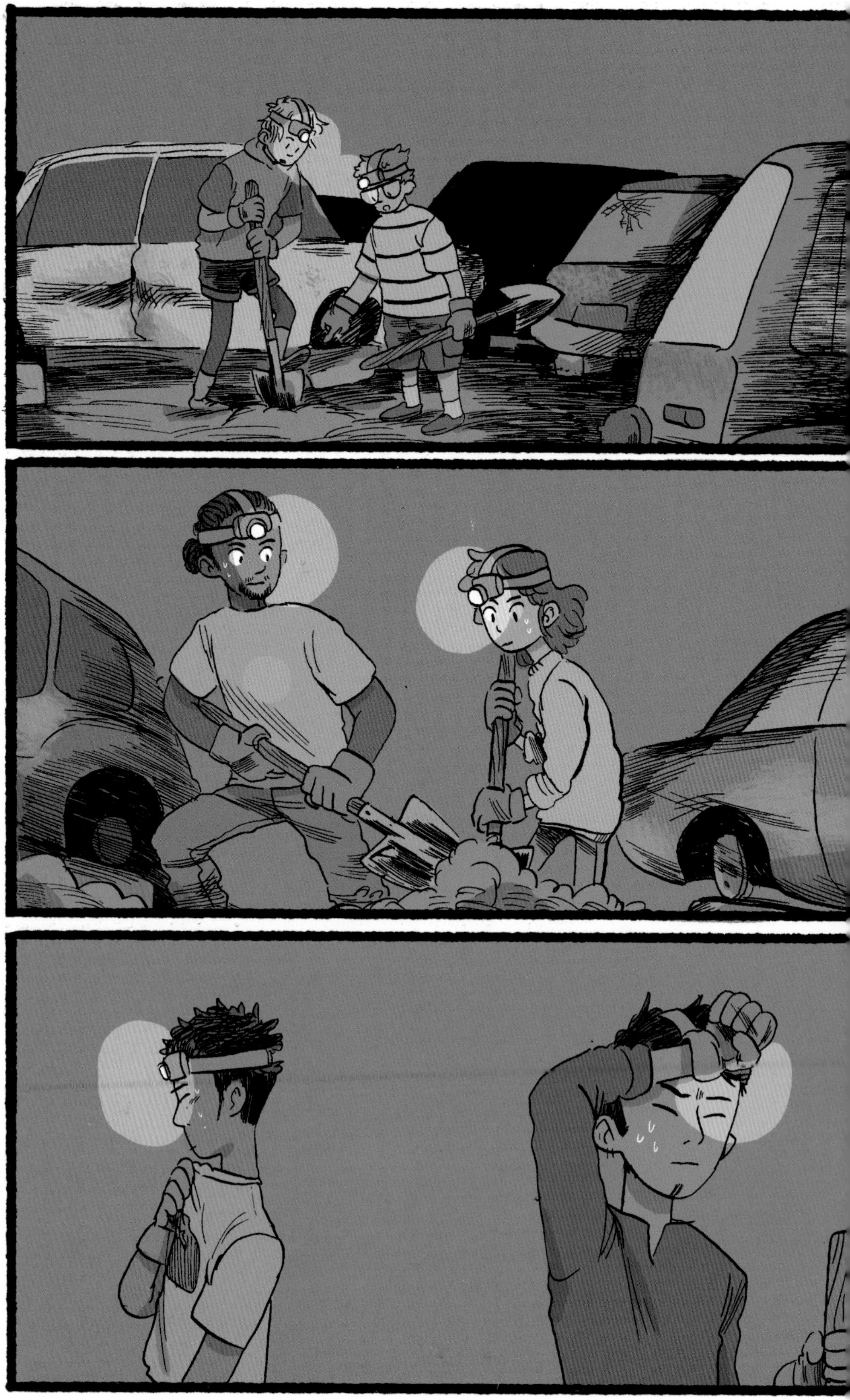

THUNK

!

HEY! I FOUND SOMETHING!

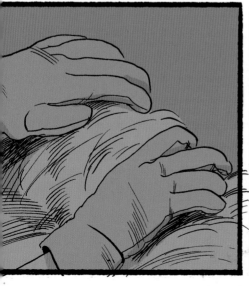

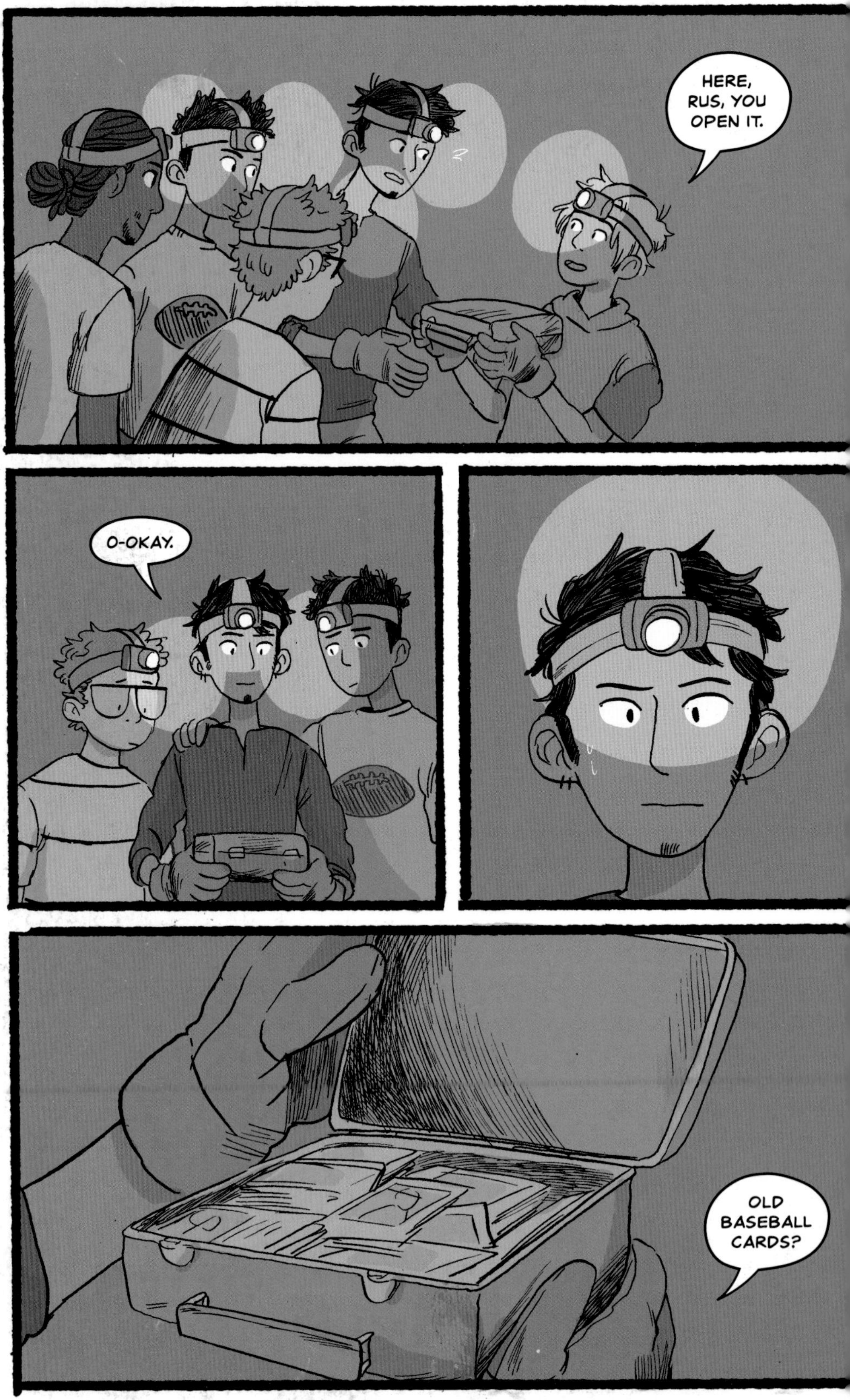
HERE, RUS, YOU OPEN IT.
O-OKAY.
OLD BASEBALL CARDS?

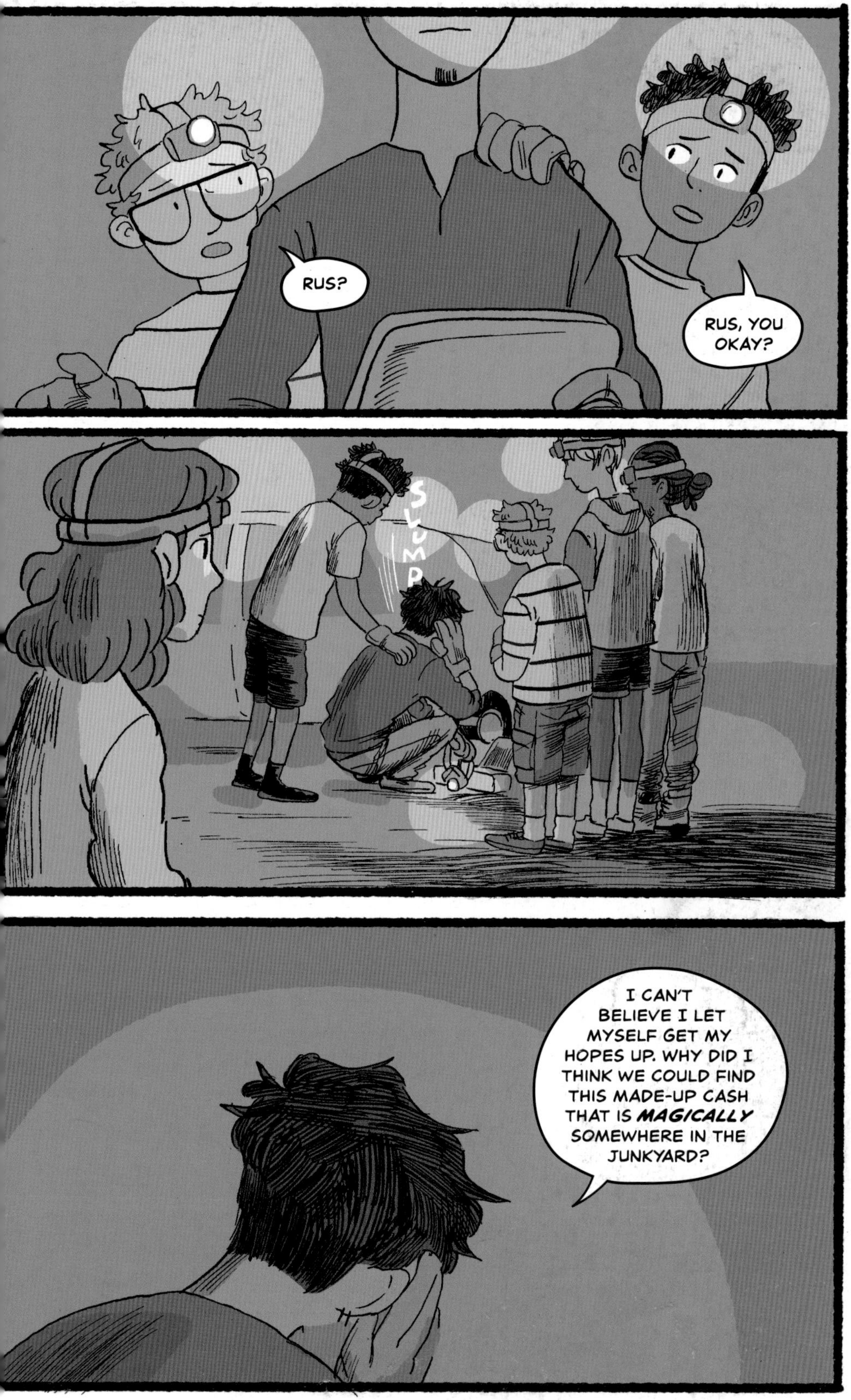
RUS?
RUS, YOU OKAY?
SLUMP
I CAN'T BELIEVE I LET MYSELF GET MY HOPES UP. WHY DID I THINK WE COULD FIND THIS MADE-UP CASH THAT IS *MAGICALLY* SOMEWHERE IN THE JUNKYARD?

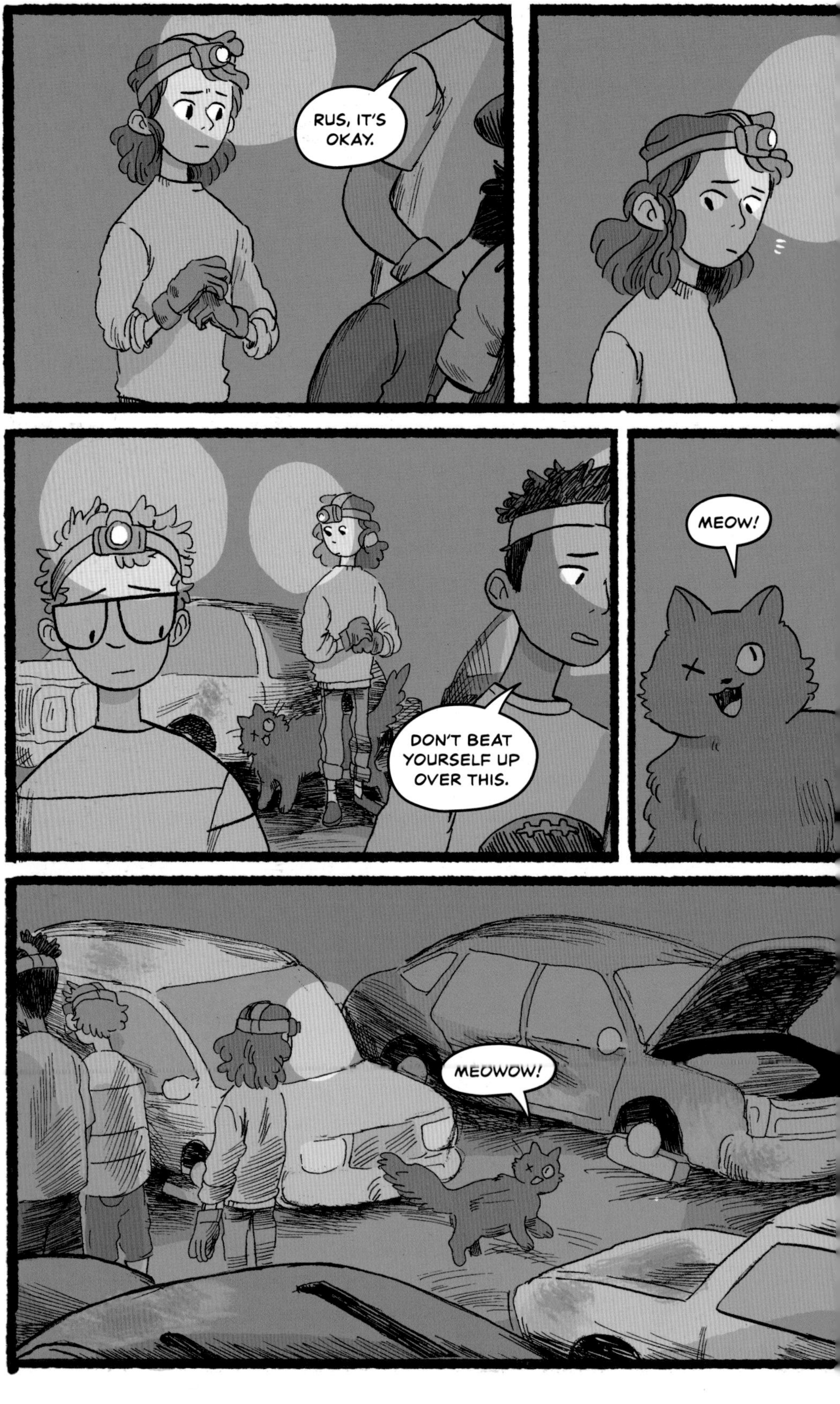
RUS, IT'S OKAY.
DON'T BEAT YOURSELF UP OVER THIS.
MEOW!
MEOWOW!

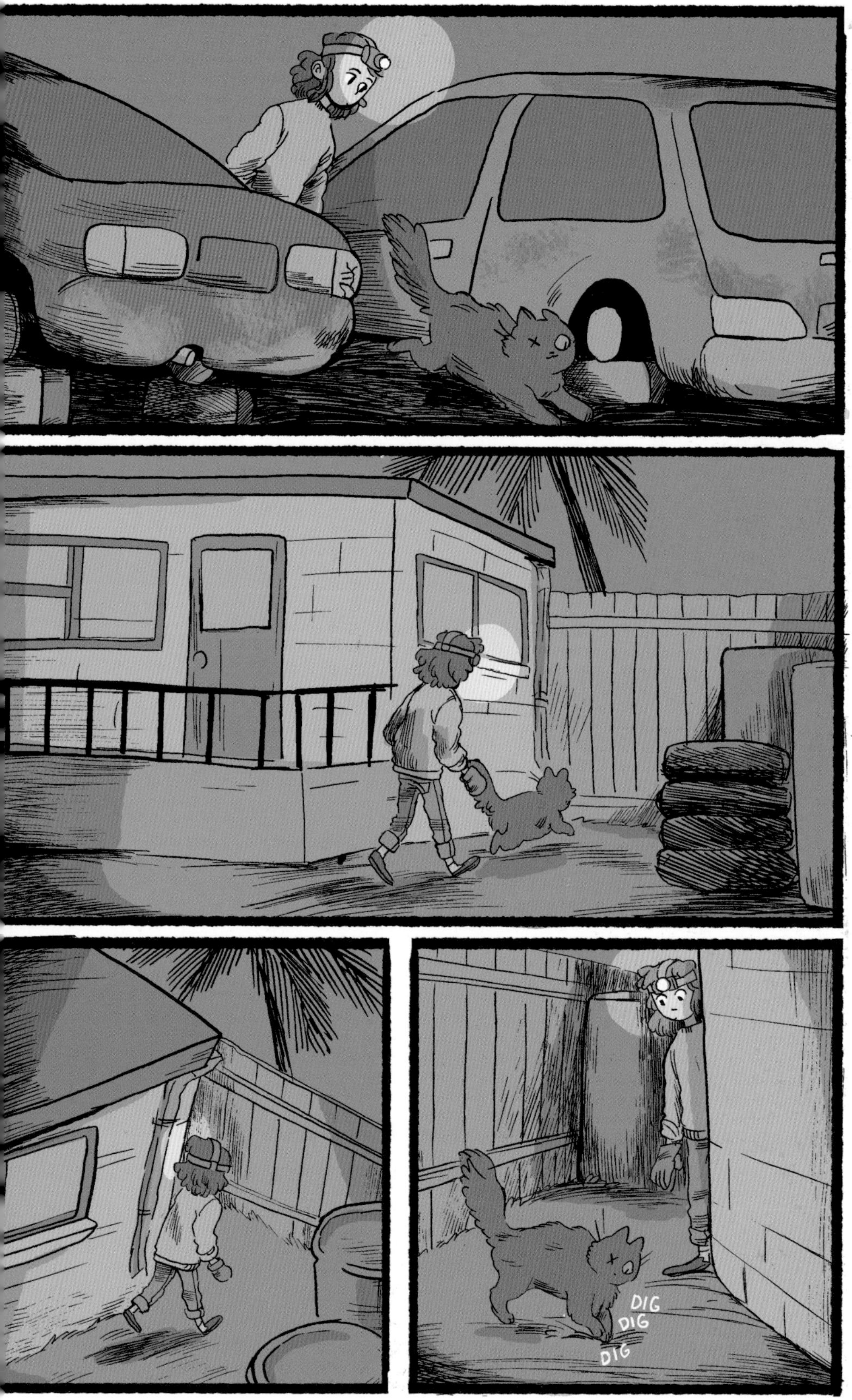
DIG
DIG
DIG

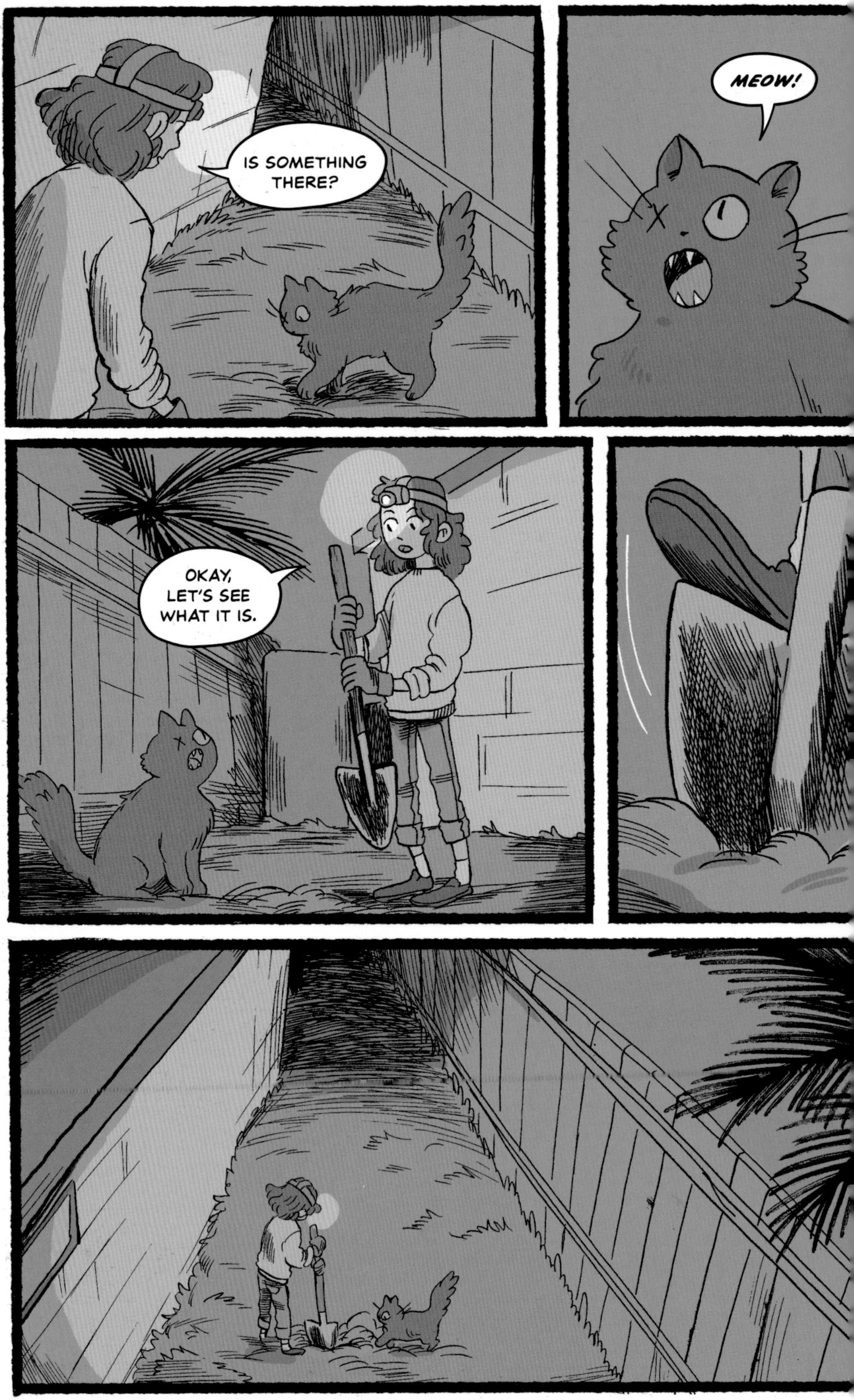
IS SOMETHING THERE?
MEOW!
OKAY, LET'S SEE WHAT IT IS.

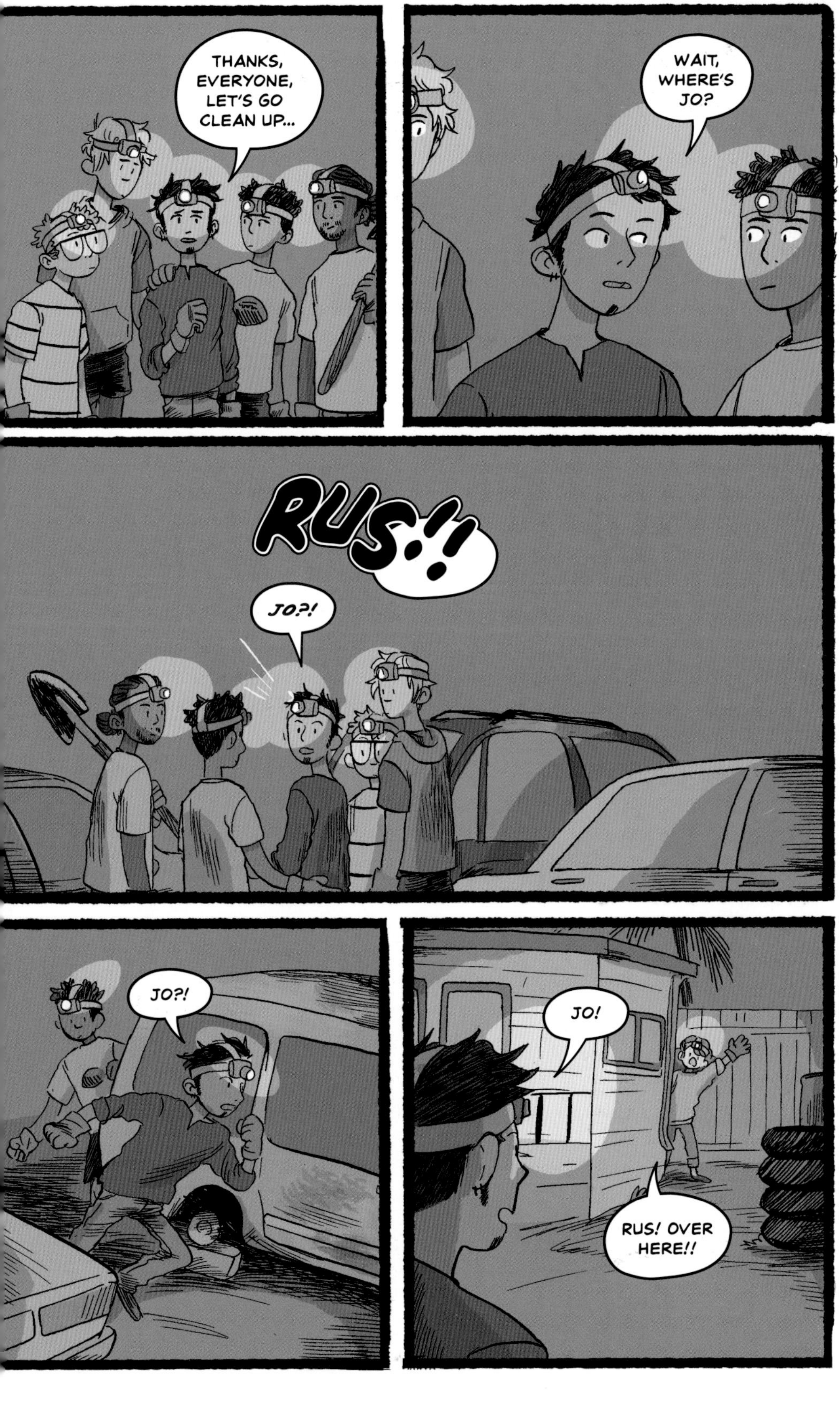

THANKS, EVERYONE, LET'S GO CLEAN UP...
WAIT, WHERE'S JO?
RUS!!
JO?!
JO?!
JO!
RUS! OVER HERE!!

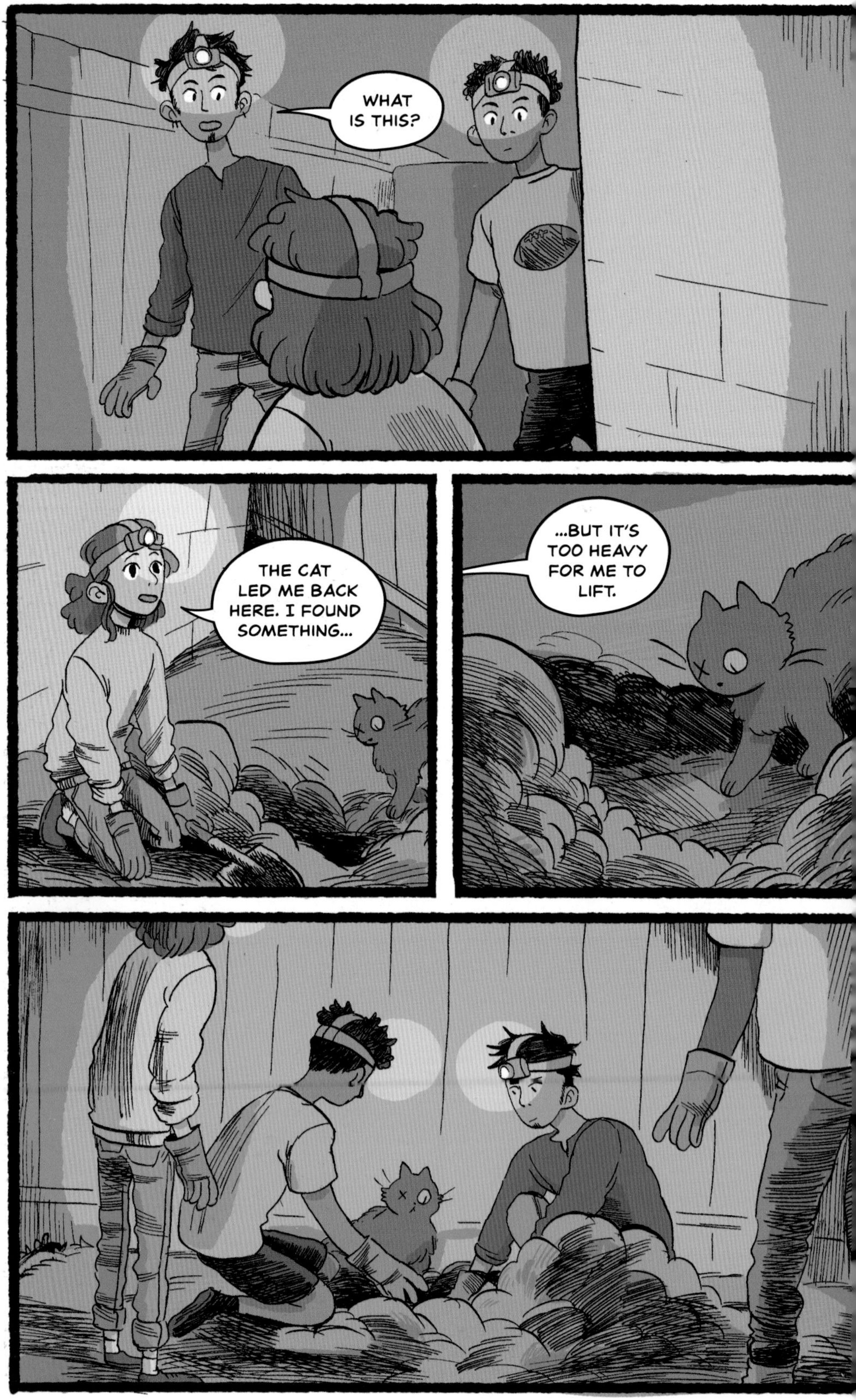
WHAT IS THIS?
THE CAT LED ME BACK HERE. I FOUND SOMETHING...
...BUT IT'S TOO HEAVY FOR ME TO LIFT.

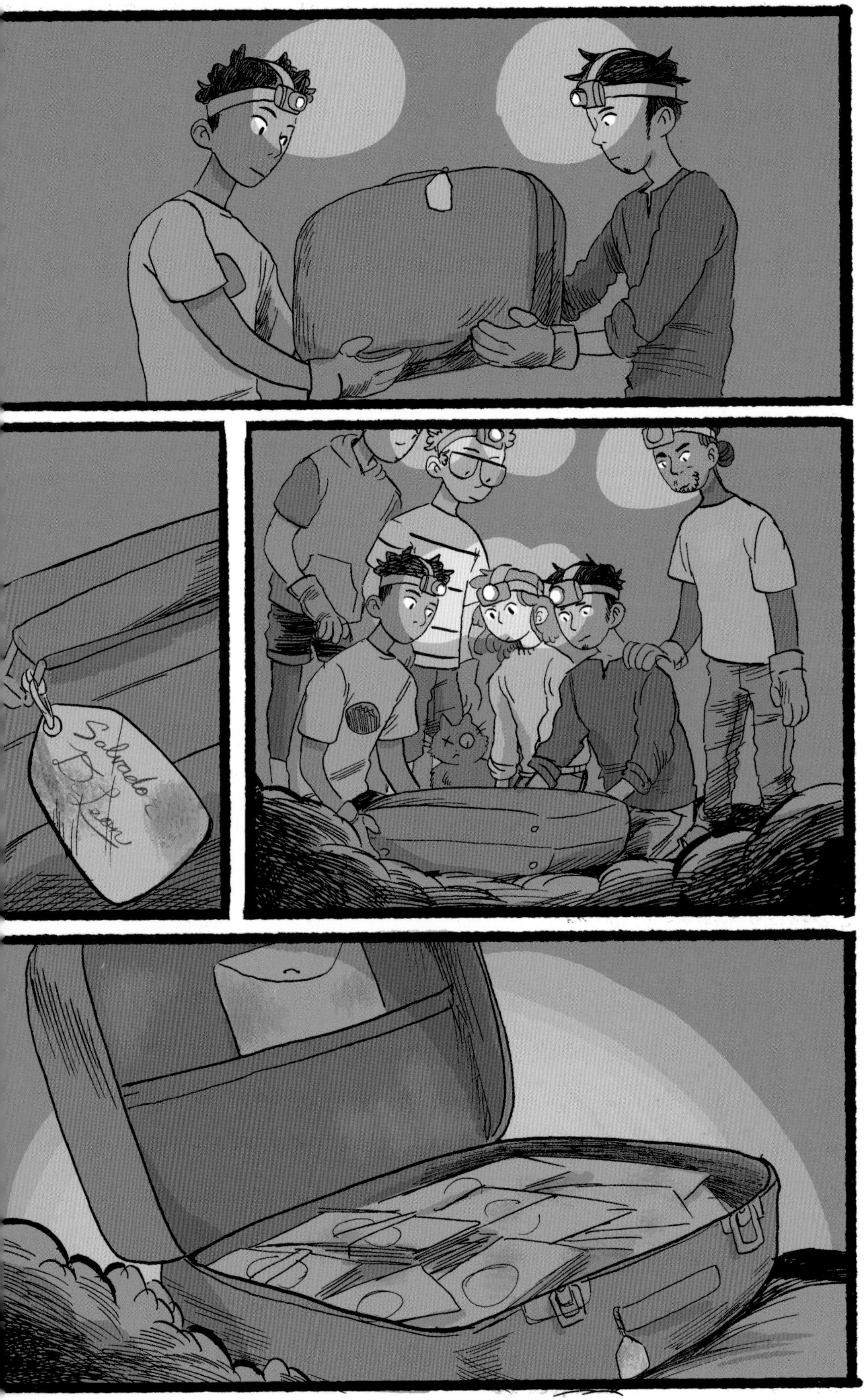
Salvado
D. Leon

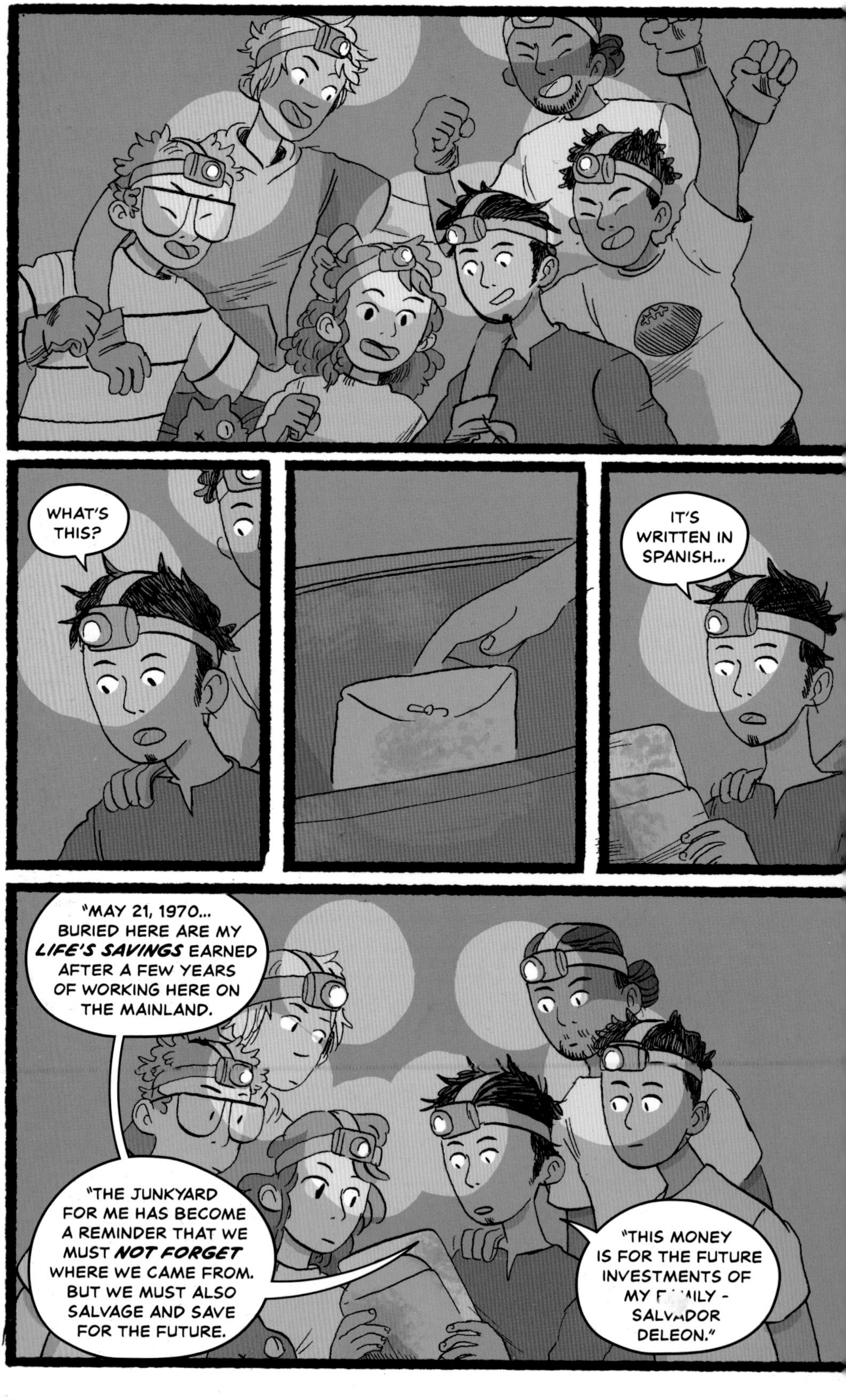
WHAT'S THIS?
IT'S WRITTEN IN SPANISH...
"MAY 21, 1970... BURIED HERE ARE MY ***LIFE'S SAVINGS*** EARNED AFTER A FEW YEARS OF WORKING HERE ON THE MAINLAND.
"THE JUNKYARD FOR ME HAS BECOME A REMINDER THAT WE MUST ***NOT FORGET*** WHERE WE CAME FROM. BUT WE MUST ALSO SALVAGE AND SAVE FOR THE FUTURE.
"THIS MONEY IS FOR THE FUTURE INVESTMENTS OF MY FAMILY - SALVADOR DELEON."

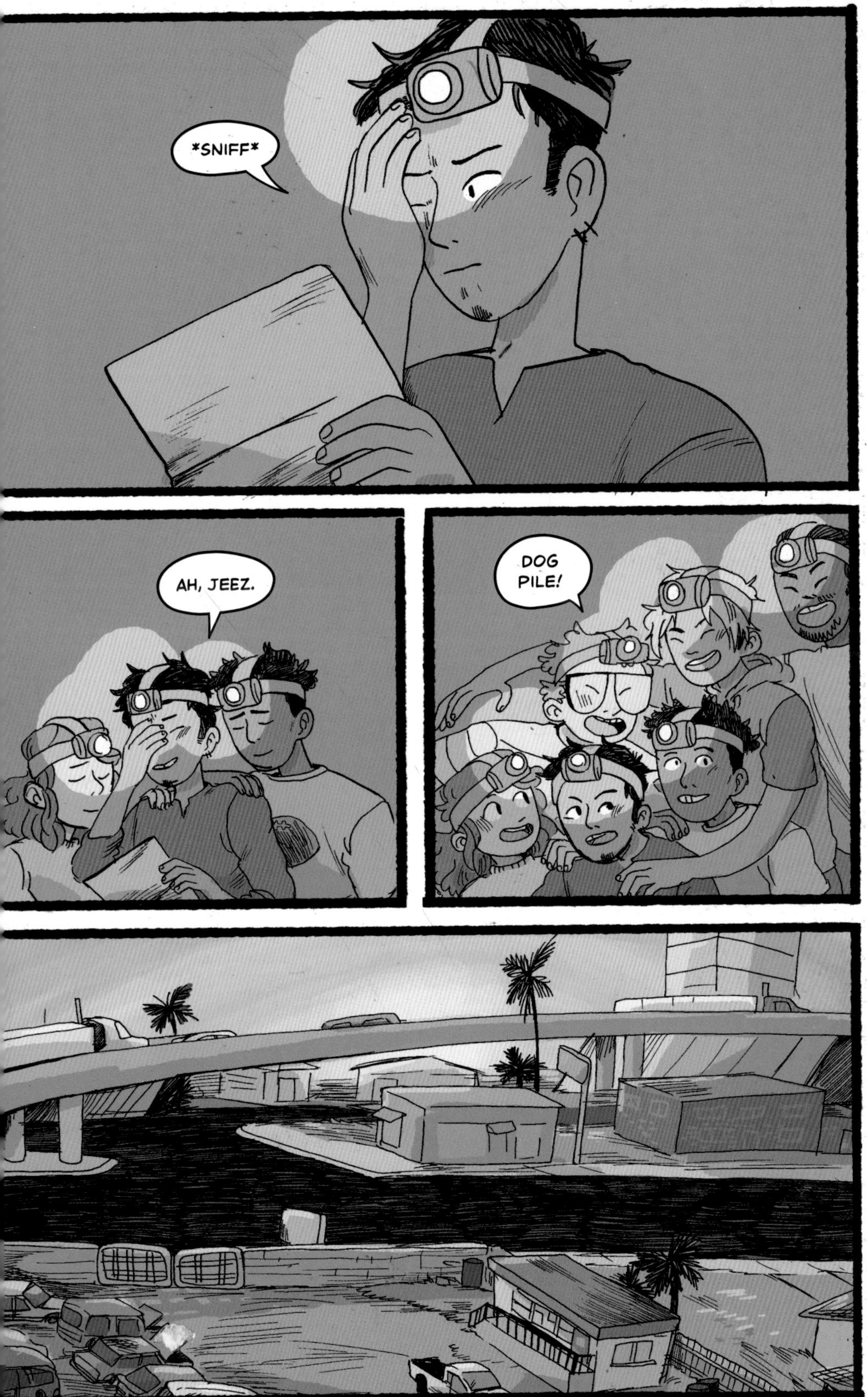
SNIFF
AH, JEEZ.
DOG PILE!

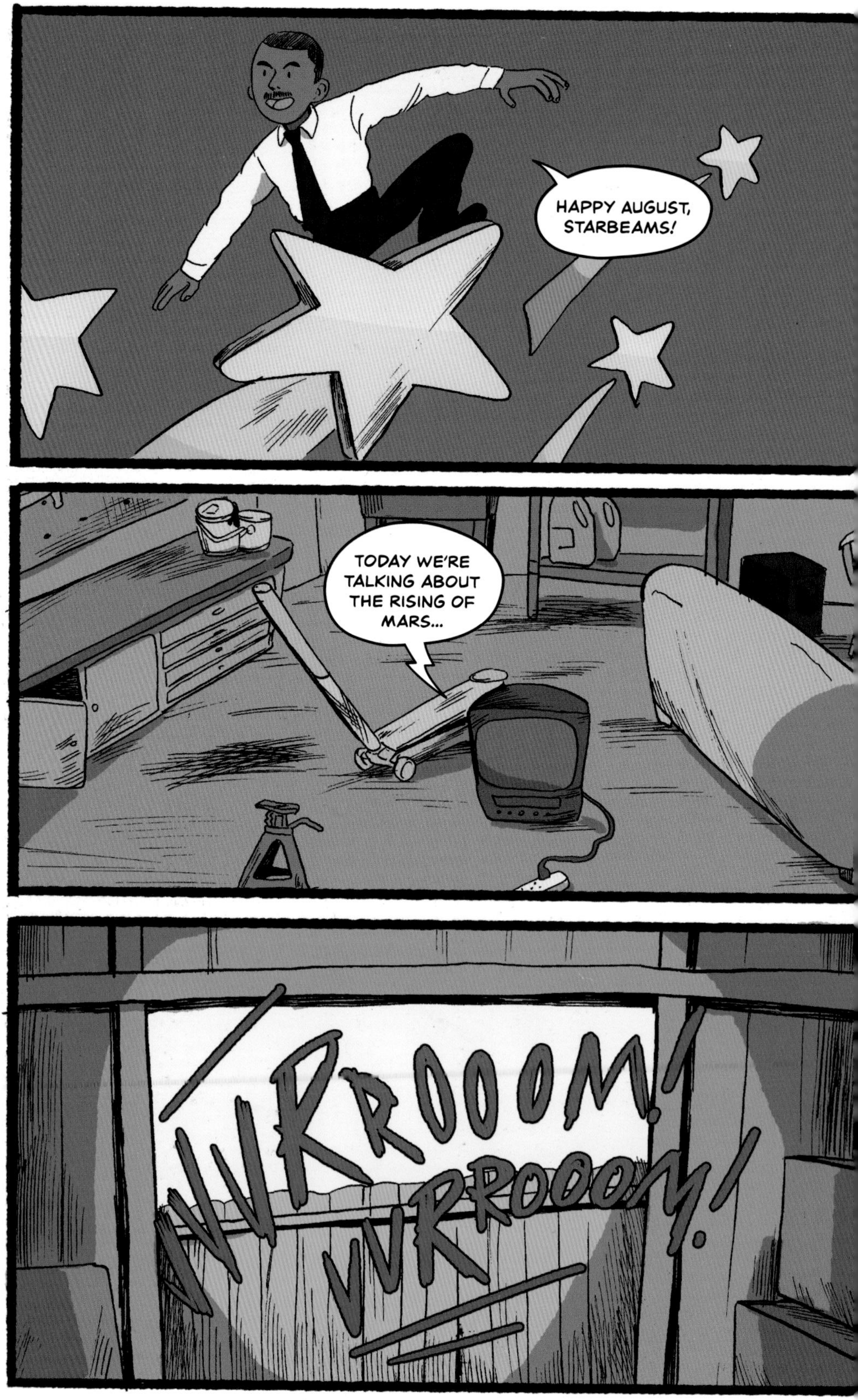
HAPPY AUGUST, STARBEAMS!
TODAY WE'RE TALKING ABOUT THE RISING OF MARS...
VVRROOOM! VVRROOOM!

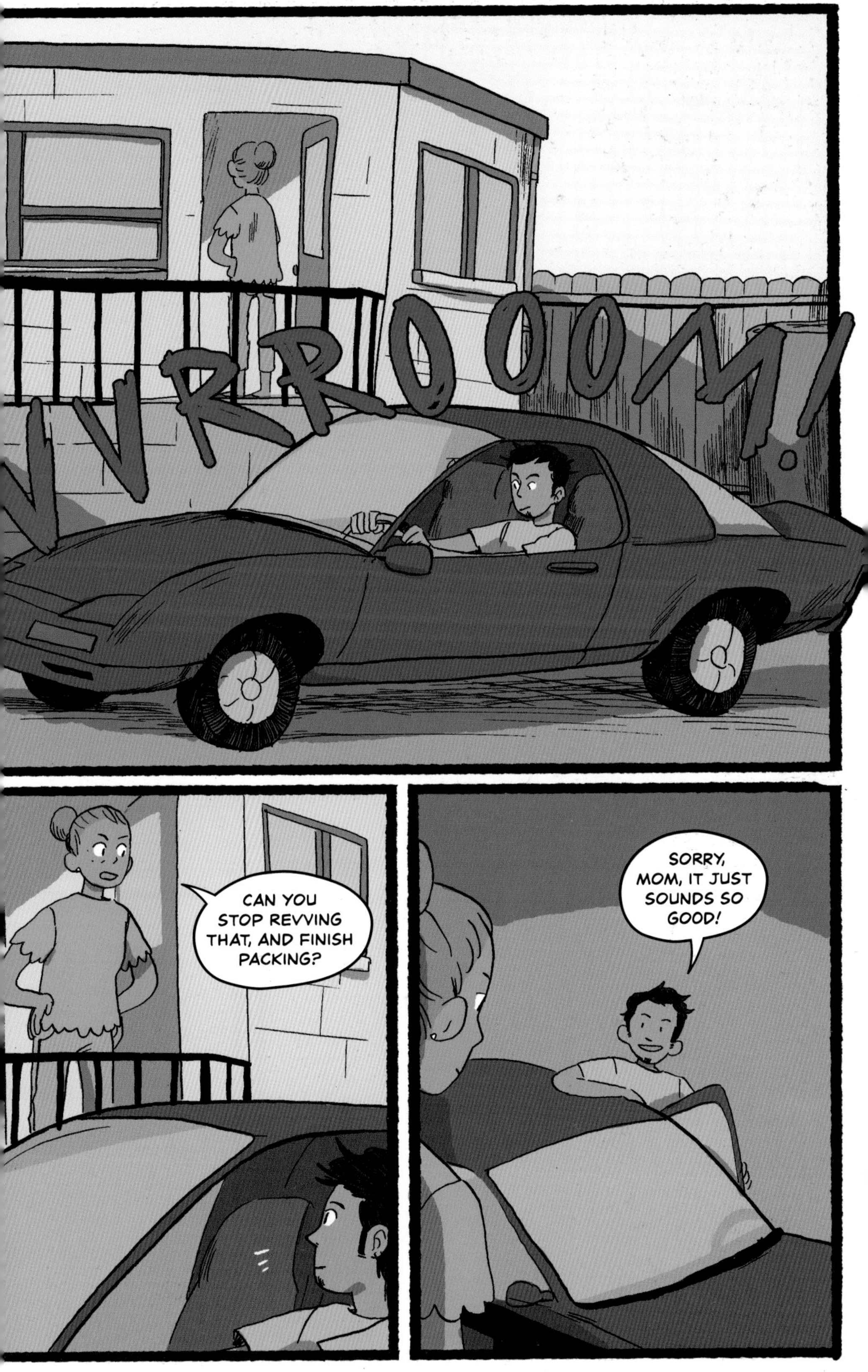
VVRROOOM!
CAN YOU STOP REVVING THAT, AND FINISH PACKING?
SORRY, MOM, IT JUST SOUNDS SO GOOD!

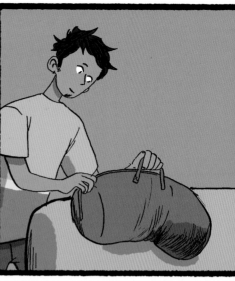

MEOW!

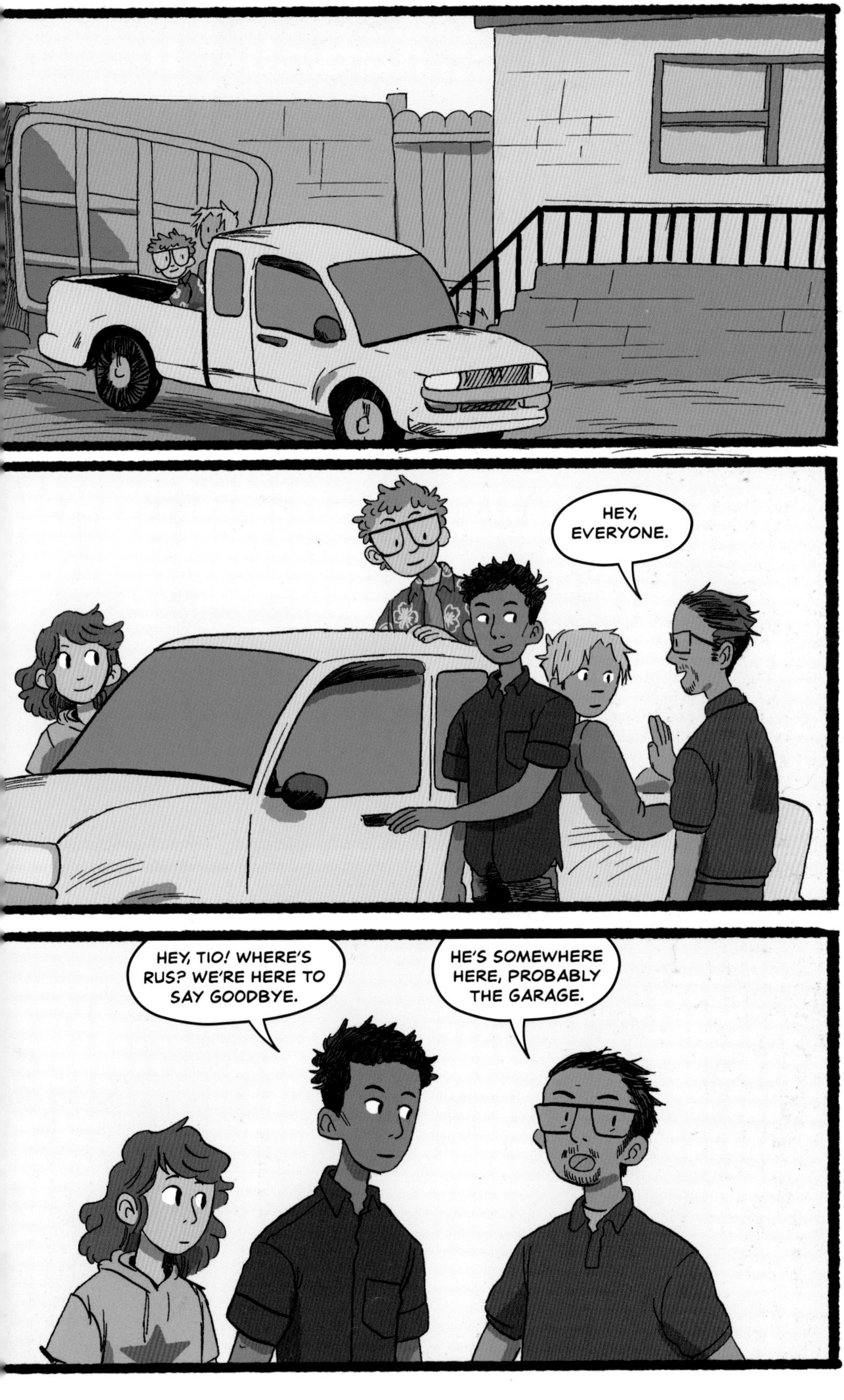
HEY, EVERYONE.
HEY, TIO! WHERE'S RUS? WE'RE HERE TO SAY GOODBYE.
HE'S SOMEWHERE HERE, PROBABLY THE GARAGE.

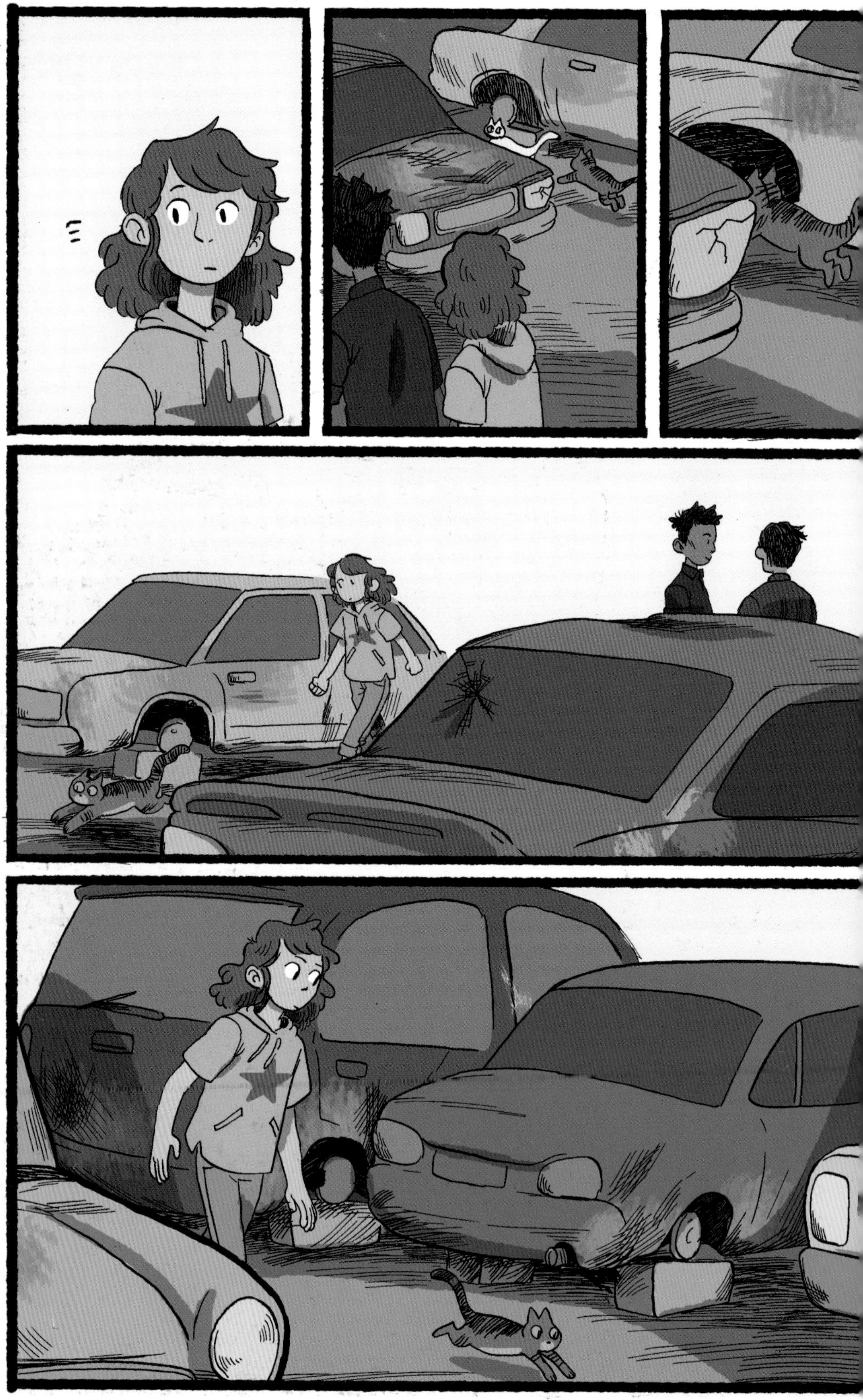

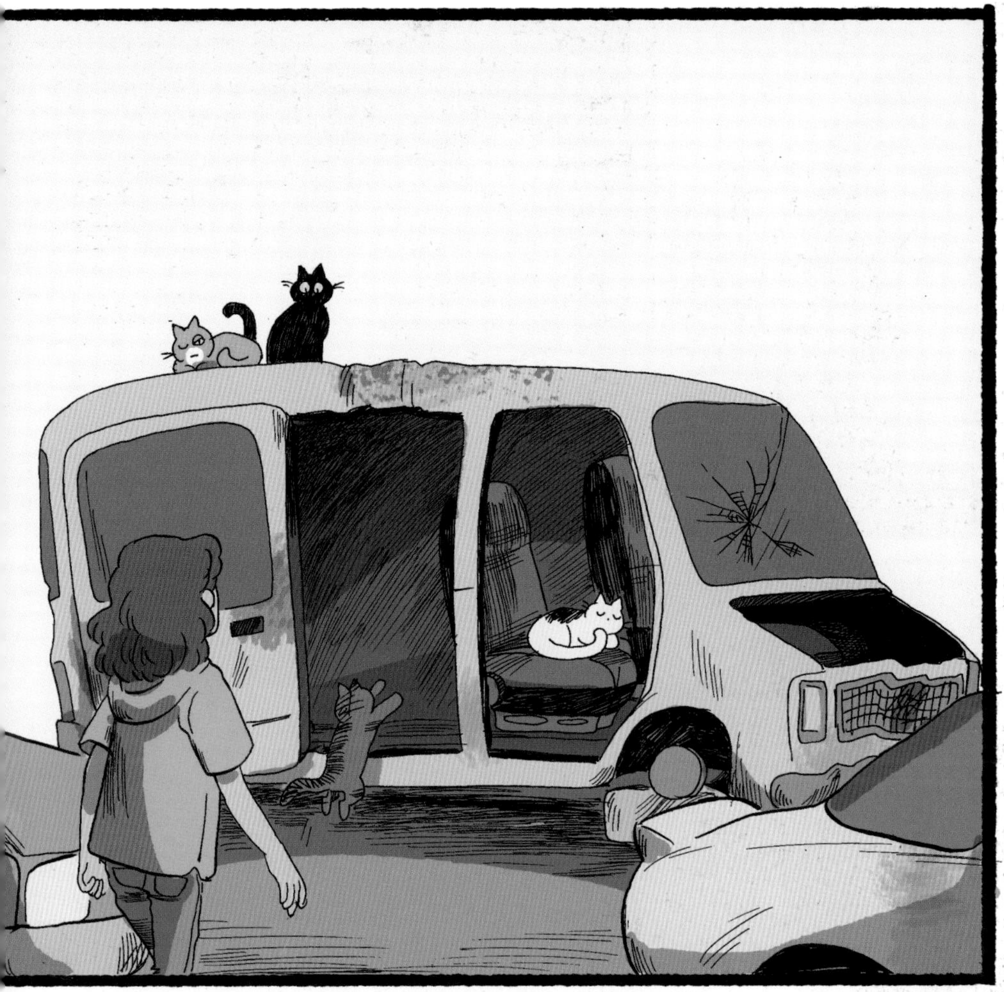

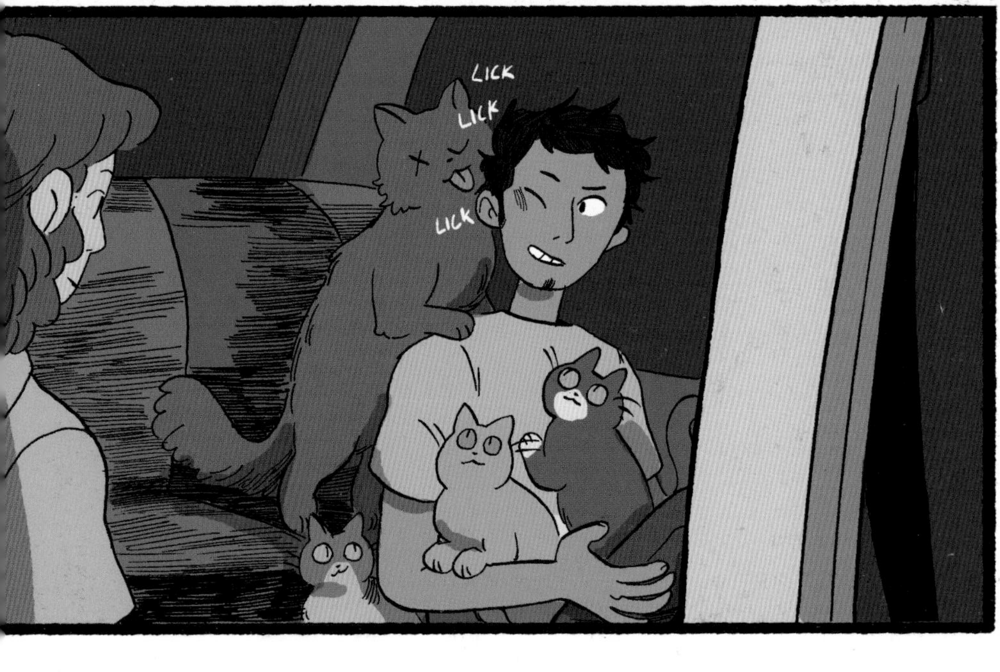

LICK
LICK
LICK

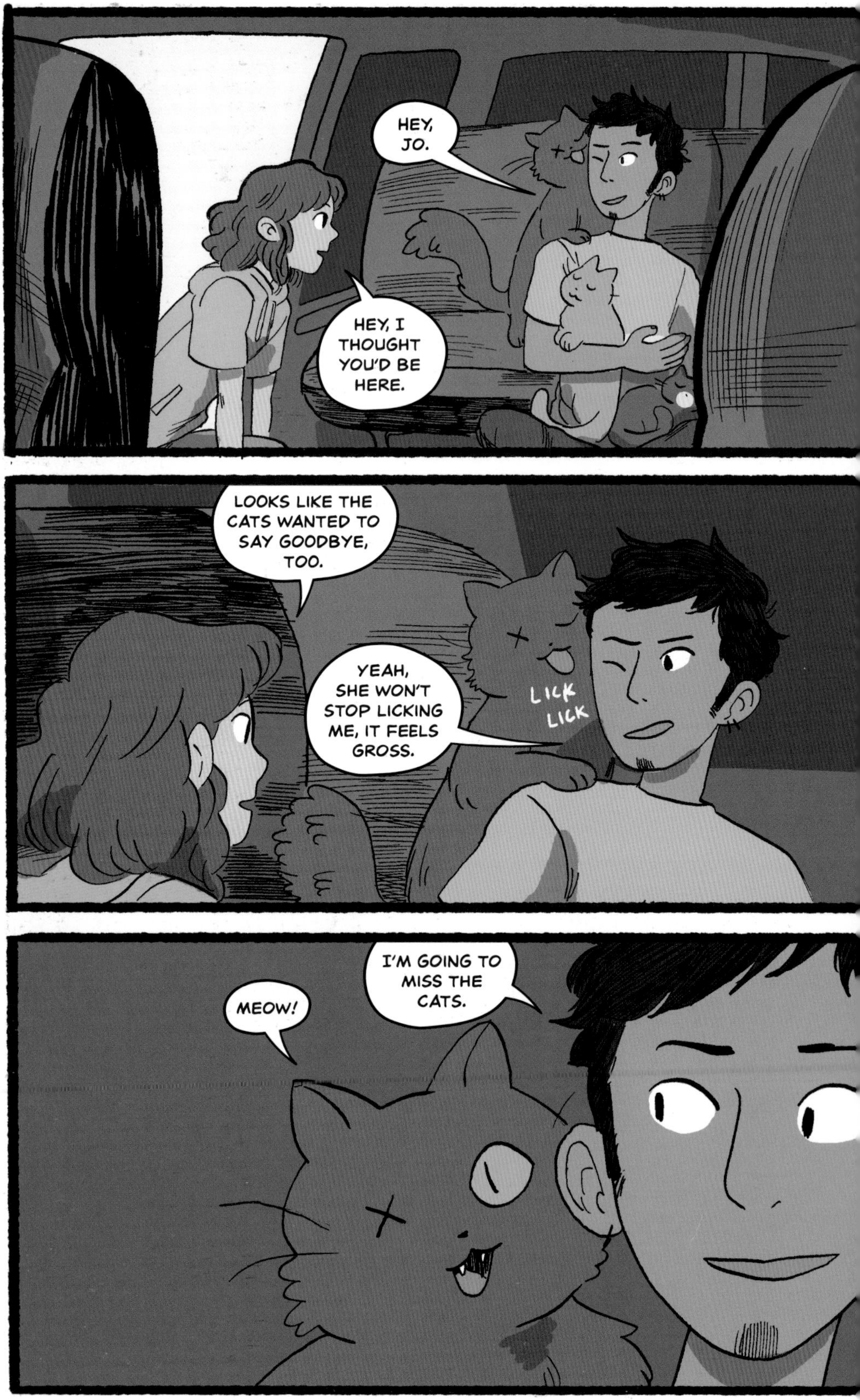
HEY, JO.
HEY, I THOUGHT YOU'D BE HERE.
LOOKS LIKE THE CATS WANTED TO SAY GOODBYE, TOO.
YEAH, SHE WON'T STOP LICKING ME, IT FEELS GROSS.
LICK LICK
MEOW!
I'M GOING TO MISS THE CATS.

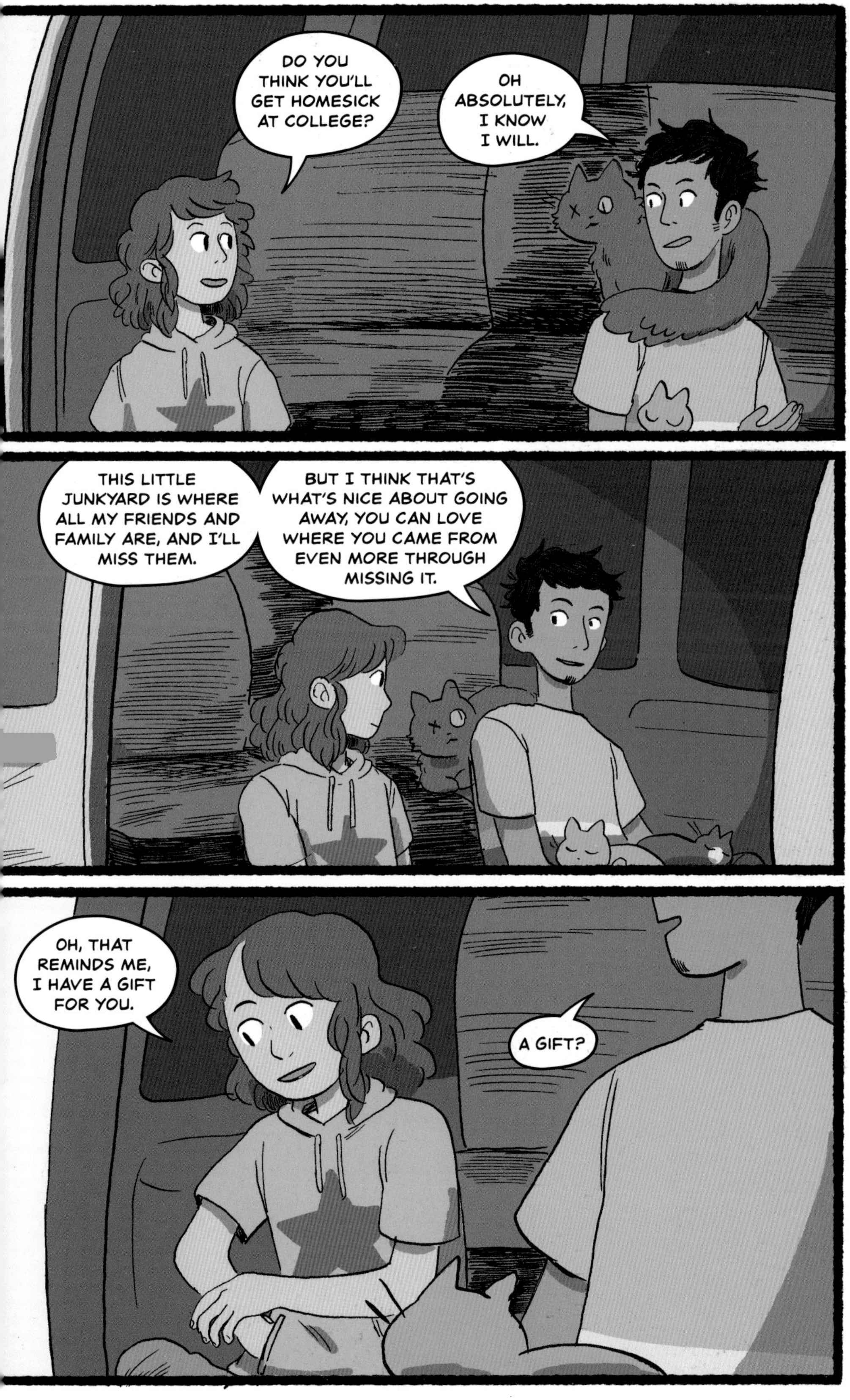
DO YOU THINK YOU'LL GET HOMESICK AT COLLEGE?
OH ABSOLUTELY, I KNOW I WILL.
THIS LITTLE JUNKYARD IS WHERE ALL MY FRIENDS AND FAMILY ARE, AND I'LL MISS THEM.
BUT I THINK THAT'S WHAT'S NICE ABOUT GOING AWAY, YOU CAN LOVE WHERE YOU CAME FROM EVEN MORE THROUGH MISSING IT.
OH, THAT REMINDS ME, I HAVE A GIFT FOR YOU.
A GIFT?

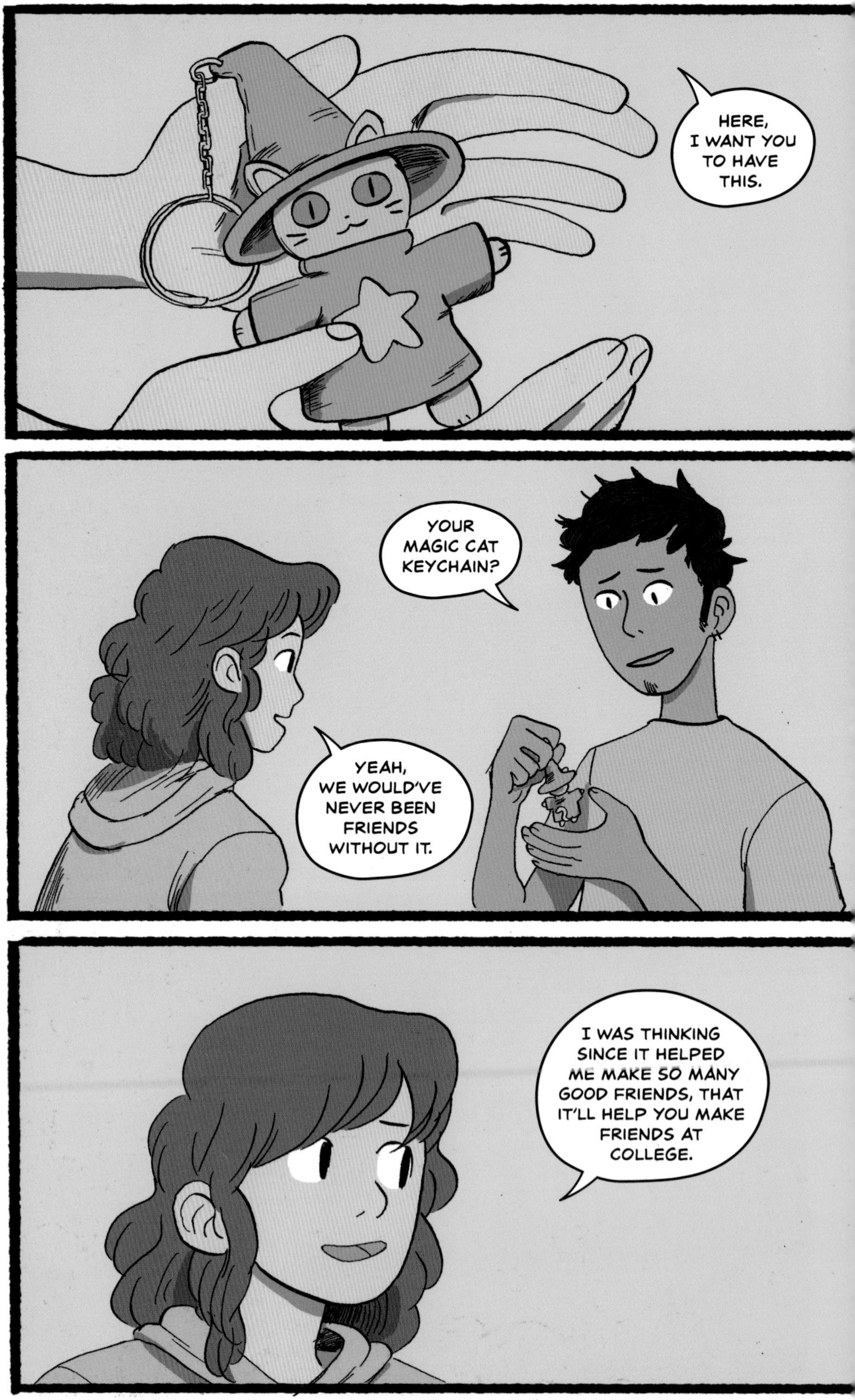
HERE, I WANT YOU TO HAVE THIS.
YOUR MAGIC CAT KEYCHAIN?
YEAH, WE WOULD'VE NEVER BEEN FRIENDS WITHOUT IT.
I WAS THINKING SINCE IT HELPED ME MAKE SO MANY GOOD FRIENDS, THAT IT'LL HELP YOU MAKE FRIENDS AT COLLEGE.

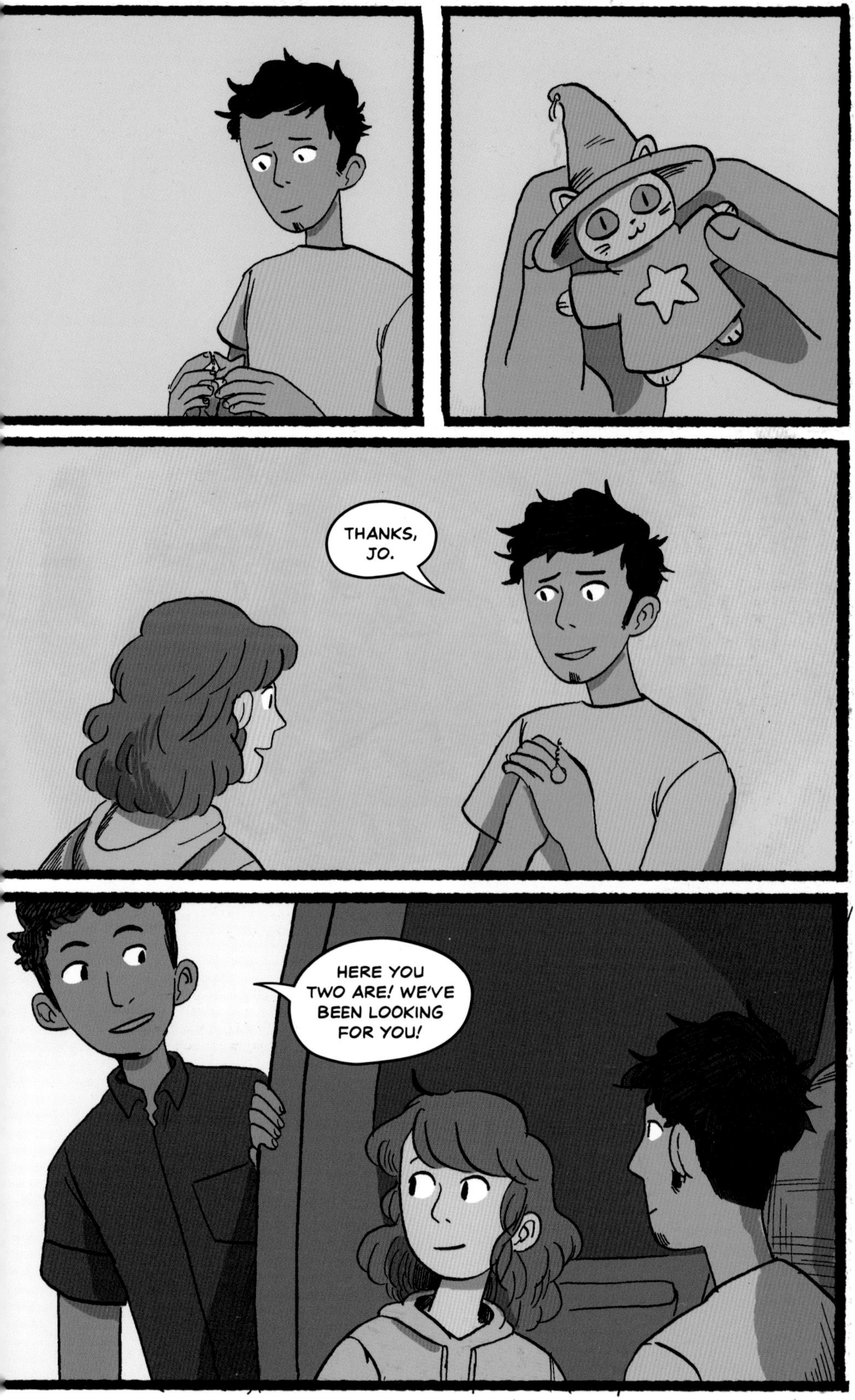
THANKS, JO.
HERE YOU TWO ARE! WE'VE BEEN LOOKING FOR YOU!

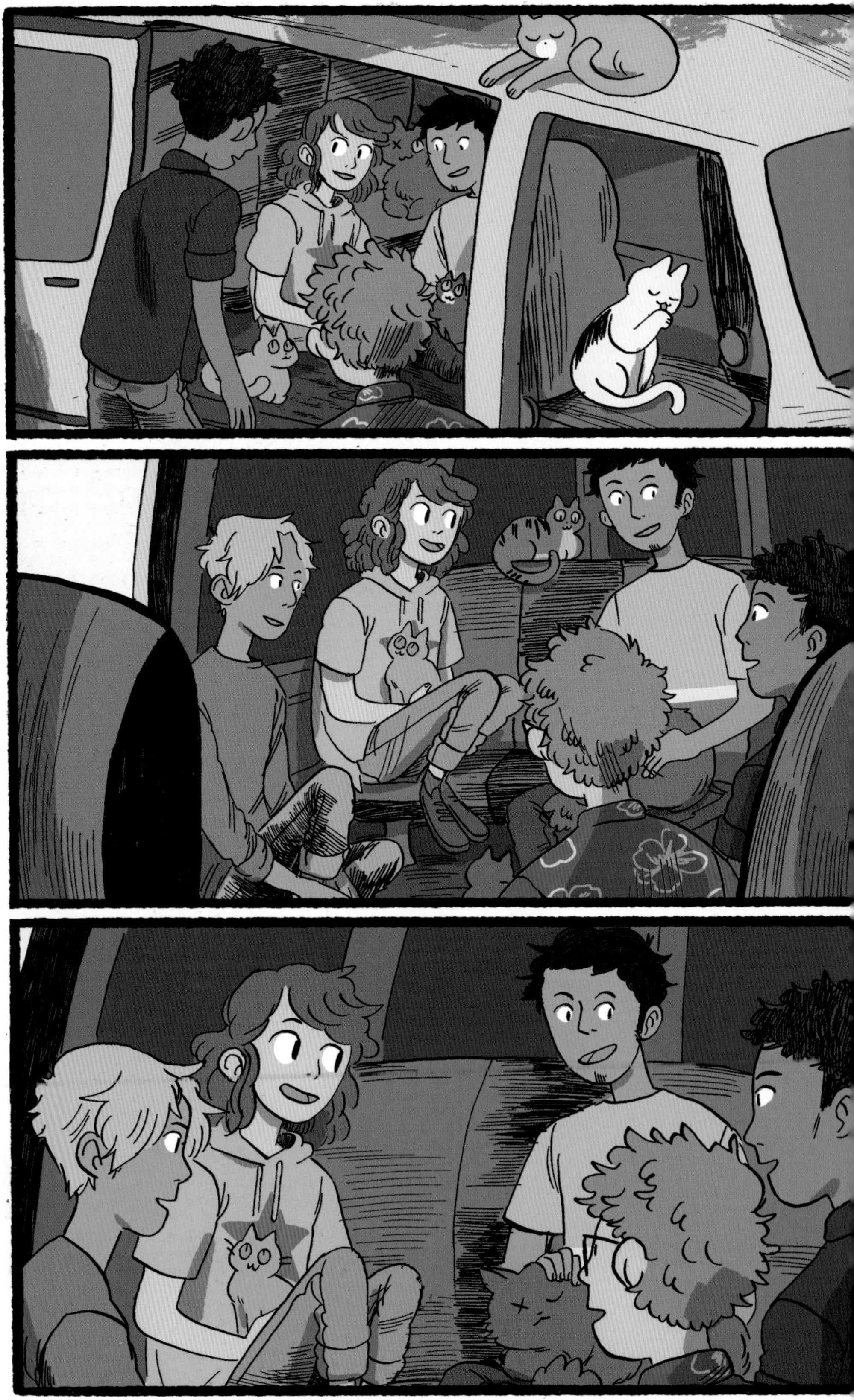

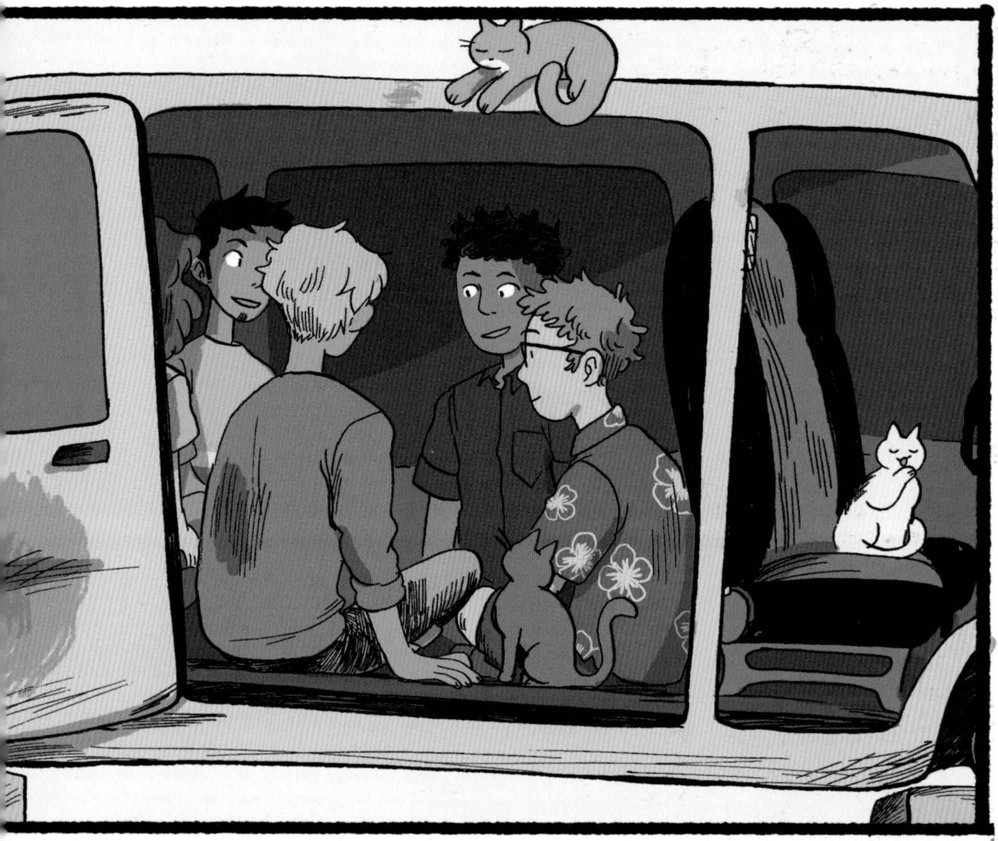

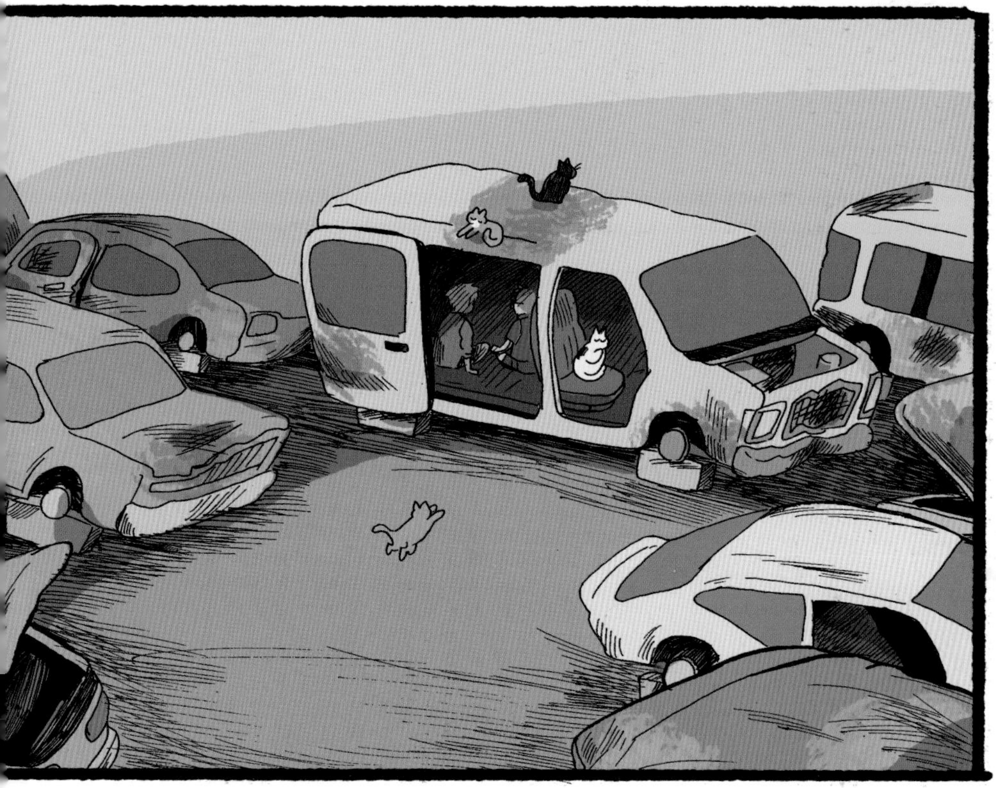

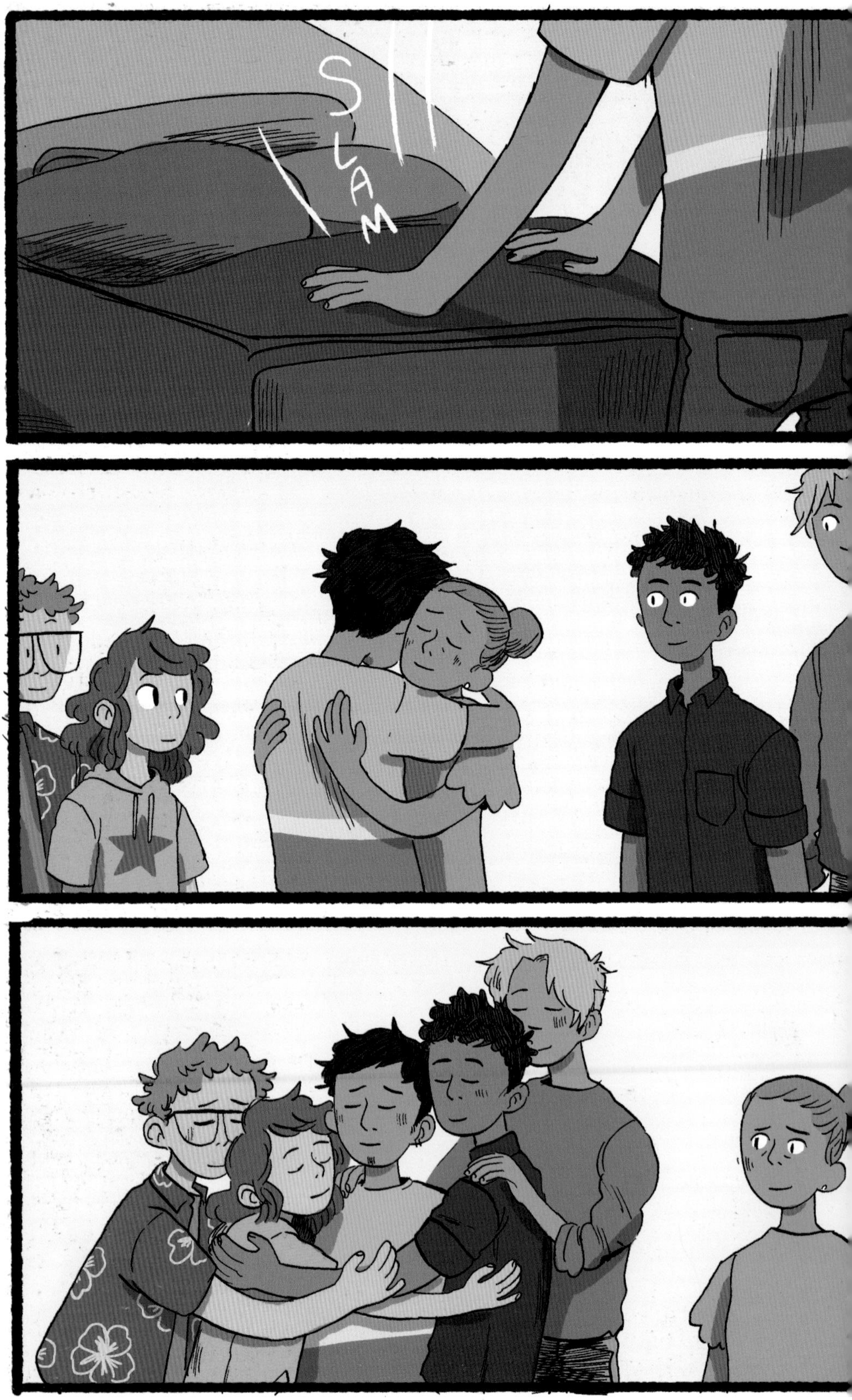
SLAM

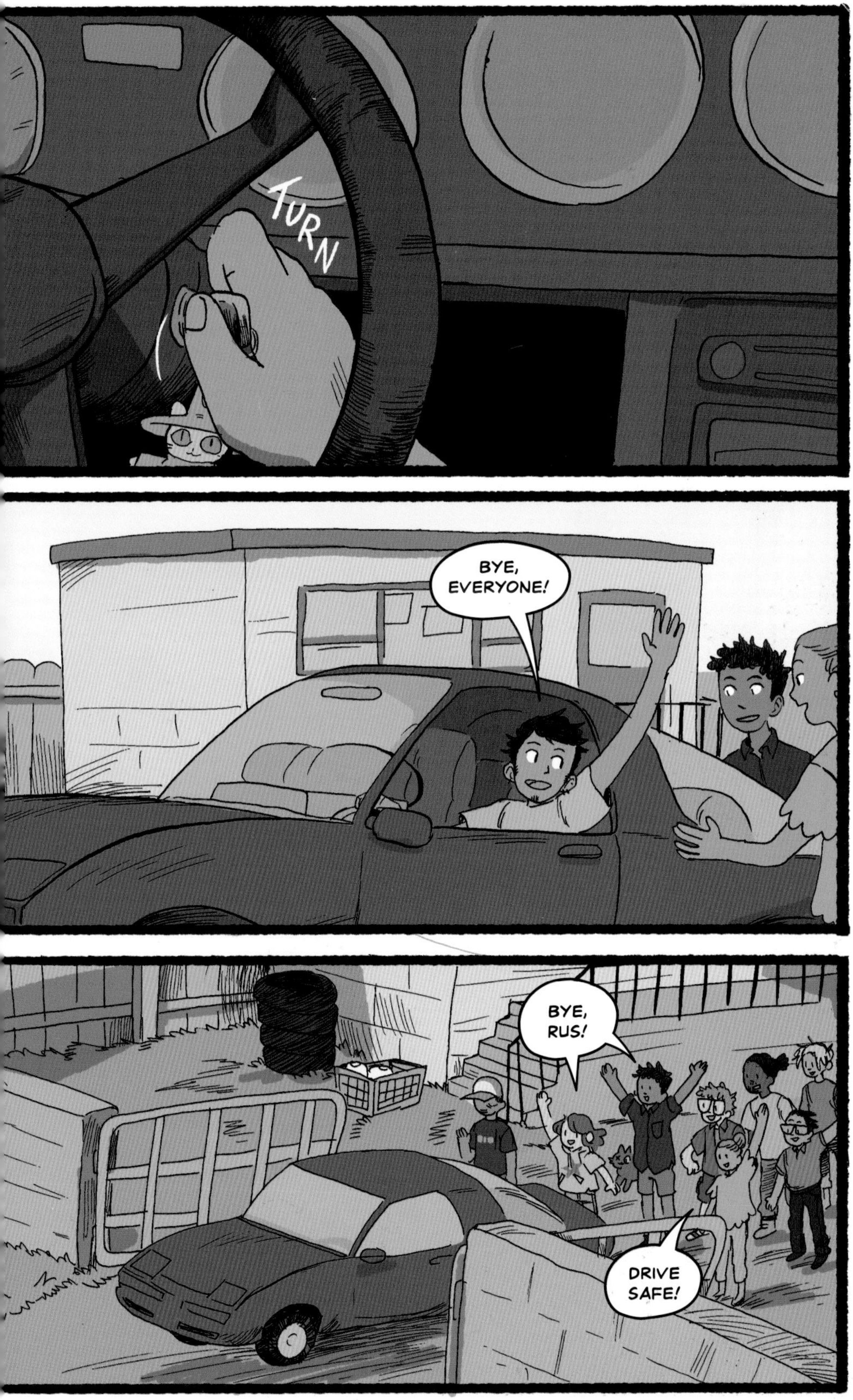
TURN
BYE, EVERYONE!
BYE, RUS!
DRIVE SAFE!

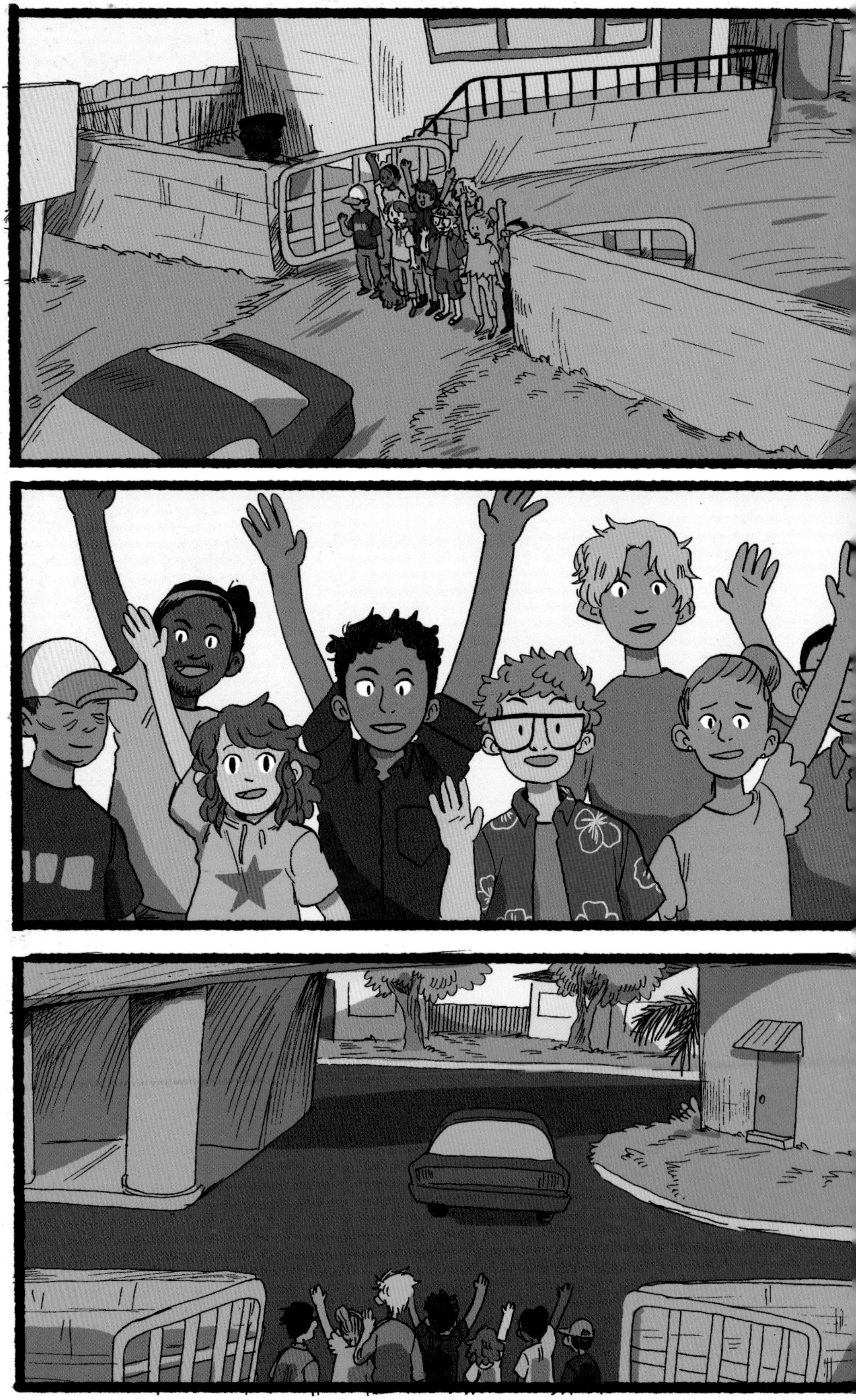

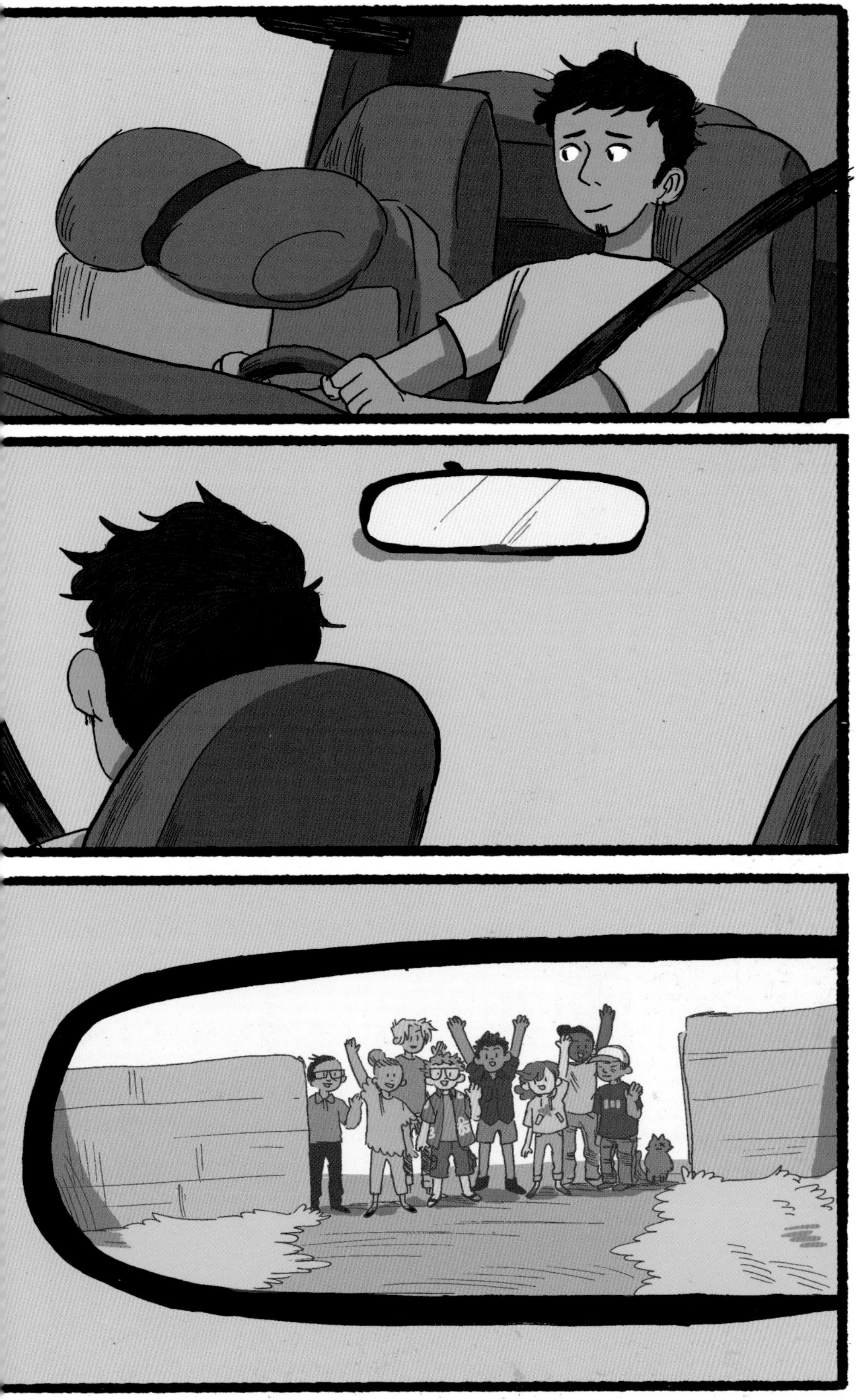

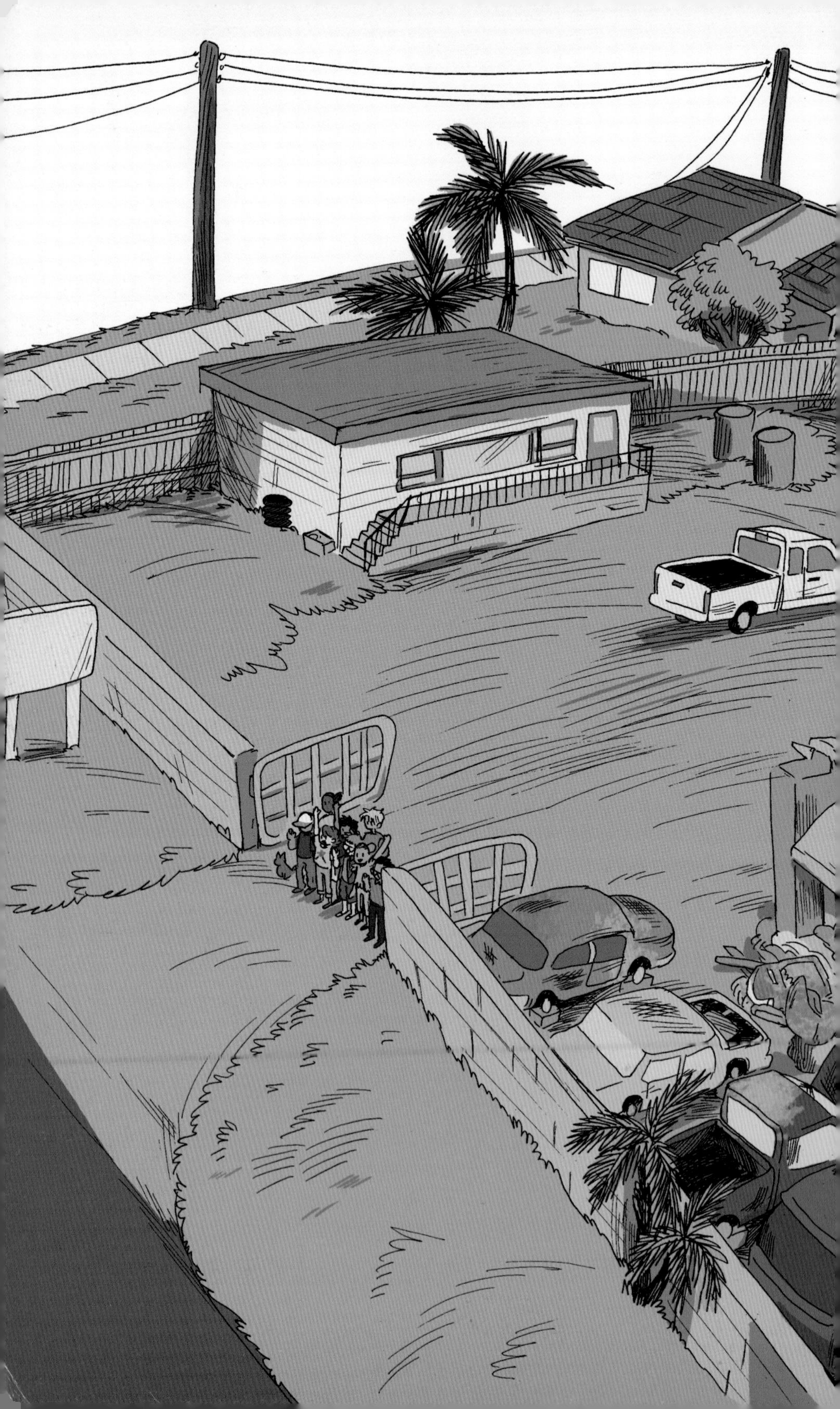

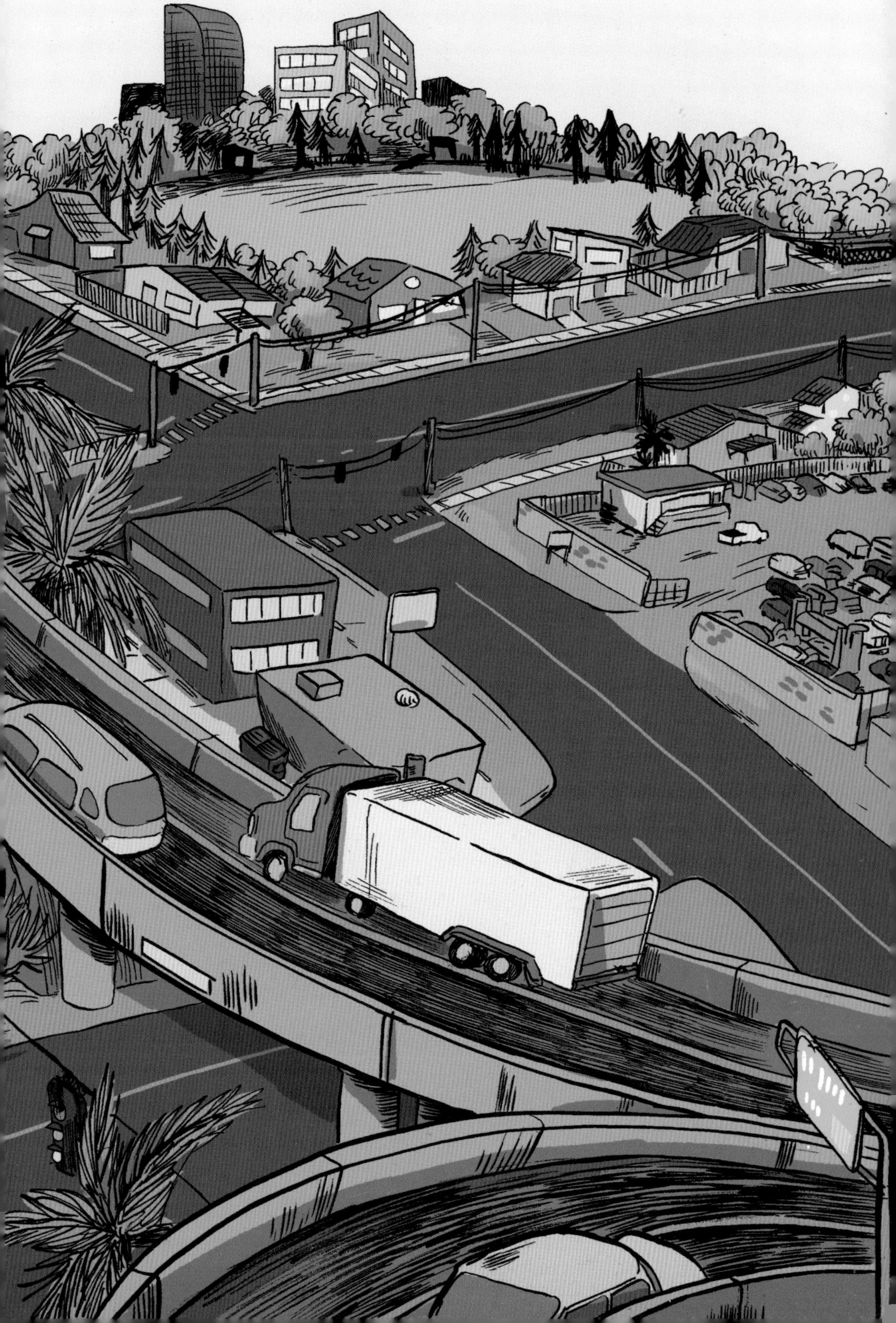

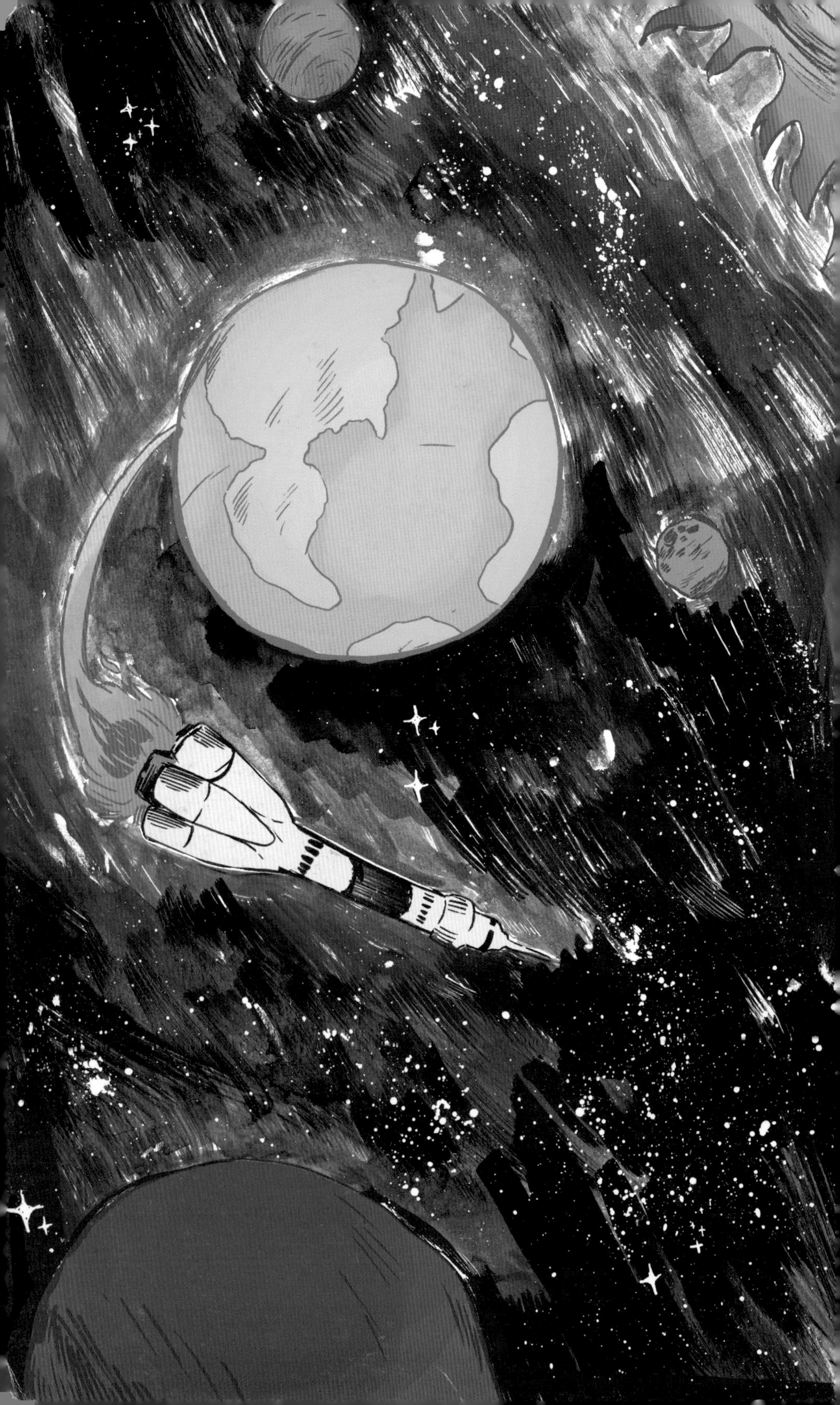

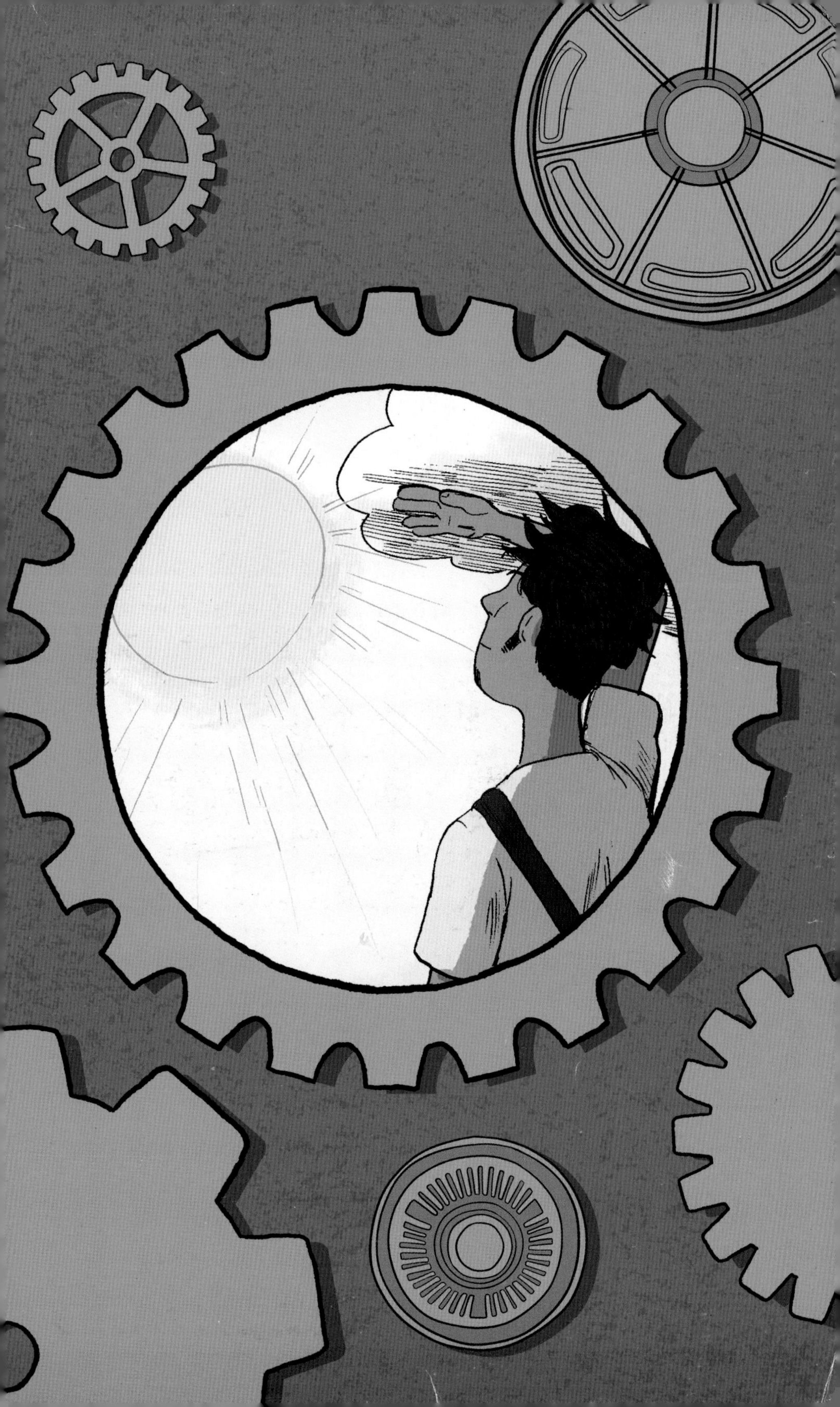

Author Bio

Audra Winslow lives in Florida and every day, they just want to stay at home and draw comics.